OMAHA STAKES

PRAISE FOR
MARK EVERETT STONE

OMAHA STAKES

"This action-packed urban fantasy follows the brooding Kal Hakala, human head of the Bureau of Supernatural Investigation in an alternate contemporary America, to what promises to be the first of many confrontations.... [Stone] writes in a brisk, conversational style .... The setting fuses magic and technology in appealing ways that will hopefully be developed in future installments.... Kal's frolic through a nifty supernatural world is enjoyable."
—Publishers Weekly

CHICAGO, THE WINDIGO CITY

"*Chicago, The Windigo City* is jam packed with action but the heart of the story is Kal's love and concern for his girlfriend and his best friend .... An original and refreshing tale that leaves me wanting to know more about Kal, Jeanie, BB, and Canton. I look forward to reading the other books in the series."
—Debbie Wiley, Fresh Fiction

"Urban fantasy infused with Native American legend takes an excursion into the bloody horror genre in this fast-paced, exciting story.... Tight prose, a meticulous plot, and good editing set this book apart from countless competitors .... Stone has written a novel difficult to put down. Endless tension along with well-implemented action make the reading experience a necessity, not an option. Even a jaded critic will shudder over descriptive passages that bring to life the ghastly crime scenes, and certain explanations may unsettle a few stomachs."
—Julia Ann Charpentier, ForeWord Magazine

"Mark Everett Stone has hit another home run .... The action is non-stop, and the magical/technical gadgets are incredibly

imaginative. Fans of this series will not be disappointed. The BSI series remains one of my absolute favorites, and I'm looking forward to the next installment."
—M. E. Franco, author of the Dion Series

I LEFT MY HAUNT IN SAN FRANCISCO

"The third in a series, *I Left My Haunt in San Francisco* is lively and smart. It is packed with action and just enough goop and gore to please fans of the genre without turning away newcomers to this subset of modern fantasy demon-busting .... Stone's book moves fast and reads quickly. It is well-written and nicely paced, with a few short rest stops built in to allow the reader to catch his breath, all to better appreciate the at-times purple but always entertaining prose .... It is just great, grand fun."
—Mark McLaughlin, ForeWord Reviews

"Another high impact, fast moving story from Mark Everett Stone. I am really enjoying seeing his growth as a writer reflected in the strength of his characters and am looking forward to seeing what the future holds for Kal."
—Michelle Herbert, Fantasy Book Review

"The third episode of the Files of the BSI series is told with Mark Stone's trademark tongue in cheek humor. It keeps you wanting more with each turn of the page, to not only uncover the mysteries of the story, but also to enjoy Kal's quick but cynical wit."
—CP Bialois, author of *Call of Poseidon*, The Sword and the Flame series, and *Skeleton Key*

THE JUDAS LINE

★ "This delightful Catholicism-infused quest fantasy stars a likable and original duo. Fr. Michael Engle, a pragmatic Catholic priest, and Jude, who has a considerably more uncertain relationship with God, are unlikely friends, but when a blood-covered Jude runs into Mike's church asking for help, Mike listens to him, believes him, and joins

him on a quest to find the Holy Grail, which Jude hopes will help him destroy a legendary and dangerous family heirloom. Along the way they encounter Cain, the Norse gods (drinking and watching *Bridge over the River Kwai*), and a Valkyrie with the requisite 'chainmail-covered pillowy breasts.' When Mephistopheles shows up, Jude manages to label him an Arch-Fiend of Hell without irony and without irritating the reader. Stone's depiction of magic is realistic and intelligent and his treatment of Catholicism refreshingly informed and three-dimensional. Even the obligatory near-apocalyptic ending is coherent, surprising, and exciting."
—Publishers Weekly Starred Review

"This evil mystery is a heavenly read! *The Judas Line* creates a believable mystery which links the ancient past to the present. By building on the ancient story of the betrayal of Jesus Christ by Judas, Market Everett Stone crafts a dark versus light drama which will keep readers hooked. I loved how Stone makes Jude an unwilling member of the darkest family threatening mankind. Simply brilliant!"
—Elizabeth Crowley, Fresh Fiction

"A fast-paced book which does not lack for history or adventure. The inclusion of death and destruction are a given and it is good that there is a lot of humour instilled throughout. I would say that if you're a fan of Jim Butcher's *Dresden Files*, you will enjoy Mark Everett Stone's work. Recommended."
—Michelle Herbert, Fantasy Book Review

"Blending paranormal and biblical ideas, *The Judas Line* is a riveting thriller that should prove hard to put down."
—Midwest Book Review

"I have come to expect a lot from this remarkably talented writer, but Mark manages to please yet again by bringing new elements to his latest work. *The Judas Line* is, as anticipated, a lightning-paced thriller that is equal parts non-stop action and intelligent musing. This is, in fact, a surprisingly introspective book that delves into many interesting questions about the nature of good, evil, and faith.

It's an enthralling read certain to delight and entertain, a well-crafted gem worthy of a place on any bookshelf."
—Michelle Izmaylov, author of *The Galacteran Legacy: Galaxy Watch*

"Mark Everett Stone takes the classic good versus evil plot line and puts his own unique spin on it. He effortlessly merges bible canon with the world and people he's created, adding off-the-wall humor to help break the tension. This book makes you laugh while making you think about the nature of evil and the power of faith."
—Jamie White, author of *The Life and Times of No One in Particular*

★ ★ ★ ★ ★ "A fast-paced read, with nail-biting moments and some humor thrown in. The characters were compelling, I often find myself picturing them in my head .... I can't recommend this book enough."
—Lisa McCourt Hollar, Jezri's Nightmares

"Once in a great while, a book comes along that challenges you to think outside the box. *The Judas Line* is one of those books. I was absolutely amazed at the way Mark Everett Stone has taken religious stories and beliefs and intertwined his own tale of power, evil, friendship, sacrifice and redemption. The action is nonstop and the characters will stay with you long after you finish the last page."
—M.E. Franco, author *Where Will You Run?*

"The pacing is flawless in every respect .... Never before have I found a work of fiction to be so captivating. It picks you up, sits you down, and it does not let you even think about getting back up. A word of warning: Hide your pocketbooks, because once you read this, you will spend your next paycheck on every Mark Everett Stone book available."
—Grace Knight, author of *Sun And Moon* (2013)

WHAT HAPPENS IN VEGAS, DIES IN VEGAS

★ ★ ★ ★ ★ "*Things To Do In Denver When Your Un-Dead* was one of the most refreshing and original books I have read in a long time

and the sequel is just as exciting as the first. In fact it may just be better than the first .... Exceptionally well-written and entertaining."
—Jerzri's Nightmares

"Vegas is non-stop action that will leave you with whiplash.... Stone leaves you gasping for breath by the end and of course, enjoys taunting the reader with the prospect of a third book in the series, which I will be waiting anxiously to read."
—Shay Fabbro, award-winning author

★★★★★"A cracking good yarn from first to final page, no question .... Mark has cemented himself solidly into the position of Master in my self-created niche of Paranormal Suspense Thriller writing. His command of his art grows exponentially with each work of his that I read....Two very enthusiastic thumbs up for a job well and properly done."
—Jeffrey Hollar, The Latinum Vault

"Don't expect a minute of down-time, for Stone is a zero tolerance taskmaster who brings a complicated plotline and well fleshed-out characters to heel and makes it look easy. What you *can* expect is for Stone to surprise you repeatedly, satisfy you completely and leave you wanting more."
—AJ Aalto, author of *Touched*

THINGS TO DO IN DENVER WHEN YOU'RE UN-DEAD

★★★★★"If you crave a really enjoyable Paranormal Suspense Thriller to read, THIS is your book. It grabs you from the very first page and drags you along (snarling for you to keep up) and dumps you at the feet of one of THE most unexpected plot twists of an ending that I have ever read."
—Jeffrey Hollar, The Latinum Vault

"If you like quick wit, sadistic charm, and bad-ass gadgets, then you will enjoy the hell out of this book."
—Shay Fabbro, award-winning author

★ ★ ★ ★ ★ "An absolute pleasure to read. It is witty, funny, dramatic and a well thought out paranormal with very fine storytelling. I couldn't put it down!"
—Clarrissa Lee Moon, author of the series, *The Nightwolves* and *Celeste Nites*

"I have really enjoyed reading this book .... The story could just be one of guns, blood and guts and magic, but ... Mark Everett Stone has made these characters seem real."
—Michele Herbert, Fantasy Book Review

"This is not a story for the faint of heart or stomach, nor for those wanting a plot with any connection to reality. Personally, I'm really looking forward to the promised sequel."
—Gordon Long, TCM Reviews

"The way Mark combines magicians, zombies and super ghouls with a Bogart-style ultra sarcastic officer of the 'Bureau' makes you want to keep on reading. I highly recommend this for everyone—not just those into stories of the un-dead."
—G.R. Holton, author of *Soleri*, *Guardian's Alliance* and *Deep Screams*

"Five stars, two thumbs, fantastic! From the moment I began the first page to the final flip of the last, I was hooked .... The writing is sharp, fast and engaging."
—Patti Larsen, author of *Fresco, Wasteland, The Diamond City*, and *The Ghost Boy of MacKenzie House*

"The fastest paced action horror that I have read in a very long time."
—Suzannah Burke, aka Stacey Danson, author of *Empty Chairs*

"In a first and quite brilliant novel, Stone proves himself equally adept at feverishly fast-paced action, edgy wit and banter, and the weaving of a richly satisfying and fresh world of mystery and intrigue. Write on, my friend."
—Michelle Izmaylov, author of *The Galacteran Legacy: Galaxy Watch*

OMAHA STAKES

FROM THE FILES OF THE BSI
BOOK FIVE

MARK EVERETT STONE

Seattle, WA

Camel Press
PO Box 70515
Seattle, WA 98127

For more information go to: www.Camelpress.com
www.markeverettstone.com

Cover design by Sabrina Sun

Omaha Stakes
Copyright © 2014 by Mark Everett Stone

ISBN: 978-1-60381-931-2 (Trade Paper)
ISBN: 978-1-60381-932-9 (eBook)

Library of Congress Control Number: 2014948222

Printed in the United States of America

This book is dedicated to all of those
wonderful readers who have actually spent
money on my books:
you know who you are.

Also by the Author

Things To Do in Denver When You're Un-Dead
What Happens in Vegas Dies in Vegas
I Left my Haunt in San Francisco
Chicago, The Windigo City

Living Legend

The Judas Line

Acknowledgments

I would like to recognize the following for their help: My best friend Dave, who came up with the title ... thanks, man. Also, AJ Aalto, the Fabulous Shay West, CP Balois, Jaime White, Lisa and Jeff Hollar (who are far more talented than they even realize), Mandy (because she's cool), the New Zealand All Black rugby team for their outstanding performance of the Haka (which inspired a chapter in this book), Evil Brain Trust, Ltd (don't ask, trust me ... they're cool) Camel Press for being awesome and to the best editor and sounding board a writer could have ... Catherine Treadgold.

Thanks.

PROLOGUE

Kal

Just Like Starting Over

ONE OF THE PERKS OF being the boss is having your own place. When you're the boss of the Bureau of Supernatural Investigation—even just the boss *pro tem*—that means a two-thousand-square-foot penthouse apartment in DC furnished at Uncle Sam's expense. In other words, the loyal taxpayers foot the bill.

That seemed only fair to me, seeing as how I had devoted over a decade putting myself in harm's way to ensure their safety. And that was about two times longer than any other Agent of the BSI had survived. Of course the taxpayers should ensure my comfort.

And the comfort of my girlfriend, Jeanie, who was sawing logs upstairs while I rose early to keep the U S of A safe from Things That Go Bump in the Night. Jeanie was the love of my life, a time-traveling refugee from 1943 who found more acceptance in 21st century America than in World War II England, where they hadn't appreciated her silky chocolate colored skin any more than Americans at that time. She also found acceptance with my parents, who loved her more than apple pie and baseball. Mom called almost daily wondering when she would become a grandmother—not that I minded the idea of children, but I'm only [NEVERMIND] years old, far too young to be listening to the pitter-patter of tiny feet.

Aren't I?

Another perk was free taxi service, also on the taxpayer's nickel. Of course, by *taxi* I mean late-model sedan service with my own personal chauffeur. And by chauffeur, I mean a Green Pea who found him or herself on Kal's Fecal List for the week. Today it was a tall, pretty Pea with long, blonde hair and more dimples than should be legal.

Those dimples were on full display as I exited the luxury apartments in my customary jeans and black Police concert t-shirt, and a pair of black Converse sneakers covering my size thirteens. I looked like a Viking beach bum, something I knew really cheesed off the brass I hobnobbed with. The last few weeks—ever since the Windigo crisis that killed millions worldwide—had messed with my sense of decorum. I was tired and cranky and it was Friday. Everyone loves Casual Friday, don't they?

"Howdy, Spud," I said cheerfully as the blonde pea held open the door to the black Ford Fusion she was using to tool me around town in. Spud ... I gave her that name because when she arrived from Coronado, all lean and mean, she had the personality of a potato. The name stuck and she was less than thrilled. It was only a matter of time before she snuck into my apartment and strangled me in my sleep.

Still, as far as nicknames went, it was one of the least offensive I'd plastered on a Green Pea. Ask Rat or Dildo, they'd tell you.

"Hello, Kal," came the frosty reply as the dimples disappeared. She knew better than to call me 'sir'—that brought dire consequences. 'Sir' is what they call my dad and officers ... and I'm neither.

The early morning sun warmed my face even through the pimp tint on the Ford's windows, and I had a hope, a faint one, that Friday would be a Good Day. No emergencies. No Supernatural buggers crawling out of the woodwork to chew on hapless Straights, and no more paperwork. Just me and a bowl of Lucky Charms and a bottle of Tommyknocker cream soda.

Thanks to the aforementioned Windigo crisis, I had been short of sleep lately, so I took advantage of the moment and conked out in the Ford, waking only when Spud opened the door. From the ice in her blue eyes, I groggily concluded that she'd been tempted to leave me in the car to asphyxiate. She could damn well get in line. There were a whole slew of baddies out there that wanted to break a chunk out of my hide … the Sidhe, vampires, Nazis, undead, and ghosts, to name but a few.

My sneakers hit asphalt that was already almost hot enough to melt rubber and I stood, stretching my tall frame and hearing joints snap, crackle, and pop like a bowl of Rice Krispies. The place where I worked loomed over me like a whitewashed mountain made out of right angles.

Warehouse. It's what we called it and that's what it was, a warehouse big enough to house and train the one-hundred Agents, eleven Receptionists and the small horde of R&D Magicians and brainiacs of Special Branch. The headquarters of the BSI. My home base for so long that I really had no idea what I would do if I left.

That thought followed me in past all the rigmarole and security measures even the Director of the Bureau of Supernatural Investigation must suffer.

Now for the third perk … the office. My temporary office. The word 'huge' damns with faint praise, but it's as good an adjective as any. Plenty of space to run a marathon or to host Congress. It's size daunts visitors and what really takes the taco is that it is actually smaller than the office of the Director when I first joined.

Yeah, we're *that* well funded.

I settled back onto an overstuffed leather office chair that molded itself to my backside quite nicely. The desk I sat at was actually the world's most advanced computer conveniently disguised as a piece of furniture. In it rested the entire history of the BSI, ready for viewing in Virtual Reality through a pair of wire-rimmed spectacles called a DRAFT (Data Retrieval and Forensic Technology unit). It was better than premium cable TV. It was also how my predecessor, Benjamin Bauer, managed to keep his eye on the ball as Director.

Through the DRAFT I saw no waiting calls, no urgent messages, nothing. Everything seemed quiet on the BSI front, a rarity these days, and so I eased back in my chair, ready to relax the day away.

The familiar droning voice of Ghost came from the desk's hidden speakers. "Kal, there's something you must see."

There ... hear that? That was the sound of the other shoe landing on the carpet with a sickening thud. I cracked an eyelid and checked the time on the DRAFT. Damn, two whole minutes of calm and now time for the storm. "What is it, Ghost?"

A picture formed on the DRAFT, the body of a young man, his throat torn and bloody. "The police in Omaha, Nebraska, found the body of Jacob Astorman this morning in a warehouse downtown."

I studied the boy's throat carefully. It had been savagely mauled. "Werewolf? Vampire?"

"The manner of Mr. Astorman's death is not the relevant issue; the manila envelope found on his body is." A piece of eight-and-a-half by eleven-inch paper came into view, crammed with writing scribbled in a tight, crabbed hand. The words seemed to be a mishmash of numbers and characters.

"What is it?"

"It was flagged when entered into evidence, one of my sniffer programs performing a routine search for the unusual. This qualifies in spades."

I scratched my head, but I couldn't make head or tail of the note. "Code?"

"Asymmetric-key algorithm."

Cryptography. Not my strongest subject. Now chemistry, there was something I could sink my teeth into. "Any clue as to who uses it? What does it say?"

A long pause. "It was utilized over fifteen years ago."

Uh-oh. I had a bad feeling. "One of ours?"

"No. It is an old MI-7 code and the key is one that had been used during the Lindauer-Kowalski incident, the joint Bureau-MI-7 mission in New York. The only time a foreign Bureau operated with permission on American soil."

This was getting worse and worser. I verbally accessed the Bureau database with the DRAFT and scrolled through the relevant file while Ghost waited patiently.

"Holy crap," I muttered once I had the gist of the report, awed by what it implied. "The British Ambassador and the German Ambassador to the United Nations? This is friggin' unbelievable."

"Let me show you what was decoded."

A herd of mice with tiny cold feet were tap-dancing up and down my spine. "Don't suppose I can refuse to read it?"

"Not really."

Crap. It had been worth a shot. "Go ahead."

On the DRAFT, the jumble of gibberish faded and reformed into coherent sentences. It turned out to be a letter. To me.

By the pricking of my thumbs …

Mr. Kalevi Hakala:

I have been amusing myself in Omaha for quite a while now, preparing for the day when we would meet. The thought, I must confess, warms the cold cockles of my heart because I have been an admirer of yours for such a long time. Watching you work has been an oft-enjoyed pastime that has aided me in avoiding the ennui inflicted upon me by this weary world.

You have been an inspiration. I had thought myself to be the perfect hunter, the ultimate predator, but we both know that is a lie, one born of arrogance and the need for self-aggrandizement. You, Kalevi Hakala, are the greatest hunter to roam this earth, a man who can defeat any monster, the one Bureau Agent all Supernaturals fear.

Although I hold you in the highest regard, I cannot have that; it is intolerable to me that one, a mere human, has proven to be so perfectly lethal. So we must meet, you and I, and settle the score once and for all. Only the best will survive the confrontation. Nothing personal, mind you; it's simply the way things have to be, the natural order. There can only be one sentient Apex Predator on this planet and it must be me. Because I hold you in such high esteem it will be an honor to take your life. Should I fall before you (an unlikely event), I will die content that only the most deadly could defeat me.

And so, onto the rules of The Game: come to Omaha within the next five days, or every day thereafter I shall kill ten humans in many inventive and disturbing ways, engaging in a spree so terrible and bloody that the creatures who inhabit this dung heap of a world will speak of it forever. Come soon and come alone. You may bring what weapons and magic you wish, but if I even suspect that you have enlisted assistance from other Bureau agents, I will commence the aforementioned killing spree. I will be watching and I will know if you break these rules. Do not force me to drastic action. Do not attempt to spoil The Game.

Please do not disappoint and know that we are, *au fond*, kindred spirits.

No signature. Nothing.

It was creepy as hell, and in its own way, quite terrifying. A mystery person or Supernatural wanted to kill me, presumably by ripping my throat out like the man in the photo. It begged only one question: why wasn't I scared, ready to change my shorts? I knew the answer straight off, without even thinking about it: I wasn't scared because I was too excited. It was time to play.

I guess Friday turned out to be pretty good, after all.

Chapter One

Kal

Gifts That Keep On Giving

Come to Omaha within the next five days or every day thereafter I shall kill ten humans in many inventive and disturbing ways, engaging in a spree so terrible and bloody that the humans who inhabit this dung heap of a world will speak of it forever. Come soon and come alone.

"Kal, are you all right?"

I raised my head and took a deep breath. "What?"

Ghost's buzz held a digital note of concern. "I asked if you are all right."

Good question. The answer would have to be a solid 'no,' though. Some maniac in Omaha was killing people and leaving notes for me in an old MI-7 (the British version of the Bureau) asymmetric-key algorithm. The bastard not only knew who I was and all about the Bureau, but it seemed that he knew a lot of our secrets.

The note contained clues. The writer referred to people as 'humans' or 'creatures,' which implied that my foe was a Supernatural and therefore right up my alley.

I'd been killing the monsters from the World Under (the world behind ours where the Bad Things come from) for over ten years. It was my job as an Agent for the Bureau of Supernatural Investigation to keep the ordinary citizens (the Straights) oblivious to all things magical and monstrous, thereby keeping mankind's fragile social sanity in balance. Straights who witnessed a Supernatural incident were subjected to an Interdiction—a Spell that would render them unable to reveal, in any way, the existence of Supernaturals and the World Under.

I reckoned I must have killed hundreds of bad guys in the last decade or so.

And I am damn good at my job.

Enough was enough. This person, this Supernatural, whatever, wanted me to come to Omaha and compete in a little Apex Predator dustup, and if I didn't show, he was going to kill even more people. I couldn't have that.

The adrenaline pumped through my system as the realization hit me with sledgehammer force right between my baby blues. How did this Supernatural know about the Bureau, MI-7 code, and such? Was it a Sidhe, the race of beings people called Faëries or Faë? Or was it something else? How could an outside entity keep tabs on me without insider information? How could it know so many secrets?

It took a few seconds, but the answer finally popped into my dense skull. I'm slow, but I get there.

It was best to err on the side of caution. "Ghost," I said casually. "This note looks like a Code B.A.G."

It was a code phrase, one that had never been used. Born from the paranoia of the Cold War and the onset of the computer age, it was every Director's nightmare scenario come true.

B.A.G. means Barbarians at the Gates. The term wasn't in any database or written anywhere. It was oral code known to a select few. Those people were BB, yours truly, Ghost, Alex, and POTUS.

In the unlikely case of cyber attack, where the Bureau's computer system becomes compromised and communications suspect, a code is needed to activate countermeasures. Said countermeasures were Ghost and the bevy of cyber-response programs dreamt up by the best programmers money can buy and a few that were subject to blackmail.

I knew that as soon as the letters B.A.G. left my mouth, Ghost would initiate a shutdown of all Bureau servers, leaving any team currently on mission status without Bureau support for a minimum of fifteen minutes. That doesn't sound like a long time, but for a team that relies on a steady stream of information and cyber-assistance, it could feel like a lifetime. Or result in a deathtime. However, the prospect of some outside enemy gaining access to the Bureau servers was almost too horrific to contemplate.

It's not paranoia if they really are out to get you.

China had attempted to hack the Bureau systems several times, but Ghost and his CIC (Cybernetic Intrusion Countermeasures) programs had been more than up to the challenge, not only stopping the hack, but also spamming the Chinese servers with ads for discount Viagra. Strange thing, though … Ghost said he received over one million orders for the erectile dysfunction medication. Imagine the kind of bank he would've made if he'd had the supply.

Better living through chemistry was alive and well in the Far East.

Ghost didn't bother to acknowledge me. The DRAFT simply powered down, becoming nothing more than a pair of useless wire-rims. I knew he would alert all team members and Receptionists of the current state of affairs and everyone would be on pins-and-needles for the next few minutes.

I sure was. The bottle of vodka sitting pretty on the wet bar was looking mighty attractive. Surely one snort couldn't hurt, right?

My hand stopped mere inches from the teardrop shape of Kauffman Vintage Luxury vodka. I wanted that fiery liquid—my cells screamed at me to let the alcohol slide down my throat—but the small, rational part of my mind that was almost drowned out by the gross *need* for drink stayed my hand.

I had spent a good part of my career drinking like Prohibition was about resume, drowning harsh memories with liquor and women. I cared nothing for the women, but the booze …. Damn, the booze always made me feel better.

And that was the problem.

The booze was my hook, the metal barb through the cheek that dragged me to and fro as I tried to get away. It used my need and desire to reel me into a dark place of forgetting and regret.

I stared at the crystal bottle—a work of art that promised beauty inside and out. It would be perfect, I knew, *perfect*. Clear, crisp with just the right amount of fire to heat the throat and warm the belly.

A hook and a trap both, one that would take Jeanie away from me. Jeanie, one of the most powerful Magicians in existence and possibly my last chance at a serious relationship. She was more important to me than the booze, more important than the forgetting and I knew she'd have no truck with someone who crawled inside a bottle.

Ah hell, I was in love.

"Sorry, Mr. Kauffman," I said to the bottle, hand dropping limply to my side. "Not today. Perhaps not even tomorrow." Perhaps never again.

Was I growing up? Heaven forbid!

I sat down at the desk, the bottle and its divine contents still tugging at me. I held my head in my hands, fingers covering my eyes, in an effort to resist its siren song. I was still sitting there, elbows on the desk, face in my palms, when Ghost returned.

"Diagnostics complete," he said sounding almost … tired.

"And?"

"There is a passive threat, a thread of code embedded into our server like nothing I've ever seen before. Whoever wrote this program knows subtlety. It is dormant, camouflaged as a payroll algorithm, and from what I have been able to discern, becomes active only when certain conditions are met."

"What conditions are those?"

"When a team is listed as MISSION ACTIVE. The program then transmits the details of the mission, personnel, equipment, everything, to places and persons unknown."

Perfect. Just freaking, bloody, abso[CENSORED]lutely perfect. "Ghost, walk me through what happens when a team is chosen for a mission. Don't skip the details."

Brief pause. "As you know, when a team or persons are chosen for a new mission, the Director inputs the threat location and who is assigned to that location into the MISSION ACTIVE file. From there all equipment removed from ARMORY is tagged and logged as part of that mission for inventory control, including Spell gems. From there, as the team leader and Receptionist log ammunition and items used, the items are then noted and counter-checked. When the team returns, all remaining items are logged back into inventory."

I rubbed my eyes. "And how are items removed from ARMORY traced?"

"All items are tagged with nanolocators, and when removed from ARMORY, are noted into the MISSION ACTIVE file. Also, as each item is removed from ARMORY, it is logged into the MISSION ACTIVE file by the Agent on ARMORY duty as yet another redundant security measure."

"So this little 'passive program' knows who becomes MISSION ACTIVE and what they take?"

"As well as the status of all the Agents, although it transmits a MISSION ACTIVE status only—it does not transmit the current health and welfare status of each Agent, should he or she be killed or injured in the course of performing their duties."

Okay, please bring your seats to an upright position. "What do you mean by 'the status of all the Agents'? There's more than MISSION ACTIVE status?"

When Ghost answered, his voice lost much of its droning quality. He sounded much more subdued and human, like the man he used to be before he accidentally translated himself into cyberspace. "Yes. As you know, all Agents are tracked with nanolocators implanted into a buttock. In order to adequately track the Agents based on probable threat or urgency, each Agent is given a status: OFF DUTY, VACATION, MEDICAL LEAVE, PSYCHOLOGICAL LEAVE, INACTIVE, MISSION ACTIVE, RETIRED or MISSING IN ACTION. In no way shape or form is a team or person to be labeled MISSION ACTIVE if that is not the case and vice versa. The system is designed that way and was, until just a few minutes ago, considered foolproof. The MISSING IN ACTION status is granted if the Agent disappears and the nanolocator is no longer active. However, if an

Agent is verified deceased, or retires, a signal is given whereby the nanolocator is disabled."

That damn nanolocator ... given under the guise of an inoculation. I was none the wiser until BB informed me a few months ago of its existence. I'd faked my death so I could pursue the Finnish quasi-deity Iku-Turso, the being responsible for my sister's death, without the Bureau's knowledge. Turns out that BB knew all along I was alive and kicking and was more than happy to have me haring off to kill a Class Five (a being of Mythic or God-like proportions) Supernatural. If I died, oh well, no harm no foul, but if I was successful (and I was ... sort of), he could disavow the event to the Finnish government, who didn't *want* their precious monster eliminated because of its cultural significance. Blah, blah, blah.

To say that the Bureau and I have a twisted relationship is to damn with faint praise. We could give Oedipus, Hamlet, Alexander the Great, and The Manson Family a run for their dysfunctional money.

But, hey, if it ain't broke, don't fix it.

"So let's assume that murderer in Omaha wrote and implemented that program," I said, leaning back in my chair with hands behind my head. "That means he or she would know if I went MISSION ACTIVE and if any other team followed because of the information on the destination, right?"

"Yes, if your assumption is correct."

"How long has that intrusion been in place?"

"When Warehouse is relocated, the servers are scrubbed and all the data reloaded, so I would say any time within the last four months."

Hmmm. Four months. Long damn time in cyberspace. "How long will it take for you to scrub the intrusion?"

Ghost didn't answer and I felt a stirring of unease. "You can do it, can't you?" I mean, Ghost was the super cyber spook, TRON on steroids. The thought that he couldn't remove the thread from our system gave me the galloping heebie-jeebies and just when I thought he'd buggered off in shame, his annoying buzz resumed, louder than ever.

"One week, Kal."

One week? "Uh, Ghost … you hacked the DGSE's mainframe in five minutes and posted naked pictures of Gerard Depardieu all through their server. He's not my first choice of actors I'd like to see in the raw, but aside from that, *how come so long?*"

"Kal, I have never seen anything like this program. It shows a level of sophistication, genius and subtlety rarely seen these days. While passive, it includes a secondary program, a diagnostic, which runs every second, testing the integrity of the program. As far as I can tell just from my cursory assessment, if the program is tampered with or abruptly terminated, a virus will be uploaded into our system that will erase or corrupt all our data. Not only that, but there seems to be an element of magic at the core of the code I cannot access until I carefully strip away the outer layers. But there is more.

"In the 1800s, each telegraph operator had their own style when manipulating the telegraph key. It was a particular way of sending Morse code that allowed other operators to know who was sending the message. This was referred to as a 'fist.' When it comes to programming, I can tell if the origin of a program is Chinese, Japanese, Indian, Australian, French, what have you. I can narrow that field down to individual programmers whose work I have encountered before. Currently, I have documented 47,383,956 different 'fists,' or programming styles, matching them to country of origin, city, state, county, province, district, shire, or boroughs. I believe I have catalogued the style of all the professional and amateur programmers on the planet as well as pinpointed their current whereabouts. *This program does not originate from any of them!* I do not recognize the 'fist' displayed in this code. It is an entirely new thing and that alone gives me pause.

"Because of the program's elegance, its complexity, and the magic at its core, I have ascertained that it will take me one week to neutralize it without tripping the diagnostic program into releasing the virus or the programmer finding out his creation has been compromised."

Wow. Double wow. Double wow with a cherry on top. "So it will be difficult. I get that." Deep breath, Kal. Don't let Ghost see how rattled you are.

"More than difficult. One week is a *very* long time to a being such as myself."

"Understood. Well, let's assume that our bad guy is behind this intrusion. I want you to begin the process of dismantling it. I'm still heading out into the wilds of Nebraska to confront this douchebag. I hope I can outwit him."

Ghost said, "I will pray for luck."

Sarky spook. "Har-de-har-har." I had a thought, something that might give me an edge. "Ghost, can I take the DRAFT with me?"

"I am sorry, Kal, but they are slaved to the desk. Only Director Bauer has a portable computer of sufficient processing power to use the full potential of the glasses while on the move."

Perfect. The DRAFT would have been handy, but I've done fine with less.

"Can you alter the MISSION ACTIVE function without the hostile program knowing about it? What I want is to check weapons and supplies out of ARMORY without logging it into the system."

If anything, Ghost sounded rather sorrowful. "Sorry, Kal; I cannot. Not only will the intruder know of such tampering, but I also do not have the clearance to perform such an act. If I were to try, bad things would happen to me, a result I do not wish to occur."

Bad things happening to the most powerful being in cyberspace. What the hell did BB have on Ghost to keep him in line? It was just another reminder that no matter how clever I thought myself to be, BB was in a whole different class of sneaky. "Okay, Ghost, get hold of Alex and brief him on the situation and tell him to meet me in ARMORY in fifteen. I'm going to need some serious mojo. Especially if this evil genius is going to know what I'm bringing with me."

"Done."

In the HUD of the DRAFT, which was back online, I tapped a virtual icon.

"Yes, Director?" asked Andrea, who was BB's, and now my, Receptionist.

"Get me Matt Alba. I want him here five minutes ago."

"Yes, sir." If she was startled, I couldn't hear it. Then again, all Bureau Receptionists were tougher than overcooked steak, so I'd be surprised right off my comfy chair if anything less than global thermonuclear war were to harsh her mellow.

The Bureau had just finished dealing with one of the most deadly Supernatural cases the world had ever known since the great Tunguska Event of 1908. The Unseelie Court of the Sidhe (think of them as the Faërie Mafia, but with magic instead of Tommy guns) had unleashed the Windigo Curse on the world, turning millions of innocent people into cannibals whose bites infected their victims and turned them into cannibals as well. So many people died that it seemed inevitable that the truth about the World Under and Supernaturals would be revealed, but thanks to some creative media spinning the public knew it only as a terrible outbreak of a virulent, weaponized, rabies-like virus. Some were calling it the Aborted Zombie Apocalypse. If you can lie convincingly enough, people *will* believe. I mean, people still believe that Earth is flat, politicians are honest, and Lee Harvey Oswald acted alone.

During the whole shebang I was *pro tem* director while the boss, BB, had been at a summit meeting with the heads of all the other Bureau-like agencies on the planet for a conference on the Sidhe problem. The irony was thick enough to spread on toast. Now BB was on his way back and Ghost had just found out that a psychopath was in Omaha killing people in order to lure me into a duel.

It was enough to make me want to hide under the bed for about fifty years or so.

By the time Matt arrived, I'd finished a bowl of Lucky Charms and a bottle of Tommyknocker cream soda, and was feeling the sugar rush buzz through my body.

"What can I do for you, Kal?" hollered Matt from across BB's enormous office. The echo hit a split second later.

After hearing the *Reader's Digest* version of the Omaha note and the cybernetic intrusion, he scratched his shaved skull and said, "So when do I leave?"

"Oh, I didn't summon you here just to send you out." I stood, handing him the DRAFT. "I am merely appointing you as interim Director until BB comes back. Which should be soon. Ghost will fill you in on how to use the glasses."

Matt's face had gone from light mocha to pale gray in about three seconds, and I wondered if his heart was starting to fibrillate. I guess the news of his hasty promotion didn't sit well. I knew *exactly* how he felt.

"Kal, you have to take a team," he said finally, conceding defeat. He'd been around long enough to know when not to fight. "Or at least have one shadow you." Matt sat slowly, his butt impacting BB's chair. Looked good on him.

I shook my head. "No can do. This perp knows when a team becomes MISSION ACTIVE and where that team will be deployed and I have no desire to have him kill more innocents because I disobeyed instructions. This perp might actually be able to track a MISSION ACTIVE team." My voice became husky as anger fueled my adrenaline. "No, I have to play this straight. Promise me you won't let anyone become MISSION ACTIVE to Omaha."

He nodded, face in hands.

"Good. Ghost?"

The familiar drone popped into the air. "Yes, Kal?"

"Walk Matt through the DRAFT and bring him up to speed on the latest developments concerning cleanup on the Windigo Curse. Also, have a plane ready, and I need a plausible story with the local LEOs, both federal and state. Call FBI Director Shields and brief him on the situation. I'm off."

Matt's voice was muffled by the cage of his fingers. "To Omaha?"

I gave him my best Bond impression, à la Sean Connery. "Why no, M, I'm off to see Q first."

DEEP IN THE HEART OF BSI headquarters lay ARMORY, housing the bulk of the Bureau's weapons, both magical and technological. It consisted of a sixty-foot square room with eleven-inch-thick steel walls accessed through a vault door that would make an Antwerp diamond merchant dizzy with envy. Inside was all a body could want for killing Supernaturals or conquering Indonesia.

That week's vault minder was a three-year veteran nicknamed Ice, a big guy of Irish descent with black hair and the palest blue eyes I'd ever seen, hence the handle. It was a cush gig; all one had to do was guard the ARMORY from intrusion from any non-Bureau entities and make sure that all who entered had the proper authorization.

Those unnerving eyes bored into me as I walked down the hall, and his round face refused to crack a smile when I showed him my pearly whites. As the *pro tem* Director, I couldn't be refused admission, although he seemed reluctant to place his hand on the black access plate.

My own big mitt landed next to his, and we both cited our *bona fides* out loud for the security programs while our handprints were scanned and our auras read by Spell Shapes embedded into the plate. Had either of us not been who we said we were, our remains would have fit into a shoebox.

"You are cleared, Director," he said, barely moving his lips. His muscles bulged under his gray t-shirt with the letters USMC stenciled on the front.

I opened the door. "Thanks, Ice. Send Alex Dumont in when he arrives."

He barely nodded and went back to imitating a statue. A big, overmuscled statue.

The interior of the vault was a sterile white, all weaponry carefully locked away in white bins and cupboards. White cabinets running the length of the room offered a marginal pathway which men far skinnier than I would've had trouble navigating. They mostly hid the bright, white linoleum floor.

Every container was labeled in black lettering indicating their contents, from Spell eggs to handguns, rifles to the latest and greatest in electronics. It was a smorgasbord of potential deadliness offered in one locale.

I was in heaven. For a few minutes I squeezed down one of the aisles reading labels and making my Christmas wish list. My idea of

Santa was a tubby NRA member dressed in red handing out M4s.

The door opened and Alex entered.

Alex Dumont. Short, skinny, nerdy as hell and possibly the most brilliant mind of his generation. Smarter than a closet full of Einsteins, he was the head of Special Branch, which handled techno/Magical research and development for the Bureau. If you needed anything—from creating singularities to Magical cold fusion—Special Branch was where you went and Alex was probably the guy who figured out how it could be done.

He must have been in the shower because his dark brown hair was plastered to his skull and his birth-control glasses had been left behind. The only thing he wore was a pair of athletic shorts and an Adele concert t-shirt. No accounting for taste.

I gave him my best crap-eating smile. "Really? Adele? And here I thought you were heterosexual."

"Are you out of you mind?" he asked, frowning.

"No, I really thought you were heterosexual."

Alex crossed his arms, covering the singer's bouffant. "You know what I mean. That Omaha thing is a setup."

"Well, *duh*." How could he think I didn't realize *that*? "C'mon, Alex, I created the most kick-ass Paladin in *World of Warcraft*. Of course I know it's a setup." McComas the Relatively Unstable was a legend in the Eastern Kingdoms and fun as hell to play.

His stare lowered the temperature by about a hundred degrees. Okay, no time for friendly banter. I crossed my arms and gave him a dead level stare. "No choice, Alex," I said softly. "I need you to help me select the right equipment."

"Don't do it, Kal," he urged, thawing. "Please."

The poor kid was worried about me. How nice. "Sorry. Ghost must have told you about the note. If I don't go, a whole lot more Straights will die."

That earned me a squint-eyed look that he held for about five seconds. "You want to go!" he accused. "You're excited about the entire thing."

Yep, smart kid all right. "Yeah," I grinned. "I am. I've been neck deep in politicians and other fecal matter thanks to the Windigo Curse, and I need to get me some fresh air. The exercise will do me a world of good."

"But you don't have your sister's help anymore."

Aye, there's the rub. No more spectral assistance in the face of unspeakable danger. The kid wasn't sure I could cut the mustard as an ordinary mortal. To be perfectly honest, I wasn't entirely sure, myself. "Do you really think I need my sister's spirit to do my job?" I asked crossly. The ghost of my long-dead sister had been attached to my psyche for over fifteen years and had only recently found its way into the light, thanks to a rather powerful Native American Magician. No more super strength and speed on tap for me; only those attributes I'd been born with.

He held up his hands in surrender or exasperation. Good enough.

"You gonna help or what?" No more time to waste.

"What's the play?" he asked.

"I have to travel light. No Bureau housing or other Bureau presence. Posing as FBI. Ghost is working on the details, but I have to do this lean and mean."

Our in-house super-genius tapped his upper lip and gave that challenge a good think while I waited patiently. To paraphrase Billy Crystal's Miracle Max: don't rush a Magician, or you'll get rotten magic.

"Armor?" he asked.

"The lighter the better."

"Guns?"

"Handguns only. The Lahti and whatever else works. Ammunition for all occasions, but not enough to weigh me down."

"Magic?"

"Yes, please."

After much hemming and hawing and enough furious thought that I could smell burning brain cells, Alex's eyes finally came back into focus and he grinned. It was one of those mad genius smiles that had my testicles running for cover because I knew I was about to be the recipient of something incredibly dangerous that could quite conceivably create a Kal-shaped exit hole in the universe.

Disappearing into the bowels of the ARMORY, Alex soon returned with a beige trench coat and a briefcase. "Here," he said, handing the items over.

I eyed the coat dubiously. "What, I'm going to make the perp sick by becoming a walking billboard for bad taste?"

His grin really had my nerves on edge. "Nope. Put it on."

It fit. I looked like a dork. Or a Scandinavian Philip Marlowe. All I needed was a cool fedora to set the whole ensemble off. "Now what?"

The little skink wouldn't stop grinning and I, the great monster hunter, was really starting to get a case of the heebie-jeebies. "Check the right front pocket," he said smugly.

Fearing that I was about to stick my hand into a Looney Tunes mousetrap, I did so gingerly and pulled out a clip loaded with 10mm rounds. "So?" I inspected the clip. Looked normal.

"Check the pocket again," he replied.

Another clip. And another. And another. On and on. Every time I stuck my hand in, I found a clip, and I placed them at my feet until there were twenty clips littering the floor.

"Alex," I said slowly, kneeling among the ammunition. "What have you done?"

"Three weeks ago one of our boys, Don Rasmussen, came up with a Spell," he said, kneeling at my side, eyes alight with geeky joy. "What it does is to create a small space inside a container which is larger on the inside than out—only by a factor of five, mind you—and the Spell will remain active until the contents are removed, whereupon it must be cast again."

I examined the pocket. Silvery thread lined the interior in an eye-watering pattern that seemed to blur around the edges. It almost made sense to me, like a half-remembered thought at the back of your mind, but after a few moments I began to develop a headache.

"Is it safe?" I asked, rubbing my eyes.

"Yes, it is actually a simple Spell Shape. The only problem is we only have two garments so far. His and Hers."

Well, I definitely wasn't going to make a fashion statement by wearing a ladies coat and I was headed to Omaha, not San Francisco. Once again I looked in the pocket and that creepy feeling of déjà-vu stole over me. Magic always made me nervous, but this was ridiculous.

"Great. Cast it again and I'll load up with all the ammunition I need." I spied a small arms locker and opened it to reveal the latest in the Colt line of weaponry.

Like most enthusiasts, I choose efficiency and reliability over flash and power, which meant my hand went right to a matte-black Colt Rail Gun. Based on the Browning M1911, it was a .45 caliber and had the sleek, no-nonsense look of lethality. Though I normally sported an eight-round clip, I chose one of the new fifteen-round loads. Less is never more. More is more and I was going to need all the more I could get.

My other weapon was my grandfather's Lahti M-35, often mistaken for the German Luger, or P-38. Built solid and heavy to withstand sub-freezing weather, it was as durable as they come and hideously accurate. It was my favorite weapon and I knew I would break before that thing did. The trigger pull was heavy, but the craftsmanship was second to none. It was my primary weapon, so I'd had hundreds of 9mm rounds specially made, bullets for every Supernatural occasion. I started loading up on 8-round box magazines.

Next I turned my attention to the briefcase. It turned out to be filled with polyfoam into which egg-shapes had been cut. A briefcase made for holding Spell eggs.

Perfect.

Spell eggs are polystyrene egg-shaped cases that house precious and semi-precious gems infused either with magical energy or Spell Shapes designed for a single Spell function. On the bottom of each egg is a detachable slip of paper that holds the activation word for the Spell. Each gem has a sort of 'if/then' statement built into the Spell, like a line of computer code. *If* the activation word is uttered within the proximity of the gem, *then* you get a result.

Alex caught the expression on my face. "Yep. This case was made during the Cold War when the Soviet Bureau Agents were infiltrating the U.S. Simple, really: you put your Spell eggs in the case and you're ready to go." He pointed to a shiny brass plate under the handle. "This is a fingerprint sensor, but I've added DNA and aura reading Spells as well. Press your thumb here and the case unlocks." He took my hand and pressed my thumb to the plate, closing his eyes and concentrating. The skin of my thumb tingled for a moment. "There. It's coded to you." He then pressed the releases to the side locks and opened the case.

Empty. Nada.

"An illusion. Anyone else opens this case and they will see nothing. However, don't let them touch because they'll feel the Spell eggs."

I nodded. "Nice. I'll take it." Snapping the case shut, I checked out several drawers of Spell eggs and began to pick my magical artillery. Most I had used before (like the Hellfire Spell—dangerous but obscenely fun), but some were brand new with Spell effects that looked interesting. I took a double helping of those. Call me a masochist, but I live to field-test unfamiliar Spells … keeps me on my toes.

When I laid the last Spell egg in the case (a Hellfire Spell, of course), I turned to Alex. "Now, what about armor? I need something unobtrusive."

"Hmmm." He scratched his chin. "I may have just the thing. Grab whatever ammo you need; this could take a while." That said, he exited the ARMORY, no doubt on a quest for something Special Branch hadn't rated 100% safe yet.

Perfect.

At one of the electronics cabinets I discovered a MagniGlass, a rectangular lens for determining the nature of an object, one of the newer toys for us intrepid field types. I never had the opportunity to use one, but my best friend, Canton Alsate—a Mescalero Apache and one of the bravest men I'd ever met—had and it seemed like just the gadget I would need in the Heartland.

It actually didn't take long before Alex returned with what looked to be a thin Kevlar vest. Far too thin, actually. He proudly held it up for me to admire.

I raised an eyebrow. "What is that?"

It flew through the space between us and I caught it reflexively. Very light indeed, with rigid plates covering the back, chest, and stomach. I dug my fingers into the Velcro pouches where the plates were stored and pulled one forth.

Light gray metal, shiny, it looked a little like aluminum, but was *much* lighter. And thin, too ... less than one-sixteenth of an inch and slick, almost frictionless, as if it had been covered in a skin of oil. For a second I thought the shiny piece of metal might actually be plastic, but it was like no plastic I'd ever seen. One side had a Spell Shape drawn on it in what I supposed was dark gray indelible ink, and this Shape was so complex that my mind shied away as soon as the electrical impulses from my eyes reached my brain.

"What is this?" I asked, staring at the unmarked side. Shiny, yes, but not reflective. I had to hold it up to my nose to catch my image.

Alex looked fit to bust. "Guess."

I didn't have the time, but you don't irk a guy like Alex too often. I needed all the miracles I could get. "Lightweight, absurdly so." I let it *thunk* to the floor. "Sounds almost like ceramic when struck. Hmmm." After picking it up, I gave it a good hard twist using both hands. Or tried to. It vibrated in my palms, but I couldn't bend that ridiculously thin bit of metal the slightest bit. "Jesus, kid, it's tougher than titanium or even NewTanium."

"It's the strongest metal ever created." The light of pride showed in his eyes.

Well, what the heck is a master's in chemical engineering good for if I couldn't figure the puzzle out? Determined not to have wasted my money and years of study—when I wasn't engaging in collegiate naughtiness—I put my mind to the task.

Clues: lightweight ... disturbingly so, strong as all get-out, slick as oil on a glass plate and definitely metal, not plastic or ceramic. What metals or alloys could be made with such properties? It took a good three or four minutes before the answer hit me so hard that I reeled.

"You crazy son-of-a-bitch," I swore, appalled. "Tell me you didn't—"

Proudly, Alex took the metal from my numb fingers. "Yep, I sure did, Kal. You are holding in your hand the very first piece of metallic hydrogen ever created by man."

I whistled low and long, stunned. Hydrogen is the lightest element and the most abundant and is at the top of the alkali metals column on the periodic table. It's not, under normal circumstances, an alkali metal. However, it's been theorized that under immense pressure—about three *million* plus PSI, or twenty-five GigaPascals—hydrogen would begin to display metallic properties. To put that in perspective, it's thought that large gas giants such as Jupiter might contain metallic liquid hydrogen, but at those pressures, a human being would be compressed to size of a raisin and therefore unable to enjoy its superconductive capabilities.

The pressures and temperatures required to make that one thin piece staggered me and sent my mind reeling in fifteen different directions until I came to the only conclusion I could, considering there was no *way*, even with our advanced technology, anyone could make the stuff. "You used magic!" I blurted.

"Of course," Alex said equably. "It took a long time for us to figure out the Spell Shape to create metallic hydrogen. In fact, the basic Shape came from one of the government's think-tank Magicians in Oregon." He spun the piece of impossible metal around in his hands, and it blurred, the harsh florescent light winking along the edges. "The hard part wasn't creating the temperatures or pressure required to form the metal. No, the really difficult part was to keep it stable." The small plate spun until the side with the mind-bending Spell Shape faced me. "You see, without this Spell Shape stabilizing the metal, it wouldn't remain so and the results would be ... severe."

I kept my eyes away from the Shape. "How severe?"

"This one piece of metallic hydrogen would destabilize until the resultant explosion could destroy an area of at least four city blocks, perhaps much more."

"So if I erase that Spell Shape?"

Alex laughed. "No way you could do that, Kal. That gray material used to make the Shape is actually silicon, which has been bonded to the hydrogen on an atomic level. Don't ask me how, because that particular secret has been classified above TOP SECRET. No, as long as there is magic in the world, metallic hydrogen will be safe as houses. The stabilizing Spell Shape is *permanent*."

Chapter Two

<hr/>

Canton
The Buddy System

"**I**s he out of his everlovin' tiny mind?"

I was seeing ten kinds of red at Kal's foolishness. Ghost had just filled me in on the situation after Kal's plane had taken off for Omaha and I was plenty riled up. How could he do such a thing, going at this op alone? There was a crazed killer out in the Midwest gunning for our best man and he just *obliges* the nutty sonofabitch without saying a word or looking for any kind of advice.

Matt stared at me from behind his newfangled glasses—what was it with those specs anyway?—and grunted noncommittally. Jeanie, who'd been with me when Ghost told us the story, merely glared. And that woman can glare. The heat of her gaze could cook a Brahma bull. She had a full head of mad going and I wouldn't want to be Kal when she caught up with hm.

"Didn't you try to keep him here?"

Our new temporary Director laughed. "You ever try to stop him when he got a bug up his ass about something? Not even BB can stop him when he's in a mood; you know *that.*"

Of course he was talking about the time Kal faked his death so he could confront his ancient enemy, Iku-Turso. Kal's Finnish stubbornness had kicked into high gear, putting years of planning into motion so he could fight that monster without interference from the Bureau. But back then he had a team with him—former Agents he'd worked with and trusted to have his back. Now … now he was on his own and I didn't cotton to that one bit.

"So send a team," I said, cracking my knuckles. My friend deserved a good swift kick and I aimed to deliver one when I caught up with him. If I was lucky, I'd miss both legs completely. "There will be plenty of volunteers, me for one."

Jeanie coughed.

"And Jeanie, of course." I'd rather arm wrestle a minotaur than try to argue with her when it came to Kal's safety.

Matt shook his head sadly. "Can't do that, Canton, much as I want to. Whoever this killer is, he or she knows about the Bureau and how we work, that much is obvious. He will be watching out for another team and will certainly know when a team becomes MISSION ACTIVE, especially since the perp monitored Kal's inventory taken from ARMORY. Can you imagine what that loon would do if he saw a team set out so soon after Kal? Hell, the perp might not be alone in all this and we could be under active surveillance *right now*."

"But what about Kal?" Jeanie's voice—like silk sliding over razors—sent a shiver down my spine.

"What about him? He's a big boy and the best at what he does." If Matt felt any trepidation at rousing her anger, he sure didn't show it.

At that moment, Alex barged through the door to BB's office with Dove Jacobs and Dom Rigione in tow. Jacobs was a short Agent with an angel's face who packed some serious muscle in her petite frame and had more attitude than sense. Dom was a four-year who'd been part of Kal's team for two of them. Short, stocky, and covered in coarse black hair, he was liquid death with a rifle.

"If'n you all are taking volunteers to chase after Kal," said the hairy Sniper, "then count us in." His grim expression was set in stone and I could tell that mind was well and truly set in concrete.

For the first time Matt looked nonplussed. "Ghost!" he yelled. "How many people did you tell?"

Our in-house genie in a bottle chimed in. "Just one more. She will be here in a minute. And do not worry; I am in contact with Kal through one of the new smartphones recently developed by Special Branch. It will allow me to communicate with him via the bone induction receiver behind his left ear."

Matt scrubbed his face with his palms. "Why am I not comforted?"

"Because you, Director Alba, are not an idiot."

"You all aren't starting this shindig without me, are you?" said a voice from the doorway.

And there was the last member of our little soiree standing in the doorway, bold as a bull and twice as tough.

Patricia Brannon, a one-woman big brass band with wild, curly, carrot red hair that was the first clue to her temper. At just a shade under six feet, she was a former Receptionist of Kal's who decided to join the ranks of active Agents after half the Bureau was wiped out over a year ago by a psychotic Magician named Margaret Whitcombe. I wasn't there for that little brouhaha, but I sure wish I could'a been. Kal put paid to said Magician with extreme prejudice via a shotgun blast to the head that no amount of magic could fix.

The former Receptionist took the long walk across the plush carpet and enfolded Jeanie in a bear hug, which was returned with interest.

"Don't worry, hon," Pat said softly. "We'll get the big lug back safe so you can kick his ass."

Jeanie smiled. "Thanks, luv."

I was dumb enough to plug in my two cents. "Hey, that's my boy you're talking about."

The look Jeanie gave me could've fried bacon. "You want something kicked, buster?"

"Hell no," I replied hastily, throwing up my hands in surrender. "I know when I'm outnumbered."

"Smart man," Pat said, giving me the once over. "There's hope for you yet."

"You all done, or should I leave the room for a Spell?" Matt looked less than enthused.

The two women turned their attention to the director and I almost felt sorry for him. "We need you to send us out."

"No." Firm. Unshakeable.

You could've heard a mouse's heartbeat. Then, "No?" Jeanie sounded way too quiet. If I were Matt, I would've hidden under the desk.

"No."

It became a staring contest: a former MI-7 field Agent from 1943 versus a tough-as-nails, entirely competent Bureau Agent of Hispanic descent and unshakable moral fiber. I would've made a small fortune selling tickets. One stared with eyes so dark brown they were almost black and fairly sparked with magic while the other looked back calmly, his orbs soft and velvety brown like deer hide. Jeanie was the first to look away, defeated. That's the thing about Matt; he's like Ayers Rock—you can climb all over him, but you can't move him.

"So you're saying we can't go?" She might have been beaten, but Jeanie still had her mad going and wasn't about to let the subject drop.

"What I am saying, you bunch of insane misfits, is that *I'm* not sending you." Matt leaned back in his chair, staring off at God-knows-what in the middle distance through his new cheaters. "I have my hands full of the Windigo Curse aftermath, but fortunately, there are no other emergencies that we know of. There's only one team in the field, Beta, so I have a lot of Agents underfoot getting in my way and causing me no end of grief." He ran a palm across his bald dome. "And you guys are really getting under my skin. So here's what I suggest: I don't need you all hanging about looking down-in-the-dumps about Kal, so I suggest you take some vacation time. Plan a hunting trip, perhaps." I felt a surge of hope as he continued. "Only thing is, you have to bring your own personal firearms for this little trip of yours, seeing as how I can't authorize equipment from the ARMORY for personal time or you'd all be listed as MISSION ACTIVE."

There were smiles all around. Hell, all *I* needed was my Bowie and I'd carve my way through the Midwest if necessary. Alex was practically vibrating. "I know just what to bring," he said.

"No."

Once again that negation hit like a sledgehammer and Alex's face fell.

"No?"

Matt shook his head. "I can't authorize vacation time for you, Alex; you're too valuable. BB would skin me alive and salt the wounds."

Alex got that look on his face he gets when he goes for stubborn while Pat and Dom muttered consoling words.

"Well, then, Matt ... I quit." The little Magician crossed his arms, grim-faced. Done and final.

Jaws dropped, Matt's farthest of all. "You can't quit!" he yelled, a crack showing in his granite veneer.

"Wrong. *You* can't quit because you have a contract that binds you to the Bureau for another couple of years. I, on the other hand, *don't* have a contract and haven't had one for over a year." A whole lot of smug was packed into those sharp little features. "One of the perks of being head of Special Branch and quote, 'invaluable,' end quote."

Dove gave Alex a one-armed hug that nearly squashed the little dude and he blushed clear to his hairline. The look he gave her was part proud, part adoring. It was then that I realized they were sleeping together. While no longer forbidden, fraternization within the ranks was at least frowned upon. I really didn't care, just wondered how he avoided being accidently flattened into strawberry jam. Dove was so strong I wasn't sure *I* could beat her at arm-wrestling.

"Might as well give up on this one, Matt," Pat said gently. "Alex learned sneaky from the best."

"Kal is gonna give me a heart-attack one of these days," Matt sighed. "You know that, right? First saddling me with this lousy job, then making me deal with you lot." He waved his hands in surrender, totally disgusted with the situation. "Get out of here and stay out of ARMORY. Although I suggest that if someone is watching, you all rent a private plane. Remember, the perp told Kal to come alone."

Our enthusiasm was dampened somewhat, but we were still rarin' to go. One of our own was heading straight for the lion's den and we had to make sure he didn't wind up as an entrée.

As we left, Jeanie gripped my hand tight and I squeezed back hard enough to grind bones together. We shared a glance and I realized she was as excited as I was, blood pumping and heart racing at the thought of taking down whatever bad dude was foolish enough to get in our way. It was going to be messy. It was going to be bloody and intense, I could feel it. Mayhem galore.

I love my job.

Chapter Three

Kal

No Rest for the Weary

"Take care of them."

My shirt was off and the cool air of ARMORY had the scarred, gnarly flesh of my torso taut as it tried to break out in goose bumps. The spiraling swirls of burned skin up and down my back and chest looked like melted, flesh-colored wax.

Warm hands touched the mass of tissue. "It's softer and more pliable than scar tissue should be." Alex sounded detached, clinical. "Have you used lotion to keep it this soft?"

"No. Never."

He followed a trail of wrinkled scars across my shoulder and around my left bicep and I could barely feel the pressure. The patch of skin didn't feel like part of me, more like a skintight shirt made of thick latex. "I am puzzled at the condition of these scars. They should be harder. They have split open at least once or twice while you exercised, but I don't see any tertiary damage."

"My sister … her magic kept my scars from tightening." Before Leena had finally … well, gone to where the dead go, escorted by Canton's grandfather, she told me that it was her magic that kept the scars around my torso from growing tight. Now that she was gone I needed some professional healing. I could already feel the tissues becoming stiff. If I didn't do something, they would soon begin to split and bleed. I sighed, missing my little sister, her smell of summertime grass and her warmth—the warmth of unconditional love.

If only Iku-Turso hadn't killed her. If only her spirit, in desperation, hadn't latched onto mine, her magic giving me the power of berserker rage.

If only.

Glowing, liquid warmth flooded across my body, coating me like soothing oil. It felt soooooo good, so right, and I groaned as my skin loosened, drying, cracking, flakes breaking away and falling to the floor like off-white snow. Alex's magic was a balm that should come in six-packs.

"Kal?"

Who was calling my name? I looked around the ARMORY at all the sterile whiteness and stretched, arms straight up over my head, reveling in the feel of my t-shirt sliding against my skin. Damn, but my poor, damaged hide felt *good*, better than it had in a long time. Sensations were closer, mitigating the distant sensation of partial numbness. It wasn't a perfect healing, but good enough.

"Kal?"

A fly must have entered ARMORY, and its buzzing was really starting to get on my nerves. I kept my eyes shut, focusing on the crisp feel of cotton against soft skin.

"*KAL!*" The buzz became a bone saw burr that tore through my skull. My eyes snapped open and I would've started from my seat except I was belted in.

"Wha ...?" I said none too intelligently.

I finally recognized the buzzing as Ghost, communicating through the bone-induction patch behind my ear. "*The plane has landed. You may disembark.*"

Oh. Perfect. The Gulfstream G550 had seats so luxurious, so soft, that I'd fallen asleep as soon as the wheels left the runway. I must've been more tired than I thought. All those weeks dealing with politicians and FEMA and whatnot over the Windigo crisis had taken a toll on lil' ol' me. Note to self: never take the job as Director of the Bureau of Supernatural Investigation again. *Ever*. It wouldn't matter to me if both BB and POTUS begged, pleaded, threatened, or bribed. Some things just weren't worth the payoff.

I stretched, enjoying the sensation. Alex couldn't remove all the scarring. A faint spiraling line still covered my torso and upper arms, but it no longer looked like melted wax, more like someone had drawn a corkscrewing pattern around my body with a flesh-colored Sharpie.

Ghost ruined the moment with, "There has been another murder. Another note."

Ugh, perfect. "When?" I asked grimly.

"The body was found while we were en route, about an hour ago. The data has just been logged into the Homicide Department mainframe."

"And the note?"

"That has not been logged yet. You will have to find out when you arrive at the scene. This case is now under a joint FBI/OPD task force, and Director Shields has placed you in charge. You may have to field a few questions from the local LEOs, but the FBI will stay out of your hair, although the director has offered what resources the Omaha field office has available."

I scratched my head, flattening my bed-hair, which had gone all Billy Idol while I slept. "Where is the vic?"

There was a moment of silence as I snapped open my seatbelt and stood. My new Kevlar/hydrogen body armor was light and snug and hadn't impeded my nap at all.

"In an apartment in the old downtown area," Ghost said. "A place called Jobbers Canyon."

I knew Jobbers Canyon. Used to be The Place To Go way back when—a historic district full of old brick warehouses and cobblestone streets. It had been converted to a sort of outdoor mall with fancy-schmancy eateries, mom-and-pop shops, and one-of-a-kind craft stores. The streets were still cobblestone, but the warehouses had been converted to luxury apartments and condos for the yuppie crowd. And since ConAgra had taken up residence next door, real-estate prices had skyrocketed. Not more than a hundred yards away, the muddy Missouri river oozed on by, a sluggish line separating Nebraska from Iowa.

"Victim?"

"A Mr. Simcha Lowenstein, Esquire, age 31."

"A lawyer? How is our boy picking his victims?" The sole flight attendant, a thin young man with tired eyes dressed in blue slacks and blazer, opened the hatch, letting in a rush of stale, humid air. It smelled like hot asphalt and diesel fuel. The attendant gave me a polite but neutral smile, and I tipped him a nod as I descended the passenger boarding stairs to the tarmac.

Thanks to Ghost's efficiency, I waited only a minute or two for my car to arrive.

"A Hyundai? Really?" The long automobile gleamed with fresh wax and purred to a stop a few feet away, sleek and sexy beneath mother-of-pearl paint. If it weren't for the emblem, I would've mistaken it for a Mercedes E-type.

"A Genesis, Kal," said Ghost as the rent-a-wreck attendant exited. "A much better automobile than you realize."

I took the keys and headed out, my FBI badge clearing the way for me to exit Eppley Airfield. Omaha was no mystery to me because I had attended college in Lincoln at the University of Nebraska (Go Huskers!) and had done my fair share of partying in the city by the Missouri river.

Had to give Ghost some credit, the Hyundai drove like it was on rails and the engine hummed with eager life, responsive and powerful. But it was too flashy, its pearl color not quite the norm for your average FBI agent.

Then again, I wasn't your ordinary agent, so a little flash couldn't hurt.

Jobbers Canyon was only a few minutes from the Airport, and Ghost provided the address via my new smartphone, the latest from the technogeeknerds at Special Branch. I wasn't quite sure of all its capabilities, but Alex seemed pretty excited about it. As long as

I received free long distance so I could call relatives in Finland, I wasn't going to complain.

Finding the correct address was not a problem; I used the GPS app on the smartphone and followed its directions, passing the venerable Baum Iron building. Shortly thereafter, I saw the flashing red and blue lights of a brace of patrol cars and an ambulance. They were parked in front of a trendy three-story warehouse-turned-condo with windows bigger than the Hyundai. Two uniformed officers were standing out front, keeping the lookie-loos at bay. They didn't seem to mind the humidity that threatened to suffocate this poor Minnesota boy.

I parked the Hyundai in a nearby pay lot and approached the scene. "Stay back, sir," said one of the officers as I bypassed the curious bystanders.

I flashed my badge.

"What kind of fed dresses in jeans, a t-shirt, and a trench coat?" asked the officer, who was one solid slab of blue-uniformed muscle. His bullet-proof vest enhanced his corn-fed bulk. The other one— leaner, but no less intimidating—kept his mouth shut and narrowed his pale blue eyes into a dubious squint.

The badge on cop #1's shirt read REED. "Well, Officer Reed, I am the kind of fed that just flew into this city, which has more humidity than should be allowed, and has no patience for standing around sweating his balls off." The air was so sultry I was tempted to draw my Bowie to cut it into manageable chunks.

My answer didn't sit well, but there was nothing he could respond except, "You're expected, Agent Pike. Third floor, apartment 303."

"Thank you."

A serviceable, but aging, elevator took me to the third floor where finding 303 was easy. All I had to do was follow the murmurs and spy the uniformed officer standing guard outside the door. More badge showing and I was let into the apartment.

White. Dazzlingly, blindingly white. The kind of white seen in sci-fi flicks and mental hospitals. My retinas nearly went into overload from the assault. Walls, ceiling ... painfully white. I looked at the soft brown of the cork flooring just so my head wouldn't explode.

Perfect.

While I forced my eyes not to water, I took note of the light blue corduroy sofa and ottoman, the glass and steel coffee table, the kitchenette to the left and the doorway to the right. The apartment wasn't that big, but it was clean and had high, vaulted ceilings. The only thing disturbing in the cleaner-than-clean scene were the obvious signs of a struggle. The blue couch was ripped in three places, the cushions strewn about, and the coffee table had been rendered into twisted steel and shattered glass. Even the fifty-two-inch flatscreen mounted on the wall directly ahead was busted to hell and gone.

Mr. Lowenstein had put up quite a fight.

"Sir?" The voice came from the right, so I tracked my peepers that way and saw a short, slightly tubby guy in an ugly, brown sports jacket standing in the doorway leading to the next room. He was wearing purple latex gloves and had a neutral expression on his thin, florid face. Homicide cop … had to be.

"Not a 'sir,' " I replied. "I work for a living."

He grinned, sending the black and white moustache on his upper lip a-squirming like a caterpillar. He was proud of that moustache, I could tell by how neat it was. It looked like he used a ruler to measure each hair precisely. "Yeah, my Gunny used to say that all the time."

"Devil Dog?" I was surprised. He looked about as dangerous as the Michelin Man.

He took a long step forward and held out a gloved hand. "Corporal Nihsen, 3rd Battalion, 4th Marines."

I gave his hand a squeeze and he nearly ground my bones into powder. He was *strong* for such a little guy. "Lieutenant Christopher Pike, Navy Special Warfare Group Two, also retired." The cover story should hold up. Chris Pike was in the FBI database, listed as an active agent drawing a paycheck and everything. Sometimes my job was just too cool.

Mercifully, he let go of my hand and I shook it to regain circulation.

"You got here quick." Those hard cop eyes of his took in my outfit.

"So you're the FBI specialist sent in to help us poor local cops?" he said, all friendly-like but with some attitude thrown in to tell me he wasn't entirely happy.

"Hey, I'm here to help, not to take your investigation away from you." No need to anger the LEOs. Besides, the police deserved respect, not attitude, that is, unless they intended to hinder my escape from the Midwest summertime heat and humidity; then I could become a little cranky. "Anything I find will be given directly to you. Even the collar will be yours. I'm just along for the ride."

Nihsen's shrewd brown eyes searched my face for a split second before he nodded. "Not how the FBI usually works."

"I'm not the usual FBI type."

"How come I don't doubt that? And not just because of the 3 Doors Down concert t-shirt you're wearing."

"They put on a hell of a show in DC last year."

"Was always a Toad the Wet Sprocket fan myself." He sighed and shook his head, perhaps missing '80s and '90s music. "Ready for ugly, Mr. Pike?"

"Chris. Please."

"Okay, Chris. You ready?"

The blood smell wafting from the room told me it wouldn't be pretty. " 'Once more unto the breach,' " I quoted.

"God save me from the classically educated," I heard him mutter as I followed his black buzzcut into the next room.

Quick inventory: Bed, slightly rumpled, check. Framed print of Picasso's *Don Quixote* hanging over said bed ... decorated with fine droplets of blood, check. Beige cut pile carpeting, very lush, very bloodstained, check. Two forensic guys in blue plastic jackets, check. Nihsen and some beefy bald guy in Sears clothing, another Homicide cop, check. Headless, naked body on the blood-soaked carpeting, check. A chest of drawers, honey oak, with the victim's head perched on top, check.

Perfect.

Simcha Lowenstein had been a big guy. And when I mean big, I mean Green Bay Packers *big* and in pretty damn good shape as well.

Muscles lay like thick cut slabs of beef on his chest and abdomen and it looked, from the signs of struggle, like he didn't go gently into that good night.

"Damn," was all I could say. The ragged stump on Lowenstein's shoulder's told me that his head had been ripped off. I was slightly nauseated and a little pissed. Ripping heads off is my bag. This guy was stealing my moves. It was almost insulting.

"Yeah," said the other homicide cop in thick deep voice. "Damn is right."

"What happened?"

One of the forensic techs replied, "Mr. Lowenstein struggled with his opponent and got his head ripped off for his troubles."

"Thank you, Captain Obvious." I knelt next to the body just outside one of the large bloodstains and took a closer look. The other forensic tech handed me a pair of purple latex gloves and I nodded in thanks.

No clean slices or even edges, just ragged strips and torn bone. Judging by the volume of blood soaked into the carpet, he'd been alive when it happened. The fight must have started in the living room then progressed to the bedroom.

But why? Did the perp toss him in here before decapitating him or was there some other explanation? I stared at the bloody stump as if it would provide an answer.

I looked up. "Did you search this room yet?"

The fat cop in the Sears suit shook his head.

"We were waiting for the techs to finish," Nihsen offered.

"Bet you'll find a gun." I squinted at the closet, the type with dual sliding doors. "Or a knife."

"We'll be done in a few minutes," said one of the techies, who turned out to be a woman under her baggy blue jacket and blue cap. Upon closer examination, she turned out to be cute as a button and I had to force myself not to ogle. Jeanie doesn't like me looking at the other dishes on the menu, even though I have no intention of ordering.

Nihsen nodded to the female tech and turned his cop eyes to me.

"What makes you think our vic came in here? He could've been thrown through the open door."

"No damage to the door frame or door. You don't just throw someone as big as a Mr. Lowenstein through a doorway and not hit it or the frame. There are no marks, no scuffs." I shook my head. "Looks like the fight started in the living room, then Lowenstein ran in here for a weapon, which I'll bet dollars to donuts is in the top drawer of the dresser." I stood. "But the perp was too fast, got to our vic, who was hurting something fierce, and tore his head off." A long pause. "And that takes a vicious amount of strength to pull off, no pun intended."

Nihsen nodded and padded over to the dresser where the grisly trophy on top stared blankly at the policeman. Using a mechanical pencil to flick through the top drawer, he removed a Glock 19, holding it up by the trigger guard for all to see.

"How did you know?" he asked while the fat cop in the bad suit stared at me suspiciously.

"Pure deductive reasoning. I keep mine in the top drawer also."

More staring.

"Okay, okay," I conceded. "On the drive over I had my guys check out Mr. Lowenstein and they found that he has a license for a 9mm." Ghost had filled me in on the life of Mr. Simcha Lowenstein in the Hyundai. Most of what he said flew in one ear and out the other, but a few tidbits of data had caught in the cobwebs in-between.

Nihsen chuckled, the fat cop grumbled, and the cute tech flashed her pearly whites in my direction. I avoided almost certain temptation by not returning her smile and cast my gaze to the ten percent of Mr. Lowenstein resting on the chest of drawers.

The wide-eyed lifeless head stared at me, a somewhat surprised look on its slack face, now rendered pasty and pathetic in death. I'd be plenty surprised too if I felt my head being ripped from my body. Mr. Lowenstein's eyes were a soft hazel and glazed, but his face still showed signs of deep character. It was an honest face, the face of a trusted friend or colleague. A handsome, kind-looking man. Or used to be.

Next to the torn shreds of the neck lay a cheap plastic cellphone, an incongruous element in a place that must have been valued at over 300 grand.

A framed photo caught my eye—Mr. Lowenstein in a white gi tied with a black belt. He was wearing black headgear and padded gloves and the photographer had caught him mid-punch against an opponent roughly his size, but more slender.

Ideas began to form as I realized there was a message here. A grim, nasty message.

"What are you thinking?" Nihsen asked from behind.

Good question. I didn't bother to turn around. "He's making a statement," I said simply, without hesitation.

"What would that be?"

"Look at this photo."

Nihsen stared. "Martial arts guy."

"Tae Kwon Do."

Those shrewd cop eyes fixed on mine. "How can you tell?"

"The letters ITF on the pant leg of his gi. International Tae Kwon Do Federation. Our Mr. Lowenstein was a black belt. A serious badass."

"So?"

"Think about it."

It didn't take long. "Our doer is telling us he can take out a brute like Lowenstein. He's telling us he's a tough guy and has the strength to rip off a tough guy's head."

"Got it in one." Yeah, this perp was strong. Stronger than Lowenstein, and Lowenstein—if all that heavy muscle was any indication—was stronger than me. My opponent wanted me to know he was stronger. He was taunting me, but I couldn't tell Nihsen that.

"I hear Mr. Lowenstein was an attorney?" I asked.

Nihsen frowned. "Yeah, worked at the DA's office as a prosecutor."

"Any good?"

"Pretty damn good from what I've heard. Had a high conviction rate and rumor had it he was a pretty straight arrow."

Perfect. He was absolutely the right guy to help my opponent prove a point. The killer must have stalked him for a while to make sure he was the kind of prey to send the appropriate message: 'Look at this. I've killed a powerful opponent. I am strong. You should be very afraid.'

I relayed that message to Nihsen, who nodded thoughtfully. The forensic techs and the other homicide cop stared at me, rapt. For the rest it was news, but for Nihsen, the cop with shrewd eyes, it wasn't. I could tell he'd already figured it out.

To deflect the attention, I asked, "Was there a note like in the murder of Jacob Astorman?" The note left at the Astorman scene proved to be a taunt and a challenge.

Nihsen kept his eyes on mine, but held a hand out to the techs, one of whom handed over a piece of paper encased in a clear plastic evidence bag. Wordlessly, the cop passed it my way.

I used the camera function on the smartphone to take a picture and it took Ghost only a second to offer an analysis. *"It is the same coded message as the one left at the Astorman murder. Word for word."*

Perfect.

Chhhiiiinggg, chhhhiiiiinggg! I almost jumped. It was the cheap, plastic cell. I answered it before Nihsen or the others could object.

"This isn't even my phone," I said into the cell. "So speak."

"Hello, Kal. So glad you could make it. You arrived in town sooner than I expected." The voice that slithered from the cell was smooth and dry like snake scales.

I snapped my fingers at Nihsen, mouthing the word 'perp.' "Yeah, I'm pretty damn fast when motivated. Hey, since you know my name, mind telling me yours?" Nihsen and the fat cop got on the horn to the PD to trace the call. I held out no hope it would work; our perp was too smart for that.

Laughter, dry and malicious. "You may call me Maydock."

"Maydock? *Maydock?* What kind of villain name is *that?*"

More of that horrible, dry laughter. "You will not be able to make me angry, Kal. Do you mind if I call you Kal? I feel like I know you *so* well." He continued on without waiting for me to answer. "Please remove your earwig and your subvocal mic. Sharpish now! Any attempt at a delay will result in the death of a young man named Nelson."

Cold slithered into my gut as I took off the dime-sized subvocal throat patch and reached behind my ear.

"Kal, do not do it!" Ghost almost sound scared. "I will not be able to communicate with you."

His voice disappeared as the bone-induction patch joined the mic in on the dresser next to Lowenstein's head.

"Very good, Kal, you just saved young Nelson's life. For now."

"You're watching me, aren't you?" Had to be. How else could he know I'd removed my subvocal equipment?

Nihsen looked up from his cell, startled, and began to search the bedroom, motioning the others to assist.

"Of course. The camera is in the Picasso. I don't need it anymore. But before you destroy it, you must also destroy your smartphone. I have no desire to have Otto monitor our conversation or your location. Then … then the game begins in earnest."

I bit my lip. "I do this, then no more killing innocents? Just you and me, big boy, okay?"

"Oh, Kal, you are so idealistic. These lesser beings should be of no import to you, just as they are as ants to me. But I give you this promise, one predator to another, out of professional courtesy: any lives threatened will be yours to save, if you can."

Red clouded my vision as anger replaced the icy worm of fear. "What are you?" I snarled, my Interdiction twinging a bit in the presence of Straights. I was moving into dangerous territory here. "Did I kill one of your … friends?"

Maydock's dry laughter was really starting to chap my ass, but he kept up his chuckling for a few seconds. "Kal, I am something new under the sun, the first of my kind. An incipient species ready to stride the world like colossi."

Perfect.

With no further comment, I smashed my smartphone against the corner of the chest of drawers, sending shattered plastic and delicate components flying. Lowenstein's head fell to the floor with a dull *thud* and rolled to a stop next to Nihsen's size nines. I put the cheap phone to my ear.

"Good, Kal," Maydock purred. "Now … three eight three one."

"What?"

"Three eight three one. That's the code that will disarm the bomb attached to young Nelson."

My skin began to crawl. I knew what would come next, but remained silent.

"He is three blocks away. Two blocks directly south, one directly east. A warehouse under renovation and is currently unoccupied by human prey. He is on the roof. You have ten minutes. Come alone or he dies. Oh, and destroy the phone." *Click.*

I didn't think twice. The cheap cell joined the detritus of the smartphone as shards of plastic and paper circuitry rained down upon the carpet.

"What are you doing?" shouted Nihsen, grabbing my arm.

"I have to go."

He wouldn't let go. Damn, but he packed some muscle beneath that tubby exterior.

His eyes blazed with mistrust. "What did he tell you?"

"Check the Picasso," I said, pointing to the crudely rendered, spear-wielding Spaniard. "Camera is in there somewhere." While everyone looked toward the print I hightailed it out of there, taking the stairs instead of the elevator.

My sneakers hit concrete at a run and the too-humid air walloped my face like a wet slap. The car was close, but so was the warehouse. I briefly considered raiding the Hyundai's trunk but realized that time was short and I had plenty of lethality hidden about my body. At least, I hoped so.

Three blocks passed in a blur; the only sound I was aware of was the flapping of my trench coat. I spied my destination. It was the only building large enough to be called a warehouse—a three-story brick monstrosity surrounded by shorter structures, equally old and worn. An ancient, weathered Gulliver surrounded by storefront Lilliputians.

Most of the small windows decorating the warehouse were either boarded up or broken. As I approached, I became aware of an aura of decrepitude and abandonment that practically shone from its crumbling russet façade. If it was being renovated, it must've been from the inside out.

I knew it was a trap. Had to be. Maydock was toying with me, putting me through my paces for his cruel amusement. It would be up to me to spoil his fun.

Side door. Steel … gray and graffitied and solid as a rock. I pulled my Lahti and tested the knob.

Unlocked.

Perfect. Just what I needed, a 'Here be booby-traps' sign. Bastard was inviting me in. I checked my watch. Five minutes until young Nelson became one with his environment. What to do?

Damn, should have stopped at the Hyundai for some Spell gems. I mentally kicked myself a few times until I spotted a window five feet to the left and seven feet up. *That* I could use; there was just enough lip to pull myself up. It was broken, the frame weathered and cracked, with no boards to hinder my entrance—just some jagged, insanely sharp pieces of glass.

A few seconds spent grabbing hold of said lip and one solid pull-up later, I managed to brace an arm and use the Lahti to clear out the glass shards. I prayed the trench coat was tough enough to protect me from remnants and I hammered my way through the frame, the dry wood cracking easily against my onslaught.

Roll in; hang from the marginal sill and drop, easy as pie. My knees bent and my ankles stung from the short drop, but I was in—my nightvision contact lenses compensating for the minimal light. The warehouse was large enough that the far wall with its dusty, cracked windows seemed impossibly far away and the echo of my every step haunted my ears.

Checked the steel door … *not* booby-trapped. Frickin' Maydock was already messing with my head. At least I looked pretty cool making a gymnastic entrance.

A flicker of motion, and the Lahti came up, my senses alert, ready to put slugs into whatever might come. I was acutely aware of the time ticking away. Nelson needed me, but I needed to live through whatever Maydock had in store. A drop of sweat stung my eye.

"Well, well, well …." came a hissing, loathsome voice. "For a moment I'd given up hope for visitors."

I could feel the hair on my arms and neck stand up as five hunched forms came into view—warty, pebbly, green skin shining under coatings of transparent slime. They were a good fifty feet away, but I was seriously wishing for fifty miles.

"The boss said we would be fed soon," said the figure in the middle, its voice dripping bile, "and I am *hungry.*"

Ghouls.

Perfect.

Chapter Four

Canton
Team Building

Good thing the Bureau pays so well, or we wouldn't be flying in style. Not that my family wouldn't have helped, mind you. Thanks to the Bureau, Dad started up a modest concern in Manhattan and within ten years turned it into the largest construction company on the eastern seaboard. However, I didn't need to call Dad for a loan of a few grand because I was easily able to afford the lease of a private jet to fly my impromptu team to Omaha.

Yeah, my team. Once again I found myself with the dubious honor of being the boss of a fractious bunch of hardheaded, gun-toting, bad asses with serious attitude problems. And I had no say in the matter; both Patricia and Jeanie nominated me for the position and there was no way I was gonna object to *them* when they had their minds firmly set on *anything*.

The bossman's chair was not my favorite place to plant my butt, let me tell you. In fact, I'd been avoiding that seat my whole career and it wasn't until just a month ago that Kal stuck me into the role as leader for that whole Chicago mess. And now I was going to back up that wily sonofabitch on his wild quest to take on a mysterious murderer in Omaha. I was seriously thinking of having my head examined.

Not that it would do any good.

Jeanie and Pat were thick as thieves, chatting away a mile a minute at the back of the plane, while at the front, Alex was hunched over in his seat. He was concentrating real hard, eyes closed and face screwed up tighter than a miser's purse.

Jacobs sat by her lonesome staring out the window at the ground far below, not that there was anything to see at six miles high. Dom exercised the time-honored tradition of soldiers everywhere: sleeping. He snored like an asthmatic Doberman.

Stowed about the cabin was enough firepower to take over a small city, from handguns to SMGs to sniper rifles. Not to mention the odd grenade or three. Our being private citizens, most of the impromptu armory was illegal as hell, but for Agents of the Bureau, such things were par for the course. We weren't gun nuts, just pragmatic. Thanks to some hastily acquired IDs, no one would bother to confiscate our weaponry. Alex was head of Special Branch, which included LOGISTICS, where such items originated. Matt said take nothing from ARMORY, but he didn't forbid LOGISTICS. A technicality, but you take what you can get.

I leaned back, sucking on a bottle of Guinness and massaging the bridge of my nose in a vain attempt to forestall a headache. Always happened when I was forced to take responsibility for others. Had a funny feeling that by the time this latest dustup was over, my head would probably either implode or explode, whichever was more painful.

The intercom crackled and the pilot's voice emerged from the state-of-the-art audio system, loud and clear as if he was right next to me, speaking into my ear, "*Mr. Alsate, you have a call on the satphone. The receiver is in your right-hand armrest.*"

God, I hoped it wasn't BB calling. I'd hate to have to disobey orders.

Wouldn't be the first time, though. I guess a bit of Kal had rubbed off.

"Hello?"

"Canton, it is Ghost. Kal is offline."

My shout of alarm rang through the cabin like a shot. "Dead?"

Cries of alarm almost drowned out Ghost's next words. "No,

Canton, he is offline. The killer, who identifies himself as Maydock, has forced him to remove his subvocal communication equipment and to destroy his phone. He is off alone and has just entered an abandoned warehouse. For what reason, I do not know. I am attempting to monitor his movements via traffic and ATM cameras."

"Jesus," I breathed. One, two, then three seconds of breathing room while the rest of the team gathered 'round, faces pinched with worry. "Keep track of him, then, and keep me informed." A thought occurred to me. "Oh, and tell BB what's what. He'll want to know what his favorite genius malcontent is up to."

"I already have. What he said does not bear repeating, but he will not be back in the States for a couple of days yet. One thing I should note … when this Maydock person was talking to Kal, he mentioned Otto."

It took a moment for that to sink in. It had been years since I'd heard the name. "You mean that old simulated AI program that the Bureau used before you came along?"

"Indeed, although a newer, more advanced version of Otto does assist me with Bureau issues from time to time. Basically, it is a cloned version of myself with certain restrictions programmed into its code that curtails … independent actions. The salient point is that Maydock does not seem to be aware of my existence."

"So you're Kal's ace-in-the-hole. Good." Although it was interesting to note how dated Maydock's information was, considering the cyber intrusion into the Bureau's servers. "Then let's make sure he doesn't find out about you, Ghost."

"Indeed. Maydock is using a burner phone to communicate with Kal and I have attempted to ascertain his location. However, he kept his conversation with Kal brief enough that I could not fix his location."

"Kal's okay," I said to the others. Jeanie let out a sigh of relief, sagging down into her seat. "Ghost is with him.

"All right, Ghost," I said into the phone. "Keep me informed of Kal's location and do your best to locate this Maydock character."

"Indeed, Canton. I will contact you on your cell when you land.

I've made arrangements for a rental car and hotel rooms."

I said my goodbyes and leaned back into the seat. Kal was safe, but that didn't reassure me none. Knowing my friend's penchant for trouble, I had no doubt I'd have to pull his bacon out of the fire.

And soon.

CHAPTER FIVE

Kal
Ghoul Trouble

GHOULS. WHY DID IT HAVE to be ghouls?

A couple of years ago I fought ghouls in Denver, except those baddies had Spell gems implanted into their flesh that gave them unmatched speed and strength. I almost died from having my shoulder gnawed to the bone. Not an experience I recommend for a slow Wednesday night.

These ghouls didn't have Spell gems, but they were plenty nasty enough all on their own: strong, needle teeth, black on black eyes, and more attitude than I liked to see in an ambulatory corpse. Usually separating head from shoulders would be enough, but ghouls have bony plates around the neck that prevent decapitation. Connor MacLeod of the Clan MacLeod armed with a Hattori Hanzō sword couldn't chop through a ghoul's neck in one swing.

My mind kicked into overdrive, noting every detail in sight, looking for an advantage: five ghouls that must have been hiding behind the two rows of I-beam pillars … catwalks twenty feet overhead, no help there unless I got bit by a radioactive spider … an empty warehouse, virtually spotless except for the scaffolding a hundred feet away with a large drop cloth draped bundle of whatever at the bottom … no good unless I could get past the undead defensive line … and nothing else. I was short of help, short of time and had been given the short shaft by Maydock.

Perfect.

While all this clever perception and strategic calculation was taking place in my head, my body was reacting of its own volition. Moving quickly as possible before the Supernaturals charged in to begin their Finnish buffet, I whipped my trench coat off and wrapped it around my left arm. Left hand grasping the loose end, I drew the Lahti with my right just in time to see the ghouls reach the halfway point.

When did they start running?

Cursing myself for being too slow, I fired, hitting the centermost monster above the right eye. Enough damage to the brain and even a ghoul will drop. Unfortunately, spraying a modicum of brain matter out the back of its head only slowed it a tad and *really* pissed it off.

Shoot and move, shoot and move, try to keep the I-beam pillars between me and the ghouls. But there were too many of them and only one of me and a ghoul came barreling in from my left, so I jammed my coat-wrapped arm into its needle-toothed maw and it bit down ... *hard* like a vise edged with jagged splinters of glass. The thick fabric of the trench coat stopped most of the teeth, but a few pointy bits made it through, punching through the tender flesh of my forearm. The ghoul had begun to worry at the coat when one or more of its teeth must have mucked with the Spell Shape lining the special pocket.

The jacket *exploded* outward with a rush of air and magical force as the convoluted extra dimensional space suddenly ceased to exist. Energy was released suddenly, violently as carefully structured magic unraveled. Colt/Lahti clips shot everywhere, quite a few passing my skull at warp speed. A Missouri mule smacked my forearm, knocking it against my chest and throwing me backward ten feet. Something in my shoulder tore and bones creaked as I landed hard on my outstretched arm, sliding the last few feet across smooth concrete, fire shooting through my chest and shoulder.

Damn, that hurt.

As for the ghoul, it jabbered and jibbered for a second before falling lifeless—or more lifeless—to the floor, its skull ripped wide open above its lipless, toothy mouth. Death by pistol-clip explosion. Had to be a first. If I lived, my version of this story told over cocktails would be that I *meant* for that to happen.

I had no time to savor the victory as the other four were on me a second later. I'd barely reached my feet when ghoul #2 attempted a mid-field tackle that could've put me out of the game permanently. Fortunately, time spent playing college football turned out to be well spent as I straight-armed the Supernatural on top of its slimy, crocodile-skinned head and slammed it hard to the floor, firing the Lahti at the back of its neck. Bony plate met 9mm Parabellum at 1,100 feet-per-second and bone lost big time. It didn't die, but it spent some time thrashing as it tried to deal with a shattered, inch-thick gap in its spinal cord.

I knew it wouldn't be long before it regenerated and returned to action, but I had bought some time, which I used to run like hell.

"Stop!" yelled one of the pursuing monsters. "I promise you will die quickly."

Yeah, right. These guys needed better dialogue.

Shoulder muscles screamed as I tried for a cross draw on the Colt, but adrenaline and fear are the best anesthetics and my left hand was filled with my trusty .45. I spun, shooting from both hands, and just barely clipped one of my three pursuers. Keeping in shape paid off because I was faster than the undead and began to pull away, only to realize the end of the warehouse right *there*. The large, drop-cloth-draped bundle lay only a few feet in front and I spun again, slowing enough so I could aim at the ghouls forty feet away. I pulled both triggers several times and rounds tore into a ghoul, tearing through flesh. A lucky shot took out a kneecap and it fell, rolling end over end.

Both guns *clacked* empty. I dropped them, grabbed the paint-stained drop cloth, and *heaved*, hurling the bundle at my attackers. The heavy white cloth ballooned out, and the ghouls, unable to stop quickly enough, found themselves draped head to toe in thick linen.

I dodged out of the way as they collided with what had been hidden.

Paint. Three pallets loaded with five gallon buckets of paint. Water weighs eight pounds per gallon, but paint—depending on the composition—starts at a minimum of *ten pounds* per gallon. Each bucket represented at least fifty pounds attached to a wire and plastic handle.

Perfect.

As the first ghoul extricated itself from the heavy cloth, I introduced its skull to a speeding paint bucket, the whole weight of my body swinging the heavy bucket around at the end of my good arm. A normal human would have been killed instantly, neck snapped or skull crushed, but the ghoul took the blow like a champ, rocking back on its heels as the cheap plastic bucket burst apart, sending industrial gray paint a-flying.

The thick, gooey substance hit the ghoul square in the eyes, blinding it briefly as the final ghoul emerged only slightly marred by the sticky gray paint. A good chunk managed to stain my t-shirt and get into my hair, turning my do into a don't.

I knew the follow-up would hurt. When I'd taken the fall earlier, it tore up my shoulder something awful. Being snacked on by a ghoul, however, was a worse fate. My left hand gripped a handle and I spun, the paint bucket blurring around as my shoulder *screamed*, white-hot agony ripping across my deltoid. The bucket connected with the second ghoul's skull accompanied by a solid *crunch*. More bursting, more industrial gray everywhere and the ghoul was on the floor, coated head to toe. I drew my Bowie from the sheath strapped to my back and knelt, quickly plunging seven inches of steel into its brain and twisting violently, doing terrible things to the rotten mass inside. It spasmed powerfully and I withdrew the Bowie and plunged again, this time deeper, into its remaining eye. The smell was *incredible*, a mixture of grave mold, rotting meat and sour milk that had my stomach rebelling in an instant, but I firmly kept my insides from becoming my outsides. More twisting and the monster ceased moving.

My left arm a lump of dead meat hanging from my shoulder, I

sheathed the knife and retrieved my precious Lahti. I calmly ejected the mag, reloaded with a clip from my shoulder rig, and emptied it into the first ghoul's head. It juked, it shuddered, but enough damage was done and it fell, still covered by thick, gray paint.

Damn, I *hurt.*

The third ghoul whose kneecap I'd turned to guacamole crawled toward me. The Lahti was empty, so once again I had to rely on the Bowie.

"Now *that's* a knife," I panted, trying for my best Paul Hogan.

Three quick stabs and a couple of twists later and the third ghoul was out of the picture.

Four minutes left.

The ghoul I'd shot in the neck took some steel to the skull through the point just above the bony plates surrounding its throat. Stab, stab, twist. Done.

Three minutes left.

The roof. Maydock said Nelson was on the roof, but there were no stairs to the catwalk, only a steel ladder. Considering the state of my arm, my ascent wasn't going to be pretty. Or easy.

Climbing a ladder with three limbs is harder than it sounds and the swelling pain from my shoulder threatened to rob me of much-needed focus. Finally I blundered my way to the catwalk.

One minute to go.

There! A roof access. Steel stairs to a steel hatch. I drew back the dead bolt and shoved on the square hatch with my good shoulder, sweating and grunting.

Seconds left.

A long pebble and tar roof decorated with a single chair whose occupant was securely duct-taped. Several plastic gallon jugs ringed the chair with wires trailing from a five-inch square block covered in electrical tape snaking through the plastic caps of each jug. Taped to the block was a cellphone, one of those new smartphones that crop up every three months or so.

The cellphone and block were firmly taped to a sweating, crying teenager whose head twitched spastically from side to side as I crunched toward him, my shoes scuffling through pea gravel.

"Who's there!" he screamed. Shiny silver duct tape covered his eyes and was wrapped several times around his head, pressing his long black hair tight against his skull. "Are you Hakala?"

I almost stopped, alarm thrumming through my poor, tortured bod, but I soldiered on. "Pike. Christopher Pike."

"Aw, man," he wailed. "The dude said somebody named Hakala would save me." The kid began to sob, snot trailing from his nose into his peach-fuzz mustache.

Thirty seconds.

I knelt at his side. "Easy, kid. I can save you." I punched the numbers Maydock had given me, three eight three one, onto the dialer display on the smartphone, praying that it would work. The smartphone began to blink rapidly and a chill raced up my spine despite the warmth and humidity.

Riiiiiiiing.

Both Nelson and I nearly jumped out of our skins and a heavy lump formed in my stomach. The ringing continued, coming from beneath the folding chair the kid was duct-taped to, behind one of the plastic jugs. The bitter, musky odor of urine assaulted my nose.

"Stay calm, kid," I urged.

"You stay calm! I'm strapped to a bomb and I just pissed my pants!"

I couldn't fault his logic.

Riiiiiiiiing.

I fished around for the phone and put it to my ear. "Hello."

"Congratulations, Kal, you defeated the ghouls in record time. I am impressed. You really are the best. I had my doubts, I really did, but no longer. By the way, how's the shoulder? When your coat blew up, it really looked like it hurt. You should have that tended to."

"Screw you," I snarled. "Now what?" For once I was all out of smart remarks. My shoulder hurt too bad and my temper was frayed to the breaking point.

"Go to whatever apartment or hotel you have secured, Kal. Have some dinner, see a movie, I don't care. Tomorrow at 9 a.m., be at the bus stop at the corner of 15th and Jackson. Don't be late or someone else will die. Do you understand?"

"Yeah, I do. It seems you're the boss." The words were broken glass in my throat.

Maydock actually purred, the sonofabitch, and it sounded like a sandpaper orgy. "And don't you forget it. Need I remind you what will happen if I see any of your confederates? I know who your friends are, Kal, and they should stay far, far away."

"You've been watching me for quite some time, haven't you, Maydock?" *Please, Ghost, please be there. Find this bastard ....*

"Have a good night, Kal. Destroy that phone. Now." *Click.*

Perfect.

I ground my teeth in frustration and smashed the hell out of the cell.

"Mister," Nelson said plaintively, snot and sweat running down his chin. "Can you please get me the heck outta of here?"

"Pike."

"What?"

I began to use the Bowie on the kid's bonds. "Pike. Chris Pike. My name."

"Like the Admiral in *Star Trek*?"

"Well, I consider myself more Jeffrey Hunter than Bruce Greenwood."

"Jeffrey who?"

And *that's* the problem with public schools today ... not covering the classics.

"Never mind, kid. Just call me Chris."

More snot and tears. The chair was beginning to drip pee. "The dude said it was Hakala."

My teeth began to ache as my jaw muscles clenched. "There is no Hakala, kid. As far as you know, you've never heard the name Hakala. Got me?"

He nodded as his legs came free. Soon he was peeling the tape from his eyes as I removed the device from his lap.

I lifted one of the jugs and took a sniff. The smell made my eyes water and I sneezed. "Grab a jug."

"Why?" His lank, black hair would have to be cut. That duct tape would not release no matter how hard he tugged.

"Because we can't leave these here in the sun, and I only have the use of one arm." And it throbbed and burned. Something was torn deep inside the shoulder and I couldn't lift it more than a few inches without burning shards rocketing to the base of my skull. Score one for Maydock.

When a person has been through a traumatic event, they often fail to fully appreciate their surroundings, so intent are they on leaving the scene of trauma. It wasn't any great feat to distract the kid once we finally descended the ladder with two of the plastic jugs of Maydock's homemade explosive—two gallons of soap and gasoline mixture, a poor man's napalm. Had the wires inside sparked, they would have exploded just enough to cover Nelson in a sticky, fiery, mess. His lungs would have slowly cooked as he breathed superheated air and his skin would have sloughed off like an old quilt as the juice in his eyes boiled and burst from their sockets. Of all the ways to die, burning topped the list for my least favorite. Perhaps Maydock knew that and wanted to push my buttons.

"There you go, kid," I said, gently steering him toward the steel door. He fiddled with the duct tape still stuck to his hair, which distracted him from the five ghoul bodies littering the warehouse. God bless vanity.

As we exited—leaving the napalm inside—we were met by one angry Omaha cop. Nihsen's bristly moustache practically sparked with ire.

"You received another call from our doer, didn't you?" he demanded.

I actually expected him to have arrived sooner. My brain must have been on slo-mo, because it took a few seconds for me to figure out why. "You called in on me, didn't you?" I grinned through the pain in my shoulder. "And your boss told you to leave me alone."

Direct hit. His normally florid face turned a bright shade of crimson as I led the stumbling Nelson down the stairs to the parking lot. I left the teen with Nihsen's fat partner, who gave me his best cop glare, which bounced off the shield of my indifference.

"My Captain told me that if you wanted to arrest the governor and sleep with his wife, I was to back off and let you do whatever you needed to do," Nihsen admitted. The words hurt, I could tell.

I turned to the irate detective. "Listen, David, you're a good cop, I can see that, but you have to let me do my job."

"Your job seems to entail tackling this psycho all by yourself."

I nodded. "If necessary."

Nihsen grabbed my arm, the bad one, which ignited a fire in my shoulder. "You don't need to go this alone, Pike."

Biting my lips so I wouldn't scream, I answered, "You are dealing with things that are far above your pay grade. Things you don't want to know about, things that will keep you awake at night. Believe me, Detective, I'm doing you a favor." Why were cops so damn stubborn? Forget that, I already knew the answer.

That earned me a stare. "Don't do me any favors."

I started up the steps. "Wait right here. I'll be back. While I'm gone, talk to young Nelson there, I haven't had the time to yet." Without further ado, I entered the warehouse, shooting the bolt on the door behind me.

Five ghouls, all in states of disrepair. Five disgusting, slimy bodies that I slowly dragged into a heap in the center of the floor. I had to destroy the evidence, didn't want Mr. Nosy Parker Homicide cop discovering greenish undead covered in transparent goo and gray paint. Hard to chalk that up to industrial accidents or radioactive waste.

The ghouls left snail-like trails of slime across the warehouse floor, along with bits and pieces of unidentified flesh and thick, greasy black blood. That didn't worry me; there are ways of disposing bodies that corporations would kill for.

The tinkle of broken glass alerted me to the nosy Nihsen clambering through the window I used earlier. Apparently he was as determined to get in as I was. Funny, he looked far too tubby to make the climb.

"I'm not done with you … yet … Pike," he grunted as he performed a credible descent and the mystery of his aforementioned flabbiness was solved. It looked as if he'd lost a good twenty pounds or so.

"You were wearing a bulletproof vest," I stated, feeling all kinds of stupid. As soon as the words left my mouth I wished I could take them back. Big heaping genius Kal Hakala forgets that most cops *don't* want bullets anywhere near their precious selves. I was sure glad Jeanie wasn't there to hear that gem fall from my mouth. Note to self: next time avoid stating the obvious.

From the look the suddenly slender Nihsen gave me, he was thinking the very same thing, but chose not to hurl it back into my face, which brought him up another notch in my estimation. Instead, the short cop stamped toward me in high dudgeon. I could almost see the smoke wafting from his delicate, shell-like ears.

Then he saw the ghouls. Let me tell you, the look that came over his face was one I'd seen dozen upon dozens of times: incredulity, amazement, disgust, horror, more disgust and the sort of morbid fascination you see from onlookers at traffic accidents.

One shaking hand pointed at the pile of undead. "W-what … what the [EDITED] is that?"

"They," I replied blandly. The rabbit was out of the hat; time to see which way it jumped.

"What?"

" 'They,' not 'that.' You should've said 'what the [CENSORED] are *they*.' " Okay, so I was being a smart-ass, but it usually helps the subject if I can focus their attention on me and make them exhibit an emotion other than bewilderment.

"Are you out of your mind?"

I laughed. It hurt and felt good at the same time. "According to my last psych eval … yes."

Chapter Six

Kal

Challenge

Hot water splashed across my body, a counterpoint to the heat throbbing in my shoulder. I raised my face to the spray and let the water wash the grime from my skin. It stung, but felt so good as my mind wandered over the day's events, sifting through the data.

Fact: Maydock wanted me to know he was stronger than me, deadlier.

Fact: Nelson was kidnapped in broad daylight and never laid eyes on his attacker.

Fact: Maydock knew when I had arrived and had everything set up for me.

Fact: He wanted me to know I'd have eyes on me at all times.

Fact: He referenced 'Otto,' the Bureau's old AI program, in relative disuse thanks to Ghost, which meant that much of his information might be dated.

Fact: Putting me through my paces was part of his master plan, but what part I still didn't know. Perhaps to wear me down, force me to use all but my most basic of resources.

Fact: I needed a lot more facts.

Damn, my shoulder hurt deep down to the bone. Pretty sure I'd torn a muscle. Perhaps Maydock was trying to wear me down to a nubbin so I couldn't fight back, but I had a trick or two up my metaphorical sleeve.

A quick towel off and I half-stumbled my way into the bedroom of my suite at the downtown Red Lion. My cheap-looking briefcase lay beneath the bed and I opened it to stare at the Spell eggs nestled within. Such a smorgasbord of magic.

Out of the thirty-four eggs resting in their foam nests, five were for healing. My eyes went to a pale gray egg with a drawing of a flexing bicep. Just what the doctor ordered—a healing for muscle. Healings for bones and organs required different Spell Shapes. I shook out a small diamond from its protective casing and cupped it in my palm.

"FLATDOG." I uttered the activation word quietly. So very tired. Long day and I had the feeling that tomorrow would be even longer.

A golden warmth flooded my body, centering on my damaged shoulder. Muscles shifted and twisted deep inside. There came a sharp twinge, a short *pop*, and the throbbing ache left the swollen joint, which once again returned to normal size.

"Oh, that's the stuff," I breathed. Over the years I had taken a lot of damage. In fact, I'd come a gnat's hair close to death more than half-a-dozen times. If it hadn't been for magic, I would've been reduced to a few lumps of meat lying on a hospital bed. Or in a casket.

After ordering steak and eggs from room service, I sat down to review the events of the day.

IT HAD BEEN A BITCH getting Nihsen to leave the scene. "I can't tell you what's going on." Fatigue had robbed the vigor from my voice, but the detective remained unmoved. Every fiber of my being screamed for a shower and about a month's worth of sleep.

He walked around the piled bodies of the undead, the leather soles of his shoes softly slap-slapping against concrete and echoing across the warehouse. His nose wrinkled. "You can't or you won't. Damn, smells like wet ass and rotten guts."

The tentacles of the Interdiction Spell lurking in my mind twitched slightly as if to warn me to keep my fat mouth shut. "Can't. I really, really can't, so don't bother asking."

"What are these *things*?" he asked, ignoring my denials.

I opened my mouth and nothing came out but a low burble. It sounded like I was gargling with rocks. The Interdiction had taken hold of my ability to speak and was strangling it.

"What? You okay, Pike?" Nihsen almost sounded concerned. He knelt and ran a finger through some of the transparent slime that dripped from the bodies and gave it a sniff. "Bleh. That is grosser than you can imagine."

Suddenly the Interdiction let go. "You have no idea how good my imagination can be."

He chose not to respond.

I informed the good detective of the two other gallons of homemade napalm, citing my injured shoulder as the reason I wasn't about to help. While he scurried off to retrieve the evidence, I hightailed it to the Hyundai. In the trunk were some supplies I desperately needed.

The mood inside the warehouse hadn't improved by the time I returned, but at least Nihsen kept his partner outside, debriefing Nelson. Perhaps he was afraid to share in the plethora of weird inside. Two jugs of napalm had joined their brothers on the cement near Nihsen's Crown Vic.

One silvery vial, seemingly delicate but stronger than steel, was clasped tightly in my hand. Utterly stable, just a tube of metal until the cap was removed; then it was more sensitive than nitroglycerine. When the Spell detonated it would disintegrate all organic material within a ten-foot circular area and all it would take for a quick trip to nowheresville was one misstep or ill-timed sneeze. Le poofe, and you're one with ... well ... nothing.

"Leave, please," I asked the detective.

"Why?" He still circled the pile of greenish corpses.

This was becoming tedious. "Because I can't do what needs doing if you're doing whatever it is you're doing here."

It took a second or two for him to decipher the sentence's tangles and convolutions, but when he did, he merely crossed his arms over his chest and glared as if daring me to move him.

At that point I was in no shape to wrestle a verb into the past tense, let alone a solid little chunk of pissed off former marine. "Please." There, maybe that would work.

Then again, maybe not. Nihson kept on glaring. He was good at it … must practice in the mirror.

I decided to deal my last card. "I'll call my boss and ask that you be read into the situation."

And that worked. With a final hard stare, Nihsen left me to my business, which was turning the bodies into a big heap of nothing at all.

Unscrewing cap to the vial, I set it gently amid the ghouls. Fifteen seconds before show time. I trotted out the door and closed it gently behind me. Five seconds.

I had time enough to note the ambulance that had arrived. Apparently Nihsen's partner felt that Nelson needed a thorough check out at the local hospital.

Through the broken window came a bright flash of blue/white light.

Nihsen raised an eyebrow. Had I showed him that trick?

I shrugged. "All yours, Detective." Deep breath. God I was tired. "Just make sure you include the slime in your report." Ghost should pick up on that if he was paying attention. "You can leave out the bodies—they're not there anymore—but once again, please do mention the slime."

THE PHONE RANG, STARTLING ME out of my reverie. "Hello?"

BB's voice emerged tinny and tired from the hotel phone. "I have been brought up to speed and have talked to Agent Alba. Seems you're in a spot."

Of course BB would read the situation. "Ghost informed you?"

"Of course."

I wondered once again what BB had over Ghost to make him step and fetch, but it must have been quite impressive. Best guess was that if Ghost became too big for his digital britches, BB would exorcize him out of the Internet using his true name. As for where the electronic eidolon would go after that is speculation best left to theologians. "You calling to cuss me out?"

"Nope," he replied. "Calling to see if you need anything."

"Not really. Who's shadowing me? At a guess I'd say Canton and Jeanie, but I'm not sure who else."

"What makes you think anyone is following you?"

I let my silence speak for me.

BB relented. "Canton, Jeanie, Jacobs, Dom, Patricia, and Alex." When he mentioned Alex, his voice hitched slightly. For BB, that subtle sign was akin to screaming his frustration to the heavens.

Strange, I never took Dove Jacobs as the caring type and Dom was just a few short weeks from the end of his contract. I knew he had a villa in Florence waiting for him and whatever Italian boy-toy he happened to have charmed. That he was willing to take such a risk for me even though he was now a short-timer was quite touching. As for Patricia ....

She and I shared some history. Three years as my Receptionist and friend, which meant three years of watching the team's back and secretly performing psych evals on each and every one of us—part of her job description. Despite the rigors of the profession and the massive turnover rate, we had become friends. When I faked my death a year ago after the Bureau suffered massive casualties, she joined as an Agent. From what I've heard, she'd become one of the best.

"I take it they're following me via the nanolocator?"

"Yes."

"Of course. Listen, boss, tell them to hang far back." I proceeded to catch BB up on the events of the day. "Maydock has me under constant surveillance. He's controlling as much of the game as possible and I have no doubt he will kill and kill and kill until Omaha is awash in a sea of blood if we don't follow his script." And he'd do it in record time so as not to get caught. I had a few ideas on how he'd accomplish that. Explosives, for instance, or poison gas. Maybe at a political rally. "Have Detective Nihsen attached to the team. He has to be read in on the situation; he's seen too much."

"Agreed."

"What's wrong, boss? You seem more tight-lipped than usual."

"I am very angry. There is a Supernatural out there killing people and messing with the Bureau and my best Agent. No one messes with the Bureau or my best Agent except for me."

"Did you just make a joke, boss? Did you?" Surely the first sign of the Apocalypse.

"No, I did not."

Click.

No, I guess not.

Flopping back on the bed, I used the remote to turn on the television. Ahh, just what the doctor ordered for mindless television fun: *Phineas and Ferb*. Reality began to take a back seat when the show hit its second half-hour.

"Hey Ferb, I know what we're gonna do today!" shouted the exultant triangle-headed Phineas to his stepbrother as his overactive imagination gifted him with a brilliant idea. My eyes closed to half-mast. So sweet the hypnotic sedative of the boob tube … so sweet. The world began to blur around the edges.

Words scrolled on the bottom of the TV. "Are you there, Kal Hakala?"

Wha—? Wide awake now …. Houston, we have a problem.

While Phineas and Ferb ran around ordering rocket parts from a local retailer, the words kept on coming. "Hello, Kal, I hope you are watching, as this little trick took some time to achieve."

Okay, ladies and gentleman, I prefer my fictional characters to remain so. My arms goose-pimpled and I was getting ready to draw my Lahti and plug one through the screen.

Then the penny dropped. Ghost … had to be. Most major hotels had servers that coordinated room, housekeeping, and concierge services for all their guests. Every television in every room was basically an extension of the hotel server and of course Ghost had hacked the system. Ghost could hack China if he had a mind to.

"By now you have ascertained that it is I, Ghost," the words read.

"I cannot receive verbal communications and I suggest you do not speak aloud lest Maydock have the room bugged. However, you may use the remote control to access the hotel's MENU function. I have provided a virtual keyboard there for your use. I assure you it is quite safe. I am monitoring the servers here for any intrusion."

Easy enough. When I hit the MENU button, a keyboard appeared, and after just a few moments of experimentation, I was able to type out a simple sentence: HERE. GOOD JOB.

"Thank you very much. As you know, I have alerted BB to your situation and am in communication with the team shadowing you. On a personal note, Jeanie is worried and very angry with you."

Good lord, it was like being married. I grinned. Oddly enough, the prospect didn't bother me one bit. J WOULD'VE TRIED TO TALK ME OUT OF IT OR COME ALONG. NO WAY, I typed.

"Understood. And I believe she understands as well, but that does not mitigate her anger."

No, I guess it wouldn't. TELL J EVERYTHING FINE. MUST SEE THIS THROUGH. PLAY WELL WITH THE OTHER KIDS.

"Indeed. It was very clever of you to have Detective Nihsen mention the foul-smelling slime in his report. We will join forces with the detective tomorrow. Do you have any further instructions for the team?"

I gave that a good think and came up empty except for IF I DIE MAKE SURE MAYDOCK FOLLOWS.

"Very well. Leave the television on so we can communicate. I will leave you to your rest."

GOOD NIGHT GHOST.

I stayed up for a few more minutes, counting and recounting my Spell eggs, obsessively taking inventory: Acid Bomb, Bouncing Betty, Interdiction, etc, etc. The belt I had taken from ARMORY wasn't the usual Bat Belt of pouches that was standard on an op, but a much thinner, lighter version with concealed pouches for small gems. One Spell gem per pouch along with a slip of paper on which was printed the activation word.

During the fight with the ghouls, I didn't have time to pull out a gem, throw it and yell out the activation word, but next time would be different, I vowed. Next time I'd have at least one gem handy.

My eyes kept straying back to the rarest of Spells: Void. It was used against Magicians, a Spell that created a twenty-foot globe of space where magic, for one minute, did not exist. It was the ultimate Magician killer. You didn't need a Faraday coat or a gun to kill a Magician. With the Void Spell, there was a one hundred percent guarantee you would face a Magician on equal terms.

I had a sneaking suspicion Maydock was a Magician.

Ghouls are created when a Magician summons a lesser demon, one without corporeal form, and places it into the body of the recently dead. The newly created undead has to obey the Magician, but is beholden to no one else.

Maydock must have made those ghouls and set them in the warehouse. One of them had mentioned 'the boss.'

I had a feeling I'd need that Spell.

And then I had an idea.

RIIIIIINGGGG ….

Bleh.

Riiiiiiinggg ….

More bleh. The sound annoyed me more than a political campaign ad.

Riiiiiinggg ….

Okay, whoever was calling me was *toast*. "Hello?" I mumbled into the receiver.

"Hello," said the digitally feminized voice of the hotel computer. "This is the … 6 a.m.…wakeup call that you requested. Hello, this is the …."

I hung up hard enough to crack plastic. What the bloody hell? I hadn't ordered a wakeup call. After inspecting the alarm and finding that it was still set for 8 a.m., I did some serious thinking (hard to do when your head feels like it's stuffed with formaldehyde-soaked cotton balls) and realized there was only one answer.

Maydock.

Bastard was screwing with me, letting me know he was out there, watching … waiting. He wanted me off my game, looking over my shoulder at all times.

This guy was really starting to piss me off.

I glanced at the TV. No more messages from Ghost. Everything must have been hunky dory for the following team. I bet *they* got to sleep in.

Well, no rest for the weary. I decided on a shower of sufficient length to prune my skin for several hours and room service. Two bowls of Lucky Charms, bacon (everything is better with bacon), toast, OJ, strawberry jam and a side of pancakes. Thank goodness for my active lifestyle or I'd weigh 800 pounds.

The digital readout on the bedside clock changed far too slowly and then, all of a sudden, it was time to go. I had the valet bring the Hyundai around and sped off toward my destination.

Fifteenth and Jackson. Near enough to Jobbers Canyon and the warehouse where I'd fought the ghouls. Near enough to Mr. Lowenstein's apartment. Was the downtown area significant? Did Maydock have an emotional attachment to the oldest part of Omaha? I had a funny feeling I was going to find out. There was a parking spot near the intersection and I pulled in, depositing two bits into the meter.

A fine May day in Omaha. Warm with enough humidity that I was in danger of drowning. Sweat began to bead across my forehead as the heaviness of my Faraday jacket closed in on me.

Since my mystical, magical trench coat took a dump on me the other day thanks to the toothy attention of a ghoul's maw, my only other protection (besides my metallic hydrogen armor, which was oddly cool and comfortable) was my Faraday jacket. Smaller than a Faraday coat, it didn't *quite* offer the same level of protection as magic; however, this particular jacket had double the amount of platinum mesh, which made it doubly heavy and doubly hot. I didn't look out of place wearing what looked to be a dark brown windbreaker, although if one were to look closely, they'd see that it didn't bunch or crease in the same fashion of a true windbreaker.

There … the bus stop. A three-walled Plexiglas gazebo housing a battered brown bench. Would Maydock meet me here, or was this merely the second phase of the game he'd concocted? I knew the answer.

The back of my lap hit the bench and I commenced waiting. It took less than fifteen seconds for Maydock to contact me.

Riiiiinnnggggg ….

I double-checked my watch. Yep. Right on time. I recognized the sound—another cheap cell.

Riiiiinnnggggg ….

Duct-taped under the bench. Of course. No need to wonder if I was being surveilled.

"Hello?"

The snaky dry voice slithered into my ear. "Did you get a good night's sleep?"

"Very funny joke, Mr. Funny Man," I said through clenched teeth. Yeah, fatigue was screwing with my judgment. Had to watch out or I'd unleash a whirlwind of tightly checked emotions.

"Aw, Kal, you didn't find my wakeup call amusing?"

I declined to answer.

After a sufficiently long period of silence, Maydock continued, "Well then, shall we continue?"

My teeth began to grind. "Yes." *Grind, grind.*

"Look to Woodman Tower. See it?"

My gaze shifted to the second-tallest building in Omaha. "Yes."

"Two blocks east and one south is an old building on 16th and Farnam constructed of red brick. On the west side of the building, right in the middle of some boarded up windows, is a gray steel double door that is normally locked. Today it will not be. Pass through the door and take the stairs to the top floor. You cannot deviate from that path because it is the only direct access to the top floor besides the elevator, which you don't have clearance to use. At the top, you will find another steel door, white this time, which also is usually locked but will not be. Pass through that one as well and locate the wooden door on the left. That is your destination. Enter and inform those inside that you are FBI Agent Christopher Pike and you wish to speak to Mr. Ransom."

"And this Mr. Ransom will lead me to whatever monster you have waiting for me?" What a friggin' nightmare. How long would I have to jump through Maydock's hoops?

As if reading my thoughts, Maydock laughed. "Yes, that building houses monsters galore. Omaha is much like a deep abscess; on the surface everything seems healthy, but once the scalpel lances into the tender flesh, pus gushes forth.

"But listen," he continued in a less jovial tone. "Once you pass this last ... test, I will know you are indeed worthy of meeting me in person. On this I give you my word. We will meet and *then*, my friend, the game will begin in earnest. Remember, destroy the phone."

I sighed.

Perfect.

Chapter Seven

Maydock's Journal
Entertainment Value

EVERYTHING HAS BEEN PROCEEDING BETTER than anticipated. Hakala has performed beyond my wildest expectations. He plowed through those ghouls like a sharp knife through soft butter and it was *magnificent*. It seemed such a waste of good corpses, but the drama was worth it.

For a long time I was not sure about Kal Hakala and his amazing abilities. Surely the stories were blown far out of proportion; no human could be that mythic, that majestic when it came to the art of murder. No, that is my bailiwick. I perfected the craft through years of experimentation, have devoted my young life to causing death, to thinking of creative ways to end life and to think that another, a *human*, was as good, or better, was *intolerable*.

But is Hakala human? That is food for thought.

While perfecting the technique of slaughter, I chanced upon Omaha, a sleepy Midwestern city that seems unremarkable, banal, boring. Oh, sure it has its fair share of crime, meth houses, and prostitution, but underneath its sleepy exterior is a cancer, an evil so profound it takes my breath away. Not that I care about simple human evil, no. To the contrary, the suffering humans inflict upon one another tickles me senseless and this city has been the perfect place to lay low while I expand my range, learning how to use a variety of weapons instead of just relying on my prodigious strength and speed.

I tugged at my lower lip, my smile a twisted slash.

Guns are efficient, but boring. Shooting lacks finesse and … delicacy. My smile grew wider. Yes, 'delicacy,' that is the perfect word. From a distance—even a short one—you can't see the light leaving the prey's eyes; you have to get up close and personal to revel in the artistry of death. And if anything, I consider myself an artist, one with enough panache to turn a simple act of murder into a creative statement expressing not just the pain, but the agony and ecstasy of death. What could be more artistic or just plain *cool* than that?

I stared critically at the bank of flat-screen monitors, irritated with #11. That one has been a little wonky for quite some time now, but the game is too far along to try to work out every little defect. I have learned to adapt and adapt quickly, and most of my prey does not possess this quality of resilience.

On #5 Kal stood and stretched. Hakala is a big man, larger than I, with large, impressive muscles and the grace of a hunting cat. One thing I know well is that superior size doesn't result in superior lethality, especially not in this case.

I watched Hakala throw the cheap cell against the sidewalk, enter his rental car, and speed off north, even though he was close enough to have walked. Is he becoming lazy, like most of humanity? Or was he in pain from the beating he took yesterday? If he was, he showed no sign. No, Kal Hakala is far from lazy, of that I am sure. No more lazy than I.

Lazy is not for hunters who need sharp reflexes and minds to outfight and out-think their prey. Why, it has taken me nearly a year to learn how to hack the local government and banking software so I can access both ATM and traffic cameras. Thanks to the several talented programmers I've docilized in the last three years, I myself now possess the skills to crack any database, corrupt any server. Once my agile and brilliant mind learned all it could from the docilized humans, they no longer held any value and joined the long list of my victims. Although, as a thank-you, I was swift, showing uncharacteristic mercy. Let it not be said that I lack compassion or gratitude, even to the lesser beings.

I know that I can hack any one of the big banks, shuffle around some code and have millions, if not billions, deposited into a Cayman Islands account before lunch, but money holds no interest to an apex predator such as I. Only the hunt, only the game can hold my attention for any length of time. It provides the stimulation that really causes my juices to *flow*. Life is boring without sport and the taste of blood on my teeth. Setting up the game has taken many years of study and surveillance, hundreds of thousands of dollars in computer equipment for monitoring events, and countless hours of hands-on manipulation. Hakala should be grateful. I have done all this for *him*. I would never grant such a favor to average prey or those I label kin.

Then again, Kalevi Hakala is not your average prey. In fact, I long ago accorded him the label 'hunter,' a designation Hakala will no doubt accept and acknowledge. Right before he dies, of course.

"Would you like something to drink, Master?"

It was one of my many servants, a heavy-breasted blonde I docilized when I first arrived in Omaha years ago. A strong, Midwestern type with a spray of freckles across her pert nose. I considered the woman critically for a few moments and noticed that she is starting to age— stress marks bracketing her generous mouth and crow's feet marring the corners of her eyes. Soon her looks will fade and I will have to dispose of her.

Not now, I thought. *I can use her a while longer.* When I smile, it isn't pleasant. The girl cringed slightly, which pleased me. No, good comfort prey are hard to find and this one has been a rare gem indeed.

Docilizing is a arduous process involving time, considerable magic, and the kind of precision found only in the finest neurosurgeons.

Thank you, Mother, I think for the umpteenth time. *Thank you for teaching me the subtleties of that Spell.* I gazed fondly at the docilized human. *A little while longer.* "A drink would be good," I said aloud. "Vodka, chilled, neat." Hakala's drink. We have that much in common. That pleases me.

The buxom blonde nodded, her long golden hair spilling around her shoulders. As she walked away, I admired the sway of her tight buttocks beneath the short, floral print dress she wore. *Very nice.*

Back to the monitors. Where was Hakala's car? Ahhh ... I stabbed a finger at monitor #4, a feed from an ATM across the street from the building where I sent my cherished enemy. The glass of the large windows on the first floor had been replaced by sheets of gray-painted steel, making the structure look like a cross between an office complex and a prison. Hakala was sauntering along the sidewalk as if he had not a care in the world; in fact he walked as if he owned it. Such nerve. Such style.

I am all about style.

Kal Hakala arrived at the large steel door and pulled. He seemed a little overbalanced—it opened more easily than anticipated—but recovered quickly and entered.

Grinning, I tapped at my keyboard, activating the camera and audio to the little 'distraction' I prepared when I saw that that little busybody Detective Nihsen was going to stick his nose where it didn't belong. Sometimes humans just don't know their place.

How dare Nihsen interfere? Most humans are sheep, meekly giving way when an alpha like Hakala comes along, but not this stubborn little man. No, he had to puff out his chest and play power games he couldn't hope to win. I have been stalking the Midwest like a panther for over two years and no one has come close to catching me. What makes Nihsen think he had the brains to compete with a real predator?

But the detective will be out of the picture for a while, and when I finally defeat Hakala—a given, considering my physical prowess and genius—then it might be just the thing to pay a visit to the nosy policeman. To docilize or destroy? Both options are ... intriguing.

Monitor #8 showed Hakala in the small lobby of the old building, and the day became a trifle more interesting.

"Don't die, Kal," I whispered, "not before I can kill you."

I hate you, Kalevi Hakala.

I love you.

Chapter Eight

Kal

Once More unto the Breach

WOW, THE DUDE WAS *BIG*.

I'm not talking linebacker big—more like semi-truck big with a generous dab of Black Angus steer thrown in for good measure. His blue blazer, large enough to double as a two-man tent, covered arms thick as my thighs. A prodigious gut preceded him by a generous foot or so, though there was obviously serious muscle beneath all that blubber.

Black hair like a slice of midnight was pulled straight back and hung six to eight inches in a ponytail, held there by a little wooden clip. Factor in a round, olive-skinned face with intricate tattoos covering cheeks, chin, and forehead, and you had one mean looking guy as big as a house.

"You must leave, sir," said the apparition in a deep voice. His broad, fleshy face was devoid of emotion and dark brown eyes that some would call black shone from deep within a swirling, tattooed motif. Those strangely looping lines hurt to look at.

"You're Māori!" I blurted, identifying the tattoos.

He continued to stare at me, those eye-bending patterns lending additional power to his glittery gaze.

Yeah, another stupid statement. *Obvious much, Kal?*

The Māori are the indigenous people of New Zealand. Their ancestors arrived at the island about 1250 AD from eastern Polynesia on canoes. Thanks to several centuries of isolation, they developed their own unique culture and language. A growing population led to competition for resources and increased warfare and the development of a strange brand of magic not found anywhere else: tattoo Spell Shapes.

Ta moko, the traditional Māori tattooing, is considered a treasure (or *taonga*) to the Māori people, the application of which is sacred. Each tattoo has a specific meaning to the wearer; they record family history and declare tribal affiliations. Then, at the height of Māori warfare, some enterprising Māori Magician stumbled upon a way to imprint Spell Shapes upon skin by including special ingredients in the ink, thus creating ink that could store magic.

To this day no Magician had been able to replicate the art of Māori Tattoo Magic, much to the frustration of the various Bureau-like agencies across the globe. And the Māori weren't sharing, either.

Most magical *mokos* were used to enhance strength or the natural healing ability while a few, a very few, were created to keep the spirit bound to the flesh regardless of damage sustained, making the warrior virtually unstoppable, much like a horror movie zombie. Because of those Spell Shapes, warriors began to eat their defeated enemies in an attempt to incorporate their magic and their spirits.

Hoped this big guy didn't feel the need to continue the practice.

I hauled out my badge. "Christopher Pike, FBI. Let me in."

"No, sir. You must leave and procure a warrant before I can let you pass."

None shall pass! The line spoken so menacingly by the Black Knight from *Monty Python and the Holy Grail* echoed crazily in my mind. *I'll bite your legs off!* I almost had a giggle fit. Probably not the appropriate response from a big he-man secret agent type. "Sorry, Slim, but I'm coming through. I suggest you get out of the way."

Slowly, deliberately, the big man reached into his blazer and drew forth a foot-long flat club made out of a greenish stone. My Lahti was in hand before the club cleared the blazer.

"Drop that right now!" I barked.

The club was a *patu*, a Māori weapon that could shatter or crush bone. At only a half-inch thick, a Māori warrior of sufficient strength and skill could remove the top of an opponent's skull with one swipe. I had a funny feeling that Mr. Big-and-Wide had plenty of practice.

"Go, sir," came the deep voice. The man barely moved his lips. "Go or I will be forced to use this."

I aimed the Lahti. "Don't make me shoot you."

Instead of complying like any sane person, the big Māori spread his legs wide in a semi-crouch, causing his cotton slacks to groan in protest, and began to chant, slapping his chest and gesticulating ritualistically. "KA MATE! KA MATE!" he bellowed, the first light of emotion hitting his face. It looked like lust. "KA ORA, KA ORA!"

Perfect. He was performing a Haka, the Māori war dance and song meant to intimidate enemies. Believe me … I was plenty intimidated.

"TENEI TE TANGATA PUHURUHURU!"

It wouldn't be long now before he stopped dancing—his movements a cross between Sumo wrestler stomps and a victory dance after a touchdown—and started attacking. His eyes—dark, dangerous eyes—were glazed with battle fervor. I knew I had only two choices: go through him or through the door behind me.

I chose him.

The Lahti spat, a short, sharp bark that echoed loudly in the small lobby. It tore through the blazer and into the Polynesian's big belly.

Nothing.

"NANA I TIKI MAI WHAKAWHITI TE RA!"

Blam! Another bullet, this time dead solid center in the right kneecap where I *knew* it would stop him cold.

It didn't.

A hole was punched into cheap beige cotton slacks followed by a half-dozen smaller holes as the bullet, traveling at a mere 1,100 feet-per-second, shattered into shrapnel which tore its way back out through the slacks. The Māori warrior kept chanting.

"UPANE, UPANE, UPANE KAUPANE."

Blam … one to the face. The swirly tattoos flared bright blue for a moment, highlighting the bullet fragments that fell harmlessly to the scuffed, black and white checkered linoleum floor.

I knew I had about a second-and-a-half before the chanting was over and the big Polynesian attacked, and it looked as if my guns were a no go.

"WHITI TE RA!!!"

With one last stomp, the warrior posed, eyes wide and mouth open, tongue thrust out and down. It was the ritual facial rictus that was supposed to frighten the enemy. Looking at the twisty tattoos and the sheer bulk of the man, I could see how it would frighten the average Straight … but then I had an idea.

Perfect, I thought, moving forward and doing the one thing that my instructors in hand-to-hand combat told me never, *ever* to do.

I kicked.

When you kick at someone, especially a high kick like I was performing, you're simply inviting your opponent to grab your leg and play wishbone with it. It was the gift that kept on hurting and I prayed that the big guy hadn't had the same training I'd received or this was going to be the shortest fight in history.

The tip of my sneaker arced under the protruding tongue and made solid contact with the Māori's chin, snapping his mouth firmly shut.

Snickt.

A few ounces of bloody meat flew through the air, leaving a trail of crimson droplets. The tongue flew up, up, up and hit the drop-tile ceiling, leaving behind a red smear. It fell to the floor with a wet *splat.* Both the shocked warrior and I watched the whole thing in stunned silence.

"I can't believe that worked," I said softly.

Two dinner plate-sized hands covered the Māori's thick-lipped mouth just as a gush of crimson jetted out from between his teeth, staining his chin. Mewling, gurgling sounds issued forth along with a spatter of blood.

It was my chance. I followed the kick with a straight right beneath the chin. The big guy might be bulletproof, but perhaps not fist proof.

Crunch went my knuckles as they were stopped cold by harder-than-steel flesh. His neck muscles gave a fraction, but not the tissues my digits hit.

"Owwdammit!" I cursed, jumping back and shaking my damaged fingers. Nothing broken, but the joints began throbbing something fierce. Apparently his skin was tough, but his muscles still had to react to whatever force was applied, which was why I could snap his mouth shut without damaging his chin. I filed that under 'things to know when fighting a big-ass Polynesian with magical tattoos.'

The Māori's back arched and he sprayed blood in an anguished scream that shook the tiny lobby. Dropping the *patu* to the floor, he slowly straightened, his black eyes focusing on me with blazing fury, his chin a small waterfall of blood.

"Oh crap," I breathed just before the metaphorical feces impacted upon the rotary oscillator.

I dove for the *patu* and managed to snag the flat club just as a hand the size of a wrecking ball clamped hold of my belt. The next thing I knew I was airborne, the floor and ceiling changing places several times in my line of sight.

This is going to hurt.

Thump!

The wind was knocked from my lungs as my spine met the wall at a high velocity, and I fell gasping to the floor behind the Māori's generic, pressboard desk. My face hit the edge of his steel chair, threatening to squish my nose through the back of my head, and the resultant cramping agony tried to put my lights out.

Lungs desperately clawing for air, I managed to rise to all fours before the big man tossed his desk aside like a tinker toy where it exploded into splinters upon hitting the opposite wall. Next thing I knew I was in the embrace of a pain-maddened giant who wanted to squeeze my guts out through my ass. Arms like steel cables hugged me tighter and tighter to a torso that felt like pillow-wrapped iron.

I gurgled something, not having the breath to do more, and flailed wildly. The edge of the *patu* smacked the Māori across the cheek. A bright flash of reddish light erupted where flesh met greenstone.

Howling, the Polynesian once again threw me across the room to become reacquainted with the wall while he grasped his cheek in agony. I stared dumbly from the floor, the *patu* still clutched in my hand, as he shrieked, spraying a red mist from between his teeth.

A small burn mark scored the flesh of his cheek where the *patu* made contact and the tattoo there leaked acrid, bluish smoke. I stared at the greenstone club, surprised. *Note to self: keep hold of that club.*

I stood, a bit unsteadily, spine on fire, limbs shaking, but ready to do some damage. "Okay, big guy, surrender now and I'll let you off easy." I spat out a gobbet of blood.

His answer was an inchoate cry of rage. He charged. I swung the *patu* and connected, hitting him on the shoulder. He grunted in pain, but it didn't stop him from landing a blow to my stomach.

Fleshy fist met metallic hydrogen armor, and while the armor held, there was enough *oomph* behind the swing to send my stomach on a vacation to Agonyville, population: Me.

Meanwhile, the Māori screamed in pain as the force of his punch against the armor shattered the small bones of his fingers. I was too busy gasping for breath to really appreciate the irony.

Eventually, after much muffled cursing and whimpering, we both squared off again. The ten-by-fifteen lobby seemed far too small to house the two of us.

The Māori had a chin full of blood, a three-inch burn mark on his left cheek, and knuckles swollen to the size of bratwursts. He held his right hand gingerly. Every third or fourth breath he wheezed and spat out a glob of bloody saliva.

I hoped I didn't look half as bad.

We circled, him wary of the *patu* I held in my right hand, and me extremely wary of all of him. There was a lot there to be scared of.

I smacked his left hand, not hard, but hard enough to cause a couple of tattoos I hadn't noticed before to spit reddish sparks. He hissed in pain and greenstone crumbled to powder as a fraction of the *patu's* edge disintegrated. I guess I'd been too busy being flung around like a rag doll to notice it happening earlier. If I hit him often enough I'd wind up holding a useless greenish nubbin of stone.

The light of understanding flooded the Māori's eyes and he charged, hand outstretched for the *patu*. There came a soft *squishing* noise and the big man did his best impression of a Buster Keaton pratfall, feet flying up while his body seemed to be suspended in air for a fraction of a second before falling heavily to the floor.

Vibrations from the impact traveled up my legs and aggravated my aching gut, sending a wave of nausea through my body and bile to the back of my throat. Meanwhile, the wide load lay on the ground, momentarily stunned.

Without a second thought I was all over him like a politician on a bribe, swinging for the cheap seats. The flat of the *patu* smacked him hard on the side of the skull above his ear, sending forth a shower of carmine sparks. His eyes crossed, glazing over before closing in the blessed relief of unconsciousness.

I raised the *patu* for the *coup de grâce*.

And did not strike.

It wasn't in me to kill the big guy. Was he just a man doing as he was told? Or was he complicit in whatever shenanigans were being conducted deep within the building? Nah ... I could easily shoot a man between the eyes for being a bad guy, but not an innocent soldier. It's always the guys on the front lines who get bloodied while the generals sit back and tally the butcher's bill. No, Maydock was playing a deep game here and I wasn't going to wade through gore for his amusement. Not if I could help it.

Sure that my nemesis was watching, I looked around for a camera but found nothing, only the shattered remains of the Māori's desk and bits and pieces of a black telephone. Other than that, the room was sparse with only the shiny metal doors of an elevator shooting my reflection back at me and another gray steel door, no doubt the one that Maydock wanted me to enter through.

So I did the merciful thing: I used a pair of zip ties on the big man's wrists—zip ties, never leave home without 'em—and a couple more on his ankles. That would keep him out of my hair for a while. I then expended a lot of energy rolling him onto his side so he wouldn't choke on his own blood. Nice touch, that.

As I hobbled away, I caught sight of what had tripped the Māori up and caused him to fall heels over head. There was a small, pinkish strip of something slick and slimy on the bottom of his size sixteens.

His tongue. The man had stepped on his own tongue and it had caused him to slip as if it were a banana peel. What was left of his mouth muscle looked like a ridiculously flattened, pink slug.

Okay, gross out time.

I left the World's Sickest Practical Joke sticking to the big guy's overlarge shoe and began to check the status of my weaponry, including the Spell gems stuffed into the mini pouches of my belt. Everything looked good, nothing missing, just a few scratches on the fender, but otherwise A-Okay. I opened the steel door Maydock told me to pass through.

Stairs, of course, leading up.

Up. Okay, I could handle up. Up was doable, but down would have been better.

Whoa. No windows, just landings, but as far as I could tell each landing was a half a story and by the sixth landing my thighs were beginning to burn. I really needed a Stairmaster workout; the old hams were getting flabby. The price of resting my fundament on the Big Boss Chair, with no time to work out.

Each footfall on concrete echoed eerily, the gray steps bouncing the sound of my sneakers back to my ears. What was up here? I feared the answer as much as I looked forward to learning it.

The stairs came to an abrupt end at a white steel door on a five-by-five landing. A camera was mounted above the door on the ceiling, hidden behind one of those black plastic hemispheres you see in every Vegas casino.

I guess my entrance would be seen. Squaring my shoulders, I opened the door that Maydock said would be unlocked and found myself staring down a long hallway lit by fluorescent lights. Cheap black and white checkered flooring, the same as downstairs in the lobby, trailed off some fifty or sixty feet before the hall turned to the left. On the right were more steel doors spaced every fifteen feet. On the left was a single door, wood, with the words TTG, LTD stenciled on the frosted glass.

As I walked toward the wooden door, I noticed the strange crosshatched texture on the wall, as if extra fine chicken wire had been placed there and painted over in industrial gray. Frowning, I ran a thumbnail across one of the fine lines and the paint peeled away easily. Gleaming silver wire met my eyes.

Silver mesh.

By the pricking of my thumbs ....

What the hell kind of place had Maydock sent me to? There was only one use for silver mesh that I knew of, and that was for a Faraday cage, one to keep magical energy from entering or leaving. I palmed a couple of Spell gems, half-carat diamonds, and read the slips of paper that accompanied them, their activation words. Had a very bad feeling that I'd need some magical firepower but soon.

Back to the door marked TTG. Time to get a move on. I smoothed my unruly mop of blond hair as much as I could without water and comb, adjusted my Faraday jacket, checked my punch daggers disguised as a belt buckle, made sure my Bowie was still secure in my back sheath, and opened the door ....

Straight into a scene from *Office Space*. Cubicles everywhere stretching across an enormous room lit by ugly, flickering fluorescents. Each little workspace seemed to be equipped with a cheap, black office chair on rollers and a laptop. The cubicle walls were four feet high—high enough to hide a seated person—and the people inside those cubicles all stood at once in a wave of hostile, glaring humanity the moment the door opened.

"Uh ... hi?" I began, sweat suddenly sprouting from my forehead.

Two things brought that sweat to the surface of my skin. Number 1: every single worker, man and woman, had the sour look of a hard, miserable life in their beady little eyes. A tightening of the skin and a narrowing of the lids as if they had spent the last few years of a hardscrabble existence squinting into the sun. Each person, dressed in office casual, looked like they could chew up nails and spit out staples. They looked like dangerous sonsofbitches ready to do serious damage at the drop of a hat. Number 2: none of them was under 30 years of age. I saw more gray hair, crow's feet and age spots within a twenty foot radius than I would all day at a nursing home. But even the eldest—a man who looked at least 80 with a *Spitting Image* puppet face and a caustic expression—had the wiry build of a career soldier. Despite their grizzled faces, they were fit, agile and mean.

"You lost, son?" asked the old man, not kindly. Each word implied hazard and pain.

I pulled out my ID. "Agent Christopher Pike, FBI. I need to speak to Mr. Ransom."

And then, of course, all hell broke loose.

Chapter Nine

Maydock's Journal
Better Than Television

On the monitor, Kal Hakala dropped the *patu* next to the bound form of his opponent and exited the lobby, heading up the stairs and out of sight. There are no cameras in that section of the stairwell. None were needed, and the tiny ones with built-in transmitters I could have used would not have penetrated the silver-sheathed walls.

What a fight! Hakala dispatched the Māori faster than I thought possible, although the fact that he let the Polynesian live is a sign of weakness. Perhaps it's something I can exploit? Or is it a sign of respect? Perhaps dominance.

Yes. Dominance. I understand that well, the exhilaration of having power over a foe, holding their fate in your hands. You can kill an enemy, or you can let them live and let them fear your return, sweating each day, knowing each tick of the clock is a borrowed moment that will be collected sooner or later.

That is it. Hakala wanted the Polynesian to live with the pain of his lost tongue, knowing that he would never perform the Haka again.

What a cruel and cunning adversary. My respect for the Agent grows greater.

Shaking my head, I leaned back and laced my fingers behind my neck, staring blankly at the wall of monitors that graced the smallest part of my home.

Fifteen large, flat screens stared back, all but one of the split screens showing a whole lot of nothing. The exception was a camera mounted among flowers resting in an ornate vase placed carefully atop a mantle. Monitor #13. The scene it revealed showed the nosy detective Nihsen and his overweight partner inspecting a crime scene, a blood-spattered room specially prepared—yet another work of slaughter art by me, Maydock the Artist. Blood Art. A little distraction to keep a pointy nose out of my business.

Four black-suited SWAT team members stood clustered in the center of the room, away from the pair of bodies thrown carelessly in one corner like so much refuse, the detritus of a messy kill—limbs and heads detached from torsos. Blood pooled beneath the corpses, a reeking stain on honey-oak hardwood floors. I knew from my hack into the police mainframe that SWAT was there in case the perpetrator happened to be close by. A lesson learned from the last crime scene.

A gout of dry laughter exploded out of my throat. As if Nihsen is worth the effort of my precious attention. It is Hakala I am devoted to, not some over-the-hill police bum with a donut fetish. Still, it amuses me no end that Nihsen might think himself, or others, worthy of such notice. Humans tend to be an arrogant lot.

"I cannot have you interfering now, Detective," I said softly. "Afterward ... after I deal with Kal, then you and I shall have a very interesting conversation and it will be *epic*."

One of the SWAT team members caught my eye: a medium-sized man with ruddy skin and a graceful roll to the hips. That man knew how to handle himself—that was evident from the casual yet alert way he held the Benelli M1 in his gloved hands and from the set of his powerful shoulders. There was something about him, though, something familiar that raised the small hairs on the back of my neck, but the black helmet and goggles partially obscured his features and impeded recognition.

I closed my eyes and sifted through multiple lifetimes' worth of memories. It nagged at the back of my mind, but for some reason I could not tease the memory forward. It remained stubbornly out of reach.

Sighing, I ran a hand through my thick red hair; the long locks curling through my fingers like fine copper wire. I am proud of my hair, so long and lustrous, but I know that such hair would be a disadvantage in a duel with Kal Hakala. More than once I've witnessed Hakala using long hair as a convenient handle in a fight.

The Mountain Dew at my elbow was warm, so I chugged the syrupy liquid down and tossed the can in the trash receptacle resting on the floor a few feet away. "Drink," I said, just loud enough to be heard in the other room.

The blonde appeared, wearing a skimpy blue silk teddy and a travesty of a smile. She quickly headed for the small kitchen and returned with a cold can of Mountain Dew, which she opened and handed to her master.

I eyed her breasts straining against the soft fabric of the teddy and felt myself begin to stir. *You have to love these corn-fed Midwestern girls,* I mused as the cold liquid bubbled down my throat. *So much nicer than those skinny East Coast wenches.*

Monitor #13 once again caught my attention. The ruddy-faced SWAT member was talking to Nihsen while holding a cellphone to his ear. Once again I felt the tug of memory. *Who is that man?*

Oh well, probably not important, I thought. Humans really aren't that interesting, except as food. I stared at the blonde for a moment. *Or as vessels for my lust.*

It will be a while before I find out if Hakala survived the next hour or so. I wish that I was able to place microcams in the TTG offices, but the company took its privacy seriously and had the best anti-surveillance tech money can buy. Using their own computer webcams against them was impossible, in that they didn't have any. In fact, I couldn't find any electronic point of access, which hints at a level of sophistication and paranoia that surpasses mine. It took all my considerable genius and stealth to place the stairwell cameras on a feedback loop so they wouldn't see Kal Hakala coming. It was delicious. Oh, the surprise, the mayhem!

I felt the thrill of arousal. I ran a long-fingered hand down the blonde's arm and watched as goose bumps marred her white flesh. Full arousal hit me in a rush and I grabbed her arm, dragging her into the bedroom.

Chapter Ten

Canton
The Way Things Work

ALL IN ALL, NIHSEN TOOK the news of the World Under pretty damn well.

Thanks to Ghost, we had a pair of rentals, twin Yukons big enough to hold a football team each and a suite of rooms at the downtown Hyatt. We ate dinner together at the Leo Club, a fancy-schmancy eatery a block from the hotel. The food was supposed to be wonderful, but we had a powerful lot on our minds with Kal in trouble and all, so to me it was pretty much a plateful of tasteless mush.

By the time we made it back to the hotel, we received the update from Ghost. Kal had killed five ghouls in a warehouse downtown. Five! Good to see that the old boy had kept his skills sharp. Turns out some ass-hat named Maydock was the creep leaving bodies around town and he was the one putting my friend through his paces.

We had our next course of action laid out for us as well: BB wanted some cop named Nihsen read into the Bureau and Interdicted. We were to stick with the cop like glue and to disguise ourselves as a SWAT team just in case Maydock had the old hairy eyeball on Nihsen while the detective continued to investigate the murders. The killer was watching the crime scenes via cameras, so having a tactical team nearby wouldn't seem out of line. With the detective as a front, BB and Matt were sure that our movements wouldn't look too suspicious.

As for Kal, Ghost downloaded an app to our smartphones that could track him via his nanolocator. Clever.

Captain Henshaw of the Omaha Police Department was more than willing to have five more FBI agents assist in the capture of Maydock. It helped that we had the full weight of the federal government behind us.

"I don't know who this guy is, but we need to catch him fast," he'd told me when we entered his office. His long face was haggard and I would bet my last buffalo nickel that he was facing some serious crap rolling downhill his way. Deep wrinkles had been made deeper by lack of sleep and worry. "Anything you need, Agent. Anything you need."

As for Nihsen's partner, a man named Clemens, a largish, overweight guy who seemed to have been born without an imagination, he only nodded once and went back to drinking coffee and eating bagels, totally uninterested in visiting Feebs and their agenda.

Why couldn't more cops be like him?

So we found ourselves in a SWAT van with Nihsen, who had been safely Interdicted by Alex, wearing full combat gear and armed to the teeth with the best weapons the local LEOs could provide and a few others they didn't know about. It was decided that Jeanie should fill him in on what's what.

He chewed the inside of his cheek as the van rolled on, following Clemens' vehicle as we headed for another one of Maydock's victims on the south side of town, almost bordering the neighboring city of Belleview.

After a bit he sighed and said, "Two things."

"Only two?" asked Alex.

Nihsen gave the younger man a nod. "Yeah. First off." He pointed to Jacobs. "Your name is Dove? *Really*?"

The van became deathly quiet as Jacobs tensed. Everyone knew she had a load of powerful hate going on for her name. More than once she'd been reprimanded for starting a scuffle over some good-natured ribbing, and we all waited with bated breath for her to lash out and start breaking some detective bones. Although, to give Nihsen credit, he had a grip like a vise and wouldn't go down easy.

"Yes," the muscular pixie grated through clenched teeth. "My parents were from Boulder, Colorado. It's a hippie thing."

"Hmm ... well, how about that?" Nihsen said, chewing on his moustache and not noticing, or downright ignoring, her clenched fists. In her bulky, black SWAT armor, she looked more dangerous than ever. Even Alex, that most oblivious of humans, tensed with worry.

Jeanie leaned over and tapped the detective's hand. "What's your other concern?"

"Hmm, what?" Nihsen shook his head, and everyone relaxed a trifle as Jacobs looked away.

"Your other concern?" she repeated.

"Oh, that. Yeah, I don't believe in magic. There has to be another more rational explanation for its existence. You can't just wave a wand and say 'abracadabra' or 'wingardium levi*ohsa*' and expect flying monkeys to shoot out your ass. It just doesn't make sense." He chewed on his moustache a bit more. "So I guess what I'm asking is ... what the hell is magic anyway? Really?"

Everyone groaned as Alex leaned forward, his face eager behind his protective goggles. "Don't ask him that," I complained. "He lives for that."

"Have you ever heard of dark matter and dark energy, Detective?" Alex began.

Nihsen nodded. "Sure, I watch the Discovery Channel. Those two things are everywhere holding the universe together or something. So what?"

More groaning. I hoped we'd get to the crime scene soon.

"Everything we can see in the universe—all matter, all those nebulas, stars and the whole sweeping panorama of the universe with its 1.2 *million* galaxies—only account for about four percent of its total mass and energy," said Alex, rubbing his gloved hands together like an excited school kid. He nearly dropped his shotgun, but Jacobs managed to snag it in time. When Alex starts on a roll, the only thing real to him in that moment is his audience and the subject matter. It was like watching a dog with a bone. "Dark energy comprises roughly 68 percent of the total mass of the universe and only shows itself on a large cosmic scale. Dark *matter*, on the other hand, comprises roughly 27 percent of the total mass of the universe and exerts itself on each individual galaxy and the universe at large. The remaining five percent is ordinary matter.

"In simple terms, dark matter attracts and dark energy repels, two opposing forces that keep the galaxies out there, including ours, from spinning apart. Instead we have a pinwheel dance of stars that manages *not* to break up.

"Current theory states that dark matter might actually be a subatomic particle that hasn't been discovered yet."

Nihsen gave the younger man a skeptical look. "And this means what?"

"Well, it's just background to my theory, which is that magic is merely the manipulation of dark matter to achieve a result that cannot be explained by the 'normal' physical laws of the universe. Either that or magic is really the manipulation of the recently discovered Higgs boson, or God Particle, to achieve miraculous results, but I don't subscribe to that particular theory." He paused, pursing his lips. "You know, current theory holds that it was the Higgs boson that was responsible for the big bang, and the Higgs Field, the invisible energy field that exists throughout the universe, might be the origin of magic—not dark matter or dark energy. It's also posited that it is the manipulation of all three—dark matter, dark energy, *and* the Higgs Field."

"Oh, I think I'm starting to get a headache." The detective rubbed the bridge of his nose.

I knew the feeling. I was about to tell Alex not to strain our brains any more, but his mouth was faster than my wits.

Alex's eyes were far away. "You know, gamma rays from the core of our galaxy may come from the explosion of dark matter, which is made up of WIMPs."

Nihsen's eyes were beginning to glaze. "Wimps?"

"Weakly Interacting Massive Particles. When they approach other WIMPs, they annihilate one another because they're their own anti-particles, like matter and antimatter. There are enough WIMPs that they collide all the time and produce gamma rays."

"What does that have to do with the price of eggs? Wait ... don't tell me, I don't want to know." Nihsen grimaced. "You can prove that wimpy theory?"

Alex's face fell. "Well, not really because, like I said, it's all theoretical, but I'm developing—"

"Then it's just a theory," the detective said quickly, eager to put an end to all that concentrated brainpower before he got singed. "Call me when you can prove there's no such thing as magic, that all that Spell Shape stuff is just science misunderstood as magic. I'll leave all the smartitude with you brain guys and trust you'll figure it out."

The little magician looked a trifle sad that his spouting off had been nipped at the bud, but it sure did please our ears. Don't get me wrong, I like the little guy, but sometimes he doesn't realize how much his vast intelligence intimidates the rest of us. Think about it like this: the rest of us in that van were closer to an orangutan in IQ than we were to Alex.

Our destination was on the border between Belleview and Omaha, a nice house, two stories with a white picket fence and neatly trimmed lawn and hedge. There were even some rosebushes to complete the Norman Rockwell-esque scene. The front door was painted a glossy, cherry red, reflecting the lights of two cruisers parked in the driveway. This was the scene of more murders, courtesy of Maydock.

Alex stayed in the van to talk to Ghost while the rest of us headed for the front door with Nihsen, acting like a SWAT team ready to spray bullets at the slightest provocation. A good indication of what lay inside was the state of the two burly uniformed officers guarding the door—faces white and hands shaking. I smelled puke. Someone had lost their lunch and from the spatter, it looked as if the rosebushes were on the receiving end.

The red door gave way to an interior splashed in the same color.

A lot of red. More than one person, more than two. The walls and ceiling of the modest living room were liberally coated, but it was the mottled orange carpeting that held the biggest bounty. It was soaked through enough that puddles of crimson pooled between the fibers. The air was thick and the odor cloying.

What was left of the victims was thrown into the corner of the front room, chucked there by an indifferent hand. I kept the others back in the foyer breathing the fetid air while Nihsen and his partner went to join the forensic team who were examining the remains.

The cell in my jacket rang. "Hello?"

"This is Ghost."

A dark, sucking pit formed in my gut. "Please tell me good news."

The pause was long enough that I grew afraid. "No. Not good news. I tracked Kal to an old office building at 16th and Farnam. The signal from the nanolocator disappeared shortly thereafter."

"What could stop the signal from a nanolocator?"

"Destruction of the locator, several feet of rock or metal, or—"

"Or what?"

"Or a Faraday cage."

"You think the building at 16th and Farnam has a Faraday cage?"

Ghost made a harsh buzzing sound that sounded like a snort of frustration. "I would not put it past Maydock." Nihsen entered the room, looking at me curiously as I continued to yoggle-doggle with Ghost. "My guess is that he knew Kal would have some sort of tracking device upon his person. I thought you should know just in case …."

"Keep me apprised, Ghost," I said quietly. "I think it's time to head back downtown."

"Agreed," he said before hanging up.

Nihsen wandered in close. "What's going on?"

"Kal might be in trouble," I murmured. "We have to go."

The detective stared at the floor a moment. "I should come along."

"It's bound to be rough," I said. Last thing I needed was to fill out paperwork on why a homicide cop got himself dead on a Bureau op. BB would chew my hide up one side and down the other and probably salt the wound for good measure. "You aren't trained for this. No disrespect."

Brother, he was sure good at tossing out the evil eye. The gaze he slapped me with woulda roasted a steak clean through. "Listen, son," he grated through clenched teeth. "I went through the first Gulf War while you still had your hand on your pecker dreaming of the prom queen, so I've seen my fair share of what floats in a toilet." His face was flushed with emotion. "This is *my* town and I will be double-dipped if I'm not part of what's going down. Count me in."

What could I say? I considered him counted.

Chapter Eleven

Kal

Behind Closed Door

OVER A DOZEN PAIRS OF eyes went from hostile to downright ugly as I announced myself and I was damn glad I'd palmed some Spell gems.

Quick motion as several ducked behind their cubicle walls and my instincts, honed by years of wading hip-deep in blood, screamed at me to crap or get off the pot. I flipped a gem out far into the big room just as several people popped up from their cubicles holding weapons, more than I thought I could safely deal with.

"HORSEFENNEL!" I yelled as I ducked out the door.

A clap of ear-ringing, room-shaking thunder and bright light followed me out as the magical flash-bang grenade detonated, sending debris after me and addling everyone in the room, rendering them temporarily deaf and blind. I had maybe a minute or two before the effects wore off.

Back through the door and the only person who wasn't writhing on the ground grasping his ears in pain was a tall, rugged looking guy in a Sears blue blazer and khaki slacks. The second I barged in, Lahti in one hand and Spell gem in the other, he fixed me with a hard-eyed gaze from all the way across the room, a hammer stare that I felt to the roots of my hair. My jacket began to smolder.

Magician! A powerful one, too, to heat up all the platinum mesh in my jacket enough for the lining to begin burning. I took a quick shot that missed and ducked back out.

My jacket was good for stopping a Charm or Sleep Spell, something that would affect me directly, but I really didn't want to stick around in case he decided to use his magic to make a phone or a printer explode and shred my hide with plastic shrapnel. No amount of platinum stuffed in a jacket will keep a body safe from *that*.

I ran down the hall, checking the other doors. All were locked; no joy there. At the end was a turn to the left which I took at speed, trying not to become one with the wall, and raced down another long hallway. No doors on the left into the big office room, thank God, and boarded, painted windows to the right. I was skirting the outer wall with only one other door in sight: straight ahead. This one was an ugly brown with faded black lettering I didn't bother to read because I had no other options left. It seemed that Maydock had dropped me smack dab into a hornet's nest of ugly.

The brown door was unlocked and opened easily, revealing a square plastic floor sink and a host of cleaning products and utensils. Janitor's closet. Perfect.

I was trapped.

"Think, Kal!" I urged myself while spinning around in the small space. Time. I needed time. Time and a way to call for help. My eyes scanned the hall and lit upon the silvery heads of the sprinkler system dotting the ceiling. An idea began to form, one that I didn't like, but beggars can't be choosers. Gritting my teeth, I riffled through my belt pocket, produced a two-carat diamond, mouthed a quick prayer to whatever kind deity might be watching, and tossed it down the hall.

Tickety, tick, tick, tickety ….

It stopped ten feet from the right turn. Good enough.

At that moment a man in black slacks and a white, short-sleeved, button-down shirt complete with pocket protector sailed around the corner, shoulder banking off the outside wall. One hand gripped a very large pistol, which spat lead my way the second he laid eyes on me. One bullet came close enough to my ear that I could feel the heat of its passage.

Time for the activation word. I quickly looked at the slip of paper in my hand and yelled, "HORNFLOOGLE!" Hornfloogle? Really? Was Special Branch watching *Fraggle Rock* reruns again?

Whooooosh!

The hallway erupted in white flame that raced to the turn and back toward me. It stopped thirty feet away, creating a wall of such intense heat that my eyes dried out and my jacket began to smolder all over again. The Hellfire Spell, one of the most dangerous in the arsenal because, even though the area of effect was limited, it burned at temperatures exceeding thermite.

As for the man, he was instantly engulfed. I heard a brief scream followed by the sharp *cracking* sounds of several rounds of ammunition cooking off all at once. His momentum carried him to the edge of the blaze, where he collapsed, half in half out. What was left of him looked roasted well done and the pistol seemed fused to the bones of his right hand.

I ducked into the closet just as the sprinkler system kicked in. It wouldn't douse magic flames burning at 5,000 degrees Fahrenheit, but hopefully Ghost would take it as a sign to send in the cavalry, because I was cornered at the top of an office building full of baddies. I had no exit strategy and maybe forty-five seconds before the Spell wore off.

While the fire burned outside I took inventory of the janitor's closet. Neatly stocked supplies: an unopened box of garbage can liners, shelves with gallon jugs of bleach, some sort of liquid soap, ammonia, window cleaner, and bags of stringy green mop heads. A mop hung neatly over a yellow plastic bucket that rested in the small square white plastic sink on the floor. Nothing useful there, just a clean little cubby at the end of the hall.

Wait a minute. *Clean*? Way too clean. When was the last time I'd seen a janitor's closet that didn't look like hell? Never, that's when. And it smelled clean, like disinfectant.

Speaking of disinfectant ... my head swiveled to plastic gallon jugs of bleach and ammonia. Bleach and ammonia.

Of course. Years of college chemistry and working in the restaurant business told me that people never, *ever* stacked those two chemicals near each other. Apart they were relatively harmless, but together? Watch out, bubba, because you mix those two and you have an instant deadly reaction. One of the worst is Cl2 (chlorine gas) or bertholite, which was used during WWI as a chemical weapon. Other byproducts, depending on the mixture, include: HCl (hydrochloric acid), NH2Cl (chloramine vapor), and N2H4 (hydrazine). Nothing you want to bring to a party. People have been killed by *accident* from mixing the two.

I quickly unscrewed a jug of each chemical and opened the door. Heat blasted against my face and I noticed that the sprinklers above my head had failed, probably due to the fire melting through the water pipes embedded in the ceiling. No surprise ... there wasn't much on this planet that could withstand magical fire. I had seconds left before the Spell wore off and people risked the aftermath to investigate. I shattered the jug of bleach on the linoleum, with the jug of ammonia following shortly thereafter. As soon as the ammonia splashed against the floor and the chemicals began to mix, the fire died abruptly, vanishing as if a switch had been thrown.

Closing the door again, I pulled out another Spell gem from my belt. Flat, round, the size of a quarter, it was an almost perfect piece of polished rose quartz. I activated the semi-precious gem and placed it against the left wall. It was as if I held a small hole between my thumb and forefinger and was able to peer through the wall at the space beyond. A See-Through Spell, allowing the user a peek through any wall up to three feet thick. Everything in vivid Technicolor, but no audio.

Back corner of the big room. Several people in office wear: white shirts, black slacks, and pant suits. All of them looked a little frazzled, but radiated the kind of hard-core determination only seen during a firefight. Water still rained down upon *them*, which caused them to look both miserable and ferocious at the same time—like wet, rabid dogs. Speaking of ferocious, every single one of them was armed. I saw just about every handgun imaginable plus some assault weapons such as AR-15s, AK-47s, and the occasional M-1 thrown in for good measure—enough letters and numbers to stage a coup of a small Latin American government.

The tall guy I'd seen earlier—the one I assumed was a Magician—was barking orders concerning the destruction of several documents. His well-cut black hair was plastered against his scalp and he had the kind of rough good looks you'd associate with the Marlboro Man. Because the sprinklers rendered shredders useless, the Magician stared at each stack of paper placed in front of him then concentrated for a moment until they crumbled into soggy ash. Neat trick that.

No go there. I'd get my fundament shot off. I placed the gem against the back wall.

Bingo.

Semi-dark room, no water falling from the ceiling, three or four geeky-looking guys, two of them wearing horn-rims. A large flatscreen monitor on the wall displaying a series of numbers and words like MIDLANDS, MIDWEST, LONDON, NEW ENGLAND, PRIORITY BIDS ACTIVE (8), PARIS, ISTANBUL, WON BIDS (17), BUY ON DEMAND (25), and EMERGENCY RUSH DUBAI.

Something told me *this* is what the whole shebang was about. I licked my lips, all too aware that soon my hiding place would be discovered. The charred corpse out in the hallway wouldn't fool anyone for long. Oh, it might buy me some time, but not enough.

Think, Kal! I urged. Without the rage that had been my sister's gift, I wouldn't have the strength or speed to win against such numbers. *You're in a janitor's closet that's never been used. So why is it here? Answer: it's a prop.*

But for what?

The answer that occurred to me left me with a swiftly sinking heart. I checked the See-Through before the Spell winked out and turned the quartz back into pretty polished stone. *Yep. No doors in that room. This must be the entrance.* The back wall had to be a secret door, but it would be locked, protecting whatever activity occurred just a few short feet away. I didn't have time to search for the opening mechanism.

How to get through?

There was a way. My hand strayed to the right-end pocket in my belt. A ruby the size of my thumbnail lay in my palm, winking a lurid red in the harsh light of the 100-watt bulb overhead. I knew what to do and I knew it could be done, but there was a good chance that in succeeding I would be killed.

Perfect.

"Do you have all the Spell eggs you need, Kal?" Alex had asked while I placed the polystyrene wonders gently in their foam nests. The bright light of ARMORY was starting to give me a headache.

"I need all of them," I answered with a small smile. Less isn't more ... more is more. "But I don't have that kind of carrying capacity."

The little magician peered into a cabinet chock-full of Spell eggs covered in descriptive pictograms. The tip of his tongue was stuck between his teeth as he concentrated, index finger moving from egg to egg. Finally, as I tucked the last of the Spell eggs I chose away, his face cleared and he said, "There it is!"

Whenever Alex slipped into his 'eureka' voice, I always felt the short hairs on the back of my neck rise, a sure sign of the End of Days For Kal. It's not that he's not smart enough or doesn't have great ideas that can fundamentally change the way we look at the universe, but when he's *wrong*, he's so spectacularly wrong it could cost millions of lives and billions of dollars. I think that's why BB only lets him out of his cage some of the time. He's like a fluffy, lovable nuclear device.

"What now?" I asked, afraid of the answer.

"This is new," he said, tossing an egg my way. I examined the casing and the pictogram of a stick-figure person stuck halfway inside a rectangle. Once again the hairs on the nape of my neck waved like seaweed in a current.

"What have you done, Alex?" I held the egg as if it were Marvin the Martian's Illudium Pu-36 Explosive Space Modulator.

"It's nifty."

Nifty? Just what I wanted to hear about a potentially lethal device, that it was *nifty*. "Care to elaborate or do we play Twenty Questions?"

His grin could only be categorized as 'crap eating.' "It phases the holder to a tangential plane of existence so that he or she can move through barriers such as walls and floors."

It was a 'holy crap' moment for me as I stared at the little stick figure embedded halfway through the rectangle. The pictogram did the effect no justice. I'd seen phasing before—vampires could do it— and it was referred to as going 'discorporeal,' something I had no desire to try.

I asked the only question I could think of. "How can you travel through an object if you are out of phase with reality? There's nothing to push against. I imagine you'd simply float away or downward as gravity takes hold."

Alex was shaking his head before I finished. "No, not at all. It works by willpower alone. Just think about the direction you want to take and there you go."

Oh, if only it was that simple! Years and years of experience with Special Branch's gewgaws and thingamajigs told me that they usually worked, but on those rare occasions when they didn't, Very Bad Things happened. When those Bad Things included explosions and transformations into unsavory puddles of goo, one developed a healthy skepticism of new developments in the Spell gem department.

"How safe is it?" I asked, staring at the glittering ruby.

"Pretty safe."

"Perfect," I said with an extra helping of sarcasm sauce. "I'll take two."

PRETTY SAFE, HE'D SAID. THE door behind me began to rattle as bullets *plinked* against the heavy steel. That made up my mind for me. I could try a door buster, but not in the close quarters of the closet. I needed at least five feet of space or my internals would become jelly in an instant.

Plink, plink, plinkety, plink.

Well, the bad guys knew I was in the closet, but my guess was that the only reason they weren't trying to bust the door down was the lack of floor from the fire. Those 5,000 degrees must have charred a hole straight through to the story beneath and perhaps through the outside wall as well. It was only a matter of time before someone either made it to the door or used a weapon that could shred the steel that was my only cover. Hopefully my little chemical cocktail would delay them some. Bleach and ammonia, the gifts that keep on giving. *Do I hear an Amen?*

"Hell," I muttered. "Here goes nothing." The activation word tumbled out from between my lips and everything became seriously weird.

The world fuzzed all around. Sharp angles and straight lines became a blurry mess and colors dulled and blended. It was as if I was looking through a haze of milky water. I raised my hand, which appeared crystal clear and unchanged, and placed it against the blurry back wall.

It disappeared up to the wrist.

I hastily withdrew my hand. No pain, nothing. It remained stubbornly hand-like and unmarred.

Perfect. Time to go. I thought about what was on the other side of that wall, concentrated on moving forward, propelling myself with my legs and entering the room beyond. The wall approached, drawing closer and closer until it was the world in front of my eyes, then the world all around. Darkness enveloped me for a moment before hazy, flashing lights hit my out-of-phase eyes.

Wait! Alex didn't tell me how long the effect would last or how to turn it off. And I hadn't asked. Looked like I would have to cancel my MENSA membership.

Okay, Kal, time for some more thinking. I know it's hard, but try. Not taking my eyes from the blinking and flashing lights, I concentrated on being one with the world I'd just left.

And bam! I was back, good as ever, not a dent in the fender, not a scratch on the paint.

The big screen monitor was on the wall directly in front with three laptops on a long table underneath. A black office phone sat toad-like at the end of the table, but other than that, the room was

Spartan. Three men in standard geekwear sat at the table, furiously typing at the laptops. All three had .22s holstered at the small of their backs—not the usual adornment for the computer nerd on the town. The light provided by the big screen flashed half sentences and city names, augmenting dim fluorescents overhead.

The Colt and Lahti hit my palms at the same time in a double cross draw from my shoulder holsters.

"Gentlemen, if I may have your attention."

As one, all three men spun, hands reaching for their little pop-guns. The one on the right managed a credible draw, the tiny automatic rising toward my torso, but my Colt and Lahti spat fire and twin flowers of blood bloomed on his chest. He stared stupidly at me for a moment before the Lahti finished the argument with a round between his eyes.

"You all better set those guns carefully on the ground," I said as my auditory system began to reassert control. The reports of my weapons were *loud* in such a small space. The other two watched, stunned, as the first man collapsed. His left leg kept twitching, like a cricket's does after it dies. Kind of creepy, but I kept my eyes fixed on the other two.

They nodded hastily and complied. Both were older men well into their forties, hard-faced, with mouths twisted from the bitter fruit of wrong choices. I'd seen expressions like that before, not only on the faces of these men in the large cubicle room, but on the faces of those who had done things most of us would call evil. On Nazis I'd killed while time-traveling, on serial killers and demagogues, the venal and the corrupt. Habitual criminals who sat in little ten-by-ten cells in the gray bar hotel awaiting execution. Whatever these two were into, it sure wasn't for the betterment of mankind.

This is what Maydock had been talking about: the abscess beneath the skin ready to gush forth a torrent of pus, smelly and foul. I knew that when I found out what these people were up to it would take all my self control to keep from putting a bullet into each and every brain pan until the walls ran with pink and gray.

"On your knees." Liquid nitrogen was warmer than I. The two

complied. "Who are you guys? What is this place?"

The oldest one, a man with salt and pepper hair and a curious X-shaped scar on his chin, replied, "This is The Trade Group. We're the investment branch of The Trade Group Insurance Company."

Even to my horribly limited knowledge of big business and finance, that sounded lame. A five-year-old could've come up with a more plausible story and by the look on his face he knew it. I risked a quick glance behind. Just as I thought: a secret door disguised as the back wall of the janitor's closet. From this side it looked to be all shiny, brushed steel with a highly polished latch and was held closed by an electronic lock with keypad. It was the type of door that a howitzer could hardly dent.

"Riiiight," I drawled. "Hiding in a small secret room behind a door of solid steel in a room with no other visible exits?" My eyes became winter. "Tell me the truth."

The other guy, shorter, chubby, with acne scars marring his cheeks said, "Go ahead and shoot, Mister. We're dead men anyway." His face matched mine in resolve and temperature.

I gritted my teeth, more than a little frustrated, and looked at the laptops. All top-of-the-line and connected via Ethernet. A cable outlet connected to a modem rested next to the phone. It seemed a little low tech considering the dollars put into the computers themselves. Why no Wi-Fi?

Because Wi-Fi signals could be intercepted. Of course, and then there was the Faraday cage surrounding the floor …. They sure were paranoid about something.

"Cellphones. Now!"

X-scar shook his head. "We're not allowed cells."

Duh. Must be getting a little rusty in my old age. Cell signals wouldn't penetrate the cage and if they could, there was a possibility of interception. Well, there was more than one way to skin an offender.

I sauntered over to the two and shoved them into a corner, where they stared at me sullenly, hands still raised. "Mind if I make a call?"

X-scar snorted. "Go ahead. Won't do you any good; it's encrypted."

Perfect. I lifted the receiver from the cradle and dialed 666. *C'mon, Ghost, be there or be square.*

The hard-core nerds kept up their glaring as I held the receiver to my ear. It didn't take a telepath to read their thoughts. Hate mixed with anger and a dash of embarrassment, an interesting mix. Mr. X-scar looked like he was nerving himself up for some violence, possibly rushing the guy with the gun. I lifted the Lahti until it was pointed right between his peepers, a casual gesture to let him know that I knew what he was thinking, and his shoulders relaxed in defeat. Funny how a gun pointed at a skull makes even the hardest bad-ass tame as an itty-bitty kitty.

"Kal?" The voice was tinny and scratchy, but definitely belonged to Ghost.

Relief flooded me. "Buddy, you have no idea how glad I am to hear your"—*Drone? Buzz? Whine?*—"voice. What's with the static?"

"There is some ..." *hkkkt* "heavy duty interference, some sort of security protocol. Hold ..." *hkkkt* "moment."

While I waited for Ghost to do that voodoo he did so well, I kept an eye on the two hard-core nerds, who seemed surprised that I was actually able to use the phone. The chubby guy's eyes were wide and round with apprehension. Perhaps he was worried I really was a Fed. He shouldn't have been. I was much worse.

Keeping the Lahti leveled at my two sullen prisoners, I reached into the pocket and pulled out the MagniGlass.

"What's that?" asked Chubby suddenly, eyes bright with interest.

A mysterious smile was his only answer. Placing the MagniGlass on the keyboard of the first laptop, I activated the device. Several icons appeared and I tapped the screen a few times until reaching the appropriate app. I gave it a tap and watched as a progress bar appeared on the shiny surface of the MagniGlass. ONE PERCENT.

It was X-scar's turn to pipe up. "What are you doing?" SIX PERCENT.

"I reckoned you were in the middle of deleting files." My voice was frosty as the gaze I gave him. "This will clone what data you have left on the drives. Thanks for linking them with the Ethernet cable. Saves me from having to do this three times." TWENTY PERCENT.

"There," said Ghost suddenly, his voice much sharper. "The line is clear now. I did not know there were any data streams to and from this building. To me it looked dead. Even the city records say it is under renovation, although I see the fire department has been alerted to a situation at that location. Is there a fire? I am very glad to hear your voice, Kal."

My, he certainly was chatty today. The electronic equivalent of worry, perhaps. "Yeah, me, too. I need your help, pal."

"Yes?"

"I'm in a room with three laptops and a large, flatscreen monitor mounted to the wall. Seems to be hooked to the Internet via cable. You might not be able to hack in, so I'm using the MagniGlass to clone what data I can. I need you to retrieve it and let me know what's going on."

"Hmmm," he buzzed. "Canton and a few others are on their way to you right now. They should arrive shortly. I must say, the level of security in this system is far more sophisticated than I would expect. It is almost as good as the Bureau's."

"There may be magic involved." Quickly, I outlined my situation and told him about the Magician. When I was done, there were a few moments of tense silence. SIXTY PERCENT.

"Yes," he buzzed finally. "I can see the magic sheathings on what data streams I can detect. Very sophisticated stuff here, Kal. I have not seen anything like it since Las Vegas."

He was referring, of course, to the Desert Pride Casino, where the owner ran a top-secret fight club. It's a tale involving a planet in a galaxy far, far away, time travel, and Nazis—lots and lots of Nazis. Not the cute, cuddly guys from *Hogan's Heroes*. Think *Schindler's List* on crack—a literary giant from Great Britain and a crazed Finnish demi-god. It was thrills and chills and I hated every moment of it except for meeting Jeanie. She was the best thing to happen to me in a long time and I felt a pang deep inside because she wasn't here to keep me sane.

Oh well, sanity is overrated.

"How soon will they be here?" CLONING COMPLETE. SHUTTING DOWN ....

I checked out each laptop and saw that whatever programs the geeks had been using were still erasing the hard drives. Most people think that if you drag a file to the wastebasket icon on your computer and hit EMPTY the information is history. Not by a long shot. The info is still there; the computer just removes the markers that keep it from recording over the data. No, erasing gigs of data takes time and I was praying that the MagniGlass was able to retrieve something worthwhile.

"They will be in the building in just a moment. I am currently sifting through the data on the main server, which is undergoing a system purge, although there seem to be blocks of data I cannot decrypt at the present time. My, I am impressed at the coding involved. However, I can access the general records and—"

"And?"

"And ... and ... and ... oh my ...."

That familiar feeling swept through my body as I heard the horror in Ghost's mechanical drone.

By the pricking of my thumbs ....

"Kids, Kal." His voice carried such a weight of dismay and disgust that my skin pebbled in response.

"What kids, Ghost?" My glance shifted to the two nerds. Chubby licked his lips nervously while X-scar stared daggers.

"They're selling kids."

Chapter Twelve

Kal

The Poison in the Mud Hatches Out

I, *Claudius*.

That was my first thought, a crazy-as-hell first thought, but it's nonetheless true. *I, Claudius* was a PBS miniseries broadcast on Masterpiece Theater in the U.S. back in the late '70s. It was inspired by two books written by Robert Graves, *I, Claudius* and *Claudius the God*. In the one of the series' last segments, the aging Tiberius Claudius Caesar Augustus Germanicus (played by Derek Jacobi), fourth Emperor of Rome, is sitting on his couch drinking wine and staring off into the distance, pondering his life and the current circumstances of the Empire. It is obvious he is tired and dissipated, worn out from a lifelong struggle against murderous family intrigue and the unsavory things he's had to do to sustain the Roman Empire. His face is vacuous and seamed, his heavy head covered by thinning gray hair. He seems so sad, so very *alone*.

Two of his advisors circle the aging Emperor, arguing about the available noble women he should marry because the Empire needed an Empress and his children need a mother. (His previous marriage did not end well.) They squabble and spit like feral cats, firing off names of women they deem worthy to be Mrs. Emperor.

Meanwhile, Claudius merely stares off into the distance, a faintly vacant expression on his face, wine and spit dripping from his chin. The voices of his trusted councilors drone on and on as he slowly drinks his wine and then one of them says, "The lady Agrippina." This causes a row between the two councilors because Agrippina is Claudius's niece, the daughter of his late brother, Germanicus, assassinated years earlier.

The councilor who opposes the idea, a smallish man with thin features, objects, saying the union would be incestuous, would destroy Rome.

Claudius's eyes narrow and for the first time in the scene the viewer sees the keen intellect behind the boorish, aging façade. Derek Jacobi, at that moment, seems to be channeling the spirit of Tiberius Claudius Caesar Augustus Germanicus, the very essence of the man oozing from the actor's skin. He fixes those bleary but shrewd eyes upon the objecting councilor and declares that he doesn't care; that the "lurking" poisons in the mud will hatch out.

That is what I saw in the eyes of the two men kneeling before me—their indifference to the lurking poisons oozing their way out—and that realization sparked something within me, a deeper rage than I had ever felt before. Not a fiery rage—no blast-furnace heat and sudden, violent reaction. No, the rage I felt was an icy thing, cold and deep and boundless.

My voice emerged, emotionless and steel-hard. "Ghost, what do you mean?" It wasn't brain surgery, I knew *exactly* what he meant; the answer was in the eyes of Chubby and X-scar plain as day and ugly as sin. Sometimes you pray that you're wrong, that for some reason you misheard or misunderstood what the other person was saying and you'd both have a good laugh about what a dimwit you are and everything would be fine and dandy, yessiree! And you can carry on as if the hideous thing born of a few words had never existed.

Not this time. "Kids, Kal," he said with a curious little break in his buzz. "Kids. They sell kids to bad people all over the world. This place is an auction house, the eBay of human trafficking."

God, no. Pain speared through my temples, the onset of an epic headache.

Each word that passed my teeth felt like broken glass and acid. "What kind of bad people, Ghost?"

"The worst kind, Kal." Ghost's voice was a shard of anguish. Very few things could faze him emotionally. He didn't have the glands for extreme feelings, but this tore at his electrons worse than anything else I'd known in our long history together. "Pedophiles, I believe. I-I ... cannot be sure. I will need more data."

There comes a point where the mind just shuts down, when there is a TMI overload that requires a mental reboot or you go from sane to bonkers in three-point-six seconds flat. This was one of those times and for the next few seconds I was on autopilot.

"Tell me more." The words came out of their own accord. I really did not want to know, yet a part of me needed to know and it was that part—the part that was on autopilot—that was calling the shots. The rest of me just wanted to face a Supernatural, to kill a non-human monster and rip it to pieces, destroy something not wearing human skin. Facing the human monsters of the really real world was last on my 'to-do' list because deep down I knew they were the worst monsters of all. I'd learned that lesson while killing Nazis a few months ago. Let me tell you, they made the worst Supernaturals look like sock puppets from *Mister Roger's Neighborhood*.

"This is their central base of operations, Kal," Ghost droned. He sounded a little ... off. I didn't blame him. "According to what I have been able to skim so far, this 'Trade Group' has other offices in Seattle, Tallahassee, Austin, and Fargo, but Omaha seems to be the hub. I do not know why."

Oh, I knew why. Omaha, Nebraska, a city in the Heartland, a conservative, *nice* place to live that most people never thought about twice. It was perfect: big enough to be modern and small enough that you'd forget what you saw once you left. The festering boil of infection and poison beneath the skin of the city was well hidden, masked by Midwestern charm and the lacquer of middle-class values.

Ghost continued, "As for the children, they seem to be held in houses in various metro areas. They are labeled as 'stock.'"

Stock. They labeled children they were selling to perverts 'stock,' as if they were chickens at market. I almost pulled the trigger right then and there, shooting my anger at Chubby and X-scar, not because it would be a sort of frontier justice, but because I would feel so much *better*. "Send it all to the feds, Ghost." My throat hurt. "Hell, send it to *everyone*. The local cops, CNN, MSNBC, *everyone*. This thing needs to be shut down hard." The autopilot me had an idea. "But first send what you have to the Bureau and tell them about the Magician; that way Maydock can't object to a team coming out." Backup if I need it. I had a funny feeling I would.

"What about Maydock? Aren't you afraid he will start his killing spree?"

My smile was a tight, ugly thing that caused Chubby to begin a-blubbering. Can't say I blamed him. If he knew what was going through the space between my ears, he'd have run away screaming. "Maydock's not watching. No, there's too much security; it's too well insulated. He just wanted to see if I'd exit the hornet's nest alive. Besides, once 'Otto' informs the Bureau, he can't really object. All he can do is tell me not to meet them. I don't think he knows about Canton and Jeanie."

"What about you, Kal?"

"What about me?"

"Are you going to wait for Canton and his team?"

I shook my head mechanically, then realized he couldn't see it. "No. I have other things I have to do." While Chubby blubbered and X-scar glowered, I began to have the faintest glimmer of an idea. "In fact, keep the info restricted to the team for right now and see if you can halt the system purge; salvage what files you can. Canton needs to stop this *now*." I pitched my voice lower so my Interdiction didn't hit me with a brain-freeze. "The team needs to put the kibosh on this Magician before the Straights arrive, and I need you to lead him to this room to pick up my prisoners and the MagniGlass so you can start scanning the data from these hard drives. The Bureau will arrive later to investigate, but I want action taken immediately. Where is Canton's team?"

"They are approaching the building as we speak."

Good. "Later, Ghost."

"Take care, Kal."

I gently set the receiver on the cradle. My head felt light and disconnected, as if I'd downed large amounts of DayQuil—what my dad would call Medicine Head. Nothing seemed real and everything echoed strangely. The world wasn't the world and I wasn't the same man who'd entered the room just a few short minutes ago. The game had changed and nothing would ever be the same.

Kids. They were selling *kids*.

Months ago I had traveled back in time—yes, it can be done but I don't recommend it as a vacation option—and fought Nazis. You heard me, Nazis. It was 1943 and I found myself working with the French Resistance against the VGG—the *Verteidiger gegen Geister,* or Defenders against Ghosts—the Nazi equivalent of the Bureau, except they had no problem with torturing and killing people to harness the magical power of life energy. Necromancy ... a word with ugly connotations for those in the know. It was easy to kill the VGG and Nazis; they treated whole cultures as less than human, so it was simple to consider them just more Supernaturals to put to grass. Just point and click, bang bang, thank you ma'am.

This ... this was another kind of evil altogether.

"You bastards," I growled, my blood singing with the energy of righteous wrath. I was cold and dead and implacable as a glacier. "You sick bastards."

It was Chubby who broke under the force of my gaze.

"I didn't know at first, mister," he whined. "They had me design the system, do all the programming. I thought it was for a legit insurance company."

"Shut *up*, you weaselly little [CENSORED]," snapped X-scar, face flushing bright red.

"You shut up!" Chubby yelled back. To me, "By the time I found out, they *owned* me!"

X-scar hit Chubby with a solid right that put him out flat, his fist making a dull *thwap* as he spread the other man's teeth across the floor. Lights out for poor old Chubster. Can't say I felt any pity.

"That's enough." My voice could've cracked granite.

"No," snarled X-scar. He stood to face me. "I've had enough of this crap. Arrest me, cop, or shoot, just hurry the hell up." He threw a twisted smile my way. "I'm bored."

I knew what he was doing the second those words popped out of his foul little mouth. He was trying to goad me into a killing. But the rage that once fueled me was long gone, had fled with the spirit of my sister to whatever just reward awaited the innocent and the kind. That rage had given me great strength and uncanny speed—a sort of spiritual nitrous oxide for the engine of my body—and in the void left behind was an icy anger. The kind of anger I knew I could use to my advantage because it offered clarity as well as resolve.

"I'm not a cop," I said, letting the tip of my fury show. "At least not the kind you ever want to meet. I'm not going to kill you." Before he could jump at me, I'd pointed the Lahti at a region eight inches south of his navel. "So I expect you'll rethink any hasty words."

Cold, so cold where once before if you touched me while I raged you'd have blisters on your fingers and the smell of cooking pork in your nostrils. But now ... now there would be only a curious sizzle and skin left behind, crystallizing. My thoughts were clear and emotionless, and I knew what I could do, *would* do to X-scar if I didn't get *exactly* what I wanted. A tiny portion of my mind—the touchy-feely, human bit—was screaming at me, but I didn't want to listen.

The Lahti barked once, twice and black polyester blew apart, exposing ruptured skin and broken bone. Contrary to what happens in the movies, sometimes you don't immediately start bleeding. Minutes can pass before the blood begins to gush.

I stared at X-scar's ruined kneecaps as he fell screaming to the floor, while Chubby lay in a pool of blood and drool, still unconscious from the right he took from the bigger man.

"I know you have a bolt-hole," I said, loud enough to be heard over the screaming, "so you can evade the law, just in case."

He was so busy screaming, thrashing, and leaving trails of blood on the nice checkered linoleum floor that he wasn't listening. How rude.

The next shot landed less than a half-inch from his right hand, close enough that he felt the heat. He snatched his digits from the floor and clutched them to his chest whilst continuing his god-awful shrieking. From beyond the walls of the room I heard a massive *boom*. Dust fell from the drop ceiling as tremors rattled the bones of my ankles.

"They're heeeeeere," I crooned in my best little girl voice.

X-scar gritted his teeth and ground out, "Who?"

"My friends. And they don't play nice."

What was wrong with me? I was being deliberately sadistic, and I couldn't seem to stop myself. The sane Kalevi Hakala was yelling and putting up a fuss in the back of my mind, but the cold thing that animated my body wasn't listening. "Where's your bolt-hole?" I urged with a smile that refused to meet my eyes.

He raised a bloody hand, finger pointed at the far corner behind me. "Th-there, on the f-f-floor," said X-scar, thickly, through a mouthful of pain. "P-push down, th-then release. Th-the, ugh, door will open. Get out! Oh God!"

God had nothing to do with what was going on in that building. The world revolved slowly, and the air was thick as honey as I knelt, keeping the Lahti casually pointed in his direction. "I'm leaving now." *Boom!* The floor shook again and faintly, through re-enforced walls, I heard the popcorn pelting of gunfire. "If you live through the next few minutes, think of your sins." I leaned in so I could spear him with the cold fury of my eyes. "You really don't want me to come back."

X-scar was tough, a man whose soul was scarred by evil and malice and things no human should bear, but my stare broke him. As he looked into my eyes, something crumbled and he flinched.

"Good boy," I whispered.

The trapdoor opened like he said it would, revealing a steel ladder leading down into darkness. I holstered my weapons and began my descent. The blackness gave way to the power of my nightvision contact lenses. It was a square shaft; the walls were thick and sturdy—

not the flimsy support of galvanized duct work, but a hefty, custom-built bolt-hole that would last as long as the building.

All I needed was to follow gravity. I wished Canton and the team the best of luck and hoped they'd put a few dozen rounds in that Magician. For the briefest of instants I pondered climbing back up to help the team out—seeing Jeanie would do me a world of good—but I couldn't be entirely sure Maydock *didn't* have any spies or spy gear in the building, and the pressure to leave, to run far and fast from the horrors above, had me flying down the ladder. I had to get out, I couldn't breathe, something was constricting my throat, choking off my air, and my breath wheezed. My hands trembled and sweat was starting to pour down my face. The dim, sane part of me realized I was in the grip of a full-on anxiety attack. It was my first one and damn if it didn't suck, big time.

Light came from below—another square growing slowly as my sweat-slick hands fumbled on the steel rungs. At least thirty feet had gone by and by my guess the ladder would lead me to the first floor, most likely next to an exit. The closer I got to the hole, the more my breathing eased, although cottony straps still seemed to be fastened about my neck and chest.

Concrete met my sneakers, followed by a soft *click*.

"I don't know you." The voice was calm and detached. The voice of a human robot.

Damn, I cursed inwardly at my stupidity. *Go figure they would have the exit guarded as well.* "The new guy, mister," I said. "I'm the new guy."

"I don't know you." Cold steel touched the back of my neck and I knew instantly that Mr. Robot had made a mistake.

My body took over as I spun to the left and back, beyond the gun that barked near enough to my ear that my head rang and a hot spike of pain shot through the eardrum. I didn't care; I was in the flow of things, reacting as my left arm rose and fell, trapping Mr. Robot's gun arm in my armpit. My right fist slammed into a pug nose, breaking it with a harsh *snap*. Another spin back and a lift of his arm out of my pit and a knife hand strike to his gun hand. The weapon, a matte black Ruger, spun away, out of nerveless fingers.

He was short, Mr. Robot. Short and wide and powerful, with thick, strong, rending fingers. A buzzcut presided over dead blue eyes and a seamed and weathered face where blood spurted from a now broken nose and a lipless mouth.

Then he smiled. It was genuine, that smile, hitting his eyes and lighting them up like lamps. "*Good*," he breathed, no longer sounding robotic and detached. In fact, he sounded … delighted.

I saved my breath, watching the set of his shoulders. The eyes may be the windows to the soul, but the shoulders are the signals of intent. We circled each other carefully, me trying to breathe in and out evenly and him blowing blood bubbles and snorting clotted liquid to the floor.

My ears rang, still stinging, and I shook my head slightly to clear it. That's when he chose to attack, like I knew he would. He was a trained professional, but even professionals make mistakes. Instead of killing me instantly like he should have, he decided to question. Instead of commanding me to turn around, he laid the barrel of his weapon to the back of my head, allowing me to spin toward him and avoid a bullet.

I took a kick aimed at my liver to the shin as I blocked reflexively. It was followed by a jab to the chin that never landed, but the force of it nearly numbed my blocking arm. Damn, but that guy could *hit*! Felt like a Ford F-150 took a chunk out of my forearm. I let him have an elbow straight to the chin and he shrugged it off like it was nothing.

His flurry of blows never landed solidly on my chest, face, and gut, but blocking them sure hurt. If he kept it up, he'd win by default, battering my defenses down to the point where he could beat me to death.

Screw that noise.

I had his measure and his timing and when the next flurry of blows came, I juked to the side, hands moving to my waist. A second later my fists were grasping a pair of punch daggers, their 50mm blades shining in the dim light, high-tensile steel, their T handles flat, disguised as part of my belt buckle, which was thick and wide, a perfect hidey hole for weaponry. I lashed out quick as a striking snake and a razor tip sliced clean through the shoulder of Mr. Robot's white button-down, leaving a long, shallow cut that bled profusely. My follow up took him in the left bicep, and I twisted the blade, which grated harshly against bone and sliced clean through the thick muscle of his arm.

Blood gushed and Mr. Robot screamed, a deep animal roar that shook my already abused ears. One of his big paws clipped the side of my head and something tore—a sharp, bright shard that resulted in a hot flow into the collar of my shirt—but before I could register the pain from what was probably a torn ear, my other fist flew straight and true to bury a punch dagger into Mr. Robot's left eye.

Any amusement he'd felt vanished in an instant as he hollered loud enough for my good ear to wish for a vacation to quieter climes. Keeping the dagger firmly fixed in his skull, I wrenched the other from his bicep and plunged it into his throat, over and over, coating my hair, face, and shirt in thick, arterial spray. The knife cut his shrieks to a wet gurgle, which trailed off into nothing as his body slumped, pulling the one dagger buried in his head free in a splash of eyeball juice. Arterial spray continued to drench me as blood arced across the room in weakening spurts, timed to the beat of Mr. Robot's rapidly fading heart.

Done.

Hands trembling, I stripped off my Faraday jacket and removed my black t-shirt with its picture of John Cleese in the Ministry of Silly Walks. Ruined. I used it to wipe off what blood I could, reversed the jacket, and zipped it up over my bare torso. I still looked a horror— my face smeared with drying, brownish blood—but it would have to do until I made it back to the car. I just had to walk a block in bright daylight to where my car was parked without women fainting, children screaming, and the rest of humanity dialing 911.

Two doors. One wood, one gray-painted steel. The steel door was latched with a push-bar, and I gave it some elbow grease. An alarm sounded faintly from deep within the building, but I paid it no mind. I needed sunshine. I needed reality. I needed a world where for at least a few hours someone wasn't trying to remove my guts through my nose.

An alleyway. The stink of dog turds, garbage, and piss. In that order. My internal compass told me to head to the right and I did, keeping my bloody head down. My spiky blond hair was stiffening as the blood dried, vampire styling gel. There were no convenient puddles of water to help wash out the smelly gunk. Nothing but a half-empty dumpster, a good place for the Monty Python t-shirt and the memories associated with it.

As the black cotton landed on a pile of shredded paper, I thought about the shooting of X-scar and the cold fury that allowed me to do so and felt a rising horror at my actions. Had I really tortured a human being? Sure, he was a corrupt, venal douchebag who sold kidnapped kids to perverts, but what did that make me?

A sadist.

With that horror up came breakfast, fast and furious, along with a generous helping of self-loathing and fear, adding an acidic stink to the already smelly dumpster.

What was I becoming?

What?

Chapter Thirteen

Canton
Breaking the Dam

NIHSEN RODE SHOTGUN.

I removed my helmet and ran a hand through my wiry black hair, wiping the sweat away while keeping an eye on the rest of the team riding in the back of the van with me. Jeanie looked grim, her normally unlined face set in harsh worry lines. Alex had his eyes closed, lips moving as if he was counting to a million, while Dove Jacobs looked pissed as all get out. Dom looked like, well, *Dom*. I didn't know him well. Kal had said he was a stand-up guy and that was good enough for me.

That left Patricia. Man, she looked as tough and as pretty as my buddy said, all hard as steel and smooth as velvet. She sat there with eyes closed, pretending to nap behind her SWAT goggles, but I'd been doing this gig long enough to tell she was wide awake. Probably assessing us while we stewed in silence as the van headed toward the building Kal done got himself lost in.

This was nuts. Nobody was talking, all tense and stuff, strung tighter than piano wire and out of tune as well. Sure not the best way to run a railroad, if you don't mind me mixing my metaphors.

I decided to chip away at the dam holding all those emotions back, because if we didn't come together as a team, we were about as useless to Kal as a crap-flavored lollipop. "When I first met Kal a little over ten years ago he was asleep in his apartment in DORMS, snoring so loud it sounded like the End of Days." I grinned as several pairs of eyes suddenly speared me. "We ate together and then I watched him take down Thomas Mace in a fight that's still talked about to this day.

"By damn that white boy was fast, taking old Mace down in the fight ring, coming out all busted up to hell and gone. It was a test, you see. The director back then had a psych eval of Kal before he was recruited. Knew he had 'anger issues.' " I snorted in amusement. "Anger issues indeed. We all have anger issues; Kal has a whole passel more than that term can cover. The Bureau didn't know half of what they were dealing with, but they had all his aptitude tests and he scored off the charts on most of them.

"From that day I knew who he was, who he would be to me. He is *Jlin-Litzoque,* Yellow Horse, named by my grandfather Marcus Alsate who was Nantan Lupan, the Gray Wolf. Nantan Lupan worked for the Bureau as a magician and when I was born he performed magic to See into my future. My mom, also former Bureau, put him up to it." It felt strange to open up like that, but the only way to make others bare their souls is to show them yours. "Old Nantan Lupan Saw that I'd find my brother warrior among the whites, find the other half of my spirit. Damn me if it wasn't Kalevi Hakala, and he's been a friend, hell … more than that, a *brother,* ever since. That's why I'm here. He and I are family and family is the most important thing there is.

"I know why Jeanie is here: she loves him." I pointed to Jacobs. "My question is, why are *you* here, Dove? What's got a bug in your ear to help out Kal? What is so damn important about him that you'd be willing to risk your life to watch his six? You've never worked with him, or anything like that."

Jacobs didn't bother to look up. In fact, she seemed unusually subdued for a woman who carried such a darn huge chip on her shoulder. I was surprised she wasn't permanently hunched from carrying all that weight.

"At first I wasn't sure why I came," she finally said. A small crack that began to leak. "Seemed like the thing to do. I don't know Kal that well, but I ran into him a few times studying up on various Supernaturals. Read his files, all his adventures." Her lips barely seemed to move.

Alex kept up his silent counting, the only one whose eyes weren't burning into my skull, but there was a set to his shoulders that told me he was listening, just like everyone else, as Jacobs chipped away at the dam a little further.

She continued, her cutesy face all screwed up like she was chewing on bitter leaves. "You know, you can't walk five feet in Warehouse without hearing about the amazing Kal Hakala, how tough he is, how brave and strong. It's enough to swell a person's ego to the size of an aircraft carrier, but that wasn't the case with him. When I met him a couple of years ago he was at the range, practicing with that antique Finnish pistol of his. He smiled and waved as he finished and went about his business and I realized all that talk about him, the fact that he's a living legend in the Bureau *hasn't* gone to his head. I think it was then that I began to look up to him a little."

Her eyes snapped wide open as if she realized what she'd said. "He's the best killer in the agency and I think that earns him some back up from the second best." She crossed her arms under her breasts and glared, daring us to say anything.

As for me, I had to hide a smile that threatened to rip my face in half. In a few short sentences Dove Jacobs had revealed more about herself than she had in the past two years. For her, that was practically gushing uncontrollably.

"He always gives me grief," Alex broke in suddenly, opening his eyes and staring at each of us in turn. "Every day we worked together was another that he gave me crap about something. I really thought he hated me."

I opened my mouth, but managed to stuff the words coming out back down my throat.

Alex continued, "During that mess in Denver I had a chance to enter his mind, once for a healing after a ghoul savaged his shoulder, the other when I removed a curse." He licked his lips. "Moving into the mind of another is not something I wish to experience again, that much I can tell you. Both times I felt something that surprised me, though. I was taken aback." A look of wonder crept into his eyes. "He *cares* for me. Kal thinks of me as the little brother he never had. All that time he ribbed me, teased me, it wasn't because he hated me … it was because he *cared* about me. He treated me like he thought a little brother should be treated and that's why I'm here. Like you said, Canton, he's family and I have to take care of family."

Quiet settled upon the scene as we drank in Alex's words, and the little Magician sat there with moist eyes behind his protective goggles, looking anywhere but at us. Jacobs gently took one of his small hands in hers and held it tenderly. That dispelled any lingering doubts about their relationship. It was a gesture loud as a shout.

"He didn't care when I told him I was gay." Dom's voice was a thin rasp, like sandpaper on silk. His skin was parchment white beneath all the hair on his face. "I tell everyone I am; it's practically the first thing out of my mouth. I say it just to get it out of the way, to get the looks of disgust or hate or fear over and done with so we can focus on the job of killing Supernaturals. A few years ago when I joined Team Epsilon, I met Kal and when I shook his hand I said, 'By the way, I'm gay.' He just blinked slowly and nodded as if I'd told him I was Episcopalian or a Buddhist. For that I will always respect him. And the fact that he's the most wily, sneaky buggar I've ever met. Man's got more brains and guts than most and he might drink too much, but he's all about the team and for me, that's enough."

We waited for more, but Dom just leaned his head back and closed his eyes. *Well, well.*

Pat seemed to sense it was her turn. "He's fragile. His experience with the Class Five Supernatural when he was fifteen broke his mind and somehow he managed to put it back together, albeit imperfectly. Only recently did I realize it was his sister who saved his mind, kept it glued together during that shattering event. But ever since she passed on, his psyche has been evolving. He's slowly changing. For years he drank and womanized, relying on childish behavior and sarcasm to deflect deeper emotional entanglements, but now he has no excuse but to grow up or …" she trailed off, leaving the rest of us on the edge of our seats, "… go nuts, devolve instead of evolve and I really *need* to be here to counsel him because there's only so much Jeanie can do as his girlfriend. He will do anything to protect her—that's his nature—even from the growing fissures within his mind, so opening up would be difficult if not impossible. But I've counseled him in the past and he listens to me. He has to … he's my friend …." Her voice trailed off.

Use whatever cliché you want—hearing a pin drop, a mouse fart, whatever—the back of that van was the place for it. The only noise was that of the tires chewing up pavement and the occasional bump of a weapon against the uncomfortable steel of our seats. Emotional water was flowing freely now from the dam and we were all aware of it.

But nobody expected Jeanie to put in her two cents. She was in love with the big lug and that was a plenty good reason for her to sit next to me. Hell, all of us loved or respected the man; that's why we were willing to put ourselves in harm's way. After all, we sure as shooting weren't getting paid for this little rodeo. Not that we needed the money. The Bureau was never about the money. Well, maybe at first … that and the excitement of seeing a Supernatural, to know that the fairy tales *were* true, even if they were a lot leaner and meaner than the Brothers Grimm ever realized. This was a world where Little Red Riding Hood met the Big Bad Werewolf and became an hors d'oeuvre wrapped in a cute crimson cloak. No brave woodcutter to save the day and cut grandma free; she was slowly working her way down the monster's lower intestine.

That was our reality, and it was one we'd accepted, despite the bloody horror and danger and pain and death and the soul-wrenching fear. It was not a job or a career. It was a calling. And it was ours.

"I hear my late husband's voice," Jeanie said, her eyes hooded. "In the odd parts of the night, when I least expect it. He died long before I met Kal, and his name was Desmond." Drip, drip, one tear then two. "Like Kal, he was a big man and he was gentle, but he was tough, too. Very tough. Taught me how to fight with a knife, how to defend myself because back then a black woman in London was more a target than a person, so he wanted me to be able to defend myself. He died in the factory he worked in and they paid me one hundred pounds. That's how much his life was worth. He'd sweated and labored there for five years, yet when a catwalk collapsed and killed five men, including Des, one hundred pounds was the blood price, guilt money paid to the families.

"For years I was torn apart, wanting only to crawl inside a hole and die, but instead I worked across town for a rich couple who never bothered to see me as a real person. To them, I was merely furniture or a dog they could bark orders at." She nodded. "Yeah, a dog that would fetch and clean and never talk, never be seen, because I was one of the help, not worth mentioning. I wasn't one of *them*; I wasn't white. After I revealed my talent for magic, Sir Ian Fleming himself, who I've since learned became a big deal in the literary world, recruited me.

"MI-7, as you call them, gave me a purpose. To kill. A lot. And I did. In France, I killed VGG and I enjoyed it because they were right bastards what deserved a good killing. When Des died, the part of me that gave a damn about things like love, decency, and hope died, too, so I filled that dead spot in my heart with the corpses of my enemies.

"Then Kal came along, flying through the window of a little inn in Natzweiler. He was living death. None of the VGG could touch him, no matter how hard they tried, and he put them all *down* like the rabid dogs they were. When the blood work was done, he noticed me for the first time and what I saw in his eyes stunned me."

Jeanie looked around, tears streaming down her cheeks, and I felt my heart was like to bust wide open. Her look was raw and hurting and it racked me, clear down to my soul. "Desire. It was the first thing in his beautiful blue eyes. Desire. He wanted me like a man wants a woman. He didn't see color, he didn't see the potential for violence, or the magic that sang across my skin, he saw me, Jeanie Morrow, a flesh and blood woman to take in his arms. At that moment I felt the dead thing in my heart begin to breathe again.

"That's why I came to this wondrous future. I fell in love with a man who made me feel something besides hate and rage and I wanted to explore that. And all this time my late husband's voice would pop up with words of encouragement, telling me I'd made the right decision, telling me he wanted me to be happy and to find some fulfillment." Jeanie shook her head ruefully. "I know the voice isn't real, it's just a part of me that wants to be happy, but I like to think that Des is out there and that he wants me to be with Kal because being with Kal has made me happier than I've been in a long, *long* while."

We all took a long moment to digest her words as they sank into our thick skulls. Finally I tossed her a smile and a wink and said, "Gee, hon, I thought you might have a *good* reason to be here."

We all enjoyed a full belly laugh and it felt good. Tension that had been building up ever since the flight from Washington washed away with the tide of laughter that swept the van. Finally … we were ready to be a team.

"I have some Spell gems," Alex said suddenly, producing a handful of sparkling stones along with corresponding slips of paper. The activation words. "One for each. All I could make in the limited timeframe available."

We each took a gem. Mine was an emerald the size of a thumbnail, a fortune in glittering green. I read the accompanying paper. It read simply: 'For Speed … BARNACLEBLOB.'

Speed? At my inquiring look, Alex grinned. "It's new. Instead of boosting performance, enhancing your speed—which can cause muscle strain and other damage—this Spell alters time for you, a sort of dilation field that encompasses your body and lasts for about ten seconds. Pretty cool."

"Ever been tested?"

He shook his head. "Nope. Developed it on the plane ride over here. You'll be the first."

No more did I wonder about Kal's disdain for Special Branch. In Chicago one of their little toys opened a singularity that nearly pulled me into dimensions perilous. I watched that singularity suck in a Windigo the size of John Deere tractor and swallow it whole in an instant. Now I was to be a guinea pig for a Spell that, for all I knew, would turn me into a wet blob of grease with eyeballs. I prayed that Alex was as good as everyone thought he was, because I didn't want to exit this world in a unique way.

The van slowed to a stop. "Grab your weapons, folks," I barked, sealing the Spell gem in a pocket. "Anything you need, the local LEOs have been more than generous." I patted the Benelli provided by the Omaha PD. "Remember, you can never be too well armed."

As the last word left my mouth, the van doors opened, flooding the interior with light.

CHAPTER FOURTEEN

Canton

Killing Time

NIHSEN STOOD THERE, SHOTGUN IN hand and body armor on. "This is the place," he said, pointing to a gray steel door. "This is the only entrance."

I nodded. "Stay behind us."

His features hardened. "You're not going in without me."

Gibraltar would crumble before he did, I could see that. "Fine, but this is our op." Not a question, just a statement of fact, which he took rather well, giving me a terse nod.

We swept into the tiny lobby in standard tactical formation, me at point checking for hostiles, the rest following quickly behind. Nothing.

Okay, not nothing. There was a big man on the floor. Huge, almost seven feet all. Possibly the largest human I'd ever seen, and I've seen a few doozies in my time. He was unconscious, lying on his side with blood sluggishly flowing from his partially open mouth. Stylized tattoos covered the visible parts of his body. Thick plastic zip-ties had been used to bind his hands and feet. Kal. Had to be. He always carried zip-ties.

"What's with the tattoos?" asked Jacobs in awe, gripping her MP9 tight enough that the little SMG creaked.

"He's Māori," I replied. "Polynesian from New Zealand."

"How do you know that?"

"Anthropology class. Georgetown. I'm more than a pretty face."

"Oh lord," Patricia gagged as she pointed at the sole of the big man's shoe. "Is that … is that … is that a *tongue*?"

Alex stared, horrified, while we all took a quick look. Yep, a tongue. Flat and pink and a little slimy, looking like a giant flesh-colored worm that got on the wrong side of a large foot. Explained the blood flowing from the big man's mouth.

Kal. Had to be.

Suddenly, Ghost's buzzing voice burst in through our earwigs. "Canton, team, Kal is safe, but you have to reach the top floor immediately."

I thumbed my throat mic as relief washed over me. "Good to hear your voice, Ghost. What's the situation?"

"Thanks to Kal, I have managed to penetrate the computer system and am preventing a full memory wipe of the main server. However, from the sophistication of the programming I am encountering, I do not think I will fool the programmers long and they will manually destroy the drives."

"On our way." I eyed the elevator.

As if reading my mind, Ghost said, "Take the stairs; the elevator is on lockdown. Top floor. Hurry."

Up the stairs, many landings, no doors. Before we reached the final landing, Ghost buzzed in our ears.

"I have completely penetrated the computer systems. The cameras in the stairwell have been neutralized, but not by me. Someone else had placed the cameras on a feedback loop. Perhaps Maydock. However, there are explosives wired to the bottom of the stairs. I have neutralized the remote detonators, but there is a failsafe, so I would hurry if I were you."

He didn't have to tell us twice. I went up those stairs faster than a scalded cat, taking them three at a time with the others beating feet behind. I didn't even pause to check the door at the top, bursting through with Benelli leveled, ready to shoot. The others cascaded around me, taking positions to the left and right just as muffled *booms* came from behind us, not loud, but with a deep intensity that we could feel from the soles of our feet to the roots of our hair. Gray dust blossomed from beneath the stairwell door.

Speak of the devil. The building shook as the explosives collapsed the stairs. The detonations wouldn't have killed us, but the fall and being squished into human lasagna would definitely have done us a powerful bit of harm.

"Team, I have some news to report." Ghost sounded unusually subdued, which raised my hackles more than a little.

"Go ahead," I murmured while scanning the long hall ahead. The floor was covered in a half-inch of water and it looked like a fire had ravaged the far end, the linoleum ending abruptly at a charred hole. It was a safe bet that that was more of Kal's handiwork. *Damn*, that white boy sure lowered property values when he was in town.

Ghost continued, quickly relating what The Trade Group was all about, what they did, the Magician in the building, everything in a few, succinct sentences. Jeanie and Patricia cussed up such a storm that my momma would've taken a switch to their backsides if she'd been listening. Meanwhile, Dom ground his teeth loud enough to scare the neighbors, Alex crossed himself, and Nihsen merely closed his eyes for a moment and trembled slightly, the only telltale signs of the fury that raged within. We had given him an earwig and intel on Ghost, which he took surprisingly well. On second thought, considering that he'd already come face to face with the bodies of five ghouls, maybe it wasn't that surprising after all.

It was Dove Jacobs who really grabbed my attention. Her face was chalky and strained; she seemed to have aged ten years in five seconds. The SMG in her hands trembled as her body shook and tears poured from eyes hidden behind protective goggles.

"Where ... where ... where are they, Ghost?" she rasped, clear snot running from her nose. Jeanie and Patricia both leaned in to rest hands on her shoulders, offering what comfort they could, but she angrily shook them off. "Where?"

"Ghost," I began. "Belay—"

Too late. "First door on the left. Be care—"

Again, too late. Before I could move, Jacobs burst through the door, shrieking at the top of her lungs. "Freeze, you [EXPLETIVE]-bastards, police!"

That worked about as well you'd expect. Bullets hammered through the air as whoever lurked in the other room opened fire. By the noise, there were quite a few Trade Group employees raising objections to her presence.

Holes appeared in the wall, and we all made like throw rugs, flattening out as Jacobs fell back out the door in a spray of blood. I grabbed her by the collar and dragged her toward me.

A hole the size of a plum spewed red from her hip. I didn't bother to look at the exit wound. I knew it would be the size of a softball. She was screaming and trying to stem the tide with her gloved hands. In less than a minute, she would bleed out.

A shove sent my helmet smacking against the wall. "I got this," shouted Alex as he placed his hands on her hip. "Buy me some time; this is gonna take all the juice I've got." He leaned forward and began to whisper fervently in his lover's ear.

"Grenades," I hollered over the staccato roar of weapon fire. As one, like a well-oiled machine, we pulled our flash-bangs, yanked the pins and did our level best to impersonate Nolan Ryan. Four grenades sailed through what was left of the door.

Blam! Blamblamblam!

Light and a sound like the end of the world echoed from within and the gunfire stopped and a powerful lot of screaming began.

I was through the door in an instant, just in time to catch a round straight in the chest. The SWAT vest I wore was enough to stop the bullet, but not the pain that came along for the ride. My breath left in a *whoosh* and decided to stay on vacation for a while. While my butt was hitting the wet floor hard enough to bounce, I noticed the room was pretty large, built rectangular with us at one of the short ends. Seven people on the opposite end were shooting with a variety of weapons as I scrambled away, protected by cubicle walls.

"Well, that didn't work," I said when I caught my breath and stuffed it back into my lungs. From the corner of my eye I saw Alex, helmet off and sweating up a storm, staring hard at Jacobs' bloody wound.

"What now, boss?" cried Dom as he leaned around the doorway to take a quick shot with his H&K MP5. A harsh scream came from within, indicating a hit.

Only one thing left to do. Apprehension clawed at my guts. "I'm going to use a gem. Wait … let's see … eight seconds and throw yours. Throw hard and high; you have to clear a lot of desks and whatnot."

"This gonna work?" he asked. He palmed his gem, a small diamond, and stared fixedly at the doorway.

Hell if I knew, but I wasn't going to tell him that. Nothing kills morale like an indecisive leader. "Of course." My grin felt like a scream. "Trust me."

Patricia scowled, freckles following her frown lines. "You hang around Kal too much."

Jeanie nodded in agreement.

There's no pleasing some people.

I dug the emerald out of my pocket and read the activation word. "BARNACLEBLOB!" I held my breath, waiting for it to take effect or turn me into something … interesting.

Then I noticed the change around me. There was a subtle blue tint to the light, and sound seemed to hit my ears at a lower register, as if stretched somehow. Pieces of wall that were being torn apart around us were falling at an amazingly slow pace, like flakes of ash trapped in sluggish fluid.

I stood, still moving at what was for me a normal pace, but to the others I must have looked like a combo of Speedy Gonzales and the Road Runner, a blur of Canton-sized motion. *Hot damn and fried potatoes!* The Spell worked! Relief and exhilaration flooded me in an adrenaline-fueled rush.

Bullets passed me at walking speed, metallic insects I could easily avoid, and I charged through the door, raising the Benelli. I had loaded the weapon with deer slugs, and I started unloading them at the seven men and women in business blah wear who were firing for all they were worth. Most of the cubicles in the room nearest our door had been flattened by the flash-bangs—the people occupying them on the ground, discombobulated and wailing incoherently, hands over ears, eyes screwed shut. The floor was a puke-colored industrial carpeting, soaked from the overhead sprinkler system.

The first slug exited the Benelli like a study in slow-motion special effects. The second slug only reinforced the sensation of being in an '80s action movie.

Cursing, I reckoned I had only a few more seconds left before a set of gems came winging my way. Dropping the Benelli and drawing my Bowie, I ran toward the seven, dodging bullets and jumping cubicle wreckage. Perhaps I could end it before the gems could. As I passed my own slow-motion slugs, I noted their probable destinations and cussed a bit. They would miss their targets by a country mile. Perhaps the minute vibrations in my hands translated into wide-ranging tremors at hyper-speed?

Fifteen feet from the shooters and I was at full speed, legs pumping and detritus bouncing away from my booted feet, but a curious heat was starting along my thighs, chest and face. Ten feet and it became worse, bad enough that I stopped suddenly, just a few feet away from the shooters. I stared at my arms. The fabric was beginning to brown and blacken, red lines of fire skittering around, wisps of smoke curling.

Oh no!

Friction burn. It was the only explanation. My mind raced. I knew there were only a few precious seconds left before the Spell ended and reality crashed in around me. The bad guys were just a few feet away and I could see them start to react to my blurred presence. Somehow, even though I was in a temporal slip, the friction of my insanely quick movement through the air was tearing at my clothes and skin. If I lived through this, I'd have a few choice words with Alex … all of them four letters.

Just beyond the shooters, between office doors, was a water cooler, a half-full five-gallon jug upside down in a dispenser. It looked like the answer to a prayer. No time for subtle; I raced past the shooters as bullets crawled from their weapons, the muzzle flares the slow dance of thick, liquid flame. Heat flared up my legs and forearms and I could feel my eyes stinging, drying out. Just before I reached the cooler, the strange blue tint began to fade, the long, drawn-out sounds of gunfire became sharper, more high-pitched, and the cacophony of battle started to batter my ears.

My hands touched the cooler as the Spell faded and my clothes burst into flames, sending a wash of heat into my eyes. Screaming in pain, I lifted the cooler from the dispenser and doused myself in tepid water that chugged quickly from the narrow opening in the jug. It felt cold and wonderful against my charring skin. Hisses and steam erupted from my clothing.

A sharp impact against my spine slammed me to the ground in a wash of green heat that lapped the edge of my vision. From the floor I had a mouse's eye-view of what had happened to the seven shooters.

Three words rang out through the gunfire, one on top of the other in a babble of nonsense syllables that had dramatic consequences. One gem, perhaps a sapphire, bounced into the air between the rightmost two shooters, thin six-foot electric blue lines erupting from each facet. The dozens of thin blue lines began to spin madly as the gem twirled in midair, suspended by the power of the Bouncing Betty Spell. The lines sliced though the two shooters, their guns, and their clothes, without slowing down or breaking. They sliced clean through everything, including the floor, as they whirled faster and faster between the two men. Before the sapphire stopped spinning, the unfortunates practically exploded in a shower of blood and other unsavory bodily fluids as they split into hundreds of hand-sized gobbets of flesh.

As for the other two gems, one of them was the standard grenade Spell, which I'd used on half-a-dozen or so occasions. It blasted two more shooters into strawberry jam while blowing a third clean out of her sensible shoes, sending her flying into and through a plate-glass office wall. The glass burst into a thousand pieces and those pieces shredded the woman up a treat before she fell in a lifeless heap into the office beyond. What was left wasn't pretty to look at.

The third effect was much more spectacular. I hadn't seen it before, but I vowed, if I survived, to give it a try. From an aquamarine the size of my thumb came jagged bolts of greenish electrical current that snaked through the air to touch anything metallic, which in this case included the guns in the hands of the last two unlucky shooters. They jinked and shuddered as the current flowed up their weapons and into their bodies, frying flesh instantly. A roasted pork smell filled the air and I felt somewhat disgusted as my mouth filled with saliva. Then the bullets in their guns cooked off, ripping apart metal and tearing through flesh. Fingers exploded from hands and blood flew. The two men dropped, accompanied by the sizzle of frying bacon.

A green flash grew large in my sight and I rolled with adrenaline-fueled speed. The baseball-sized globe of chartreuse fire missed my skull by inches, crisping the hair on the right side of my head. I kept rolling until a wall stopped me.

"Who are you?" snarled a tall man with black hair graying at the temples. He was dressed like the others in office blah wear, but the green fire burning bright in his fists told me he was no extra from *Office Space.* I didn't bother to reply. What good would it do? I merely stared as he raised his hands, the flames roaring higher, crackling and hissing evilly. "Never mind, it's not really important."

My body hurt too damn much, and I didn't think I could dodge another blast of that mossy fire. The Magician raised his hands ....

And a shot rang out, the bullet missing the Magician by less than an inch. The cavalry had come.

Dom, Jeanie, and Patricia raced toward us, weapons raised. "Stop," Dom commanded, M4 aimed at the Magician's head.

The Magician raised his hands, emerald flames sputtering out. "I surrender," he said.

As I levered myself slowly, painfully to my feet, I saw the man's fingers twitch and felt a thrill of alarm, but I was too late. Patricia, Jeanie, and Dom rose straight in the air and fell down to land with bone-breaking force upon the ugly carpet. The Magician began to laugh as I reached for the 9mm holstered at my hip. Not fast enough, because his eyes, dark with hate and evil, fixed themselves on mine and I knew I was a dead man.

Crack!

The shot was harsh and brutal, violence given sound and the side of the magician's head bulged outward as a flattened lump of lead burst through the skin in a welter of red and pink gore. The Magician's eyes rolled up until only the whites were showing before he slowly crumpled to the floor.

Nihsen walked into view, Dom's M4 cradled in his arms. "Nice weapon," he remarked calmly. "I need to get me one."

I grunted, slowing wiping bits of magician from my SWAT vest. "Hell, you can have his for all I care."

"Sorry, boss. My fault," groaned Dom from his prone position. Blood stained his mouth and beard. "I shoulda shot him when I had the chance. Must be getting soft in my old age."

My nod hurt and my skin felt dried, desiccated. "Yeah, you shoulda. Remind me to dock you a day's pay."

Nihsen smiled grimly and pointed to the three members of my team who had been so rudely manhandled by the magician. "That sure looked like it hurt."

Jeanie was already on her feet, swaying slightly, while Dom managed to pull himself into a sitting position, placing his head in his hands. Patricia pushed herself to her hands and knees and practiced her Technicolor yawn all over the hideous, wet carpeting. Not an improvement on the color scheme.

"I think the worst damage is to their pride," I said. "Call for backup; we're going to need a mess of handcuffs."

CHAPTER FIFTEEN

～

Kal

Here We Go A-Malling

I SHOULDN'T HAVE DONE IT. I shouldn't have tortured X-scar. The information about the bolt-hole wasn't worth the feeling of self-loathing that stubbornly adhered to my skin, despite the hot water from the shower head. Unfortunately, unlike the soapy water, the stain on my soul wasn't circling the drain. No amount of scrubbing would render it clean, only absolution. Unfortunately, part and parcel of absolution was 'solution,' and I didn't know of any for this situation.

Torture and I aren't strangers. I'd once done a Nazi dirty by ripping off his little finger during questioning; said Nazi was a member of the VGG, a man who had gutted an eight-year-old child so he could power a Spell, so don't judge me harshly. Necromancers are at the tippy top of my Hate List. The information that the Nazi possessed had been vital, but not the information X-scar carried. I could've waited for Canton to catch up; the odds favored him carving his way right through The Trade Group with his Bowie.

Maydock was right about the pus beneath the skin, and it galled me to see just how right he was and how deep the infection lay. It galled me that he'd forced me into a situation that revealed how messed up I am, how susceptible to cruelty and casual evil.

Damn him.

Damn me.

"Crap," I breathed, spitting water. "Crap, crap, crap and triple crap, crap on a cracker." I wanted to rage, to pound my fists against the white porcelain shower tiles until they shattered and my skin split, sending red down the drain with the water, but it wasn't in me. I was empty as a politician's promise, empty and numb. I dried my skin with a scratchy towel, but it didn't hurt enough. I wanted to feel pain, to feel anything but the numbness that lay beneath my skin.

No TV for me tonight; I had faith that the team had made it out of that hellhole in one piece and I was in no mood to talk to anyone, even over the boob tube, not even Jeanie—circumstances made being with her impossible right now. Actually, there was one person I wanted to talk to and even more than just talk to. Maydock, that rat bastard. Beating him to death with my fists would make me feel Jim Dandy, Yippie Skippy, and Hunky Dory.

Maydock was keeping tabs on me, knew where I lay my head, and I was tired of letting him call the shots. "I know you're out there listening, Maydock," I said calmly, staring at the window. It was likely he was using a laser listening device, a highly sophisticated surveillance apparatus that utilizes an invisible infrared laser beam to eavesdrop on a target. Sounds in the room cause tiny vibrations in the windows. Those vibrations modulate the laser beam, which is converted back into sound at the receiver.

I'd been thinking about how he'd been able to find me so quickly. It isn't hard to find what room a person is staying in, or even what hotel, as long as you have a name. I'd given my alias to Nihsen in Mr. Lowenstein's apartment and Maydock had been listening in.

"Call me quick or I'm packing my bags and heading back to DC," I continued. "My patience is at an end and I'll risk you going on a tear in this city. But know this: you start killing innocents, and I will call down every Fed at my beck and call to rip your ass off and feed it to you." My Interdiction twitched slightly, causing me momentary discomfort. I didn't know who else might be listening. "So call me, text me, send me flowers, or spit in my ear, I don't care. I am tired of games."

I waited. And waited. No answer. No phone call. Nothing.

Damn.

The bed creaked slightly under my weight as I lay down, and fatigue washed over me. My eyes closed of their own volition and I drifted away.

I KNEW IT WAS A dream. I could feel it as the sights and sounds were unspooling in front of me and I could sense my sleeping body nestled in the hotel bed, but the vision came to me with the relentless inevitability of the tide and no matter how hard I tied to shut it out, it arrived unbidden, unwanted. After several moments of struggling to wake, I gave in and watched the show.

It was 2004, a year before the iPhone was released to the public. Bush 2.0 was president. The US of A was embroiled in a Middle Eastern war that would last for over a decade, the Spirit Mars rover landed successfully, and Lance Armstrong won his sixth Tour de France with no one the wiser about his use of performance-enhancing drugs that would soon besmirch his name forever. At home it was business as usual for the BSI, killing Supernaturals and taking names.

The Mall of America, Bloomington, Minnesota. A quarter million square feet of pure commercialism packed solid with over 500 stores, the SEA LIFE Minnesota Aquarium, Nickelodeon Universe, Radisson Blu Hotel, and the Theaters at Mall of America, where you could buy overpriced popcorn as you watch the latest Disney/Pixar feature.

It was cold in the parking lot, with a strong wind howling from the north that bit through your clothing and brought tears to your eyes. My Faraday coat, heavy as it was, seemed to offer no protection from the harsh Minnesota winds. Ah, home sweet home. Up in Grand Rapids, where my parents lived, it would be even colder, and I knew Dad would have the Franklin stove lit, pumping hot air and sending a light scent of wood smoke through the house.

Thinking of Mom and Dad brought a pang and tugged at the old heartstrings. Thanks to the encounter with the Finnish demi-god Iku-Turso, they had Interdictions squatting like toads in the hallways of their minds and had been read in on the BSI. It didn't hurt that Dad was a legend in military circles and still had friends in very high places, such as General Johansen, a member of the Joint Chiefs. No one screwed with Pekka Hakala more than once.

As for my mother … well, she didn't carry much influence (except with Dad), but she was like a force of nature and had been known to make big he-man Scandinavian lumberjack-types with beards down to their bellies quake in their Timberlines. I'd been tempted to put a 'Here be Dragons' sign on the door to her kitchen, but self-preservation and fear had stayed my hand.

Five pairs of boots hit the asphalt behind me as the team exited the minivan. The parking lot was virtually empty and so was the mall. Thanks to Bureau influence, even the security guards had the night off. Darkness shrouded the lot and the enormous mall like a thick blanket, offering no warmth, just concealment for whatever baddies might be haunting the environs.

"What a lousy way to spend Halloween," muttered Two-Hit as he joined me. The others stood back, waiting for orders.

I looked at my teammate. Tall, broad shoulders, more muscle than a Kodiak, he looked like the poster boy for Armed Services recruiting. "While all the good kiddies are out Trick-or-Treating, this is the busiest time of the year for us," I explained for the umpteenth time. I wasn't too upset about repeating myself; I would only be worried if someone *wasn't* bitching about something.

Most of us BSI types referred to Halloween in the Gaelic: Samhain, the festival marking the end of harvest and the beginning of winter. For the World Under, it was the time when the veil between worlds was most permeable and they were able to cross over with greater ease. For Things That Go Bump in the Night it was kind of like Christmas, the hap-hap-happiest time of the year. That is if you thought of Christmas as a time filled with blood, screams, and horror. Sort of like the annual CPAC convention.

For the Bureau, it was mandatory overtime.

Small flakes of snow began to drift from the sky, the stars hidden behind a gray barrier of clouds that reflected city light back to the ground, giving the night a gray, twilight feel. "This is just wonderful," complained Two-Hit.

"Welcome to Minnesota, Team Epsilon," I said just loud enough for them to hear. "You should be here in January when it is *really* cold."

Chuckles and groans answered me. One of the Green Peas, Jackson, had to put his two cents in. "Why would a bunch of Scandinavians move a billion miles just to settle down in a place exactly like the one they left?"

Our diminutive team magician, Punch, snorted. "Homesick, Pea, homesick."

Without another word we started across the parking lot to the main mall entrance. Less than twenty-four hours ago local police responded to a call from one of the legions of employees. Seems that a young woman by the name of Hillary Trippleton, a cashier at the Sharper Image, had spotted a demon as she was preparing to leave after closing the store the previous evening. Thanks to Otto, the semi-artificially intelligent program that monitored all U.S. databases, we were alerted in time and a team was sent out. My team, Team Epsilon.

Gearing up, we flew to the Twin Cities and paid the young lady a visit, posing as FBI. Punch was able to fog her memories a bit with a gentle Spell used for such occasions, but not before gleaning what information we could. She had indeed seen something—a large, humped shape with glowing silver eyes—and we couldn't attribute it to drugs or alcohol because she did neither. It was a bona fide tip that we had to take seriously.

Messing with the minds of Straights was always a dicey proposition, but it was better to cause some slight psychological damage than risk stories of an eight-foot, humped, black demon roaming the halls of the nation's most popular mall. Bad for tourism. Eventually the memory would become so hazy that she'd blame it on lack of caffeine or a severe sugar low.

It was no great feat to empty the mall. All that was needed was the right badge, the right clout, and the right phone calls. The place was shut down before 5 pm. By the time onlookers and such departed it was eight, and thanks to overcast skies, gloomy as hell (no pun intended). Perfect for demon hunting.

"Damn, this building is huge," said Griffin, our team sniper, in awe as we walked through one puddle of light to the next. Each lamp in the lot looked lonely and the brightness of the halogens seemed dim somehow, as if oppressed by what lay inside the mall. Not that we really needed the light, mind you; we had our nightvision glasses and could see quite well, albeit in shades of black and white. "It's not as impressive as the Pentagon, but damn, Kal, this is something else."

"Trick or Treat, Griffin," I replied. Griffin was a good guy—steady, dependable, with nerves of steel and a lousy sense of humor.

I REMEMBERED WHAT HAPPENED TO him and silently began to shout in denial. This was a memory I did not want to recall, but it continued on despite my protests.

"WHO'S THE KID?" SAID REV, pointing a long arm at the entrance. Everything Rev said or did was done with careful deliberation and carried the weight of total conviction. If Rev said he would get something done, it got done. A rock was more emotional and carefree than Rev.

I spied with my little eye something that began with 'teenager,' lounging at the big front entrance under the enormous white 'Mall of America' sign. Thin, lanky and nearly six feet tall, the kid looked to be in his mid-to-late teens and had the large hands and feet that promised an even bigger height to come. An old pair of Ray Bans shielded his eyes.

Making sure my weapons were well hidden and my long coat covered my full suit of body armor, I strolled casually up to the young man. "Hey, kid, it's a little late to be out at the mall, considering it's closed."

"Who are you supposed to be?" he asked with the contempt and feigned ennui only the young can pull off. He looked like a longshoreman, with his ratty pea coat and black wool cap pulled down over his ears and scraggly hair. "You sure don't look like cops to me."

"And you look like a dockworker reject with crappy sunglasses. We aren't cops," I replied, crossing my arms and looming over him. When I put my mind to it, I can seriously loom. "Private security hired by the mall. I suggest you leave and allow us to go about our business."

Damn, but that kid could sneer with the best of them. But he moved away, slowly, hands in the pockets of his old pea coat. Each step was a statement, one that said 'I'm moving at my own pace and I'm only leaving because I want to, so screw you.' A battered Vespa waited for him in the muted light of a lamp and he took his sweet time puttering away.

Frickin' kid.

I removed the keys to the front door from my Faraday coat and we entered the mall.

Whoa. I'd been here before, several times in fact, but never when the place was in lockdown and all the lights were turned off. It reminded me of an enormous underground city, abandoned and lonely, waiting patiently for the return of its inhabitants. For a second I expected Gimli and Thorin Oakenshield to come strutting out of the darkness demanding we vacate this modern day Moria.

"*Keep your eyes peeled, Team,*" I said, switching to subvocal. The rule was silence from now on, lest the bogeymen had ears as sharp as their claws and teeth.

"*Check, boss,*" they said.

"*Rev, you ready?*" He was one of our secret weapons against demons. Rev was exactly that, a reverend. Episcopalian ... Catholic Light. He was a true believer, a man of near unshakeable faith that the average demon couldn't bear to be near. If there was demon punting to be done, an exorcism to be performed, or a funeral to arrange, Rev was the man.

"*Ready, boss.*" He fingered the large silver cross on a chain around his neck.

Jackson the Green Pea said, *"How are we gonna find a demon in this?"*

"We won't have to. It'll find us. We just need to locate a defensible position. Like the realtors say, it's all about 'location, location, location.'" I touched the rim of my glasses and said, *"Blueprint."*

The mall came to life with a brilliant HUD shining on the lenses—the official, up-to-date blueprints filed with the city. A glowing yellow dot on the lowest level represented the team. *"Zoom. Rotate left. Zoom. Enhance. Reduce detail."* All the commands were carried out quickly by the magical/tech apparatus perched on my nose. I knew the others were seeing the same thing because their glasses were slaved to mine.

It was time to start the hunt.

Each step echoed faintly as we quick-timed it. I had a location in mind to wait for the demon because I knew that no demon worth its name would pass up the opportunity to snack on six juicy humans. It wasn't a matter of *if,* it was a matter of *when.*

"There." I pointed.

Punch looked down my arm. *"Kay Jewelers?"*

"No, smart ass. In front of Kay Jewelers. The escalators. We should head to the second floor and park it there. The location gives us direct access to either side of the ledge, a controlled escape route down if we need it, and unless the Supernatural is in either Lane Bryant or Things Remembered, its only route to us would be down the escalators from the third floor or along the second floor walkway along the shops. That will give us plenty of time to see it coming. It will have no place to hide."

She wrinkled her roundish, pug nose. *"Gee, I don't know boss …."*

I gave her my patented Look Of Death that promised Very Bad Things if she didn't shut it right quick and she did so. The others were kind enough not to razz her about it. Not out of respect, mind you, but because it was always good policy to be on the good side of a person who could turn you into something … squishy.

We bypassed Camp Snoopy—the theme park the mall was wrapped around—and headed toward the escalators, weapons ready. In the center of the park, the beloved Peanuts character waved at us, surrounded by trees, buildings, and a roller coaster. Its normally cheerful grin now seemed rather … sadistic, as if the cartoon beagle knew that we were about to step in a load of stinky brown stuff.

In the noon light that would stream in from the massive skylights above the park, the whole family would ooh and ah at a riot of greens, whites, blues, and reds—a festive variety of colors. But in the gray world of nightvision, the park took on a more ferocious aspect. The roller coaster became a haven for all manner of evils that could easily hide in the nooks and crannies it provided, and the trees, luscious and inviting in daylight, were menacing giants waiting for our eyes to focus elsewhere so they could pounce.

The Supernaturals that inhabit the World Under are legion. Thousands of different creatures, most of them thirsting to kill the unsuspecting humans that inhabit this fragile Earth. Was it jealousy? Were they here first and unhappy about being kicked out? Or were they like sharks, predators that don't rule out certain food sources based on intelligence?

Whatever the reason, if you could name it, imagine it, it existed. I'd even bet there were Supernaturals that were helpless, motionless, when observed, but if you took your eyes off them—BAM!—they had you by short and curlies. Gives one the creeps just thinking about it.

I had a sturdy MP5, possibly the most widely used submachine gun in the world. Mine, however, came with some optional extras not found on the common floor model. Able to shoot 800 Supernaturals a minute with 10mm rounds at full auto, it would do so in complete silence, thanks to a Spell gem embedded in the handle. It also sported twin drum magazines that upped its capacity from the standard one hundred rounds to an impressive two hundred fifty.

My companions had all sorts of slug-throwing lethality as well as various sharp-edged weapons. Mine was a fourteen-inch Bowie knife given to me by my father, fashioned from an industrial file and sharp enough to cut an idea in half.

My team was stationed at the top of the escalator in front of closed shops, whose security grates were pulled shut and firmly locked to the floor. There was a straight shot up the twin escalators to the third floor, where the assailant would be perfectly exposed to fire. Good thing demons—the corporeal ones, at least—were susceptible to bullets. If lead didn't work, we had silver, which would also work against lycanthropes.

Jackson and Rev kept an eye on the escalators leading to the third floor, Griffin to the left and Two-Hit to the right, while Punch kept her eyes on the escalators heading to the first floor. She also used a silver market to draw wards on the floor that would slow down most demons, or at least make them very uncomfortable. Wards are simple Spell Shapes designed to protect, and they have a tendency to expel all their power at once when crossed. When dealing with demons— if, indeed, it was a demon—it helped if you covered all your bases. As for me, I kept my eyes a-roaming everywhere. If I could've put eyes in the back of my head, I would have. We had our backs to the stores' steel gates and a clear line of fire.

What could go wrong?

I found out quickly enough.

Chapter Sixteen

Canton
Valuable Merchandise

THE BASTARDS IN THE OFFICE, stunned by the flash-bangs, fought like crazed weasels the second they realized we were arresting them. I had to punch a little old lady square in the schnoz because she set her dentures deep in the flesh of my wrist, drawing blood. Cartilage *cracked* and *popped,* and blood gushed from her witch nose, but her lights went out and I was able to wrap her wrists in a zip tie.

Good thing Jeanie and the rest were up and about after kissing the floor and ceiling. Kal would've been plenty mad if I returned them broke. There were contusions and some mild carpet burns, but nothing to write home about. They had a good head of mad going, enough that they were none too gentle with arresting the kiddy peddlers.

Those right assholes knew full well what happened to folks who prey on children and they didn't want to see the inside of a prison cell. Not that I could blame them. Convicts have kids, too, and feel pretty much the same way any parent would when faced with pedophiles, or those who supply them.

Jacobs tottered in from the hallway, looking a little shaky and walking with a slight limp. Alex followed straight after, white, pasty, and sweaty. Guess healing her drained him a good patch.

"You two okay?" I asked.

Alex nodded while Jacobs, not one to appear weak, helped Patricia put a fat guy in an arm bar so he'd be docile enough for cuffing. Not that Patricia needed the help, seeing as how she could beat me two out of three falls.

"How about you?" I asked Nihsen, who was standing there looking both frustrated and sad.

"I have two kids," he replied absently, eyes staring out at a horizon only he could see. "Sammie and Zach. They're mostly grown up now, college age and whatnot, but when they were little the thought of them winding up like the kids these people sell …." His voice trailed away and he pointed to the dead Magician with his pistol.

"You saved our lives, Detective," I said quietly. "Killing him was the right call."

His eyes snapped back into focus and he stared at me, the fires of his rage burning bright in his face. "I know. I just wish I could bring him to life so I could shoot him all over again."

Oh. Good. Thought he might have regrets.

"Jacobs, put the fat man down and take Alex to secure the hallway." I wiped my hands off on my black pants. The whole place was dripping wet from the sprinkler system, and the carpet smelled like wet dog and old cigarettes.

Snarling, Dove Jacobs slapped the jelly belly she was manhandling into restraints and dumped him on the floor. She limped away, grabbing the little Alex's wrist and dragging him along with a startled 'squawk!'

"Damn," I muttered and took over the job of hog-tying the moaning woman I'd punched. She looked like my hometown librarian, Mrs. Kratchner. Just goes to show that evil is often wrapped in the most innocuous packages. After making sure the cursing lady was well and truly secured, I unholstered my phone and dialed.

"Ghost?"

"Here, Canton."

"Update."

"Local LEOs and FBI are on the way, along with firemen, who have been told to stand down until the building has been secured. ETA is two minutes. I have Kal on a traffic cam entering his Hyundai and heading toward the hotel. He appears to be unharmed."

Thank *God*.

"Thanks, Ghost. Keep me apprised."

"Will do. Just so you know, I am currently unraveling the encryption on The Trade Group server and it is quite elaborate, so I will be busy for a while." *Click*.

I stretched, moving tired muscles, then shook free of my body armor. That Magician had hit me with something and I needed to eyeball the damage.

The back of my jacket had a fist-sized hole burned through the fabric and the steel plate beneath had a shiny, almost melted look to it. I remembered the greenish fire and the ball of flames that had missed my skull. Magic fire. I'd seen it before, several times. It made napalm look like a Disney cartoon.

I was one lucky sonofabitch.

Jacob's voice interrupted my reverie. "*Boss*."

I thumbed my throat mic. "*Yeah*?"

"Come to the hallway. You really should see this."

"On my way."

As I entered the hallway, I noticed the bullet holes. While these holes were not remarkable in and of themselves, what did capture my attention was the exposed, glinting silver mesh. I ran a gloved finger over the ragged edge of one hole, the fine threads of silver snagging fabric. That would explain why every merlin sensor in the area hadn't alerted Ghost to the use of magic. The whole place was one big Faraday cage, and that had me worried a-plenty.

What the hell was going on here? Faraday cages? Magicians? This information yielded more questions than answers and my poor ol' brain was a-clanging and a-jangling with confusion. This was way above my pay grade.

I splashed through a thin scrim of water to where the hall turned to the left. Jacobs and Alex were staring at a hole burned clear through the floor to the story below. The hole was roughly ten feet long and encompassing the width of the hall. Its edges were melted, exposing concrete around the rim that had turned liquid and re-solidified in waxy-looking runnels. The inside hallway wall was scorched black with burned paint, and the cinderblocks beneath looked like they had started to melt. The previously boarded up windows on the opposite wall were merely gaping holes to the outside world, while rivulets of silver from the mesh lining the walls streaked cinderblocks and spread droplets to the fourth floor. Speaking of the fourth floor, its beige carpeting was pitted and scored with burn holes, not only from the melted silver, but also from melted iron—not to mention that it was soaked with water and soggy ash. Above, the ceiling had burned clean through as well, along with sprinkler piping and a heap of wiring. Soft afternoon sunlight streamed through past us down to the fourth floor.

"Hmm," I grunted. "You don't see that every day."

"What the hell happened here, boss?" Jacobs asked, staring raptly at the structural damage.

"Kal happened," I replied, raising my bulletproof vest with its shiny hole in the back. Magical fire. Probably a Hellfire Spell egg. I stated my theory aloud, and Alex nodded in agreement.

"My guess is he tossed a Spell egg into the hall," he said, leaning around the corner and pointing to a body. It was pretty much a crispy-critter; all that was left was a blackened upper body. "Only magic fire could burn a body to ash so quickly and localize the damage like this."

I spotted another body lying in the far hall near a brown steel door pockmarked with bullet dimples. "Kal made it through there. They tried to go after him and he done them a dirty."

Something about the body sprawled at the door caught my eye. It didn't look right; the skin on the corpse's face looked ... bubbly.

"Alex, what does that look like to you?" I asked.

"I was wondering the same thing. Also wondering how he crossed this great big hole in the floor. From here, it doesn't look like he was killed by a bullet or fire. Perhaps some toxin?"

There were two plastic containers near the corpse, both shattered; the only thing keeping some of the pieces together was the glue from their labels. But from my perspective, it wasn't clear what had been in them. There was no way I was going to try to jump the hole, not with the floor being so wet and slippery, but crossing the divide was merely a matter of perspective.

A minute later I was in the office room, where the rest of the team had secured The Trade Group survivors. Sixteen people were positioned against the left wall, all trussed up, awaiting transport to jail. Most were gagged so we didn't have to listen to the powerful lot of cussing they had been throwing at us.

The shared wall with the hallway was blank—no decorations or doors. I took ten paces from where I estimated the hallway turned—doing my best to guess where the hole on the other side ended—stepped back, raised the Benelli, and fired. Drywall shattered and flew out in a spray of dust. The resultant hole revealed cinderblocks pocked with buckshot. *Hmm.* They should have shattered. I loaded the shotgun with deer slugs and let fly half a dozen times, the gun roaring loud enough that I wished for earplugs.

"What are you doing?" hollered Patricia, fingers in her ears. "You're destroying the wall!"

I grinned at her. "Nah, you can't really destroy that wall, just rearrange it somewhat."

When the dust settled we all saw a torso-sized hole bordered by torn concrete. Running through the hole, blocking access to the hall was a pair of steel rebar. Apparently The Trade Group didn't want anyone busting through this long wall at any point.

"Ghost," I said softly into my phone.

"Yes?" he replied, sounding distracted.

"You know what's on the other side of this wall?"

"Apparently a secret room Kal discovered, accessed through the janitor's closet. There are three men in that room, one dead, the other two injured or unconscious. The walls of that room are sheathed in quarter-inch steel plate; therefore, punching through would be problematic. Entering through the janitorial closet would be easier.

And according to the files I have liberated, there is also an escape hatch leading to a first floor rear exit. Canton, I must inform you that I have overridden the lockdown on the elevator that was enabled when Kal arrived. The FBI and local law enforcement will arrive on your floor in under a minute. The FBI has been ordered to answer to your authority. The elevator will open at the end of the large room you are in."

"Check, Ghost. Thanks."

Backup arrived, a baker's dozen of police and feds all dressed up nice in riot gear. They took custody of The Trade Group employees, making several trips through the elevator because the stairwell had been reduced to a shaft of rubble, thanks to well-placed shape charges. They weren't too gentle with the prisoners, and the hard look on their faces told me they'd been informed about what had really been going on in the building.

Before all was said and done, I had some members of the Omaha Fire Department use a Husqvarna 16" circular saw to cut through the wall. No need to waste bullets and time when you've got professionals with the right tools.

Of course the firemen drew all sorts of goo-goo eyes from the ladies. Even Patricia wasn't immune, and I could practically see the Firemen of Omaha Calendar centerfold image in her lovely green eyes. Jeanie merely stood off to one side and tried not to stare at the sweating beefcakes with their enormous tools shooting sparks as it chewed through rebar.

"I wonder what Kal would think," I whispered out of the corner of my mouth to her. "Should I tell him?"

She didn't bother to look back as she softly said, "You realize I can lay a hex on you that would shrivel certain parts of your anatomy until they're the size of chick peas, don't you?"

Might be worth it.

Nah.

"Shoo," I said to the beefcakes when the work was done, much to the dismay of the ladies. "Fly, be free and come back no more!" I made flapping motions with my hands and escorted both the Fire

Department and the feds to the elevator, liberating a respirator from one of the fireman. They grumbled, but apparently the Bureau did its job because no one kicked up a fuss.

"What about the bodies?" asked the last fed on the elevator as he prepared to go cool his heels in the lobby. It was Special Agent-in-Charge Daniel Foreman, the local muckety-muck who no doubt was bucking for Section Chief.

"I'll call and let you know when you can pick them up," I replied. "Don't worry. It's your department, along with the local LEOs, who will get the credit for this bust. Just let me do my thing and you'll get the spotlight."

That earned me a lopsided smile. This was the type of bust that would make his rise in the FBI all the more meteoric, and we both were well aware that it would have him on the fast track out of Omaha in a New York minute. The elevator doors closed on the sight of him planning his future with a new Mrs. Section Chief and 2.5 kids in a much more prestigious location, perhaps in an oversized house filled with Restoration Hardware furniture.

"Why didn't you just break through to the room instead of the hallway?" Alex leaned against the wall. Judging by the dark circles under his eyes, he was exhausted.

"Didn't want to waste time trying to cut through steel plate. I'm not worried about the guys in that room—they're out of commission—and Ghost would've let me know if the injured one was critical. The easiest way in is through the closet. Besides, I'm curious as to how Kal neutralized the fella in the hall there."

The team granted me a collective nod and I pressed on. Kal was at the hotel and would contact Ghost via the TV if he needed anything. My guess ... he was using all the hotel's hot water in a marathon shower. I would if I were him.

Poison was the key and the skin was the clue. There was something wrong with the second victim's face. It looked wrong, almost melted, and as I stepped through the hole I was able to read the labels on the two broken containers.

Bleach and ammonia.

It took a second for it to sink in through the thick layers of my skull, but when it did, I was rocked back on my heels. Chlorine gas, had to be.

Most people saw Kal as a big, mean killing machine, forgetting that there was a pretty sharp mind beneath that imposing exterior. He'd earned a master's degree in chemical engineering at the University of Nebraska, and it looked like all that edjumacation served him well.

"Damn, white boy," I muttered to myself. "You sure don't mess around."

"What's going on?" Jeanie asked, peering through the hole.

"Everybody step back," I commanded, gauging the scene. Victim one had been caught in the fire and turned into a crispy critter. I reckoned number two somehow jumped the big hole when the fire went out to land right smack dab in the middle of a cloud of chlorine gas and now was going to spend the rest of his life dead. "Alex, I need you to neutralize the chemicals in there." I squeezed back out into the cubicle room. "No one goes in there without a respirator. The only reason the gas didn't spread further is because the fire burned clear through the roof."

I gave Alex the respirator and he performed whatever mojo necessary for allowing safe passage. Before he finished, I gave Ghost a call to see what was what.

"There is a block of data I have yet to decrypt," he buzzed, sounding pissed ... for a sentient computer program. "Very sophisticated algorithms, both technological and magical, but I will be able decode it eventually."

All that techno stuff hurt my head. Point me at a bad guy and I knew what to do, or hand me a mystery involving ancient cultures and I'm your man, but modern magic/tech is a no-fly zone for Canton Alsate. "Anything else?"

"Yes. From what I have retrieved from the main server, it seems that the little room you are trying to access is the 'nerve center' to this particular locale, where all sales are monitored and bank account transfers are confirmed. They use a series of three state-of-the-art laptops for these transactions instead of an actual small server farm. While not as fast as an actual server, it does allow for immediate portability and easy destruction of data, although Kal has managed to clone the hard drives with a MagniGlass, which I need you to retrieve. All other data in the server belongs to the 'CEO' of TTG, a Mr. Wilson Hanziger, who was, I believe, the Magician you encountered." He paused for a moment. "While there are no actual references to magic, there are mentions of 'assets particular to the officers of the Corporation.' This has me wondering if there might be more Magicians."

Chilling thought and I said so.

"The concealed door in the janitor's closet is electronically locked, but I have broken the 10-key code, and it is ready for you and the team. The latch mechanism is disguised as a faucet. Just push down and the door will open. You must excuse me; I need to give this last block of data my full attention."

After hanging up, I checked on Alex, who was finished neutralizing the toxins, and the entire team passed through the janitorial closet—far too clean, wouldn't have fooled anyone who actually worked for a living—and entered the room beyond.

"Jeanie," I barked, pointing at the big guy with a curious X-shaped scar on his chin. "Heal him." Both his knees were shot to hell and gone and I figured he must've done something to put Kal in the 'pissed off' column. My finger drifted toward an unconscious tubby guy lying in a pool of his own blood and drool. "Dom, secure him." The third guy, dressed in the same sort of short-sleeved, white button-down shirt and black pant combo as the other two, didn't need any help. He was way beyond any we could offer. Two in the chest, one in the head, just like they taught us at Coronado. I spied a trio of .22s in the corner and figured he had the bad sense to draw on Kal, which was usually a good way to discover how to get dead in a hurry.

An open trap door at the far corner of the room showed itself to be Kal's exit point. I peered into the hole to see a ladder bolted to the inside of a chute. A tiny square dot of light marked the end some thirty feet below.

Jeanie had her hands on the big guy's knees and I realized it wouldn't hurt my feelings none if she did a half-assed job of healing so he'd walk with a limp for the rest of his life. It was a safe bet Kal had used the Lahti on the guy, his favorite weapon. The thing weighed a ton and never jammed, but it was an antique and I was surprised it hadn't broken long ago.

A few minutes later, after Jacobs had secured the laptops and the MagniGlass, Kal's girlfriend opened her eyes wide. The big guy's knees were fine, only small round red marks indicating that he'd ever been shot. "Canton," she said heavily, her voice thick with fatigue. "This man is under an Interdiction."

Well, knock me over with a feather. "He's Bureau?" Silence dropped in heavy on the room as everyone turned to listen. Anger stirred sluggishly in the stale air.

Jeanie shook her head. "No, I don't think so. The Interdiction used by the Bureau is elegant, beautifully complex, and subtle. Looking at that Spell is like looking at a Rembrandt. What his man has in his mind is brutal and grotesque, a child's finger painting. It's ugly, not subtle, and doesn't have the safeguards ours has." She wiped her forehead. "But it is effective."

"Can you remove it?" asked Dom. "If it's so crude, maybe you can erase it and then we can interrogate him."

"Not likely. I said it was brutal and grotesque, but also effective. Removing it will turn his mind into an unusable slurry."

We stood there, staring at the man with the scar on his chin, flummoxed by a crude copy of an Interdiction. What could we do?

Alex had an idea. He knelt by Jeanie's side, put his hands on either side of the unconscious man's head, and closed his eyes.

"Alex," I said. "Whatcha doin'?" A bad feeling was creeping up my spine. Sort of like the ones I get when Kal comes up with a clever idea.

He replied without opening his eyes. "Benjamin Franklin spent years developing the Shape for the Interdiction Spell. He was possibly the greatest Magician of his time and definitely one of the greatest in all of human history, so I doubt a copycat could have set in place the same kind of safeguards and exceptions for causality ingrained into the Franklin Interdiction. I am going to attempt an end-around."

"Uh, will it be dangerous?"

"Only for him."

Hmmm. "Right. Go ahead, then."

And he went right on ahead. A minute passed while we all watched, the tension thick enough to slab on toast.

Twitch ... the big man's leg spasmed. *Twitch, twitch, twitch,* like the dying convulsions of a spider. *Twitch, twitch, twitch.* It was unnerving and it began to happen with great frequency and violence. It got worse, with his whole body shaking like a million volts were coursing through his nerves and it was starting to make me a little sick to my stomach. I mean, a man ought not to be a-shaking like that; it ain't natural.

After several minutes of flip-flopping, Alex removed his hands and the guy commenced to lying still once again, much to the relief of yours truly.

"Damn, Canton." The little Magician wiped his forehead with the back of his hand. "That was rough." He looked ready to vomit.

"What?"

He lowered his head and his next words were so soft I had to strain to hear them. "I stripped his mind bare."

Jeanie's voice cracked across the room like a pistol shot. "You *what?*"

When he raised his head, his eyes shone with such fury I took a step back and Jeanie's mouth shut with a *snap!* "It was the only way to get the information, to mind-rape him." He licked his lips. "That man knew everything about The Trade Group. *Everything.* He was the CFO and he made sure the money paid for the children was securely deposited in the company's many offshore accounts.

"He knew all about the magic, the Spells used to keep The Trade Group's activities quiet, the Interdictions. He also knew where the bodies were buried and what palms were greased so they could prey on unsuspecting families and take advantage of a corrupt and understaffed foster care system. I couldn't get it all, but I got enough to nauseate me for the rest of my life."

Alex slowly stood and we watched as he spat on the big man who now stared at the ceiling and drooled, showing all the mentation of a rutabaga. "He knew and he *didn't care*. His mind was an open sewer and just getting a glimpse of it made me want to vomit." Without warning, he lashed out with a furious kick that connected to the prone man's ribs. Bones snapped and the human vegetable coughed up blood. "Don't you dare touch him!" screamed the little Magician as Jeanie started forward. "Don't you [CENSORED] dare! He doesn't deserve healing; don't waste your magic on him!" Alex's breath was starting to come out ragged and twin spots of red dotted his pale cheeks. "You didn't see what I saw in his mind ... what he did to come to the attention of the TTG. He was a pedophile. Everyone who worked here is a pedophile, or some sort of deviant. It's the reason they cooperated so freely; their minds are broken, ugly things. The fact that I had to strip this bastard's mind bare to acquire this information doesn't bother me one bit. To me, all these people were as dangerous and evil as any Supernatural I've encountered."

He scrubbed his face with the palms of his hands. "But the kids, Canton, the kids aren't purchased for perverts—not enough money in that. No, these kids were *handpicked*; each and every one of them is a Magician. Or a potential Magician. Somehow this Trade Group has discovered the gene for magic and can tell which kids will become Magicians."

Damn.

Oh, *damn*. My belly rolled over and I saw the team's reactions: disbelief, surprise, shock, and horror, all mirroring my own.

"How?"

"They have people in doctors' offices and around the country, doctors who work within the foster care system," came the reply. "Doctors who draw blood, take cheek swabs, what have you, all to test the DNA for the magic gene. Those children who have it are 'tagged' for cultivation, and when they are old enough, they are taken and sold all over the globe to people who will twist the kids' minds to their purposes so that when they finally mature magically, they will be willing slaves." The last few words were spat out with such heat I was surprised the air didn't scream in pain.

I raised my hands. "Calm down, Alex," I soothed, trying not to gag, not bothering to consider the repercussions … they were too big to consider in the moment. "Take a deep breath."

"Calm down," he said, sounding anything but. "Can't, Canton, I am nowhere near the same vicinity as calm down. Not even in the same *hemisphere*. Taking a trip through this asshole's mind was like snorkeling in an outhouse. They use the foster system because when they disappear the majority of those kids won't be missed. Those that are can be explained away. And that wasn't the worst of it."

A bad feeling started right behind my navel and began to travel upward, along with a load of bile. "What do you mean?"

"What do I mean? What do I mean?" he asked absently. I noticed everyone staring at Alex as if he'd burst into flames at any second. Even Jacobs looked worried. "What do I mean? I mean to say that The Trade Group is only the tip of the iceberg, only one part, a tiny part, of a vast criminal organization that is using magic and tech to further their ends, all at the expense of the Straights."

The world just plumb dropped out from beneath my feet. "What?"

Alex furiously scrubbed his scalp with his fingernails. "He didn't know *all* about this vast organization, Canton, but he knew enough. The parts of this organization, the companies, are like terrorist cells— they operate independently—but the CEO of each company—and they are *all* Magicians—report to an anonymous central authority.

"This vast organization of interconnected, seemingly legitimate companies are into everything. Drugs, illegal arms dealing, conflict diamonds, information brokering, snuff films, and more. Every venal piece of filth you can imagine in your worst nightmares bear the fingerprints of this organization. From this septic tank of a human being I've learned that they are rich, they are powerful, they are ruthless, and they are *global.*"

Oh, my head hurt.

CHAPTER SEVENTEEN

～

Kal

Let's Dance

R*IIIIINNGG ….*

Snap! Just like that the dream ended, the last frame of the movie passing my mind's light, and the screen went blank. I bolted upright, eyes wide and staring. Mid-afternoon light streamed through the thin inner curtains that shielded the windows and tinted the room in shades of sepia.

That dream … so vivid, so perfect. Every detail, every nuance perfectly shaded, as if I were experiencing the whole thing all over again.

Riiiiiiiiiinnnnnnnggggg ….

I knew who was on the other end of that phone, waiting patiently like a spider for me to answer. My hand reached out of its own accord and snagged the receiver.

"Hello?"

"I told you there was pus beneath the flesh of this city," said the hateful, snaky voice. "It is good to see that you survived. You surpassed my expectations."

"How did you find out about The Trade Group?" *I will not throw the phone across the room; I will not throw the phone across the room.* Thinking that didn't stop the urge, but it kept me centered.

"I will tell you soon."

Out of the corner of my eye I saw the TV set and I froze. It was on, the volume muted, and I clearly remembered shutting it off. Words were scrolling across the bottom: KAL, UPDATE PLEASE … KAL, UPDATE PLEASE.

I picked up the remote to answer and continued my conversation with Maydock, a study in multitasking. "You must have some serious mojo, Docky, to set everything up like this." AM FINE, GHOST. HOW IS THE TEAM?

The response was immediate. THEY ARE FINE AND THE TRADE GROUP HAS BEEN SHUT DOWN WITH EXTREME PREJUDICE. Good, that was a load off my mind.

"Do not call me that, Kalevi Hakala," Maydock growled. Seems like he was big on respect and fear and I had neither for him. That seemed to cheese him off something fierce.

"Well, *Maydock*, I am sick and tired of your little games." GOOD NEWS, GHOST. I THINK IT IS ABOUT TIME THE BUREAU OFFICIALLY SENDS A TEAM TO OMAHA TO MOP UP THE TRADE GROUP AFFAIR. I WILL HANDLE MAYDOCK. GIVE JEANIE MY LOVE. HAVE TO GO, KAL OUT.

"You won't have to play games anymore, Kal." There was a serious edge to Maydock's voice I hadn't heard before. The snaky whisperings sounded vicious and full of hate.

UNDERSTOOD, KAL. I WILL INFORM THE DIRECTOR. GOOD LUCK. WILL KEEP IN TOUCH.

The words disappeared as Ghost signed off. I guess he wanted to make sure I was all right. "Good to know, Maydock," I continued. "What now? You realize that once the police report on the silver mesh inside that building and the Polynesian security guard with the strange tattoos, Otto will alert the Bureau. We *have* to send a team now."

Once again that disgusting laugh crept into my ear. "Of course. I planned on that. I know you will not meet with the team because you know I am watching and will do terrible things if you disobey."

He was right about that. I dared not buck his say on that matter.

He knew how to pull my strings, but I swore that they'd be cut before this dance was over. "So I ask again … what now?"

"What now? Now we meet face to face."

Heat suffused my skin as excitement thundered through me. *Finally.* "So we end this soon? Good, I'm tired of playing around."

"No, no. This doesn't end tonight, not at all." And there went the excitement. "I reasoned that it was time we met, so you know what you're up against. Like knights locked in a duel to the death, we should meet and you should get to know the person who will defeat you."

Interesting choice of words. Defeat, not *kill*. It didn't take a pop psychologist to figure out that he wanted me to squirm and plead and know who held the reins if I lost. This wasn't about who was the best Apex Predator, not by a long shot. This was personal. Maydock had a grudge and he wanted to play Hatfields and McCoys.

I kept my voice neutral. "So, where do you want to meet."

I could hear the smile in his snaky voice. "There is a wonderful club downtown …."

The Foole Moon, a club that catered to the Halloween Goth crowd. Go figure.

I parked the Hyundai near an alley across and hoofed it over to the entrance. A bouncer the size of a Sherman tank gave me the old hairy eyeball before reluctantly letting me in. Must have been my aftershave.

The inside was a study in brick walls, neon, and black lighting. The establishment's namesake glowed malevolently over a bar that stretched across the back wall, lending a sickly green light to the dance floor and the skin of the young people who swayed almost listlessly thereon. Whoever owned the place kept a very simple layout: booths on one side, tables and chairs on the other, with the dance floor smack dab in the middle.

It wasn't very busy—only a couple dozen or so in a place that could easily accommodate ten times the number—but it was a weekday and the regulars probably had to be in school in the morning.

The customers who draped themselves in the booths and danced lethargically on the floor to the sonorous John Carpenter-esque house music were dressed in the latest Goth chic. Some (both male and female) wore Wicked Witch of the West outfits while the rest looked like failed extras from *The Vampire Diaries*.

Maybe I was getting old, but it all looked rather silly to me. My white t-shirt with its picture of a bulldog named Crowbar sitting contentedly with a cat's tail drooping from its jaws glowed a greenish/yellow under my Faraday jacket, the words *'Used to hate 'em 'til I ate 'em'* standing out in stark relief.

There was a small table near the bar next to a brick wall—the same wall shared with an alley outside. I sat, keeping my back to the bar and my eyes everywhere else. A mirror was hung next to the opposite chair and I tried to use it to observe the dance floor, but the mixture of black lighting and imitation moonlight made that impossible. So I sat there and tried not to let my eyeballs bounce around all over the place like a pachinko ball.

Perfect.

A bored cocktail waitress dolled up with black and white Goth makeup trudged over in her black mini, asked what I wanted to order, and grimaced when I asked for a diet cola. I love the sugary stuff, but considering how fast I'd been putting on weight lately and how much longer it took to take it off, it was time to watch my figure.

Fifteen minutes later and I was beginning to stew in my irritation juices, frustrated over having to wait for a Supernatural psychopath with delusions of grandeur. I shouldn't have let him get to me like that, but I did have a history of anger issues.

I ran a finger along my belt, feeling the comforting lumps of Spell gems. I had each little Spell memorized, along with their activation words and where they rested in the belt. Four hours since the call from Maydock telling me where and when to meet him. I practiced palming them and tossing them, never speaking the activation words aloud but letting them jangle around in my mind. By the time ten o'clock rolled around, I could reach into the belt, flick out a gem, and say the word in less than three seconds. There was an even dozen

Spells I chose for this meet and I prayed I wouldn't have to use a one.

The waitress came back with my soda pop and I tipped her a buck, which sent her black-rimmed eyes rolling. "Is it always this … boring?" I asked, pointing to the listless dancers. "Everyone looks like they'd rather be someplace else."

She scratched the nest of dyed black curls that served as her hair and replied, "It's a weekday, go figure."

Yeah, go figure. I watched her leave, realizing that under her black skirt, black fishnet stockings, black pumps, top, and troweled-on makeup, she was actually quite attractive in a slender, Midwest sort of way. And young. Far too young to be working in a dump like The Foole Moon.

"She's a cutie, isn't she?" said a familiar snaky voice from behind me.

It was all I could do not to leap to my feet, firing the Colt and the Lahti at the same time. My palms itched to fill them with the comforting feel of my weapons, but instead I forced myself to smile blandly and turn toward the speaker.

Slightly younger than myself, perhaps thirty or a year or so older. Long face sporting a red Van Dyke, with freckles dotting his cheeks and just about every surface of his milky pale skin. Red hair buzzed close to the scalp covered his skull and his eyes were hidden behind mirrored sunglasses. He wore a plain white t-shirt, jeans and a black leather vest. It looked like he cast an eye to the '90s for tips on how to dress in tough guy chic. He walked past me slowly as if showing off his lean, powerful form and took a seat next to the mirror.

"Maydock."

He inclined his head a fraction, and his white face split wide in a grin. "Hakala."

One hand reached under the table, all slow and casual-like. "What now?"

I hadn't fooled him one inch. "If you make one hostile move, the explosives I have placed throughout this building will detonate."

The statement was flat, matter-of-fact, and I absolutely believed him because his hidden gaze was unwavering. He wanted assurances for my continued good behavior. Bastard.

A cell came at me and I caught it reflexively. Shiny. New. Cheap.

"This is how we will stay in touch from now on. It is untraceable and you will not be able to dial any number but mine, or receive any call but mine. The number is printed on a label taped to the back."

I stared at the plastic casing and put it in the pocket of my Faraday jacket. "No more games."

He shook his head. "No more games. This is for later. I want you to be well-rested and healthy when I win."

When he wins. When I die.

"Why are we here?"

"I wanted to meet you in person." His smile put a whole new meaning to the word 'feral'—a slit in his face showing far too many perfect teeth. "I think it is good to meet your enemy face to face."

Yeah, perfect.

A reddish wink of light caught my attention. A ring, thick gold clasping a ruby that had to be at least two carats surrounded the ring finger on his right hand. "Nice jewelry. You don't strike me as the kind to wear something like that."

The ruby was quickly hidden beneath a freckled hand. "An heirloom. Sometimes I can be … sentimental."

I doubted that. "Looks familiar."

"Don't think so."

What lay behind those shades? I had the feeling that Maydock was angry about something, but for the life of me I couldn't figure out what it was. We continued to stare at each other in an attempt to establish dominance, but those damn mirrored sunglasses threw my gaze right back at me.

Time for another tactic. I had an ace up my sleeve and hopefully I'd be able to draw three more. "Let me see that ring."

That pale hand clamped down harder over the ruby. "Why?"

"It clearly means something to you, an item of great worth, so I have a proposal for you."

Just as I thought, he was far too curious not to pay heed. "I'm listening."

"What do you know about medieval jousting? You know, knights in shining armor and all that. You mentioned knights before on the phone, that our thing here," I pointed a finger at his chest then back to me, "was like a couple of knights in a duel to the death."

His head cocked to the side, like a bird's. "I have a passing familiarity with medieval history." He tried to sound calm, bland, but I'd piqued his interest, I could tell.

I leaned back in my chair, a study of nonchalance. "In the High Middle Ages, from the eleventh century through the fourteenth, jousting was practiced to hone skills with lances that were also used in warfare. And they jousted not just with lances, but with shorter weapons once both combatants closed the distance and they were unhorsed. Before the time we've come to refer to as the 'age of chivalry,' these contests were often fought in groups, with the objective of winning their opponents' horses, arms, and armor."

"Very interesting." Maydock's sarcastic tone told me it was anything but.

My smile was pure mean. "Don't interrupt, it's rude." That hit him in the shorts. No one wants to be chided like a six-year-old. "Jousting was originally not so much about sporting, but about showcasing the greatest warriors. In fact, the words 'knight' or 'chevalier' weren't used as terms for a warrior of noble birth, the word was actually *cniht*, from the proto-Germanic term *knehtaz*, and it meant a male servant or attendant. In the mid-twelfth century it became a term for a military follower while the warriors of noble birth were called *milites nobiles*. It wasn't until the thirteenth century that *cniht* evolved into 'knight' and was used to indicate a junior rank of nobility."

"What is the point? Do you even have one?" He looked bored and pissed off and I felt a stab of vindictive pleasure.

"The point is History. Learn from it quickly or become Geography."

His lips twitched. "Cute."

"I thought so." My stare grew cold and my tone grave. "History aside, my point is that to the victor goeth the spoils. If I defeat you," *not kill,* "I want your ruby ring."

Dum-dum-DUM! *Take that, you psychotic dickhead.* I kept my

face neutral and my eyes on Maydock's hands, which were clasped around that beautiful ruby ring. Once again, I dimly felt that I should know that piece of jewelry. *C'mon, take the bait.*

I knew he was a clever monkey and his next words proved it. "You said 'defeat,' not kill." His gaze burned me through those mirrored shades. "Not planning to kill me *if* you win?"

"*When* I win, I plan on taking you back under three hundred pounds of chains to a holding facility where you can be examined at length." *Go for it, Kal, give him that connection he's dying for.* I channeled Ricardo Montalbán's Khan and said, "What I will do to you is worse than killing, Maydock. I will hurt you and keep on hurting you."

He stared at me for a long minute before saying, "That's it?"

Damn, no one gets my pop culture references. I nodded.

His sudden laughter startled me. It was loud and harsh, edgy with a hint of insanity and … darker things. "I didn't think I could be surprised," he said finally, wiping tears that flowed from beneath his sunglasses. "You are more than I have ever hoped, Kalevi Hakala. So much more. I thought you might be soft, limited like the cattle around us, but you are hard. Hard as diamonds and sharp as knives and I am both amazed and pleased." Maydock leaned forward, fist extended, the ruby winking in the ugly light of the club. "You have a deal."

It sucked, shaking his outstretched hand, but I did it, and just to be spiteful, gave his hand an extra squeeze. He smiled a cruel smile. "I am stronger than I look, Kal. You won't be able to hurt my hand."

Really? It was one of those moments when an epiphany hits like a freight train and you know it's right, it's perfect and ignoring it would be a crime against nature. My smile matched his and I put a little extra mustard into that handshake and slammed the back of his hand hard against the brick wall.

Thwack!

I was seated, and he was seated, so there wasn't any real leverage to apply to the motion, but I put my shoulders and arm into the swing and his hand flattened nicely against the rough, terracotta colored brick. My fingertips were mashed some, but not like the back of his hand, which left a bloody, wet imprint on the wall.

And the bastard just smiled at me. "Well," he said calmly, staring at the blood that flowed sluggishly from his torn skin. "I guess I was wrong." The blood stopped dripping and dried right before my eyes into a hard scab that turned to dust and spilled onto the tabletop. In less than a minute the flesh had knit itself whole, not a mark to be seen. "What do I get when I win, Kalevi Hakala? Your precious Lahti? Or perhaps that Bowie knife your father gave you?"

By the pricking of my thumbs ....

How the hell did he know that? I was more than a little surprised at the extent of his knowledge and the cavalier way he tossed it at my face, but I refused show it. My bruised fingers dug under my shirt and I brought out a flat plate of silvery metal the size of a paperback. It landed on the rectangular table with a light clang that I barely heard over the dolorous house music. "No, not the Lahti, which is totally cool, or my Bowie. Something far more valuable. In the interest of keeping things medieval, I offer you my armor. It's saved my life a couple of times already."

The shades came off and I saw the mossy green of his eyes. Well, one at least ... the other was curiously pink, like raw tuna. It made the white of the eye all the brighter. Not the weirdest thing I'd ever seen, but unnerving.

"What is it?" he asked almost too casually, but I could tell he was excited. He gave the plate a curious sniff.

"One part of the best armor in the world. All with its brothers secured in the ballistic cloth of my vest. With this armor I can withstand just about any bullet in the world, including armor-piercing."

"It doesn't look like much."

I put as much sneer into my voice as possible. "Pick it up. Bend it."

He lifted the plate, eyebrows hiking to his hairline as its weight surprised him. Holding it in both hands, he tried to bend it. When it resisted his efforts, he bore down with all his strength, which the metallic hydrogen resisted easily while the long muscles of his arms stood out in stark relief. Finally he quit.

"Impressive," he said, tossing the plate back to me. "What is it?"

I slid the plate back into the bulletproof vest. "Not telling you, but know this: it is part of the best body armor known to man. The ballistic cloth is the latest and greatest, a mixture of Kevlar and Bucky-Fiber, which by itself can withstand a 20mm round. With the plates the vest can withstand even a 50mm round, although it would still hurt like blazes. It saved my insides from that damn Māori guarding The Trade Group's lobby. It is the most valuable, most prized, coolest damn thing I own."

Pink and green stared at me for a goodly while before Maydock nodded. "Deal."

"Deal."

"You surprise me, Hakala, making bargains with the enemy. I was under the impression you were the 'shoot first, ask questions second' kind of Agent." That snaky voice held a wealth of amusement with just a smidgeon of condescension.

"Nice eyes, by the way. Genetic or are you wearing contact lenses?"

He smiled and looked into the mirror next to his chair. "All natural. I don't need contacts; my vision is perfect." Damned if he didn't tip his reflection a wink. "Much like myself."

A cold wind seemed to blow through my body as a sudden realization hit. I *had* him. That one simple, self-indulgent gesture he made to his reflection revealed more to me than any amount of conversation or violence. For all his claims of being an apex predator, of holding himself above the tide of humanity, he definitely shared some of mankind's flaws. Like vanity.

"You know," I said casually, rocking back on my chair far enough that the front legs parted ways with the floor a couple of inches while I rested a couple of fingers on the table for stability, "life has thrown me a few curveballs lately and I've been having to deal with some ... well, let's call them moral issues."

"The only morality is survival," he said, still regarding his reflection. Perhaps he was checking for zits. Not that a zit would dare mar his perfect, milky skin, oh no siree.

"I know people in my line of work who would agree with you, but no. No, what I'm talking about is a shift in my perception of right and wrong." I held up a hand to forestall interruption. I knew what he would say. "Please, let me finish. Where was I? Oh, yeah … right and wrong. The old me might have seriously considered drawing down on you and firing away, explosives or no, just to take care of business, but recently I've entered into a stable relationship and certain factors have led me to rethink my priorities." Factors like my sister's soul finally separating from mine to complete her voyage to the Infinite and losing Winch, one of our best Agents and the love of Canton's life, in San Francisco.

"But now … well, you have caught me in a moment of self-reflection as I enter a new phase of my psychological development." My right hand touched cold metal and the front legs of the chair gently touched the floor. *Soon* ….

Those unnerving eyes left the mirror. "You are boring me, so please get to the point." From the look on his face I was quickly losing what respect he held.

"The point … the point … yes. The point is, at this juncture of my psychological/emotional evolution, I would never knowingly endanger another human being just to kill a piece of maggot-ridden garbage like you." I let that sink in and watched his eyes widen in shock. "And back in the day, killing myself to kill you would've been an option. Hell, without a second thought the old me would've gladly died to take you out, but I know now that the reverse isn't true. You're too damn *vain*."

Blam! Blam!

The Colt bucked twice, one of the rounds tearing through the edge of the table from underneath in a spray of shredded plastic and wood to enter Maydock's body just under his sternum. The other round from the hefty .45 entered just above his left nipple, shedding burned cotton and blood.

Maydock fell backward, landing hard against the table behind before falling to the floor, his face a mask of shock and confusion. I jumped to my feet, flinging my chair back to hit the bar, and gripping the edge of the table with my left hand. Even though it was heavy, weighed down by a cast-iron pillar that ended in a large, circular foot, I managed a decent throw fueled by adrenaline.

Without the rage to power me, I was cold, like when I shot X-scar. Cold and powerful and filled with deadly purpose. The Colt rose, the Novak sight guiding my eyes to the spot between Maydock's uncanny eyes. My finger tightened on the aluminum trigger and I felt a brief burst of joy at the thought of Maydock's imminent death.

Those unnerving eyes, tuna pink and mossy green, flared slightly and I felt my Faraday jacket heat up as it soaked up his Spell. My mean smile accompanied the bullet that left the barrel of my pistol.

His form blurred, becoming nothing more than a foggy blob of vapor that the bullet passed through harmlessly to punch a hole in the floor. The blob rose in the air, then passed through the brick wall, disappearing before I could get off another shot.

... something wicked this way comes.

"Jesus," I breathed. There was only one Supernatural I knew of that could disincorporealize, and that was a vampire. And Maydock sure didn't look like any vamp I'd ever had the pleasure of forcibly shuffling off its mortal coil. Or would that be immortal coil? Still ....

Vampire.

Further contemplation of Maydock's abilities were rudely interrupted by a serving tray to the back of my noggin as the Goth cocktail waitress swung for the fans. I saw a galaxy's worth of stars as the heavy plastic connected and I was driven to my knees in time to catch a high-heeled black leather boot to the ribs. Foot met body armor and body armor won, but the air still left my lungs with a *whoosh!*

Hands and feet pummeled my body, but they lacked the strength to really cause serious damage, so I gathered my wits and surged to my feet—220 pounds of angry Finn ready to deal some serious dirt. I lashed out with a spinning back fist, smashing the face of a young tough whose nose burst like a ripe melon. He dropped, screaming, while my right foot slammed hard into a kneecap, bending a leg the wrong way with a sickening *crunch*.

A girl with vacant eyes clawed at mine and my stiffened fingers took her in the throat. The others—all the patrons and bar workers—kept coming at me with the same vacant expression, no one home, please come back some other time. I kept on striking, breaking fingers and gouging eyes, and they dropped but there were more and I hit them hard, covering myself in their blood as hands and feet tore at soft tissue and shattered bone. I was starting to bleed from minor cuts and abrasions as they just kept on *coming* at me. My blood mixed with theirs, but years and years of training was on my side and I kept striking, machine-like, all around until I was surrounded by the screaming wounded—young people forever altered by the mind numbing violence I'd visited upon their young bodies.

I was cut, blood leaking into my left eye—thick, warm, and coppery—and I shook my head like a dog, dashing the salty fluid from my face. Over the bar, through the swinging door into the back rooms—storage, boxes of booze, coasters and straws—past a walk-in keg cooler to my left. There, to my right, an exit to the alley. To where Maydock had fled.

Outside. Heat, humidity, and an alley that smelled like garbage, piss, and crap. Streetlights gave fitful illumination as if the light was afraid to dispel the dark. Maydock nowhere in sight. What the hell?

My breath was harsh in my throat as I spun, keeping the Colt up, ready to shoot, ready to kill. The powerful blow that drove me to my knees came from above, a wrecking ball of pain that shot across my shoulders. My neck snapped back, muscles protesting as I was driven to the ground.

I rolled over to see Maydock standing above me, face contorted with emotions alien to my human perception, pale face suffused with blood.

"You shot me!" he spat.

The Colt was gone, spun away into the darkness when he jumped me. I tried to draw the Lahti, but something was wrong with my arms—they moved far too slowly. Maydock's biker boot slammed down, pinning my hand to the filthy alley.

"I was amused," he said, drool dripping from his chin. "But no more. Goodbye, Kalevi Hakala." He raised his boot from my arm and lifted it over my head and I knew the last thing I'd ever see was a size eleven slamming down toward my face. I'd be damned if I'd meet it with eyes screwed shut so I looked Maydock in the face and said, "Screw you, assbag."

There came a screaming sound and the last thing I remember before passing out was a large figure in a long duster, the broken light of the city outlining his ragged form, sweeping down from the sky to collide with my killer.

CHAPTER EIGHTEEN

Canton
Memories Still Fresh

LONG, LONG DAY. I SAT sprawled out in the fairly comfortable easy chair in my hotel room, staring at the TV along with the rest of my team.

Breaking news: A joint FBI and local police task force have made several arrests in a downtown Omaha office building today, putting a halt to what is being called the most horrendous offense to the country since 9-11, a child slavery ring run by a group of individuals styling themselves as The Trade Group.

FBI spokesman Martin Allred released a statement saying that the so-called 'white slavers' have been in operation for four years, using the downtown office building as their headquarters. Posing as a legitimate insurance company, The Trade Group has been kidnapping children and selling them to the highest bidder using an illegal website known only to pedophiles and Third World slave merchants.

It is unclear how far this network of human trafficking extends, but authorities are saying that office buildings in Seattle, Austin, Fargo, and Tallahassee have been raided as well, leading to more arrests, although casualties amongst The Trade

Group have been in the triple digits.

Once again in breaking news: a criminal organization known as The Trade Group ….

I flicked the remote and the talking head disappeared.

Big news, the good guys won. And there is much rejoicing. The information about pedophiles and Third World slave merchants had been spoon fed to the FBI, of course, because the real explanation—that they were selling budding magicians to the rich and immoral—had to be contained.

We were gathered in my suite, the lot of us including Nihsen, who looked like he'd been gut-punched. Sweaty, grimy, stinky, and exhausted, we stared blankly at the television while Ghost filled in for the talking head.

"Six teams, four cities," he droned slowly. "I have frozen all The Trade Group's accounts, foreign and domestic, and have turned all files over to the appropriate agencies. As far as the world is concerned, this was an FBI investigation culminating in the downfall of the most insidious criminal organization the U.S. has ever seen. As far as the Bureau is concerned, since all the Magicians working for these assholes have committed suicide-by-agent, The Trade Group is now a matter for the FBI, NSA, ICE, and Homeland Security." It was the first time I'd ever heard Ghost swear, and I realized that his normally impersonal, buzzing voice was filled with anger. Just considering the dangers posed by an angry entity like Ghost gave me the shivers. "The Bureau is now working with all friendly nations in scouring the Internet for clues to the organization that The Trade Group was affiliated with."

"It wasn't an affiliation, Ghost," said Alex suddenly from where he sat on my bed next to Jacobs. They were holding hands and she was stroking his wrist with one callused thumb. It was an oddly tender caress, and I felt like a peeping Tom just watching the two. "The Trade Group was *part* of this larger organization, like a fast food restaurant chain is part of the larger soft drink company that owns them."

"Do we know anything about this larger organization?" Jeanie asked. She sat near the mini bar with several tiny bottles of booze—all empty—scattered on the table next to a plastic cup. Scotch mixed with gin mixed with vodka mixed with bourbon. The four fingers of liquid looked like something you'd find at the bottom of an oak beer barrel. She took a long sip and I shuddered. *Blech*. That woman must've had a stomach like cast iron and guts like steel.

Ghost said, "I will have the block of data captured from our raid decoded soon, most likely within the next few hours. It might reveal more data that's relevant to that larger organization. What they lacked in magical finesse they made up with programming savvy. This is the most complex cipher I have ever dealt with, far beyond what the NSA and CIA employs. Only the programming thread coded by Maydock shows more finesse."

Nihsen cut in. "Wait-a-minute. You're talking to us and decoding encrypted data and you said earlier you were coordinating efforts at the other sites where your Bureau teams were mopping up operations. How is that possible?"

"Mr. Nihsen," Ghost buzzed patiently. "I can talk, decrypt, fly a fleet of commercial airplanes, brief the President, plan a Kardashian wedding, read the entire works of Shakespeare and King, play 50,000 Soduku puzzles and raid the CIA files to find out who really killed JFK simultaneously. Much like you would chew gum and walk at the same time."

I hid a smile at the look of consternation on the detective's face. Ghost sure didn't like it none when the Straights questioned his abilities. Nihsen grumbled a bit but kept his trap shut. He was a whole patch smarter than he looked.

"Let's get some rest, folks," I ordered. Fatigue was dragging at my eyes and I knew we'd be worse than useless without some shuteye. "This Trade Group thing is now in the lap of people whose pay grade is substantially higher than ours."

Everyone filed out. Nihsen would be going home to his wife and kids, but he made it damn clear that he'd see us bright and early in the a.m., and from the fierce look in his eyes, saying 'no' wasn't an option.

"What are we doing, Canton?" Jeanie asked when the rest had left.

She took another swallow of her suicide cocktail.

"We're doing what Kal wants. Staying back so the bad guy doesn't sniff us out."

Her soft brown eyes were bloodshot from fatigue and worry. "My boyfriend is a genius and the best killer known to man, but his following Maydock's instructions is just plain crazy. He's going to get himself hurt or worse … killed."

"Old Kal and I have been in worse straights, Jeanie, and we've come out okay."

"Last time he nearly didn't come back." Her tone was flat, but there was plenty of worry there. She was referring to the San Francisco op where Winch was killed and a crazy detective nearly tortured Kal to death.

I remembered how after we'd just finished up that whole Sidhe business in the Farallons, Ghost had alerted me that Kal was headed toward an industrial park in Hayward, just south of Oakland. There was no good reason for Kal to have crossed the San Mateo bridge when he was supposed to head back to the hotel where we were staying.

"You sure, Ghost?" I'd asked, biting my thumbnail.

"That is where his nanolocator puts his position."

Those damn things. Kal told me that BB had them injected into our butts when we received our yearly physicals as a way to keep tabs on us, to make sure the Bureau could find a lost Agent. I had a sneaking suspicion that Kal was such an enormous pain that BB came up with that idea just to keep him in check, only having them injected into the other agents' keisters as an afterthought.

Kal is not what you'd call 'low maintenance.'

"Okay, Ghost, I'm going after him. Keep me posted."

"I will send the details to your RediPad," he replied. A blinking red dot appeared on the map displayed by the ultra-powerful ten-inch computer tablet.

By the time I hit the bridge, Ghost had a fix on Kal's location, a crapped-out old warehouse just north of the 92 toll road.

It wasn't hard to figure things out as there was only one car parked outside, a black Crown Vic with cop tires and recessed cop lights. Sarkasian, had to be. The temperamental pinhead had been riding our case ever since we came to San Francisco, poking his oversized nose into Bureau business and generally making a damn nuisance of himself. The only thing that toasted my grits was why he'd bring Kal here. I didn't know, but I sure as heck meant to find out.

Slipping in was no big chore; the locks were old and easy meat for Bureau picks. As the whitewashed steel door eased open, I heard something that took the starch right out of my shorts. A scream. Full, loud, and echoing, it bounced off the steel and concrete walls of the warehouse and had my skin all goosebumpy. That scream expressed so much pain, so much anguish that it tugged at my heart. No man should scream like that; no man should feel that much pain. But what really had the mice with the cold, cold feet trampling up and down my spine was that it was Kal's voice, Kal's scream.

I drew my weapon and rushed in, making almost no noise in my sneakers, but stealth really wasn't necessary. I could've been a herd of wildebeest and no one would've heard me over Kal's agony.

The warehouse was big, at least 80K feet, and Kal was strapped to an old office chair right in the middle of it, surrounded by the waste of hundreds of homeless, leavening the air with the funky, thick odor of excrement and the ammonia tang of urine.

Kal looked like he'd been worked over with a crowbar. Every time he opened his mouth to scream, I saw shattered teeth and lips running with blood where they'd been split. His nose looked like a tomato that had been run over by a semi and that's being generous. Sarkasian, who was looming threateningly over my friend, had worked him over right proper and mean. His body was blocking whatever torture device he was inflicting upon my friend, but I heard the sound of an electric motor between the screams and I knew something worse than punching was happening. Something I didn't want to see.

I am Canton Alsate, a member of the Mescalero Apache tribe, the most bad-ass knife fighters and guerilla warriors the United States Cavalry has ever had the misfortune of facing in combat. More than any other tribe, the Apache put the fear of God into the white soldiers in the 1800s—our knife-fighting techniques are still taught today—and let me tell you, right then and there I wanted to draw my big Bowie (a gift from Kal) and set to work on Sarkasian. I wanted to show him firsthand why we were so a-feared. My palms itched to hold the walnut handle and commence skinning that bastard up a treat, finishing with a good, old-fashioned scalping. I have a sister and a brother and I love them dearly, but, Kal, Jlin-litzoque, Yellow Horse, is the brother of my spirit, bound by ties of love and combat, and to lose him would leave me broken, just as my death would break him.

I drew my Glock.

I delivered two rounds into Sarkasian's skull from behind with the 10mm, the bullets turning the detective's brain matter into strawberry puree. He dropped hard to the warehouse floor. Blood and brains leaked from the large exit holes while his googly-eyes stared sightlessly at the ceiling.

Behind me I heard the steel door open. It was the other members of the team who'd arrived a few days ago to back us up for the second Supernatural occurrence. Jeanie was one of them. I knew she shouldn't see Kal in such a state, but there was little I could do.

"Hey bud," my friend slurred through broken teeth and torn lips. One eye was swollen shut while the other was thick with blood. "You got any ibuprofen?" With that said he passed out.

Now that Sarkasian was worm food and out of the way, I could see what he'd been doing. There were holes drilled into Kal's kneecaps with bone and marrow filling the runnels of the one-eighth of an inch drill bit chocked tight in a battery operated variable speed drill. Blood oozed from the wounds and soaked the bottom third of Kal's jeans, rendering the blue denim black. Vomit clogged the back of my throat as I took in the enormity of the damage he'd sustained.

I SHOOK MY HEAD AT the memory of my friend in a puddle of his own blood and piss and took the plastic glass from Jeanie's hand, downing the remainder of the vile mix of alcohol in one gulp.

"This is what we do," I said when the burn had faded, "what you signed up for."

Her eyes were hooded, with grief or regret, I couldn't tell. "I know."

Later, after a long shower where a gray trail of grime slid down my body and into the drain, my cell buzzed.

"Hello?"

"Canton, this is Matt."

"Yes, Director?"

There was a pause. I guess he didn't like the title. Didn't blame him none. It came with zero increase in pay and a whole passel of headaches. "Ghost just decrypted the last of the files from The Trade Group."

It's at times like these that Kal would quote *Macbeth* and say, 'by the pricking of my thumbs ....' I merely sighed and said, "What?"

"It presents the Bureau with a great opportunity."

"But?"

"It presents you with a great big crapburger to eat, if you decide to take the op."

I knew it. "Tell me."

Chapter Nineteen

Kal

Pig Problems: Minnesota, 2004

WHAT WENT WRONG WAS THAT the interior of the Mall of America had gone away, obscured by a darkness I could almost taste. Mind you, we had nightvision sunglasses, but those were of no use in a black so unnatural that even switching on a flashlight didn't help. Something drank the light. All light. It was a boiling, thick cloud of nothing that ate and ate and ate every photon, every ray that tried to cut through it. I held the flashlight to my eyes until the cold aluminum touched my nose and clicked the button several times. Nada tostada.

"Report!" I subvocaled, a drop of sweat slicking down my face.

I received five different versions of 'all good, boss' and my stomach unclenched somewhat.

Clop, clop, clop.

My stomach clenched up again. Each hard, almost metallic, *clop* caused the floor to vibrate; a tremor like in *Jurassic Park* as the kids in the car watched the ripples in a glass of water when the Tyrannosaurus Rex took a step. It was a vibration that traveled up my legs and settled into the pit of my stomach to nest behind my navel for a while.

"Where is that coming from?" I couldn't tell.

"To the left."

"No, to the right!"

"I'm not sure, boss."

Perfect. *"On your toes, people. Don't move and don't fire unless you have to. We don't want to be hurting friendlies."* Translation: Don't shoot me in the ass.

I received a *"Check, boss"* times five.

Clop, clop, clop.

"Steady."

Clop, clop, clop.

"Steady."

It was closer, but the building threw echoes from every direction so we couldn't tell where the noise came from. From behind I heard one of my team members wheeze in and out as fear spiked hard.

There came a snort, followed by a brief scream and a horrid crunching sound. Someone fired a multitude of shots, but the black swallowed even that light and then the darkness was gone.

Not gone, actually, but rather traveling down the right-hand walkway overlooking the amusement park. Frothing trails of black vapor trailed a ball of darkness that *clop, clop, clopped* away from us. I sent bullets across the mall into that black mass, but it kept moving, impervious. Cursing, I flicked the drum switch, my fingers a blur, and the magazine switched from left drum to the right, sending lead-weighted silver bullets into that black ball. There came a sound, more felt than heard, that razored into our ears, splitting our skulls, a high-pitched squeal. It spiraled up and up, echoing into frequencies no human was able to hear, but I knew it was there because it flowed across my flesh, the sound twanging each nerve like a guitar string. It hurt—oh it hurt so bad, both in my head and my body. That sound was pain, was made of pain, raw as torn flesh.

As the sound pierced me, my rage answered, roaring through me, a red haze of emotion that battled the pain, shunting it aside. I became a blur as I chased the cloud of blackness with more rounds, my throat closed and teeth clenched, too furious for words. Only action would do, only ripping and tearing and killing until all my enemies were dead. I zipped through all the silver rounds in the right drum and ejected the double drum rig, letting it fall to the floor because the left drum carried standard loads which were useless, but I had more silver in a forty-five round banana clip and my hands moved faster than the eyes could see, replacing drum with clip and sending more silver flying with almost no break in the flow; it was *that* fast. The scream, that otherworldly scream, ripped into me, but I was immune because the rage battled the scream and their collision nearly tore my body apart. More bullets streamed from the gun, my hands steady despite the pain because the rage won; the rage always won. The rage was me and I was it and together we were unstoppable. The barrel of my weapon began to overheat, shimmers radiating off of it, and I knew that if I gripped that barrel my skin would sizzle like bacon on a grill.

The blackness winked out—the way a negative image of a light bulb might wink out—the harsh vapors disappearing. A dark form, seen only for an instant, disappeared down a right turn. Whatever it was, it was *huge*. I started to give chase, but Punch's words chased the rage from my body, extinguishing it and leaving me sweating and panting.

"Boss, it's Griffin!"

Griffin.

I turned, limbs shaky, and headed toward where the team clustered around a still form lying on cold concrete. Two-Hit was wrecked with sorrow, tears streaming down his face, but he still kept his back to the body and eyes roving the perimeter, every muscle alert, taut.

Yes, it was Griffin. Or what was left of him. My knees hit concrete next to the corpse as my eyes drank in what I thought was impossible. Once pink skin, healthy, vibrant, was now a shriveled, paper-like covering that had the color and texture of dead leaves. Griffin's face was set in a grimace, dried lips pulled away from teeth. What was left of his eyes, dried like raisins, lay in the desiccated cups of their sockets.

"Jesus, boss," Punch moaned. "It looks like he's been sucked of all his bodily fluids. Blood, bile … everything." Her hands were shaking so much that she couldn't hold on to her weapon; it lay on the floor next to her knees.

"Pull it together, Punch," I grated, sweat streaming down my face. My own hands were trembling, but I held on to my weapon tightly so they wouldn't shake so much. God, Griffin looked like a mummy, a thing of leather and dust and it didn't make sense. What kind of Supernatural did *that*? There were no wounds and his armor was whole, only now it contained just fifty pounds of Griffin jerky.

"Pull it together? Pull it together?" Punch was starting to sound hysterical and tears were flowing freely down her homely face.

"Yeah," I snarled, what was left of the rage adding spice to my voice. "Pull. It. Freaking. Together." My eyes captured hers and whatever she saw there scared her down to her toes. "We are in the mud here, Punch. Against some sort of demon I've never encountered and we need to stay frosty or we will all be extra dead come morning. You got me?"

She nodded, lips quivering.

"Good." Standing took a lot out of me, but I made it to my feet without wobbling too badly and dashed the sweat from my forehead. All around me my teammates kept an eye on things, scanning the mall for the hostile, jaws clenched and faces betraying nothing but severe determination. Good people in a pinch. The best.

"Rev?"

The lanky Agent turned toward me. "Yes, boss?" he said quietly.

"I think this is your show now."

"Demon?"

I nodded. "Yes. Pretty darn sure. You up to it?'

Rev lifted his silver cross and kissed it reverently. "Of course, always. The Lord is with me."

"Good, you'll need Him. You know what to do." To the others, "Okay, Rev's handling the show. Listen to him. It's your best chance to stay alive."

Three terse confirmations, three team members who looked less than confident, but they stood their ground. One of theirs was gone and they wanted the hide of the Supernatural who'd done the deed.

Good. Too much grief robbed one of focus. I needed them angry. I needed them ready to kill.

"What are we gonna do if that darkness comes back?" asked Punch.

I raised an eyebrow. "*You* will try magic to dispel it." I raised my voice. "And the rest of us will fire short, controlled bursts to the left and right if we hear that thing coming. From the noise it makes, silver hurts it, so let's give it some pain."

As inspirational addresses went, it wasn't going to win me any awards, but I saw their spines begin to stiffen with a little bit more resolve. Good enough.

"Stay frosty," I urged, lifting the MP5.

I was ready, Rev was ready, silver cross held tightly in one big fist, mouth moving as he silently prayed. It was now down to faith, faith against something that didn't belong, that was an offense to God and His creation.

Some people wonder if we at the Bureau believe in God. Believing in God isn't the same as having faith in Him. So many of our brothers and sisters die in ways too horrible to imagine … in agony, misery, and terror. Some die quickly, but most weep, moan, and wet themselves in fear of death as it steals upon them, and it is hard—so damn *hard*—to believe that there is a kindly old guy on a cloud somewhere smiling down benevolently while his children die in a puddle of their own piss at the hands, or claws, or tentacles, of a nightmare so terrifying that most people would faint dead away just glimpsing it. No, it's easy to believe in God when you face magic every day, when you know there are demons and devils and ghosts and ghouls. The hard part is the faith.

Good thing Rev had faith enough for all of us.

Clop, clop, clop.

This time whatever it was didn't bother with stealth. The floor trembled. We knew what was coming and we crouched, prepared to fire upon whatever we needed to fire upon.

The noise seemed sourceless and we tensed, not knowing where to look. I made a slow circle. Nothing to be seen, just the clopping as it neared.

It came and once again we were suddenly immersed in a black so absolute it seemed to suck the very juices from our skins.

"Short bursts," I cried, letting loose three rounds. Bullets left our weapons without noise as the silence Spells on the barrels absorbed sound.

Between the shots, Rev began to shout. "In Christ's name I abjure thee!" His voice rang with authority and a terrible confidence. "In the Lord's name I deny thy foul magics. In the Lord's name I deny thy foul magics. IN THE LORD'S NAME I DENY THY FOUL MAGICS!"

A strange sort of pulse—like a pressure wave, but slower, almost liquid—rippled through the blackness and there came a low scraping sound, like rocks rubbing together, and an almost feminine squeal.

"IN THE LORD'S NAME I DENY THY FOUL MAGICS!" thundered Rev again and the black retreated so suddenly from the violence of his shout that the gray world of nightvision seemed brighter than staring into the sun. The darkness was torn asunder by his faith and what it revealed near ripped my soul out through my eyes.

It was a sow. A really *big* sow. When I say *big*, think of one of those monster trucks people see crushing little Toyotas and Hondas at the local civic center. Give that monster truck thick, gnarled, pebbled, black skin with bristly hair like ebony knitting needles, split hooves as big as dinner plates, a snout large enough for you to plant both fists in and teats that sagged from a fat belly all the way to the floor and you might have an idea of the vision that assaulted our eyes.

But it was the eyes that made me want to make water in my pants. They glowed a nacreous silver that wasn't really silver, but the shining of a hideous anti-life. Those eyes were a negation of all that was good and pure in the world; they rejected things like love and happiness and glowed with the crushing abhorrence of a creature that exists only to tear the most precious thing from a human being—the soul.

It swayed for a moment, startled by the holy force of Rev's conviction.

"God no," I swore.

"What is it?" screamed Punch, putting her knuckles to mouth and biting hard. Blood ran down her wrist. "Do you know what it is?"

Yeah, I knew what it was. It was evil given form, hate with hooves and bad breath. It was worse than any demon I'd ever encountered, worse than anything except Iku-Turso, the monster that killed my baby sister.

"The Cutty Black Sow." That was Two-Hit, whose face had gone all shades of pale in recognition. "The goddamned Cutty Black Sow."

Sir James George Frazer wrote in his famous study in magic and religion *The Golden Bough* (also known as 'the Bureau Bible'), "Down to the present time the saying is current in Caernarvonshire, where allusions to the cutty black sow are occasionally made to frighten children." And in Wales there is a proverb that says: "A cutty black sow on every stile, spinning and carding every Allhallows' Eve."

The Cutty Black Sow has been legend in Wales for as long as there's been Halloween; a devil—some said *the* Devil—who appears to take souls on that October holiday. Stronger than a normal demon, it could easily be categorized as a Class 4 Supernatural: 'a unique entity of less than mythic or deific capabilities, possessing an appellation all its own.' Not the best explanation, but it works.

"BEGONE, UNCLEAN BEAST!" The force of Rev's conviction *pushed* the monstrous sow back ten feet, its hooves *screeeeching* against the floor. He advanced, silver cross held high over his head, and continued to holler at the giant pig, forcing it back inch by inch, its gnarled mass braced against Rev's holy might.

Then it squealed.

If the sound it made before was a shout, then this was an explosion. I could actually *see* the pressure wave erupt from its filthy, foaming mouth, expanding in a rippling cone force and flinging Rev back as if he weighed nothing, his chest and face erupting in welter of crimson. Blood gushed from my ears and the bone-shattering wave clipped me, but I was farther away and crouched. The edge of the cone flattened the wild tangle of my blond hair and I screamed back in pain as the sound that was more than sound threatened to tear the roots of my mind free. Behind us the windows of the storefronts shattered into millions of jagged, popcorn-sized bits of safety glass.

Out of the corner of my eye I saw Punch blasted off her feet. She rolled away while Two-Hit stood at the blast's edge, yelling words I couldn't make out as he hosed the pig with silver.

The noise stopped abruptly. Two-Hit and the Cutty Black Sow stared at each other, the man with blood tears streaming down his face, the pig with thick, black ichor drooling from bullet holes in its knobbly hide.

I spied Rev's silver cross not more than a foot away and I automatically picked it up.

"He's dead, boss," said Jackson the Green Pea, staring vacantly over the side of the balcony. I could barely hear him over the ringing in my ears. "He got thrown off. Looks like his neck's broke."

It was at least twenty feet to the bottom level of the mall and the floor was unforgiving, polished marble tile. Even if he hadn't broken his neck, the impact would have shattered most of his bones like crystal.

A large hand grabbed the cross from mine. I met Two-Hit's soul-blasted eyes. "He was my friend."

I could only nod as he turned back to the swaying pig. As he stared, I emptied my clip at the demon pig and black blood spurted from its flanks. The others joined in, weapons silently delivering damage. Maybe its tremendous blast of sound had worn it out, because it stood there and took it, took the damage, and stared at us with baleful silver eyes.

"I am James Maydock Sodersohn," Two-Hit yelled as we reloaded, "and Rev was my friend, you unnatural sonofabitch!"

The sow seemed to crouch.

"Two-Hit, stand down," I barked.

He ignored me, raising the cross in one meaty hand, holding it like a knife. Screaming, he charged the Cutty Black Sow.

Maybe that's what the demon pig was waiting for because it sprang forward, quick and nimble despite its gross size and the two rushed toward each other. Two-Hit was screaming and the pig squealing and my scream followed because I knew that no matter how strong Two-Hit was, he'd get squashed into jelly under those huge hooves which shattered tile with every thundering step the beast took. But my teammate was undeterred. Two-Hit charged the sucker and within ten feet of the beast he launched himself in the air.

Pigs can't look up—their bodies aren't designed that way—and it seemed that even demon pigs had that limitation because I could've sworn I saw a look of confusion in the dead light of the thing's eyes as Two-Hit became airborne. My cry of dismay echoed around the mall as the big man landed belly first on that giant pig snout and slammed the long arm of that silver cross into one of those shining eyes, which burst like a water balloon, spraying burning fluid over Two-Hit's hand.

The Cutty Black Sow trumpeted as Two-Hit quickly switched hands and stabbed the other eye out. The pig bucked and thrashed, but Two-Hit wouldn't be dislodged, couldn't be dislodged as his body began to change from its contact with the Sow's gnarly hide. Once healthy flesh began to dry and crack and dust leaked from those cracks as Two-Hit's soul began to leak from his body like water slipping from a cracked jug. We could *see* it leaving his body, a shimmering pure mist that entered the Sow, and the beast screamed once again, but not in pain. No, that sound was beyond pain, beyond the mere agony of flesh, it was the sound of a damned thing dying, knowing it was dying and railing at its own helplessness. It *knew* that when it died there was nothing left for it but oblivion because demons have no souls, no essence that stays behind after death. For a demon, that was worse than anything it could imagine, because it came from oblivion and going home sucked.

All this I felt as it shrieked its denial. That dreadful knowledge poured into my ears from a dying Supernatural and I didn't feel one bit bad about it.

Punch and Jackson stood there, eyes filling with the information of the Sow's demise, but I didn't want to wait around for it to die. I grabbed Jackson's weapon from his hand (a KMP-45), gripped the forestock hard and emptied the clip of silver bullets into the demon pig. It was dying anyway, down on its front knees, eyes pits of foul fluid, but it made me feel better to plant several rounds into its scabby hide.

After several seconds the pig fell over, the sound of its death turning to a rasping wheeze that soon stopped altogether. Two-Hit's body was flung away, his purpose served, and the Sow began to fold in on itself, becoming smaller and smaller, wisps of dark vapor steaming from its dark form until there was nothing left next to Two-Hit's shriveled corpse but a puddle of dark ichor.

"How did that happen, boss?" Punch asked after a long while. Her eyes were wet and her skin pale. "How did Two-Hit kill it?"

I was a four-year veteran, the leader of team Epsilon. I had already racked up a sizeable rep for killing Supernaturals, so it was no surprise that I was the one everyone expected to have the answers. Not without some justification.

Every day in the Bureau, when I wasn't drinking and screwing just about everything in a skirt, I worked out and studied and trained and studied some more. I learned everything I could about Supernaturals and how to kill them until I became a walking encyclopedia of death, the ultimate reference work on doing the wet-work for the Bureau. I breathed it, felt it, lived it, and loved it. I wore my knowledge like I wore my own skin, a part of me that could be scarred but not destroyed. The Bureau was my life and I was totally dedicated to carrying out its aims … as long as it didn't interfere with my plans for vengeance.

"It was a sacrifice," I said slowly, staring at the wet spot that used to be a giant demon sow. "He willingly sacrificed himself for the team and that sacrifice purified his soul, made it something the Sow couldn't stomach. It only took souls it could steal, souls with some sort of taint." My laugh was brittle and shattered against their ears. "After a sacrifice like that, Two-Hit's soul was way too much for the beast, untainted … like an overdose of too-pure heroin."

Punch looked at me like I was on the fast track to Crazyville, but she nodded and holstered and slung her weapon over her shoulder.

"Let's gather up our honored dead and go back to base." My voice was heavy with unshed tears. "We need to rest up for round two." It was a reference to the second Supernatural occurrence that always follows the first.

Punch nodded, but Jackson had his eyes fixed on the ground floor.

"What is it?" I asked.

"Something down there," he said, tipping his head toward Snoopy.

I looked over the side to where he indicated. It took a few seconds, but I finally saw what he saw. Down by Snoopy, partially obscured by trees, was a slender figure staring up at us, sunglasses obscuring his eyes.

"Frickin' kid," I snarled. Before I knew it I was on the main floor, running hell bent for leather after that stupid kid. What had he seen? What had he heard?

By the time Snoopy loomed over me, he was long gone.

Frickin' kid.

THE LAST REEL OF MY mind's movie projector ended, and the film slap-slap-slapped fruitlessly as the memory faded away, leaving more questions than answers.

Cursing up a storm, I woke.

CHAPTER TWENTY

Maydock's journal
The Past is a Rolodex

*H*E SHOT ME!

I lay on my back, the busty blonde's fingers deep in my abdomen, while blood ran down my side to puddle beneath my body. The wooden table was cold and the blonde's fingers were blunt instruments that tore apart my insides. Each one of her fingers, daggers probing deeper.

He shot me!

How did Hakala know there were no explosives in the bar? Is he psychic? Is that the secret to his success? There are no such indications in my memories. Talking to the human face to face was a mistake, I now realize. I should have strung the Agent along, wearing him out of magical resources until he was considerably weakened, but my curiosity got the better of me, just like in Minnesota. I wanted to look into the killer's blue eyes and see the fear there.

But there was no fear. No fear, not even rage, just a kind of amusement as Hakala regaled me with the history of medieval knights and such. I did like the idea of removing that remarkable armor from Hakala's body. Such an item would be invaluable in my efforts to defeat my kin, who, although divided, are very powerful.

The blonde grunted and sliced again with the box cutter, opening the hole in my torso even wider, using one hand to keep the wound open so it wouldn't heal, but I didn't make a sound, even though it hurt worse than getting shot. In fact, I've never been hurt like that in my entire life. Never has such an indignity been perpetrated upon my person, not by predator, not by prey. Blood ran sluggishly down my torso and I bit back the urge to scream in anger.

The bullet was lodged in my stomach; I could feel it there—sharp barbs against the lining, digging and tearing with my every labored breath. My powers of healing are remarkable and the bullet wound itself was of no consequence, but I would not allow the bullet to remain in my body. When I arrived at my base of operations, I immediately commanded the docilized blonde to cut me open and remove the offending lump. It wasn't her fault that she was such a clumsy bitch, that her fumbling hurt more than I could have imagined. It was merely the price I had to pay for haste.

Once again I vowed to bring pain upon Kalevi Hakala, pain such as the human has never felt before.

Bloody to the elbow, the blonde stuck her entire hand in my torso. The pain spiked to new, searing levels and I almost cried out. Biting my lip, I gripped the edge of the table with one hand and *squeezed*. Wood creaked alarmingly, but the structure held as my muscles stood out in stark relief.

I've never bothered to docilize a physician because I never thought I'd actually be wounded. I thought I had planned for all eventualities, but the bullet in my gut and the arrival of the Ancient One proved me wrong. And if there is one thing I hate more than Kalevi Hakala, it is being wrong.

To take my mind off the blonde's hand squirming around my insides, I let my thoughts drift to ancestral memories. Not too far back, just far enough to be relevant to the present:

WAREHOUSE WAS A DUMP.

At least, that's how the Magician thought of it. Except for DORMS, the place was Spartan and unimaginatively designed, much like most of America.

The Magician shuddered, vowing never to return to the Lone Star state. Just the thought of Odessa was enough to bring bile to the back of her throat. Warehouse was a dump, but even with the juvenile American television blaring only a few feet away, it was far better than west Texas.

"You okay?" A deep voice. Very masculine.

It was Thomas Mace, a great slab of beef with far too many muscles topped with a round dome of a head that housed too many brains. He always made the Magician uneasy. If anyone could figure out the Magician's secret, he could.

"I'm all right. Just tired, I guess."

His brown eyes softened. It was strange to see in such a brutal face. "Still thinking about Vegas?"

"Naw. Y'all worry too much about me."

"It was your first time in the field and you did fine."

His sympathy and supposed understanding grated. " 'Fine' is short for Freaked Out, Insecure, Neurotic, and Emotional. All I need is some shut-eye, Mace."

"Well, you need anyone to talk to, my door is always open." He paused. "BB's too."

The Magician sank deeper into the large leather recliner, sighing dramatically. "Yes, Mom." A slender, pale finger played with a coppery strand of hair.

"My ears are burning. You talking about me?"

Dammit. Just the last person the Magician wanted to see… Benjamin Bauer, the leader of Team Epsilon. Thomas Mace was smart, but BB was in a whole different class of clever, a real bright penny and an up-and-comer in the Bureau. So clever, in fact, that he was number one with a bullet to be the next Director. If anyone could sniff out a falsehood or emotional turmoil, it was BB.

Somewhat short and balding, BB didn't look like much. You'd forget him the second you looked away. Unless you met his eyes. They were near colorless and shrewd and they looked right through a person, clinical, analytical—the eyes of a computer or an unforgiving god.

"Hey, BB. Mace and I were just yoggle-doggling about nothing."

BB stared hard at the Magician, then looked away, seemingly satisfied. "Okay. Glad to see everyone is relaxed and happy." He waved at the large, wall-sized flat screen television that was blaring some inane comedy involving two women, a man, and a series of misunderstandings. The laugh track was tinny and annoying.

"Heck, boss," said Mace, "everything is cool."

The smile BB gave was as impersonal as a robot's. "Of course."

No, THAT MEMORY WAS WRONG, not the one I was looking for. Shutting my eyes against the pain of the blonde's hands in my guts, I cast my mind back down a different path, searching for a memory I wasn't sure existed:

COMBAT WAS THE ROOM WHERE Agents trained. Men and women sparred with wooden weapons, wrestled, and punched. The large room smelled of sweat, a scent like that of stale bread and old fryer oil.

The Magician wiped sweat from pale, freckled skin, tired after an hour's worth of training. Fatigue and after-effort spasms ran down arms and legs and across shoulders. Working out was frustrating, taking valuable time from research, but it had to be done. The Magician was almost ready for field trials of the new Spell, painstakingly developed over the past few years.

No ... THAT WASN'T IT. I was close, though. The memory I needed was right there, like a fish barely seen through cloudy water or a card buried in a huge rolodex, distressingly hard to find. I could *feel* what was needed so desperately because there was a tangled thread that I hadn't accounted for, something I was missing, and it had to be found, *must* be found. It was important. Once again, I dived deep within my mind:

BETS WERE TRADING HANDS FAST and furious as the two men loosened up, wooden knives in hand. The boxing ring was surrounded by Agents ready for the evening's entertainment, a match between the best knife fighters in the Bureau: the Green Pea Canton Alsate and the reigning champ Karl 'Duke' Van der Clive.

The Magician's eyes narrowed as calculations ran through a mind as disciplined as any soldier's. Height, weight, reach, musculature were all weighed impassively. It all came down to one inescapable conclusion: the Apache would win.

Duke was a tall man with broad shoulders and long arms, muscled like a gorilla. It could easily be imagined that he could bend a horseshoe with his bare, scarred hands. He seemed to be a force of nature, and one look at his lean, harsh face beneath a cap of short black hair gave the viewer pause. For the past two years he'd trained others in knife fighting, a necessary skill when facing the creatures that vomited forth from the World Under.

His opponent seemed to be the polar-opposite. Shorter, whipcord lean, muscular but not overly so. Where Duke moved like a slab of granite given life, deliberate and unstoppable, Alsate was elegance given form—smooth motion and liquid speed. He held himself with a panther's grace, the set of his shoulders and the movement of his hands hinting at his skill.

EYES FLYING OPEN IN SHOCK, I forgot all about the pain, the tearing hole in my gut, the clumsy blonde, and the bullets lodged deep within. I had it: the SWAT team member in the house with Nihsen, the set of his shoulders as familiar as his coppery skin.

Canton Alsate. The SWAT team member. Had to be.

Anger. Rage. Limitless hate and righteous fury. All of that and more boiled up from within. *How dare he?* Hakala had been given specific instructions. He'd been *told*, dammit, and he'd disobeyed. The sheer magnitude of disrespect shown staggered me.

Something has to be done and I know exactly what.

Finally the blonde withdrew her hand, fingers gripping a flattened chunk of lead. While she smiled at the results of her handiwork, the incision below the inverted V of my ribcage began to close and within a few seconds the cut had disappeared into a thin red line that soon vanished.

"Give me that," I snarled, snatching the bullet. The blonde knew better than to pout, to show anything other than utter surrender to the will of her master. She took the box cutter and walked to the bathroom. Through the open door I saw her grab a bar of Lava soap and begin to scrub her skin raw. Her blouse was ruined; it bore a thick, dried crust of blood. When she removed it, the material momentarily stuck to her breasts. Wincing, she peeled it away from her sensitive nipples. Her chest and stomach were brown with dried blood as well. Gently, she washed her torso clean, then examined her face in the mirror. Still young, but hard lines were beginning to bracket her mouth. Lately, crow's feet had appeared at the corners of her eyes. After drying herself, she carefully began to apply makeup. It wouldn't do to look used up and haggard in front of the master. The last woman, a brunette with small, pert breasts had to be put down because her looks had started to fade.

The blonde's eyes welled with moisture as she fought hard against the tears. *Perhaps she knows her time is slipping away. None of my favorites last long. Who cares? The thoughts of animals are of no consequence. When it is time, I will dispose of her like all the rest.*

Dismissing the blonde for a moment, I regarded the bullet for a moment before licking my blood from it. "You sonofabitch," I swore. *I can't believe he disobeyed. I can't believe he shot me!*

It hadn't been fatal. It hadn't been close to being in the same neighborhood as fatal, but it hurt like a bitch and the man must answer for that.

Oh, I will make Kalevi Hakala pay, that's for sure. He will pay and pay and pay.

I'd been about to make Hakala pay in that filthy alleyway—I'd been ready to crush the life from the human's body—but the Ancient One showed up and ruined everything. I bared my very white teeth. The Ancient One, the elite killer among my relatives—that is, until I came of age, then *I* had become the ultimate killer. My smile turned even uglier as I regarded the misshapen bullet.

All the others fear the Ancient one, fear the Final Justice he brings, but not me. Had it not been for the bullet in the gut—the other passed clean through and had already healed by the time I phased into the alley from the club—I would have killed the Ancient One right then and there. That, and the fact that Hakala might have interfered in some way.

I chuckled as I sat in a pool of my quickly drying blood. The thought that Hakala might actually help a Supernatural kill me tickles me to no end. And what a Supernatural, too! One of those I hate above all others. It was precious.

For a brief moment I wondered if the Ancient One killed Hakala after I fled the alley. But first things first; I had to proceed as if that were not the case. I had to respond to the insult of Hakala's failure to obey.

I pulled a cell from the front pocket of my jeans and dialed. "Malcolm, my friend," I purred when the call was answered. "I have a job for you …."

Instructions given, I turned my mind to food. I was weak from the fight, the quick phase from reality, blood loss and regeneration. Sustenance was called for. Vengeance could wait until my stomach was full and I was well rested. I called the blonde, my razor-sharp incisors lengthening in anticipation.

Chapter Twenty-One

Kal

Frenemy Mine

THE DREAM/MEMORY OF THE CUTTY Black Sow faded and what took its place was a whole lotta hurting. My shoulders throbbed with hot weight and my head pounded to an ache that started at the base of my neck and traveled to just behind my eyeballs. From there the pressure pushed outward until it felt as if my brains would squirt out my nose and tear ducts.

I groaned, and the sound of it threatened to tear my skull apart.

"Careful, you have sustained injury."

You could say that again.

Wait-a-minute …. *Who was that?*

"Wha?" Oh yeah, silver-tongued devil me.

"You are hurt."

That I already knew. "Wha?" Again, so smooth it was surprising women weren't flocking to me like seagulls.

"Open your eyes."

The voice was rich, the voice of an actor or a narrator for a major motion picture. Deep, resonant, with a strange burr that was almost but not quite a Scottish brogue. I decided to follow his advice.

Ouch. There wasn't a lot of light. A heavy curtain covered a window, but there was enough illumination to send needles into my skull.

"I know it hurts. Are you thirsty?"

God, was I ever! My faint nod hurt almost as much as the light. A large, suntanned hand came in sight, holding a red plastic cup. I took it gratefully and swallowed the warm water. Two seconds later it was a memory.

"Thanks."

"Why were you fighting?"

My Interdiction pulsed slightly, letting me know that forbidden subjects were still forbidden. "Some guy was trying to kill me."

That drew laughter, cold, harsh and rattle-y, like marbles in a ceramic cup. "I would say that you were fighting a losing battle."

You could say that again. Maydock had hammered me to the ground and was about to turn me into Finnish hamburger when something … no, *someone*, interfered.

"That was you in the alley," I said, keeping my eyes on the covered window. The heavy drape bore a gold and green paisley pattern that hurt my eyes almost as much as my head. At least the light didn't hurt anymore.

"Yes." The red cup and tanned hand reappeared and I took the water gratefully, sipping instead of gulping. A second later the hand returned with two fat, oval pills.

"For your pain," said the voice.

Painkillers I could deal with and the stylized V on the tablets led me to believe they were Vicodin. Doubted seriously it was poison. The guy could have killed me anytime he wanted to. I downed the tablets and lay back on the pillows, my eyes swiveling to catch sight of my benefactor.

Tall. He was tall, taller than my own six-foot-four inches and whip thin, dressed like a mortician in a black suit and black string tie. Wayfarers were wrapped around his lean face. He looked like a Blues Brothers stunt double, but without the porkpie hat. Black hair cut in a flattop sat atop a strangely cruel, angular face and what a tan! Bronzed skin fairly glowed in the dim light.

"Thanks for the help."

His lips barely moved in reply. "You are welcome."

"Who are you?"

He considered that for a moment. "A hunter. Like you."

Like me? Doubtful. I'd never go for a fake bake like that. He looked like a Coppertone ad. "I mean your name."

"I am," he paused, "Marcus."

"Not your real name."

"No. My name would be hard for you to pronounce."

"Try me. I'm Finnish. My people excel at unpronounceable."

What came next sounded like a cat throwing up a heavy metal band.

Okay, hard to pronounce. Not to mention that no human could have produced that sound. I was standing before I knew it, on full autopilot, ready to kick some Supernatural butt.

And … then I was back on the bed, groaning, arms wrapped up around my stomach. I didn't remember being hit, but it felt like Babe Ruth had slammed me in the gut while swinging for the fences. I hadn't even seen the tall guy move. For the next few moments I succumbed to the numbing, paralyzing pain that strung all my muscles tight as piano wire.

While I gasped and struggled for breath like a landed trout, the tall man said, "I did not want to do that, Kalevi Hakala."

"How …?" I couldn't finish the question. It took a heroic amount of discipline not to hurl.

"Of course I know who you are. Our mutual enemy spoke about you often."

"Mutual … *ack* … enemy?"

"The one who refers to himself as Maydock. The Abomination."

I heard the capital letter, and after many a gasp and a moan, managed to sit upright. That's when I realized I was in my birthday suit. Okay, that was embarrassing … not only had I been treated like a punk, but a naked punk at that. I wrapped the bed sheet around my middle.

"I need your help and you need mine." Marcus sat on a battered green couch that was more stain than clean cloth. It creaked alarmingly under his weight. We were in a small room that included a worn kitchenette and threadbare avocado green carpeting that looked like it hadn't been cleaned since the Nixon Administration.

"Not a nice place you have here," I panted.

"Not my place. It is a human dwelling. The homes of my people are," he paused, "different."

"You're not human." I grimaced at the hot throb of pain in my gut. "What are you?"

"I am kin to the one we seek, although no one but me would dare make that admission."

And just like *that* the Vicodin hit and the throbbing in my shoulders and the ache in my gut became much more tolerable. In fact, they stopped bothering me altogether. Not that they went away, far from it. The drugs reduced my ability to give a damn and that was pretty darn yippie skippy with me.

"Kin?"

He nodded.

"So … you're a vampire."

Another nod. The potential for violence in the room ramped up as he made that admission. I knew he was readying himself for another attack, but right then I didn't have enough get-up-and-go to attack a sandwich.

Marcus smiled wide, and sticking his fingers in his mouth, removed a set of very white, very even false teeth and laid them upon his knee, revealing dentation that would've done a piranha proud. White, stake-like teeth thrusting through too-pink gums. The teeth out of nightmare. The teeth of a vampire.

"He is a … blending of your race and mine," he said after replacing the fake set, for which I was eternally grateful. Easy to see how he could blend in so people wouldn't run screaming. The tan, most likely a spray on, hid his bone-white skin. When is a predator most dangerous? When you don't know it's a predator. "Such a thing should never be and I am here to correct that mistake. He is something that should not have been allowed to be born. He is … wrong."

Amen to that. A vampire and human. How the hell could that happen?

Oh crap.

A sickening feeling started to flow through my gut that had nothing to do with the force Marcus used to hit me. "You …." I licked my lips, forcing myself not to rush the Supernatural. "You said he is a 'blending' between our races. Who are his parents?"

Marcus was silent for so long that I thought he might not have heard the question. "His mother is of your race. The race of the prey."

Oh Lord *no.* "Who was she?"

His eyes burned at me through the shield of his Wayfarers. "You know."

Yeah. I knew. In my mind's eye I caught a wink of a ruby ring.

I knew indeed:

A VAGUE MIST FILLED THE space behind Win, who still leaned over the couch, staring drunkenly at me. All I could do for a second was cock my head to the side and think, *What the heck?*

Maybe I was tired, maybe confused or maybe just inexperienced, but that one second of hesitation cost us.

When the vampire sprang into being from whatever dimension it used to phase in and out of our reality, I saw that it wore new, almost black, jeans, a dun-colored button-down shirt and a long tan leather duster, the ensemble topped off by a brown fedora. If Indiana Jones had come from the bottom-most depths of the abyss, he'd look like that thing.

Before I could move, it grabbed Win from behind and grinned at me, tipping me a pink-eyed wink. I never wanted to see that kind of smile again. It spoke of things dark and damned, of shrieking madness.

I'm never far from a weapon, one of lessons drilled into my head during weeks of training. Win barely had time to scream before the Lahti was in my hand. Only problem was, no wooden bullets, and she was in the way.

Win's scream cut off as it tightened its grip around her throat. Staring at me with eyes full of liquid hate, it spoke in a voice like broken glass in a blender, "You took mine; I take yours."

It must have heard something, a scuffle, a whisper of breath, or even the beating of another heart because it took a long step backward and swiveled slightly, eyes darting to the side.

"You got him, Kal?" BB asked softly.

Somehow I kept my voice steady. "Yeah, I got him."

It hissed and raised Win higher, her feet dangling inches from the floor.

"Kal, I still have blackthorn."

Okay, I admit it took me a second to get his meaning, but when I did, my stomach tied itself into knots. But I didn't hesitate, not with a monster in the room. Two shots, center mass, and Win went limp in the creature's arms, bleeding like a stuck pig. Startled, it dropped her.

Three shots in rapid succession from BB's revolver. Three blackthorn bullets raced toward a target that was no longer there. Instead, the bullets passed through a grayish something that looked like the mist I'd seen earlier and drilled into the drywall.

It rematerialized in time to catch two from the Lahti, but phased out—or whatever you called it—when BB fired again. It knew. It knew who had the wooden bullets and it knew who to fear.

It should have feared me.

When it phased back, my first punch took it in the nose, which broke with a loud snap. Before my next punch could connect, it had already begun to heal. That didn't matter; I kept at it, maintaining my distance, kicking and punching, keeping it occupied so BB could reload.

One punch went in its throat. It bent under my knuckles and I started to feel the rush, the frisson in my blood that accompanied my rage. Faster and faster I punched and kicked while it futilely tried to defend itself against me.

It retreated, first one step then two, then a third. I grinned savagely in anticipation of beating it to death.

It lashed out—a kick that shouldn't have connected—but it was so fast that, even though my reflexes were heightened, its size ten cowboy boot smacked me solidly on the hip, sending me flying across the suite. Fortunately, drywall stopped me from going too far.

By the time I rose unsteadily to my feet, it had grabbed Win's wrist as she lay moaning on the floor. Meanwhile, BB peppered it with shots from his .45, the wounds healing almost before any of its turgid blood could flow. BB must have run out of blackthorn.

Pushing myself away from the wall, I started for it—intending to deal some world-record carnage—when it misted again, this time taking Win with it. The mist sank out of sight through the floor.

THE VISION—OR MEMORY OR FEVER dream, whatever it was—left as quickly as it had arrived, leaving me breathless and faint. Not from the clarity of the vision, but from what I saw on Win's finger just before that vampire misted her right through the floor.

A ruby ring.

Damn it. What was wrong with me? Why didn't I see it sooner?

"Maydock's mother was a human Magician named Winnie Keener. Or Margaret Whitcombe."

Marcus, who'd been unmoving through my moment of revelation, merely nodded once.

"How? We're completely separate species. Humans and chimps have more compatible DNA."

Lips barely moving, he said, "She was a prize of combat. The one who took her should have drunk from her, drained her dry, but instead he kept her and mated with her and from that mating, thanks to her human magics, an offspring was born. The human you call Winnie was capable of foul, but potent, sorceries."

True. Winnie had been one hell of a Magician and I don't think there was any other who knew more about human biology and anatomy. Her great passion in life was to create magic that could amplify speed and strength, to create a superman, but she wasn't successful. Oh, her experiments yielded results—the test subjects did display increased speed and strength far beyond the norm—but the stresses inflicted upon the subjects' bodies resulted in torn muscles, tendons, and ligaments and broken bones. A human being can only run so fast, lift so much, before tissue quits.

So MI-7 shut her down and Margaret Whitcombe faked her own

death and reappeared in America as Winifred Keener, a Texas widow who had come late into her substantial powers. She became a valued member of Team Epsilon, a colleague and an almost-friend before that vampire kidnapped her over a decade ago.

Turns out, she held a grudge.

When I last confronted her after the op in Denver, she was bat-crap crazy and mad as hell, raring to do me and mine some serious mean. She had hinted at the things she'd had to do to stay alive, the horrors she'd seen. In the clutches of a master vampire, she had obviously been forced to take part in a human/vampire breeding program. That vampire couldn't have picked a more perfect subject to work his will upon.

Years after the vampire had kidnapped her, Winnie came back …. Well, that's another story entirely, one involving ghouls, serial killers, and Lucky Charms. Safe to say I blew her head apart with a shotgun, putting an end to her madness.

Or so I thought. Seems like Vampire Junior held a grudge as well. That would support his claim about being the first of his kind.

And that thought brought me to another question. "Winnie was kidnapped eleven years ago by that master vampire, but Maydock looks to be at least thirty, possibly thirty-five."

"The children of my race reach maturity in two of your years. For the Abomination it took somewhat longer."

A harsh wind blew across my soul. Of course … Maydock. He'd been the kid in Minnesota at Mall of America. That frickin' kid! He'd been watching my team face off against the Cutty Black Sow. That's what the dreams had been about. But despite their vividness and depth of detail, I had been slow on the uptake.

We sat there looking at each other, one a master vampire and the other the guy who killed things like him for a living, and we chewed on the silence for a while.

Winifred Keener of the BSI. Margaret Whitcombe of MI-7. Reoccurring pain in my ass.

"How does he know about me?" I asked.

"What?" The question seemed to startle the normally inscrutable Marcus.

"He shouldn't know what he knows. Win had magic in her mind that forbade her to tell Maydock *anything*. Unless she crossed over to the World Under, she should have been mute on the subject of me and mine." Traveling across time and through dimensions seemed to erase the Interdiction. I didn't know of any other way.

"The young of our species are born with the knowledge of their parents, and so on. Most 'vampires' as you call them, are born with the entire history of our race fresh in their minds. From the moment their eyes open, they have the intellect of adults."

Okay … seriously … ugh. I couldn't quite grasp the enormity of the concept—it was too alien—but it sure explained how Maydock knew about the Bureau, knew about everything, and didn't that just suck the big one?

Everything made sense now: how he knew, his ability to find Warehouse, his magic, and why he still thought Otto was in play. Ghost didn't arrive on the scene until half-a-decade later, so Win would've had no knowledge of the Bureau's resident super spook. Everything was clicking together, the pieces falling into place.

First things first. "My clothes?"

Marcus nodded slightly. "Under the bed."

Yep. All there and slightly worse for wear and smelling like wet dog ass. The cell that Maydock had given me lay heavily in the front pocket of my jeans. I was tempted to chuck the damn thing in the trash, but I stayed my hand. Instead, I left it there and shrugged into my shirt, wincing as twinges of fire penetrated the Vicodin haze. Eventually I was dressed enough and sufficiently awake to soldier on.

"Why you?" I asked. "You said you're a hunter, but is that what you do? Hunt vampires?"

The sneer he threw at me was in his voice, not his face. "I am The Justice of my people. As the oldest and strongest, I am appointed to cleanse our ranks of those deemed insane or … wrong to our way of life."

"Wrong? As in being a half-human. Oh, excuse me, half-prey." I could sneer right back with the best of them.

It was a sudden thing, the anger he radiated, pounding against my skin like heat radiating from a blast furnace, and I stepped back. The casual vampire was now an unstoppable predator filled with unyielding determination. "When you defeated the one who fathered the Abomination, it was the right of his heir, his first-born true blood," here came another broken-glass-in-a-blender noise that signified a name, "to assume leadership of the family group, what your kind calls a 'nest,' when he came of age. He was to be the new sire, but the Abomination took his life. Not in a challenge, which is how things are done, but by surprise, when his … brother … rested. That is a violation. That requires justice."

I'd killed Winnie's vampire hubby over a year ago. Seems like Maydock had been a busy boy, irritating all the right vampires. "So you're after him because he's a fratricide, not because he's 'the Abomination'?"

The heat of Marcus's anger still stung my skin. "The Abomination should have been put down years ago, but his sire chose not to do it, as was his right. But now all the Family knows of his wrongness."

"You should've done it anyway, despite what poppa vampire wanted. Would've saved me a lot of time and bother."

And like *that*, he was in my face. I didn't even see him move. Must have been the Vicodin haze. Yeah, that's it. "You have no idea who you face, prey." His breath was the wind from an abattoir, thick with rotting blood. "I came to this world when your kind was still clad in sheets of bronze and fought each other with spears. Empires have risen and I have watched them fall to dust and still I walk this world with impunity. I have learned your speech and how you people think. I have learned how to hide among you in plain sight, so do not presume to lecture me about how to fulfill my duties. I was The Justice for my entire race long before you were whelped and I will still be meting out Justice long after worms have eaten your rotting corpse."

I admit it. I was intimidated as hell by his power, speed and size, not to mention that barf-inducing breath. Up close I could see the mottled fake bake layering his skin, keeping it safe from the sun, and the too-dark color of his hair. Instead of vampire white, it was bottle black, so inky that it drank in the light.

There I was, a flawed mortal trembling in front of a titan whose anger tore at my mind's defenses. He was the terrible will of the vampire race, an unstoppable ….

Wait-a-minute.

"He's stronger than you," I said into the wind of that hideous breath. "You had a chance against Maydock in that alley and you couldn't close the deal." It made sense, and the revelations kept a-coming. "That's why you need me, why you brought me here. With my help, you can finally put Maydock into the ground, but you can't do it alone."

At that moment, which stretched so far I thought it would snap and kill us both, the cell in my pocket vibrated harshly.

"One sec," I told Marcus. "It's for me."

Chapter Twenty-Two

Canton
Back Up, Back Down

Morning sure came hard and fast. I felt like a dog that had been kicked more than once. The day after a major battle does that to a body, and I was feeling every one of my thirty-something years, plus another decade or two for good measure.

Most of the others looked as worn down as I felt, the only exception being Jeanie, who seemed fresh as a daisy—a surefire way for everyone to give her a good glare or two. She paid them no mind.

I led the team into my master suite and watched as their faces lit up a treat. During the wee hours I'd been woken by the team sent in from Warehouse, led by a tall long-timer named Ayre, who volunteered for the assignment. A four-year guy, he stood a couple inches taller than me and wore a face that Kal would call 'solemn with a helping of solemn on the side.' All soft lines and blurred angles. It didn't help that his short, brownish hair was starting to retreat against the rising of his forehead. Made him look older than his thirty years.

The new team brought enough equipment for two, and was I ever a happy camper with my choice of Spell gems and magical/tech equipment. Just what the doctor ordered. Finally … I was dressed for success and feeling good until Ayre told me I was the man in charge, and he was placing his team at my disposal.

Dang it.

"Your team, Ayre, will work on finding this Maydock creep," I said tiredly, staring at suitcases full of lethal tech. "He's keeping an eye on Kal somehow. Probably hacked the city traffic cams or some such."

"What about Ghost?" he asked, crossing long arms.

"He's out of the picture for a while." That hurt to say. I told Ayre that BB had arrived in the middle of the night to take charge of the Bureau once again and recalled our handy Internet spook. Ghost wouldn't tell me why, just that he was needed desperately elsewhere.

"You have a computer nerd on your team?" I asked.

He nodded. "Gina. We call her Twitchy. Other than Ghost, I can't think of anyone better."

"Good, have her start immediately. You'll have the run of the local LEOs and FBI, so she can go to the source and get this done. The sooner we get a bead on this Maydock scumbag, the sooner we can go home."

"Whatever you say ... boss."

Man, that sounded worse out loud, especially coming from Ayre's mouth. I gave him a sharp glare, but he only stared back blandly, easily fending off my effort.

"Get to work. Find him, kill him, blow him away."

That was early morning, before breakfast. After I ate my fill (no use driving on an empty tank) and made sure all the other kids had access to their toys, I readied myself for the questions.

"What's the play, Canton?" Alex asked, fastening his Bat Belt and holstering a Glock 10mm at his hip. His standard sweater vest was lying on the floor while he readied his body armor. I caught sight of a large bruise on his neck near the juncture of his throat and it took me a second or two to realize it was a hickey. *Oh, Dove Jacobs! You go, girl.* At least someone got lucky last night.

Hmm ... enough of that. Winch had only been dead a few months and the loss still stung, so I concentrated my attention on Alex's Standard Question #1.

"We have a new op," I replied. "One that has nothing to do with Kal."

Dead silence. Everyone stopped what they were doing.

Glares. Dagger stares. The old hairy eyeball and five pairs of stink-eyes. Choose your metaphor, that's what I got … a lot of unhappy Agents ready to kick up a serious fuss. "Take it easy, sweethearts," I growled. "I've decided to have Ayre and Team Gamma watch Kal's back and they'll do a good job—you know that—but we have bigger fish to fry."

Five sets of raised eyebrows. Kal taught them well. "This mission is straight from BB. Seems like Ghost managed to decrypt the final Trade Group files and found that a couple VIPs from that mysterious shadow organization are in town."

"In town? Really?" asked Alex. "They didn't leave when they heard the news on the TV?"

I shook my head. "Apparently not. If they have sources within the FBI and the Omaha Police Department, all they would have gleaned is that no files were recovered, that the small server in the Magician's office and the three laptops had been scrubbed clean. They would have no knowledge of the MagniGlass and the copied drives. Only the Bureau has access to that information, and it's a good bet that it wasn't leaked. So, in effect, these people, labeled Mr. G and Mr. Y, are holed up nice and comfy at a spread just outside of town, a place where The Trade Group houses visiting VIPs." I gave them all a good hard stare right back, trying without words to impart the gravity of the situation. "These are two high-value targets, and intel indicates they will depart tomorrow morning by methods unknown, to a destination unknown, so our job is to infil, then exfil these bozos. It could be they have deep knowledge of this mysterious global 'organization' that has everyone's panties in a twist, so the Bureau needs what's rattling around in their brain pans."

I took a deep breath, then added, "I know you all want to go hare off and guard Kal's back, but he has new minders now, a damn good team who can look out for him. Nanolocation has him holed up in a cheap motel in north Omaha where he's been the entire night. Let Gamma take care of our friend. I trust them."

During my spiel, shoulders began to relax and heads began to nod. "Okay, boss," Jeanie said. "It's your call, but why us? Why can't Gamma take Mr. G and Mr. Y?"

Relief about knocked me sideways. Relief and gratitude for Jeanie's support. If she was willing to back off her boyfriend's case, how could the others object? "Two reasons: One, Ghost has reckoned that since the big honcho for TTG was a Magician, these two fellas might be also. And we have two of the most powerful Magicians I know of in this very room." I pointed to Alex and Jeanie. "Always bring a Magician—or two—when facing a Magician. Also bring enough Void Spell gems, just in case. We each will carry three, and don't be shy about using them, either.

"Reason number two: aside from Kal and BB his own self, I am the most experienced Agent in this room, with Dom and Alex second-most. It is because of that experience that this team, *my* team is up for this op." Deep breath. "Remember, TTG was bad, and we helped shut those kiddy peddlers down, but these guys, G and Y, are part of the larger problem. You know the score—what these guys represent. It's up to us to go get 'em."

Rah, rah.

God, I suck at inspirational addresses.

But it worked. The team perked right up; the bleary, tired look faded from their eyes, and the beaten stoop of their shoulders testifying to lack of sleep lifted. I had them. They were *mine*.

Damn, I was beginning to think like a boss.

Silently, we inspected our armor, checked our weapons and Spell gems. All items were then tucked away, the large bedroom eerily silent as the six of us got our equipment squared away. There was nothing more to say. Things were as they were and we had to trust that our brothers and sisters on Gamma would do, could do, the job of watching Kal's six. I knew, deep down, that they would.

As the last Spell egg was tucked into our Bat Belts, there came a knocking at the door.

I reckoned it to be Nihsen. Turned out I was right.

"What the heck is that?" he asked when I answered the door, Faraday coat in hand.

"Special coat."

He gave the garment a questioning look, then eyed his own JCPenney gray suit and shook his head as if to say 'to each their own.' Then his head swiveled toward the parts of the body armor we utilized and I thought he'd have kittens right then and there.

"You planning a costume party?"

"You'd be surprised."

Nihsen changed the conversational direction without missing a beat. "I was followed this morning from the station. One of yours?"

Followed? I shook my head and a feeling of unease prickled across my skin.

Jeanie spoke up. "You led them here?"

The look he gave her could've fried bacon. "I was born during the day, but it wasn't yesterday. Whoever it was drove a late model Honda CR-V and was a lousy tail."

Alex joined in and asked, "You think it was Maydock?"

"Why would he follow Nihsen?" Dove placed a possessive hand on his arm.

It took a while and when the answer came it hit me hard enough to knock the air out of my lungs. "We've been made."

That got everyone's attention right quick. "Think about it. Why follow Nihsen? He's a homicide cop. To kill him?" I shook my head. "No offence, Detective, but there's no percentage in killing you right now. I think Maydock made us and sent someone to follow you to get to *us*. Somehow, Maydock knows."

Nihsen shook his head. "But I lost the tail, so no worries."

"Damn," I swore. "Pack up. We're leaving." At the team's stunned looks, I hollered, "*Now,* people! Like we have a [DELETED] purpose!"

Training kicked in and the bedroom was cleared in less than a minute, everything packed and racked. We decided to wear our NewTanium/Kevlar torso armor and cover them with jackets we brought from DC.

"Detective," I barked. "We are all heading toward FBI headquarters here. We have an op to plan."

He scratched his head. "What op?"

I grunted. "Oh, you'll love it. I'll brief you on the way to the car. Let's get in motion."

By the time we hit the lobby, Nihsen was caught up to speed. "I want to come," he said.

Bright light stabbed me hard as we exited the hotel, and the humidity was a hard slap in my face. New Mexico was dust dry compared to Omaha. "No can do. This has gone federal and you're a local. A homicide cop at that. Kind of out of your bailiwick."

That went over about as well as a fly in a soup bowl. "[CENSORED]!"

Our vehicles were right there, and I raised the key fob to unlock mine when it hit the fan big time.

Nihsen and I had lagged behind the others, who were waiting at the cars. I saw Jeanie's eyes open wide as she spotted something over my shoulder, and her lips formed my name before my ears heard the word. Instinct honed over years of service turned my head and there, behind me, I saw a face partially obscured by a chrome-plated pistol that seemed bigger than my head. That face was contorted with fear and hate and anger and hopelessness and I knew I was a dead man because I could see his finger tightening on the trigger, the subtle play of muscles along his forearm. I had time to think, *this is it?* when suddenly the wind was knocked from my lungs by Nihsen's flying tackle.

Boom, boom!

The two shots were deep, resonant, and as my cheek rubbed hot asphalt, the rational part of my mind figured that the guy must be sporting a Desert Eagle, like Dirty Harry would say, 'the most powerful handgun in the world and will blow your head clean off.' I almost pissed myself. Those shots were *loud.*

More shots, sounding like firecrackers in Chinatown on 4th of July. *Snap, snap, snap.* Then louder, full-throated shots and blood—hot, sticky and salty—misted across my face, and despite my protesting lungs, I rose to my feet, my eyes scanning the area.

The shooter was down, a red blossom on his forehead, throat a tangled mess with a glint of bloody spine shining in the sun. Three more men—all with weapons raised and spitting sparks—while rounds buzzed past my head. From behind, the team answered in kind and the rightmost attacker's face exploded into gobbets of flesh and bone, the back of his head ceasing to exist. He dropped, and my weapon appeared in hand and I shot from the hip. My first shot took the middle man in his thigh while another round destroyed his knee. My follow-up put him down for good—two to the chest, the last round a perfect shot to the forehead.

A punch to my own chest as the NewTanium armor took a bullet and my ribs cried out in pain, but the heavy round never penetrated. While my breath was forced from my lungs for the second time in a few seconds, I continued to shoot, and another round hit my upper arm, spinning me around and flinging me to the asphalt.

More firing, and I was trying to get up, but my arm wasn't listening none; instead it kept caterwauling as hot stabs of pain flooded my shoulder. I wanted to rise, *needed* to get to my feet, but no doing, my body wasn't gonna listen, so I decided to stop trying and to trust my team. It was hard, damn hard, to let go and I realized that sometime in the past couple of years I'd become a control freak. I cursed Kal for making me the leader of the Chicago op because that made it worse, being a leader, being the guy in charge, and it sucked, even though I was pretty damn good at it. While I came to this realization, my mind fracturing along zig-zaggy lines, the shooting stopped and something obscured the sun shining in my eyes.

"Boss, you all right?"

Stupid question. I was on the ground, wasn't I?

Apparently Alex thought so, too. "Sorry, boss."

Soon I had an audience and the blue sky disappeared behind the team that loomed over me like the monoliths of Stonehenge. Even Nihsen was there; so was Auntie Em and the Scarecrow. *There's no place like home.*

"Your body armor took the shots, boss," Alex said, squinting his eyes shut. From a distance, I heard the sound of a siren. Some enterprising soul had called the cops and a unit must have been nearby. "But the one on the arm landed between the small NewTanium plates, so you took the majority of the kinetic energy from the bullet directly to your bicep. Which, by the size of the wound, was from a .44, so your muscle is severely bruised. No worries, I'll have it fixed in a jiffy."

In a jiffy? In a *jiffy*? Jiffy wasn't soon enough.

A few seconds later an almost burning warmth swirled around the hurt on my chest and the damage to my arm. Within a few moments the pain receded and the relief was incredible, almost orgasmic in intensity.

"Oh, that's the right thing there, Alex," I moaned. So *nice*. I almost wept.

It was Dom who brought matters down to earth. "Four shooters, boss. All gone, all relatively young, all relatively dead."

"Relatively?" I sat up. No pain. Sweet.

"Well, they're mostly dead."

"Yeah," Patricia said with a smile. "All we can do now is go through their pockets for loose change."

Nihsen looked disgusted. "You guys always quote *The Princess Bride* after killing people?"

On my feet and I was feeling good, fit as a fiddle. The bodies of the shooters were littering the parking lot, leaking blood all over the place. In life they'd been vibrant young men in jeans and t-shirts, kids you wouldn't look at twice because you see them everywhere— they're part of the scenery—but dead they were gruesome sacks of meat. Lookie-loos were already gathering, drawn by horror and the macabre spectacle of it all. "We usually quote Schwarzenegger," I drawled, fishing for my FBI badge and holding it over my head as a police cruiser shrieked into the lot, "but we're branching out into new genres."

The LEOs had their weapons drawn and not quite pointed at us as they neared, eyeing the badge in my hand. There would be no inquest, no formal hearing on the shooting. Like all Bureau-related incidents, this one would quickly and quietly disappear. Large government agencies might screw up due to internal politics and squabbling, but the Bureau was small and tightly knit. It didn't make the kinds of colossal blunders that led to things like Iran Contra, and as long as it remained apolitical and relatively small, it never would.

"Thanks for the tackle, Detective." Had to give credit where credit is due.

Nihsen shook his head wryly as he presented his own ID to the patrolmen. "It's what I do." He winced. "Can't do that so often anymore. My body is less forgiving than it was twenty years ago."

Ain't that the truth.

Chapter Twenty-Three

Kal

Play Nice

"I'm still alive," I said into the receiver, hoping to prod the bear a bit.

There was the briefest pause before Maydock spoke. "Only because of untimely intervention."

Did he know that Marcus was sitting only a few feet away? "Who was that in the alley? Who could scare *you*?"

No answer.

"Maydock?"

More quiet. Should I be pleased or was this part of his game?

"Maydock?" I waited a heartbeat. "Perhaps not. Maydock was the middle name of a brave man, a better man than me and he was sure as hell a better man than you by a long shot, you fang-faced phony. I don't know how you managed to track me and my team to Minnesota, but the man whose name you took deserves someone better than you as a namesake." The cell creaked alarmingly in my hand, but I couldn't stop myself; something feral had taken over and wasn't about to be corralled. "No, James *Maydock* Sodersohn ...." I paused. How could I have forgotten Two-Hit and the Cutty Black Sow? Had I seen so many die that I was beginning to forget them all? If so, they deserved better than that from me, and for a moment, shame eclipsed anger. "James Maydock Sodersohn would kick your ass without raising a sweat."

Maydock's snaky voice finally slithered back through the cell. "He was magnificent." He actually sounded sincere, the sonofabitch. "Good to see your memory is still intact."

"Listen, scumbag," I growled. "You don't deserve his name, so give me another. What did Mommy call you? Vampy Junior? What name did that red-headed British bitch dig up for you? Edward, Harry, William? Perhaps something even more stupid like Nigel or Colin? C'mon, Red, what label did that monstrosity of a mother saddle you with?"

I could hear his breathing now, long and labored as if he'd just run a mile flat out. "You … you … insignificant insect," he hissed. "Keep your filthy mouth shut and stop insulting my mother." The words started spilling through the cell, faster and faster. "I was going to kill you quick, out of respect, you see, but no more. No, now I am going to kill you slow, Hakala, and make you beg for the sweet kiss of death, to have me put you out of your misery. I guarantee that before you die, you'll discover what your own testicles will taste like."

Okay. Gross. "Sounds like the big bad member of an incipient species, a brand new race, is a Mama's Boy." Oh, well … hell, I guess it was time to go for broke. "You know how she died, Junior? How did Margaret Whitcombe, or should I say Winnie Keener, die? I killed her. But of course you know that; that's one of the reasons you're after me, because I killed dear old Mum." I laid on a thick cockney accent and sounded a bit like Dick Van Dyke in *Mary Poppins*—one of the worst cockney accents on film, ever. "Wot? Nuffin' to say, gov'nor? You know that I put me shotgun to her 'ead and blowed it clean off, I did. Made a right mess o' the drapes."

"You lie." Several lifetime's worth of hate were packed into those two words.

"Ah, so you didn't know. You only knew that Mom was dead at my hands. Oh, on a side note: if you want to keep your ancestry a secret, you shouldn't wear your dear ol' mommy's ruby ring. Or was it just arrogance on your part, eh Junior?

"You know, Momma was a hell of a Magician," I continued before he could answer. "Right before I blew her head apart like a pumpkin, she took out a whole team of Agents armed with *Faraday coats*. Coats that should have stopped her Spell dead in its tracks and she did it from just looking at a live feed. You know, it sounds impossible, but I understand the theory behind the ability to cast a Spell on someone wearing a Faraday coat … it requires discipline and pinpoint accuracy to target the one part of the body not covered by the coat. The head. Yeah, you heard me. She was *that* good. You have to admire that kind of aim, that kind of mental focus. Too bad I startled her by not going down when she tried to use her hocus-pocus on me, thanks to some silver hidden on my body." Silver wire wrapped around my torso and upper arms like a metallic t-shirt protected me from Win's Spells, but left me overheated and cooked medium rare. "It flummoxed her enough that I managed to get within striking range and *bam*, that was the end of that. No more psycho Mommy."

I was having fun in a sadistic, almost animalistic sort of way, enjoying Junior's discomfort far too much. Perfect.

"You think you're so clever," he whispered. I could barely hear his voice, but the malice came through loud and clear.

"Clever enough to figure out the important bits, thanks to that ring you're wearing." Inspiration flooded my overworked gray matter and I started to feel almost giddy. "Clever enough to figure that you were in Denver as well, helping Mama out on the sidelines. Clever enough to realize that she was collecting blood not just for her fang-mouthed boy toy, but for you, too. There were too many murders for just one vampire; she was feeding more. You. Her baby boy. Now, isn't that the sweetest thing?" As the words passed my lips, I began to connect more dots. "I guess her boyfriend must have been Daddy Fearest, wasn't he? I killed *both* your parents, didn't I? Although, truth be told, your momma put up more of a struggle than dear old tooth-daddy. He was kind of a wuss, you know that?

"And guess what? I reckon that when I faked my death, you must've been pissed off no end. How many computer viruses did you implant into the Bureau server to see where I would be deployed?" The Interdiction didn't even twitch. It knew it was safe for me to talk. It always knows. "Damn, you must have been crapping gold bricks when I was tagged for an op in San Francisco, triggering your program and alerting you to my continued existence. That's when you put Omaha into play. That's how clever I am, Junior, clever enough to figure you out." Not to mention that I had a nudge or three from Marcus.

Almost breathless after my heroic monologuing, I waited for his response, sweating and grinding my teeth as the mixture of anger, impatience, elation, and fear ran rampant through my body.

His next words injected liquid nitrogen into my veins. "Canton Alsate is dead. I had him killed. Him and all his team."

No.

Dear God *no.* "I doubt that."

"You shouldn't," came the reply. He knew he'd hurt me; I hadn't been able to keep the anguish out of my voice. "I sent four of my docilized servants to ambush them. All they had to do was follow that homicide detective, Nihsen."

No, no, no, no, no, no …! Panic clawed at the edges of my eyes and my self-control began to crumble as the thought of losing my friends—*Canton!*—flashed through my mind. *Jeanie!*

Jeanie gone. Canton gone. With the panic came a yawning despair that filled the space where my heart used to be. It must have shown on my face because Marcus cocked his head to the side, studying me intently.

Please, dear Lord, let this be a lie. "All you've done is seal your fate, Junior. I don't know what you mean by 'docilized,' but I can guess …. They're folks like at *Foole Moon* who tried to put a hurt on me. You mucked with their minds. Magic? A little voodoo you cooked up?" *Canton, Jeanie, Pat, Alex, Dove, Dom.* Their names rattled around my skull like marbles. "No? Perhaps it was Mommy dearest who taught you how to do it? Tell me, dickhead, are you really anything *without* Mommy? You tried some eyeball mojo on me at the bar and it didn't work. Hell, if it had been Win, I'd be her drooling love-slave by now."

Hurt him, hurt him, make him squirm.

"What you don't know will kill you." Those words were delivered with such clean precision that I knew he was holding back monumental anger. I could picture him gripping his phone, knuckles white, face contorted, and it made me smile, the expression on my face cold and unpleasant.

"If you are so sure about that, Junior, then put your money where your mouth is."

"Oh, I will. I have spent the past couple of years putting together just the right place for us to meet, one which will test both our skills as predators." Maydock's … no, *Junior's* voice slowly became more pedantic, as if he was teaching a freshman English Comp class. "Tonight, 9 p.m."

"I'll be there." We will both be there, Marcus and I.

"Don't bother returning to the hotel; your belongings are not there."

Perfect.

"And I thought you wanted this to be fair."

Dry laughter answered me. "Did I?"

Bastard.

"Listen, Hakala, here is what you will do …."

I CHECKED MY WATCH. ALMOST nine. Damn, I was starting to become nervous, my foot tap-tap-tapping on the floorboard of the Hyundai. The call should be coming soon. I glanced at the cell.

You can buy disposable cells at just about any local gas station and I was sorely tempted to do so. Every fiber of my being urged me to call Warehouse or Ghost and see if the story about Jeanie and Canton was true. *God no!* But Junior cautioned that he would know if I tried and that many, many people would pay for my disobedience with their lives. I just couldn't take that chance, so I'd been stewing for hours, incommunicado, in an agony of zero confirmation. It was eating at me hard enough to make my eyeballs twitch.

I checked my watch again and hoped that Junior didn't know

about my temporary alliance with Marcus.

Riiiiiiiiiiinnnngggg.

Perfect. Right on cue. Nice to know that Junior was punctual. "Yeah?"

"Are you at the location?"

"If you mean the junction of 72nd street and Highway 36, then yes. Does this mean you don't have eyes on me?" Not that I believed that for one instant.

"It means I am waiting for you, waiting for our final meeting to see who will come out on top."

On top ... and who will wind up in the ground. "What do you want me to do?"

"You are close to the North Omaha Airport. I want you to cross 36 and take the first right onto Bennington Road, then an immediate left into the gas station next to the airport. Park next to the pumps and enter the service station. You will be briefed on your next move."

"Why the James Bond cloak and dagger bit, Junior? This is tiring."

"If you don't do this I will—"

"Stop."

That took him aback. "Wha-what?"

"Stop with the threats. I'm sick and tired of it. Damn sick and tired. You're not going to do diddly-squat and you know it. Oh, you could go on a killing spree, but we both know that if I feel it's necessary, I'll have your ugly mug plastered on every television set from here to St. Louis with the words 'Armed and Dangerous' in big bold letters underneath. I will personally put a two million dollar bounty on your head so every idiot with a gun will be hunting you. I will make it my life's work to finding you and tearing the flesh from your bones, assuming some Okie from Muskogee doesn't blow your head off with a shotgun. You get me, Junior? You feel me now?"

There was a brief pause before he answered, "Just park at the gas station and go inside. No tricks, just you and me facing down in the ultimate test of a predator."

'Ultimate test' my red, white, and blue buttocks. I glanced west along 36 toward where the sun had recently set. Overhead the sky showed stars while the horizon was painted in shades of blue and indigo. It was time to pony up and throw my chips into the pot and I hoped, hell, I *prayed* that Marcus would come through because if he didn't, there was a good chance Junior would slap the ugly right off my face.

"You better keep your word," I breathed. I crossed the 36 and turned right then left, parking next to the gas station pumps. The world slowed around me, or maybe it was just me, but every step across that cracked concrete was the ponderous movement of tectonic plates. I noticed that there was a CLOSED sign on the station door and the whole place was as menacing as the Bates Motel.

My eyes landed on a de Havilland Canada DHC-2 Beaver at the end of Runway 35. The de Havilland was an out-of-production classic rarely seen outside of a museum. Its yellow-striped white body gleamed in the light of the airport halogens. I itched to walk over and check it out, having a fondness for the classics, but I had bigger fish to fry.

As I neared the gas station's glass doors, I felt sweat trickle down my side under my armor. I was nervous as hell, excited and anxious, a furious blend of emotions that had my skin prickling as if I was in the middle of a thunderstorm.

The station door opened easily, revealing an overweight man almost as wide as he was tall, with thick black hair and a vacant expression on his rubbery face. There was a black stain on his red polo shaped like Italy.

"Are you Hakala?" he said thickly, lips barely moving.

"Yes."

The answer penetrated his slack features and he graced me with a twisted, somewhat vacant, smile. "Good. Come."

So I did, following the round man into the gas station.

What a dump. Unwashed slick tile floor, half-filled racks of potato chips that looked like leftovers from the Viet Nam era and the smell ... a cross between the first blast of burned dust when a heater kicks on for the winter and cheese mold. I didn't know whether to follow the fat man or call a Hazmat team.

Scuzzy light from dying fluorescent tubes installed in the ceiling gave my skin a scrofulous look and it didn't do much for my guide, either. "Jesus, man, this place looks … looks … I have no words." First time for that. Somewhere in heaven my sister was laughing her ass off.

"It's where the master lets me stay. It's my home," said the fat man glumly. He led me toward the storeroom in the back.

Whoops. "Sorry, dude."

He shook his head, pulling out a ring of keys, selecting one, and unlocking the back door. "It's all right. You can call me Paul. And I have plenty to eat. We all have plenty to eat here."

"We all?" Those two words gave me a cold chill.

The round man turned, an almost beatific look on his pasty face. "All of us at the airport. We all serve the master."

"All?"

"All."

Perfect. Junior mentioned 'docilize' and by the look of it, this guy was plenty docile. It fit with fang-boy's alpha predator mindset. "How many … serve the master?" The words tasted like manure and I resisted the urge to spit.

The fat man smiled wide, showing all ten of his yellow and brown teeth. "Oh, the master has dozens, perhaps hundreds. I don't know."

"How did you come to serve the master?"

He squinted at the ceiling, lost in thought, his eyes receding deep into their folds of fat. "I don't know. I've always served him, I guess."

Craptastic.

Without speaking, I urged him on. We entered the storage room, which turned out to be a well-pillaged fifteen by ten space filled with empty soda bottles, heaps of empty wrappers and the thick, salty smell of stale chips. It had a nasty looking plastic pillar sink thick with scum and a steel door that I assumed led into a walk-in cooler. I stood there in the ugly, greenish light of the fluorescents and watched as he moved a heap of cardboard from one corner, exposing a hole cut into concrete floor. It yawned like a ragged maw and I felt the back of my lap pucker in apprehension.

"What the hell is that?"

Paul gave me squint. "A hole."

Of course. Stupid of me to ask. A closer look showed that it was about two feet square—narrow fittings for a guy my size—and descended into blackness. My nightvision contacts kicked in, and I could see it descended farther than I thought possible.

"Here," said Paul, holding out a sweaty hand.

Nestled in his palm was an earwig and a hand-mic. Expensive, professional grade, but seriously old tech compared to Bureau standards. "What?"

"He wants you to have these." Paul held up the earwig. "This goes in your ear."

I nearly told him where it was about to go, but refrained. He was as much Junior's victim as anyone. Lowenstein might be dead, but this guy had zero free will.

Once in, I pressed the mic. "Hakala here."

Junior wasted no time. "Enter the hole."

"What's going on?"

The vampire's breath thundered in my ears. He was excited, breathing hard as if aroused. Perhaps he was. "I am down here on the opposite side of a rather large underground complex. We each have a task, which is to find and eliminate the other. Are you up for this, Hakala? Can you find me? Can you *kill* me?"

You have no idea. "I don't aim to kill you, Junior. I aim to let you live after I wrench that ring from your finger. But, yeah … I can do it."

"Wonderful." The bastard actually sounded *happy* now. He had more mood swings than a drunk, menopausal sufferer of a bipolar disorder. "Come on down, then. I'm waiting."

I looked to Paul. "Underground complex?"

He beamed. "Yeah. It's cool."

Perfect. I didn't know if Paul had been dimwitted before he was docilized, but there were definitely a few fries missing from his Happy Meal now. With a shrug I asked him, "How do I get down?" There sure weren't any ladders in the shaft.

Paul merely smiled and hauled open the door to the walk-in cooler. After rummaging inside, he emerged with a coil of nylon rope, which he tied around the pillar of the sink, tossing the remainder into the hole. "There you go."

And there I went, gripping the slick nylon tight. It was an imperfect fit, the shaft and I—like an octagonal peg in a round hole. The hole was just barely big enough, although I had to remove my Faraday jacket so it wouldn't get shredded against the sides.

That climb was the worst because my hands started cramping in an effort to hold onto the thin, slick rope. It wanted to slip through my palms and take flesh with it, leaving behind a bloody mess, and I kept gripping tighter and tighter to keep that from happening while bracing myself with my feet, my sneakers barely able to find purchase against the rough tunnel walls.

When I thought it was safe, I dropped the last few feet. As the shock of the impact traveled through my knees and into my ass, I took stock of my surroundings.

What I saw took my breath away.

Chapter Twenty-Four

<hr>

Canton
A Doggone Shame

WEST OF OMAHA A FEW miles. Farm country. Flat. Damn flat. Table-top flat, but at least the humidity was bearable thanks to a goodly bit of distance from the Missouri river. I crouched with the others in a ditch next to a gravel road and waited for the RediPad at my feet to finish doing its job.

Maydock. Had to be Maydock who sent those kids with their popguns after us. Put *two* tails on Nihsen so he would lead them right to us. Clever monkey.

The mess was cleaned up quick and slick with grim efficiency, the trademark of the Bureau. Bodies disposed of, evidence wiped from databases and the local LEOs told to shut their traps if they knew what was good for them. It was something I'd seen far too many times.

Fortunately, Maydock didn't seem hell bent on sending more assassins, this time with bombs, or grenades, or Sarin gas to take care of us pesky Agent types. Maybe Kal was giving him indigestion or something. Hopefully he wouldn't get his ass shot off before Maydock caught a good case of dead.

I let out a sigh and looked around. It was just us, the team. The feds were down the road a ways, fuming that they couldn't come closer, but we didn't know what kind of surveillance our target had aside from human eyes, and for what we needed to do, it was better safe than sorry. Nine times out of ten, 'sorry' was just another euphemism for dead.

The Bureau provided warrants, just in case. It felt odd, having legal documents. Usually we hauled ass on into a situation, shot anything that needed to get shot and mopped up afterward. This was to be an infil/exfil—clean and neat and all above board.

Not really my style.

A quarter of a mile away stood the mansion that Misters G and Y were hunkered down in. It was a gaudy, almost gothic affair embellished with gables and Tudor touches surrounded by a good thirty acres of land bordered by a ten-foot tall stone fence. The grounds were dense with cottonwoods and maple, a forest from which the gray mass of the building loomed like a sleeping giant.

Satellite intel showed almost a dozen heat sources moving around the spread. Human and canine. I spat.

Patricia noticed the unhappy plastered to my face. "What's wrong?" She kept her voice low, not wanting to alert the others, who were jawing a few feet away in an effort to still pre-operational nerves.

"Dogs," I muttered. "I hate killing dogs. Can't abide hurting dogs." The memory of a dog named Max loomed large in my mind. From ages ten to fifteen, I had a dog member of my family; Max was a loyal and loving pure bred Hungarian Vizsla the color of a doe's eye. Of all the companions of my childhood in the Hamptons, Max was the best, the most loving, and he was *mine*. The man who killed him hadn't cared, though. He was too busy driving drunk in his mother-of-pearl Aston Martin Virage coupe. He had knocked childhood outta me the same way he knocked the life outta my dog.

We lived a hop, skip, and a jump from school, and as I walked home that dreary fall day in October, all hunched in on myself against the cold wind blowing in from the Atlantic, I saw something lying on the side of the road that didn't look like Max so much as a soft brown bag filled with broken sticks. I couldn't quite believe it; it looked like my dog, but then again, it *didn't*. My fifteen-year-old mind couldn't quite grasp the reality of what I was seeing.

A slight moan reached me, the sound of a man in considerable pain, and my eyes were dragged ahead to the sight of an expensive import, all crumpled in on itself in a twisty mess against a foot-thick tree. A man sat on a nearby deadfall, head in hands, blood slipping through his fingers to patter against his knees, ruining his ten-thousand dollar suit. With every third or fourth breath he let out a sob and a moan.

The really real situation finally sunk through the dense bone of my skull and I felt a hitch in my chest, a spasm of shredding pain as loss made itself known. A sob burst from my throat—one, a second, and finally a third. Then the grief flooded in, filling my eyes to overflowing. Max was gone and his loss was a hole in my soul I thought I would never fill.

"Look at my car," the man said, in between moans and sobs. "My beautiful car."

That halted the sobs at my throat and straight away I felt an emotion I couldn't name, didn't recognize because it was a new thing, a fresh-birthed feeling that was almost too much for my young body. It was so *big*, so incredibly massive, that I thought I would burst apart like a rotten tomato hurled at a stone. It was too much, too intense and it needed *release*.

"My nose," groaned the bloody man. "My poor nose!"

"What?" was all I could think of to say.

"That damn dog," he answered, not looking up from the safety of his palms. "That damn dog broke my beautiful car and broke my nose."

Max? Max did that? I looked around in confusion and spotted the lie. It was obvious, really. The skid marks started at the far side of the road and swerved to where Max lay, his ribs burst by the front tire of the Aston Martin. The man had been driving all over the damn place and seemed to have gone out of his way to kill my dog.

My Max.

Next thing I knew my knuckles hurt like they'd been dipped in acid, the shredded remains of his teeth impacted deeply into the skin of my fingers. I'd beaten the man ugly and hadn't even been aware I'd been doing it. A clip of time between *here* and *there* was missing, erased from my conscious mind, gone forever.

Long story short, my dad made the whole incident disappear as if it had never happened. No police, no lawsuit, nothing to tarnish the reputation of a fiery Native American kid whose dog had just been turned into road pizza. That, however, didn't stop Dad from proving that I wasn't too big for my britches and deserving of a good stropping.

Afterward, my dad held me in his long, strong arms and told me that there was nothing like a boy's first dog. It was a special thing, like a man's first love, or his first car, and nothing in the whole wide world could ever replace it.

"The best thing you can do, son," he said sadly as I cried into his shirt, "is to cherish the memories you have of Max like they're gold, or jewels. Hoard them like a miser, only to bring them out when things are at their darkest, because that's what they're for—to give us pleasure when none other is to be found."

I've never forgotten those words and I never will.

"Canton?"

"Mmm ... what?" I was so deep into the past I'd plumb forgot the present.

Patricia gave me a look I knew so well. "I asked you about the men, the guards. Don't you feel at least a little discomfort as the thought of killing those men and women?"

Did I? "I haven't given it much thought."

"Well?"

I narrowed my eyes. "Kal told me one of the roles of the Receptionist is to perform psych evals on the Agents, to monitor their reaction to the most stressful job in the world. But the thing is, Pat, you ain't a Receptionist anymore. You don't need to head-shrink me none."

Her mouth opened and closed several times and she had the good grace to blush, crimson staining her pale cheeks. "Sorry. Force of habit, but my question stands."

"You asking as a friend or as a psychologist?"

"As a friend."

"As friend, then, I will give you an answer, the only answer I have: dogs have little or no choice but to obey their masters because their very nature makes them loyal, loving creatures, even if their masters are cruel and abusive. In that they are like children whose only notion of God is the image of their parents." I sucked air through my front teeth for a few moments before continuing. "Men, however, know who or what they serve and have the intelligence, the choice of doing so for good or ill. They make up whatever rationale they need to for doing so. Killing them, while unpleasant, doesn't sting me so much as killing an innocent creature who has no notion that what it is doing is wrong."

Patricia stared at me a moment, eyes glistening, before nearly jumping out of her skin at the sound of Dove Jacobs' voice. "How come," she said, "when you get speechy and such, you sound less like a hick from the sticks and more like a English professor?"

Hell, she practically gave *me* a heart attack. I closed my eyes in dismay. Must be getting old not to have heard her creep up nice and close. She was certainly light on her feet.

Jeanie's voice floated out from behind Jacobs. "If you all bothered to read his file like you should have, you would've found that he attended Georgetown."

When had she joined the group? Damn, I needed to get my eyes checked. "Okay, boys and girls, enough about my vast and impressive edjumacation." I checked my watch just as my RediPad *pinged*. I examined the display. "It's time to head out."

They put their game faces on and soon my team surrounded me—I still hated that term, *my* team—ready to hear the play.

"Okay, guys and dolls, we now own the security systems: motion sensors are offline and surveillance cameras have been compromised. You have the blueprint to the mansion tagged into your contacts, but let's assume that even though the place is only five years old, the information isn't accurate." If I were a vast criminal organization bent on making billions in dirty money, I sure wouldn't let the outside world know what kind of bolt-hole I had. "Anything on the exterior of the mansion is fair game, but our mission is to capture Mr. G and Mr. Y alive at all costs as they are high-value targets that must be brought back to the Bureau for interrogation." I took a deep breath. "That being said, if you suspect that G or Y is about to do you serious harm, I want you to put them down hard, like Old Yeller. No mercy. I ain't gonna bring any of you all back in body bags, not on my watch. You hear me?"

"Check, boss," was the only reply.

"Good. Split into two teams of three." I commenced pointing. "Jeanie, Patricia, you two are with me. We'll take the front door. The remaining three will take the back. Keep your ears on and your eyes open. You three," I jabbed a finger at Jacobs, Alex and Dom, "you take the rear entrance. Once we have secured the exterior, the feds will arrive and secure the grounds. They will wait for my signal to take the mansion, if necessary."

Alex raised a hand. "Why didn't BB send another team? We could use the backup."

"Because BB is still backing Kal's play," I growled, "and I agree. No more teams in case it scares Maydock away or causes him to go postal on the citizens of Omaha. People *we* are tasked to protect. G and Y might be Magicians or not, but we have the two most powerful Magicians on our team and if we can't take out two non-Bureau Magicians hiding in a big damn house in the middle of the US of A, then we should retire to Boca Raton and play shuffleboard for the rest of our useless lives." My stare could've boiled water and Alex winced as it flowed over him. "So, if the stupid question portion of our show is done, I suggest we saddle up."

We covered the quarter mile to the mansion at a steady jog, Dom, Alex and Jacobs splitting off to circle round while the rest of us ran straight off, paralleling the gravel road that led to the front gates. As one, we pulled Spell gems from our Bat Belts and prepared to make our entrance.

Forty feet from the wall. I had the activation word in mind, ready to spill from my lips.

Thirty feet. I gave my teammates a nod, their skin livid in the black and white world of nightvision.

Twenty feet. The activation words tumbled free.

Fifteen feet. Our knees flexed and we pushed off the earth.

We were over the wall in an impressive arc, our speed undiminished, our Faraday coats flapping behind us like black wings.

If you're wondering why we didn't use flying Spells, not everyone can handle 'it's a bird, it's a plane' mumbo jumbo without barfing on those staring up in wonder. It takes a strong stomach, and not all Agents can handle the acceleration, deceleration, and twisty maneuvers of magical flight.

We landed gently, lightly, continuing our run, the one-shot jump Spell from the gems having done its work. It used less magic than flying and was easier on the tummy. We had trained with jump Spells before, but this was the first time in my career I'd used one. I kinda felt like Batman and I prayed that if G and Y were Magicians, the Spell was weak enough that they couldn't feel it.

We split, keeping within line of sight, each using the trees for cover. My weapon, a Brave Bull auto shotgun, found its way into my hands and for a split second I felt a ghost-pang from my missing pinky finger.

During that San Francisco mess a few months ago a Sidhe named Olludir sliced my pinky clean off during a duel. Truth be told, it hadn't really hurt much at the time. His rose-colored glass dagger was so sharp that it cut through both skin and bone with equal ease. Every now and then, with less and less frequency, I felt the ghost pains from the missing digit, a reminder that it could have been worse.

Back to a tree, scanning the surrounding trees. Thick, like a forest, but made of cottonwoods, maples and the occasional weeping willow. Carefully planned and controlled nature.

Dim howls reached us, faraway canine caterwauling that told me the second team had been spotted. I had to assume they'd be all right.

A four-legged mass of muscle streaked toward me, and unlike the dogs after the other group, this one was silent as a ghost.

The Brave Bull spat, the flash fully suppressed, the sharp report fully silenced. The deer slug took the dog in the back, cutting its legs out from beneath it and sending the brindle body tumbling head over heels until it came to rest at my feet. It was one of those dogs people think of as Old English Pit Bulls, a Staffordshire Bull Terrier. Large muscles at the hinges of the jaw, thick, almost nonexistent, neck and square body like a fur-covered brick.

It looked at me with dark brown, pained eyes filled with confusion, and without hesitation I shot it through the skull, my teeth clenched in revulsion.

I *hate* killing dogs.

Jeanie and Patricia were flitting shadows in the forest, keeping pace with my lead, and when they flattened themselves against the trees, I knew a patrolling guard was near. My stomach met bark and I peered around the trunk of the tree I was hugging.

There. A man wearing body armor and nightvision goggles, a muscular terrier at his heels. The dog must have sensed something, because it crouched, ears flattening, a low growl issuing from its throat. Its blunt white teeth were terrifying.

Both the dog and the guard fell lifeless to the ground as flowers of blood appeared on their skulls. Their deaths were as silent as the gunshots from the ladies' weapons.

We continued forward.

Gravel from the long driveway met our feet as we eliminated another dog and guard combo, leaving their bodies to bleed into the warm spring grass. Poor dog.

The mansion loomed.

Thwp.

Pain, pressure on my calf and a hammerblow to the small of my back had me kissing dirt, while sharp tugs flung my leg back and forth.

It was a dog. The biggest terrier I'd ever seen—at least 120 pounds— had my leg in its enormous jaws and was chomping down fit to bite it in half. Covered in fawn-colored fur with a white star on its massive chest, it gave me a mean stare as it bore down. The NewTanium leg armor creaked alarmingly. I brought the Brave Bull around.

Thwp.

A blow to my chest, then another, also accompanied by the subtle sound of a suppressed weapon, and the Brave Bull dropped from nerveless fingers. My ribs shrieked at me while the monster dog tried to separate my leg from my body.

As the terrier gazed malevolently at me, the fur along its back rippled and began to expand, the skin stretching tight as if it were an overinflating soccer ball. Another *thwp* and my belly bucked with pressure as the NewTanium plates took the bullet, but not the kinetic energy, which transferred quite well to my poor gut.

By the time I could see through the pain and the tears, the dog was almost a perfect sphere. For an instant it looked like one of the Looney Tunes characters, a dog that stuck an air pump into its mouth. It was almost funny … that is, until it exploded all over me with a wet *pop*.

Blood, bits of bone and shredded organs covered me from head to toe, a thick coating of dog that smelled worse than I could've possibly imagined.

"You okay, boss?" Gauntleted hands lifted me to my feet. My gut and ribs hollered at me some for the abuse, but gentle warmth took the sting away.

"I'm fine. Thanks for the heal."

Jeanie removed a blood-coated palm from my chest. *"Sorry about that. Exploding the dog was done almost by reflex. It scared me, the way it was savaging your leg."*

I nodded my thanks and saw a dead guardsman, two holes in his forehead and sightless eyes bugging from their sockets. A Glock 10mm with suppressor lay at his side.

A quick check of my RediPad showed that we still owned the security system and that the brief fight hadn't alerted the other guards or dogs.

"Let's go."

We continued our loping run, flitting from tree to tree, keeping the driveway within sight. Two more guards, three more dogs, and we were at the front door, a line of bodies decorating our path.

Crouching, Patricia used Bureau-issued lock picks to open the door.

"Team Two, we have breached the front door."

It took a few seconds for Alex to reply. *"We are delayed by hostiles."*

"Do you need assistance?"

"Negative, Team One, we will have the field cleared shortly as long as their walkies are still out of commission."

Once again I checked the RediPad. *"Affirmative, Team Two, enemy comms are still out. We are breaching the perimeter now."*

"Understood, Team One. Good luck."

"Check that."

And with that, we were in.

Chapter Twenty-Five

Kal

It's All Greek to Me

IT WAS A CAVE. A goddamned cave. There were stalagmites and stalactites, dripstone fashioned into all sorts of melted, twisted-looking shapes. It was if the place had been carved out of gray wax, then slowly heated to the point of collapse and frozen into place. Cool humidity flowed across my cheeks, the smell of wet stone sliding into my nose. Damn, even the odor was that of an authentic cave.

Narrow and treacherous, a footpath meandered among up-thrust dripstone, traveling forty feet or so before gently curving to the right. A cave tunnel underneath the North Omaha Airport. The concept was staggering. As far as I knew, the nearest cave system was south, near the Kansas border, Indian Cave State Park.

My thumb pressed the button on the hand mic, clipped to the cuff of my Faraday jacket. "What is this, Junior?" I asked, running a hand along the cool, wet stone of the cave wall.

"Impressive, isn't it?" came the reply. He sounded all too pleased with himself.

"I didn't know there were caves in Omaha."

"There aren't?"

"Hmm?"

Junior's mirth came with bursts of static over the earwig. "I made this cave, these tunnels you will be traversing."

He made them? My mind commenced boggling.

"Yes, it took a long while, but my servants are skilled with spray-crete. It is a work of art and art is its own reward."

Jingle, jangle, jongle … thoughts bounced off the pinball bumpers of my mind. "This is the Cascade Caverns, isn't it?" Of course, it made sense. The Cascade Caverns, where I killed his 'family,' all of them except for the Master Vampire who stole Win. "That's what this is, your attempt to bring it all full circle to where it began."

He remained silent for so long that I thought he disconnected his mic. "Since you are such a fan of history, Kal, let me lay some upon you."

I shook my head. Here I thought Junior was just an arrogant prick, albeit a *powerful* arrogant prick. This little display, however, showed me that his 12-pack was missing a few cans. "Oh, this should be rich. Go ahead, Junior."

"This story begins roughly at the 15th century BCE. The isle of Crete was the strongest nation in ancient Greece and had been for nearly twelve hundred years before that. This ancient Bronze Age society is referred to as the Minoan Civilization.

"Thirty-five hundred years ago, the great King Minos demanded tribute from the great city-states of the mainland. So powerful was his nation that they complied without complaint. From Athens he insisted that every year they yield unto Crete seven comely men and seven beautiful women, whom he sent into the Great Labyrinth, a great maze constructed by the famous engineering genius, Daedalus.

"In the center of the Labyrinth was the Minotaur, a savage creature that was half man, half bull. But, of course, being the great monster hunter that you are, you know this."

Of course I did. Although I'd never actually seen a live Minotaur, in 1977 Team Beta hunted one down in the wilds of Arkansas. Its horns are on display in Records. "You're talking the Theseus legend, right?"

"Correct. Now, don't interrupt. You see, Minos, in order to placate the vicious Minotaur, fed the best the fourteen young people one at a time over the period of a year. It kept the beast pliable and dependent on the king, who planned to unleash the monster on any city that failed to deliver its allotted tribute. Eventually the monster was slain by the hero Theseus. This is my tribute to that Labyrinth. We shall see which of us is the Minotaur and which of us is Theseus. I wait for you at the end of the maze, Hakala. It is up to you to find me."

Screw that noise. "And if I refuse?"

"Then listen to this." There came a soft *click* and the sound of heavy breathing, then a familiar voice drifted into my ear.

"Hey there, Agent Hakala."

My stomach did a credible imitation of a landed trout. *Flip, flop, flippity, flop.*

I didn't recognize the voice.

When my own voice emerged, it didn't sound like me. "Who's there? You okay?"

Cough, cough. "It's Ayre. The leader of Team Gamma. I'm fine. Little worse for the wear." From his heavy breathing and the strain in his voice, I reckoned he'd had a tough time of it. "But can't complain."

"Nobody listens anyway."

Weak laughter. "Yeah."

"How did he get you?"

"My—" his next words never arrived because Junior rudely interrupted.

"That is none of your concern." Long pause. "Now, if you do not come to me, Hakala, I will play 'he loves me, he loves me not' with the good detective's body, starting with his fingers and toes. Do you understand?"

"Yeah, I understand." *Grind, grind, grind* went my teeth.

"Good. Now, hurry along like the competent little Agent I know you to be." *Click.*

"Junior? Junior?"

Nothing.

Perfect.

Sighing, I raised the Rail Gun to the ready position and began my trek down the treacherous tunnel.

Scccchh ... The sound was so soft it almost wasn't, but the hyper-alert part of me took note and spun my body around, the Bowie already in my hand and coming up and it ....

Shuunk ... plunged wetly into the stomach of a young man, a child really, eyes wide in fright and confusion ... mouth gaping, a trickle of blood drooling from his lower lip. Horrified, I stood there, staring, taking in the thin, pinched face and the long, greasy hair, the black and white of nightvision rendering him into smears of gray.

"*Oh, god,*" I whispered, agonized as he stared at the knife in his gut. "*I'm so sorry!*" A kid—just a kid, no more than sixteen—and I had gutted him like a trout.

Suddenly a hole appeared in his throat, spewing blood, while gore shot out the back of his neck and his legs gave way, gravity sliding his body off the Bowie to land in a heap at my feet. My head swiveled to see Canton lowering his pistol, a frown on his normally inscrutable, flat face.

"What the—" I began.

"*Shut up!*" he interrupted. "*Keep it subvocal, Green Pea!*"

I nodded. "*Sorry, Canton.*" My eyes traveled to the lump of bone and meat at my feet. "*Look what I did, man. Just a kid ....*"

"*Look closer, white boy.*" Even through the earwig his voice was sad. "*Look at his wrists, his neck.*"

I knelt at the kid's side and plucked a slack arm. Heavy gauze covered his forearm from wrist to elbow, as did the other arm. Next to the body lay a wicked little knife, a dagger actually, the type with a nine-inch triangular blade called a misericord. "*What the hell?*"

"*Vampire lunch box,*" Thomas announced, staring impassively at the corpse. "*Five will get you ten that that's the Renfield. Looks like he was sneaking up on you, Pea. Wanted to take you from behind.*"

The vision, so crisp and perfect, slipped away and my body was in motion before my brain had time to catch up. The silenced Rail Gun spat twice, and the man sneaking up from behind staggered, bloody holes appearing in his chest and gut. Two more shots and the man dropped, a two-foot length of piano wire fastened to wooden toggles at either end clattering to the ground. A garrote.

Had the vision been a warning? What was happening to me? Why were these memories assaulting me?

I knelt and checked for a pulse. None. At least the assassin wasn't a child like the Renfield in Cascade Caverns, the subject of my crystal clear vision. No, this was a grown man in his thirties, thick with muscle and armed with the perfect weapon to bypass my metallic hydrogen armor.

"Clever, Junior," I muttered. "History repeats." If I was lucky, history would repeat fully and I'd win this confrontation.

No more delays, time to go.

Down the tunnel, a left, a right, and another left before coming to a three-way split. The Labyrinth began in earnest. What to do? I had no ball of twine such as Theseus possessed and getting lost seemed a real possibility.

Fumbling at my belt, I removed one of my buckle/punch knives and scratched a vertical line at the left-hand tunnel. A line to mark a place I had been. I would scratch an X for a dead end and an O for the correct passage. Hopefully I wouldn't become too confused and wind up wandering for days until I died of thirst. Perhaps that was his plan—to wear me down over time.

Not gonna happen, Junior, I swore. An hour later it seemed that his plan might actually work, because I was so lost that I couldn't even find what marks I *did* place here and there. Left, right, diagonal, dead ends, loop-arounds, a crazy maze that had my brain fair tied into knots. My back hurt from crouching to avoid stalactites and my nightvision contacts were beginning to itch, perhaps from some sort of airborne irritant. Whatever it was, it was damn annoying. Eyes streaming, back grousing at me, I almost cried in relief when I saw a light at the end of the tunnel.

Savagely, I yanked back on any elation. Now was not the time to throw caution to the wind. I raised the .45 and strode forward toward the light.

Ten yards away I heard weeping, a sound filled with misery and loss so profound that the hair on my arms stood up straight.

Five yards from the light, I could tell it was a woman crying. My protective instincts kicked up a fuss.

The light of an old-fashioned oil lantern threw wild shadows on the walls of a small cave, oval-shaped with no stalactites or stalagmites, the floor and ceiling smoother than nature would have provided. Opposite to the entrance was an exit, a jagged edged tunnel that continued deeper into the labyrinth. A young blonde woman lay in the center of the cave bound in rusty chains, her tear-streaked face distorted with misery.

As I stepped in, she gave a small gasp, then began to scream in panic, whipping her head from side to side and causing her long gold hair to fan out around her. "No, no, no-no-no-no!" she sobbed.

I holstered the Rail Gun and approached slowly, talking in low, soothing tones as if she were a frightened animal. "Miss, it's okay, I'm here to help. You have nothing to fear from me, okay?" Trap? Most likely. Perhaps Junior wanted to see if I would exhibit mercy, a quality he'd certainly consider a weakness.

"Don't kill me," she wailed miserably, face wet with tears. "Oh please, don't!"

What had Junior done? Anger, fresh and hot, poured into my veins. As I approached, I saw that the woman was barely more than a girl, but put together in all the right ways. Her skintight jeans hugged her ample curves while her blouse, torn and stained, showed her large bust to its best advantage. She was definitely drool-worthy, but her face had some hard country miles on it, as if she'd seen too much, done too much. It was the face of someone life had kicked in the teeth one too many times.

I knelt at her side. "Hush now. I'm going to unlock these chains. Stay still, okay?" My hand went to one of my belt pockets.

She stared fearfully but remained still.

The ends of the chain came together at her feet and were bound together by a large Master padlock. I never had much use for lock picking, which is why the beryl I held in my palm was so handy.

"FLAPSWITCH," I intoned.

A whitish spark of light flared deep in the heart of the small stone before bursting free and zipping toward the padlock. The spark entered the keyhole and the lock gave a muted *click*, one end of the shackle popping free of the body.

"What are you doing here, miss?" *Are you a trap?*

As the chains fell away, she quickly scrambled away, crouching against the wall of the cave.

"Careful, now," I soothed, not wanting to startle her. I kept my hand near the butt of the Lahti, just in case. "What are you doing here?"

It took a minute, but she finally screwed her courage to the sticking place. Her voice emerged rough, as if her vocal cords had been sandpapered. "He left me here to die."

"Maydock?"

She flinched. Yeah, Maydock all right.

"Who is he to you?"

"My master." Her full lower lip trembled as if she were holding back sobs.

"Your master? And what do you do for your master?" As if I didn't know.

Wordlessly, she rolled up a sleeve, revealing ragged scars in the inside of a creamy elbow. Fang marks, a lot of them.

Stomach clenched in anger, I blurted, "You're his Renfield?" Vampire servant … vampire juice box, all around dogsbody. Slave.

She nodded.

Renfields did the work vampires couldn't, such as interact with the human world and stray into the sunlight. I learned a long time ago that vampires, while they could communicate, had no idea how we thought or what motivated us. We are as alien to them as they are to us and we would be better off trying to understand the thought processes of plankton than figuring out what makes them tick.

But what was clearly understood by both sides were the Renfields, the go-betweens. They guarded the vampires' secrets and foraged for their blood. Marcus was the first vamp I'd met who could communicate in any significant way besides violence and I was betting that it was his extreme age and experience that allowed him to do so. Hopefully he was the only one of his kind to be that old because the thought of a whole nest vampires thousands of years old filled me with dread.

Normally I'd kill a Renfield without thinking twice because they willingly became enslaved to a vampire, but this one, like the rest of Junior's slaves, had been 'docilized.' So instead of dealing two to the chest and one to the head, I held out a hand, ready to help or kill depending on her next move.

"He is my master." The words emerged in a mixture of resignation and love.

Docilized indeed. What I saw in the blonde's eyes bore no resemblance to sanity. "Why did he leave you here?"

Fat tears began to roll down her cheeks. "I angered him and he said it was my punishment to be killed by you." Faster and faster the waterworks flowed and her face cracked into shards of misery. "Hurry up, please. I don't want to hurt."

From Copenhagen comes the odor of piscine decay, but for the life of me I couldn't figure out Junior's play here. A quick glance over my shoulder revealed no sneaky vamps tiptoeing up from behind and I sure couldn't detect any booby traps. What was my fanged foe up to?

I found out quick enough. When my eyes tracked back to the blonde, they met the barrel of a small gun. A *very* small gun. One easily hidden in, let's say, a pants pocket, or the waistband of a pair of jeans, even one that is tight.

What she had on me was, if I wasn't mistaken, an original 1880 Remington Model 95 double barrel pocket pistol, commonly referred to as a derringer. I knew that a .41 caliber Rimfire bullet was soon to head my way at 425 feet-per-second, slow enough for eyes to track but fast enough to kill. At a range of less than two feet, it was plenty lethal enough.

"Easy there," I said softly. The small twin barrels yawned wide as the Grand Canyon in my sight. "You don't want to do that."

The tiny gun shook slightly. "I have to."

Slow and steady, Kal. Don't spook her or it will be the last thing you ever do. "But you don't want to." Fear began to eat away at my stomach.

A second hand joined the one holding the derringer in an effort to stop the trembling. "I have to. He told me to." Her voice was agonized, but she still kept the itty-bitty gun trained at a spot right between my eyes.

"How long have you been serving ... your master?" I asked. "Long time, right?"

She nodded. "A long time." The weapon steadied. "He's kept me the longest."

As long as she was talking, she wasn't shooting. "What happened to the others?"

Pride began to shine in her cornflower blue eyes. "I could please him the best. The others aged." And then her face began to crumple. "Like I am now. Getting old, lines on my face, boobs starting to sag. I'm becoming old and ugly."

"Sweetie," I crooned, "you're not old. You are one attractive *young* lady, you know that?"

My bladder nearly gave way when she screamed, "I am too old. Look at me! Look at my face. Old and ugly."

Heart racing, I slowly held up my hands. "Not from where I'm sitting, hon. You're beautiful to me."

"You're just saying that because I'm pointing a gun at you." But there was a glimmer of gratification in her eyes that spoke volumes.

I fed her ego as quickly as I dared. "Nope, saw it the second I came in here. You are a tasty looking woman I'd be proud to have on my arm any day of the week and twice on Sundays." Her tense expression eased up some and I laid it on thicker and heavier as I went. "Damn, but if you aren't one of the finest women I've seen in a while. Why, look at you, a killer body." Perhaps a poor choice of words there. "Blue eyes I could just lose myself in." Better. "And that hair! My god, girl, but there are actresses out there who'd give their right kidney for natural blonde hair like that! You kidding me?"

The gun dipped ... slightly. "You mean it?"

Yeah. Me, Captain Truthful. I nearly broke my neck nodding.

"Thank you, Mr. Hakala."

"Call me Kal."

"Call you Call?"

"K-A-L. Sounds like 'call.' "

"Sounds kinda silly." Were the corners of her mouth moving upward ever so slightly?

"It does, doesn't it? It's short for Kalevi."

"Kaa-leh-vee," she drawled, stretching my name like warm taffy.

"Yeah. But not many people can pronounce it worth a darn." Slow breath. "What's your name, pretty lady?"

Her face fell. "I-I don't remember." With glacial slowness her features hardened and the gun rose a fraction. I could swear I saw her finger tighten on the trigger. "Sorry, Mr. Kal, but I have to kill you."

"But you don't really want to, do you?" My bladder was uncomfortably full.

She shook her head.

"Then don't."

"I have to," she wailed. "He wants me to."

"What do you want?"

Silence as she mulled that over and I could hear my heart trip-hammering in my chest.

"I want to go home," she sobbed.

"Then go home, girl," I said softly. "Put the gun down and go home."

"I-I-I can't."

"Look at me." Our eyes locked and I felt a small thrill as blue clashed against blue. "Yes. You. Can."

Was that hope? I couldn't tell because her hands began to tremble furiously as she struggled with some internal demon. The struggle moved to her face, which began to twitch and spasm as if her muscles were rebelling. This internal civil war lasted for eight, nine, ten seconds, the derringer swaying with every spastic spasm of her face.

There! My hand leapt forward almost of its own volition, taking advantage of a particularly violent convulsion that juked the pistol just enough to the right. Cool metal filled my palm, and surprisingly the blonde let go, shaking and trembling hard enough to rattle teeth.

Then my arms were filled with more than a handful of female

pulchritude. Hot tears slid down my neck in a flood. I held her for a long time. She sighed and shuddered, wept and coughed while I made all the right comforting noises until she finally calmed down enough to pull away.

"Thank you," she said, staring at the ground.

"Do you have a place to go?"

She shrugged.

Damn. "Do you know the way out?"

"B-back where you came from—Jesse's gas station."

Ah, so the fat man had a name. "Yeah, go that way, climb the rope, get the hell out of here. Do you still have family out there?"

Another shrug.

"Still no clue as to your name, hon?"

She shook her head. No joy. "Don't know. Master told me to forget, so I forgot. He calls me Number Three."

Perfect. Junior was really racking up a tally on my hate list, quickly gaining ground on Iku-Turso and the Sidhe. "Get out of here, find a cop, call a cop, I don't care, but stay safe." I gently lifted her chin, forcing her to meet my eyes. I was surprised to see the crow's feet around hers. She might be young, but Junior had worn her down to a nubbin. "Go, git."

With a trembly sort of smile she got gone with barely a whisper of Nikes against fake stone.

I exited the little cave, heart hardened by the encounter and swearing anew that the last thing Junior would ever hear was my laughter.

Chapter Twenty-Six

Canton
Mind Your Manor

WHEN I LIVED WITH MOM and Dad in the Hamptons, our house, while no mansion, was pretty damn big by anyone's standards. Growing up rich had its advantages, like cool toys and the best education, and never having to go to bed hungry, but when I stepped into that monstrosity, I felt like a poor country cousin come a-calling.

"*I imagine the Queen lives like this,*" Jeanie sent in awe.

Patricia sounded like she felt the same bellyful of wonder. "*Doubt it, sweetie. Don't think she lives this well.*"

All in all, I think she hit the nail straight on the head. Our rubber-soled, Kevlar-reinforced boots touched down on black and white, hand-polished Italian marble, the faint scuffs of our soles echoing slightly up the fifteen-foot wide staircase.

"*Jesus wept,*" I marveled. The scrollwork on the banisters must have taken months to complete. "*Here I thought I was born with a silver spoon in my mouth. That's a hand-carved, hand-laid, hand-polished set of redwood stairs. Look at the scrollwork! Those stairs alone could buy you a good sized house in the Midwest.*"

Patricia gave me look of pure skepticism. "*How do you know that? And how can you tell it's redwood? All I can see are shades of gray.*"

"*By the grain of the wood.*" My smile was only slightly superior. "*I might have been born with a silver spoon, but just because my dad owns the largest construction company on the east coast doesn't mean he didn't teach me the value of honest labor. I spent five years working for the man, doing every job under the sun, including electrical work. I've helped build some of the finest homes on Long Island.*" My eyes scanned the surroundings, noting the cut-crystal chandelier and the hand-finished crown molding. "*But none of them holds a candle to this place. This makes Trump's Mar-a-Lago look like a New Delhi hovel for Untouchables.*"

"*What now then, boss?*" she asked.

"*One moment,*" I urged. "*Alex, Dom, you there?*"

"*Check, boss,*" came the sniper's reply. Dom almost sounded out of breath. "*We just finished neutralizing the guards and the dogs. Approaching the servants' entrance now.*"

I pointed to Jeanie. "*You're up.*"

She nodded and stared into infinity for a moment before a green, marble-sized ball of light flared into existence. It hovered in front of her eyes for a moment before splitting in two, the second ball flaring crimson. The balls of light began to slowly drift away, green toward the stairs, red toward a door a dozen feet to the left of the staircase.

"*Alex, we have a bogey upstairs and one on the main floor. We'll go up.*" I nodded to Jeanie, who waved a hand. The red ball of light faded into nothingness before it could touch the door.

Alex's voice came through squeaky, like he'd inhaled helium. It was disconcerting and oddly hilarious. "*Check, boss. Taking the bogey on the main floor. Casting my locate spell now.*"

"*Let's go,*" I told the ladies. "*I'm point, you two watch my six.*"

"*Check, boss,*" was the reply.

Up the stairs, each step carefully taken, my heart hammering. We moved slowly, following the green ball that remained three feet in front of my eyes. At the top it floated to the right of a long hallway, toward a thick oak door that looked strong enough to weather a nuclear firestorm. It stopped at the knob and floated there, as if waiting patiently.

I tried the door. Unlocked. Carefully, silently turning the knob, I pushed, and the green ball floated inside. A twenty by twenty room, furnished with glass display cases along the wall and in the middle of the floor. Inside were various insects pinned to white matting. Beneath each insect, a label in both Latin and English. A quick glance revealed over a thousand bugs. Hell, *two* thousand.

"Jesus wept, boss," Patricia muttered, eyes wide and horrified. *"Jesus wept."*

Didn't figure her for the squeamish type. *"They're just bugs. Keep it together."*

"That is not what is bothering her, boss." Jeanie's subvocal voice was tight as she approached one of the cases.

"What?"

She pointed to an orange, black spotted butterfly labeled 'Polygonia Interogationis/Question Mark Butterfly.' *"Look."*

I looked. Toward the body, the butterfly's wings were bright orange, darkening to crimson at the edges. Black, leopard-like spots dotted the main body of the wings, becoming smaller and less dense toward the edges. The pin was carefully placed in the center of the insect's greenish body and ... it moved.

The wings folded gently back to touch the head of the pin before opening again.

"Alive, boss," Patricia said. *"The insects are all alive. Every one."*

Each insect moved slowly, a leg here, a wing there, antenna vibrating with pain or confusion. Taken separately, it was hard to see each slow movement if you weren't paying attention, but as a whole the entire collection seemed to ripple in the cases, an insectile audience acting out a slow-motion wave of pain.

What was this place and what the hell was going on here?

"We can assume our Magician targets are here, then," I said grimly. The green ball of light had stopped next to another door and was pulsing gently. A soft glow emanated from the space between door and floor. I gestured to Jeanie and she nodded.

"In there all right, boss," she sent. A languid wave and the ball disappeared.

I checked the door … unlocked. *"Let's go."* Making sure they were ready, I opened the door quickly and quietly, the Brave Bull auto shotgun at the ready.

It was a long room, easily sixty feet. Polished teak walls, Persian rugs over Macassar ebony flooring and leather furniture. The place was cut from Downton Abbey: British parlor sensibility combined with American overindulgence.

At the end of the large room, behind a mahogany desk, sat a dapper looking man in a black, three-piece suit pecking away at a laptop. Asian, he had jet-black hair combed straight back from a broad forehead over pale, pale eyes. A weak chin marred what good looks he might have possessed.

"Don't move," I cautioned, covering the distance between us quickly. The Brave Bull didn't stray from his face. "Not a twitch, not a muscle."

He stared at me as if I were one of the insects in the other room—gently wiggling my legs and striving to escape, despite a pin through the gut.

"Who are you people?" he asked quietly in a cultured British accent. His very posture, each word as it exited his mouth told me this was a man accustomed to being obeyed. Behind him were hundreds of books standing in shelves built into the teak wall. I glimpsed an original Twain and Faulkner. What I would give for an hour or two alone, examining such precious works!

No time for that. Twenty feet from the man I quietly labeled 'Douchebag #1,' I said, "Raise your arms and place your hands on top of the desk."

He shook his head. "No."

What? "What?"

Those pale eyes pinned me to the floor and I felt a rush of heat from my Faraday coat that dissipated quickly. He frowned as his magic was absorbed by platinum mesh.

"Nice try," I said, pointing the shotgun between his eyes.

"Who are you people?" he asked again.

"Buster, we're people you plumb don't want to mess with."

That produced a smile. "Oh, yes. I do indeed want to 'mess' with you."

A cold chill settled on my bones. I didn't like that smile one damn bit. "Trust me, mister, messing with us will be the last thing you ever do. Now, place your hands on the table."

"Are you one of his?"

That cold chill just got colder. "His? His what?"

He frowned. Apparently he didn't like his question being answered with a question. "The one who has been sniffing around our facility here." Hands rose above the desk. There was something clenched in one fist and I nearly blew his head off right then and there, orders be damned. "The pesky one who kidnapped one of our top people. Apparently we weren't sufficiently paranoid, because our facility was rather forcibly shut down." Pale eyes brightened. "Or was that you? Did you do that?" Something in my face must've given me away. "Yes, it was you. You shut down our facility before we could safely terminate operations." A familiar spasm rocked his face.

I'd seen such a reaction before ... on Agents who were skirting the limits of the Interdiction. He wanted to say more, perhaps deep-down *needed* to, but the spell in his mind was clamping down hard.

"You think he's talking about Maydock and TTG?" said Patricia.

"Duh." Okay, that wasn't my most clever comeback or even very nice, but I wasn't feeling very PC or chatty right then.

The effect on the dapper dude was electric. "What are you doing?" he exclaimed, half-rising out of his overstuffed office chair. "I see your throats move, your lips twitch. Are you communicating somehow?"

Well, that threw me for a loop. Most people weren't perceptive enough to catch wind of subvocal communication. I was seriously impressed, but that didn't stop me from motioning to Patricia. *"Cuff him. Careful now."*

As she moved forward, removing a pair of cuffs from the inside pocket of her Faraday coat, the man's eyes grew wide. "Stay back!"

Patricia didn't listen.

The dapper man raised an arm, showing me a fist filled with a metallic tube, one of his thumbs on a red button sticking out from one end. "I cannot allow this," he said as I performed a decent midfield tackle on Patricia, both of us slamming onto the hideously expensive floor at the same time.

Was there a *click*? Some sound to herald the devastation to come? Couldn't say. All I had time for was one thought and one thought only: *so this is it*.

There came a noise like the last trumpeting before the end of the world, a bone-deep wall of sound that swept toward me as light and bright as the sun erupted through the walls of that room. It blossomed from the dapper man and the heavy mahogany desk he stood behind raced toward us at speed before suddenly exploding into bits—jagged shards of wood flying overhead and around, but not touching us, somehow missing us entirely. I didn't care none because the sound was everywhere and the floor—that beautiful, expensive floor—was rippling like water beneath me as light and fire and unidentifiable pieces of *something* flew all about. I was screaming—not in pain, not in shock, but in anger and denial—because somehow, in the last split-second of my life I had been looking forward to dying, to finally seeing Winch again. Now I knew that possibility had been taken, stripped from me, and I sure was raw about it. I wanted everyone to know that little fact.

Then the sound, the light, and the debris ended and all became quiet except for the ringing in my ears, the crackling of fire and pattering of small bits of wood and plaster raining down upon us.

"We're alive," I wondered aloud after about a century of marveling at my intact condition. My voice barely reached my ears, which felt stuffed with cotton.

Patricia opened her green eyes, a startling sight in a face covered with soot. "We're alive!" Her voice was almost garbled mush through the cotton.

"I said that already."

"What?"

I shook my head. "Never mind."

"How are we alive?" she yelled. "The room blew up around us, so how the [DELETED] are we still alive?"

That was a very good question. I racked my brain for an answer. Time for a rewind: the dapper man (Mr. G or Mr. Y, it didn't matter now, can't exfil bits and pieces) with a thin metallic cylinder in hand, red button on one end. Me jumping like a deranged kangaroo all over Patricia because she was right there next to me, and covering her with my body. A soft *click*, then all hell breaking loose on a Biblical scale.

Where Douchebag #1 had been was a crater leading to the lower level, a ten-foot ragged round hole that continued up to where the bookshelves and the priceless books used to be. For a brief second I felt a tinge of anguish at the loss of these rare volumes. The remains of his mahogany desk were toothpicks scattered all around and what was left of the Persian rug we sat upon was a ten-foot circle of cloth with charred edges, as if where we lay was a sanctuary, proof against explosions.

An explosion. A bomb. The realization finally drifted through the ringing in my ears. Douchebag #1 dude detonated a bomb and nearly turned me into one overcooked Apache and the only thing that would explain why Pat and I weren't dead was … Magic.

Jeanie! I swiveled my head behind and found her lying still, eyes closed and chest barely moving, looking so small and frail inside the shelter of her Faraday coat.

"Oh, no, no, no-no-no-no!" I moaned, crawling over to her body. Her skin was clammy, almost cold, and her dark skin was ashen. She looked dead.

"God no," I mumbled, placing two fingers to her throat. From behind I dimly heard Patricia gasp in horror.

There … *thump* … *thump* … a pulse. Thready, weak, but there. I nearly passed out from relief.

"What did you do, girl?" I said, stroking her hair. "What the hell did you do here?"

"She saved our lives."

I looked up and met emerald eyes. Patricia nodded once to the fallen Magician before taking her from me and lifting her as if she weighed nothing.

"She saved us." Her voice was wondering. "It must have been her. She created a safe area that kept the blast from jellying us and the strain really cost her. We need Alex."

Right. Good call. *"Alex, report."*

Silence.

"Team two, report!"

More silence … a fat lot of nothing that twisted my insides into knots. I looked around at what used to be the big room, now open to the elements through a hole the size of large sedan in the outside wall. I caught a glimpse of the third floor directly overhead and the floor below from where the dapper man had stood. By all rights the three of us should've been smeared all over the place. The sheer volume of the magic needed to shield us from harm blew me clear the hell away. No pun intended.

I said a few choice words I'd learned during training at Coronado, then hastily apologized to Patricia. If my mom and dad learned that I used foul language in front of a woman I was pretty sure a good chunk of my hide would be tanned and used to skin a drum.

"Stay here," I told Patricia. "If you don't hear from me in five minutes, set off the emergency beacon and get the hell out of Dodge. Do not let the feds enter this estate." An emergency beacon was our nuclear option. It signaled the Bureau that an entire team had been lost and to use whatever methods necessary to scrub the area clean of life. In this case, a squadron of F-35As at SAC Air Force Base in Bellevue was fueled and ready to go. Several payloads of AGM-114 Hellfire missiles would turn the mansion and everything inside the walls into the world's most expensive parking lot. Such events had happened before. For example, the Japanese version of the Bureau— their name has more syllables than a loving god should allow, but it's roughly translated as: The Division of Defense against the Horrific Rising Of Deadly Spirits Inimical to the Land of the Rising Sun— initiated a nuclear event in the ocean off their own coast in order to stop one of the old gods from rising a couple of years ago, although the Class Five Supernatural managed to create one heck of a tsunami before being destroyed.

"You sure, boss?" Patricia's face was creased with worry.

"I'm sure. Just make sure you can get Jeanie to the front gate in time." I was gone without a backward glance, a goodly amount of anger in my heart.

Down the redwood stairs to the foyer. I set my feet toward the door that the red ball of light had been aiming for and cautiously tried the knob. Unlocked. I went through silently and encountered a ballroom bigger than the one that hosted my senior prom. More shining Italian marble, a bandstand at the far end, long with a wet bar next to that. Other than that, empty.

There were two doors on the left hand wall and I chose the nearest. A long hallway. Paintings of regal-looking men and women decorated walls. All had serious or thoughtful expressions on their patrician faces. I would've preferred a few originals by Leroy Neiman or Frank Frazetta, but you can't always get what you want. Even a few velvet Elvises would have been preferable to the intense, haughty stares of the dignitaries framed in oak.

The hallway ended at another heavy, dark oak door, which opened at a touch to reveal a kitchen. Very large, with stainless steel, ultra-modern appliances. I was halfway tempted to raid the fridge—looked just like the one at Warehouse. My tummy was grumbling that much.

Back the way I came, past disapproving acrylic stares, into the ballroom and to the second door, also unlocked. A short hallway, this one devoid of decoration, which was a relief. At the end was another door, also unlocked. It eased open silently, and just as I sent a prayer of thanks for WD40, there came a loud *crunch* as it struck something … fragile.

Damn.

Third oldest trick in the book: place something easily breakable behind a door so it will shatter when opened. A primitive alarm, but effectiveed. Nantan Lupan would've been disappointed to learn that I let someone get the drop on me like that.

"Ah, there you are." The voice was hard yet very feminine. It floated to me from an open doorway across what looked to be a dining room. A very long, very dark wooden table dominated the center of the space and there had to be at least twenty chairs arranged around it. "I wondered how long it would take you."

Damn again.

Chapter Twenty-Seven

Kal

History Repeats in Unpleasant Ways

Rail Gun pointed in front, Lahti in my shoulder rig, I made my way down the tunnel, trying to be soundless. I didn't know how many traps Junior had laid for me, but I was bound and determined to be ready for them all.

Several turns, a few dead ends, and a grip of scrawling marks on the wall later, I heard the sound of running water that grew louder and louder with every step. Soon it became a rumble that vibrated the tunnel floor.

"What now, Junior?" I muttered, striding toward the sound. What met my eyes floored me.

An arched ceiling with enormous fingers of organic-looking rock pointing at a pool of clear, rippling water that was fed by a fifteen-foot waterfall. It was a mirror to the large cave in the Cascade Caverns called The Cathedral. I stood at the edge of a ten-foot drop to that rippling pool of The Cathedral and was gripped by another vision that hit with all the subtlety of a flying brick.

A geyser of water erupted from the pool's placid surface, a vampire at its head, clawing its way up from the light. Amazingly, it reached the ceiling of the Cathedral and hung there like a spider, hissing in pain, fingers and toes literally embedded in limestone. It ratcheted its head around, its pink eyes finding my goggled face, and hissed.

GONE. THE VISION HAD LASTED for less than a second, but its urgency had me in motion before I was even aware. A sapphire fell toward the pool.

"SQUIDBUG." The sapphire flared and hit the water, which instantly steamed and boiled around the gem. Another followed. "DEATHTONGUE." And another. "DIRTPHONE."

Three Spell gems, sapphire, ruby and topaz. Hellfire, grenade, and freezing Spells. The pool boiled, blew up and froze almost at the same time, spraying me in the face with freezing steam and pellets of ice. Skin stinging, I peered into the clearing mists.

Chunks of ice containing unidentifiable bits of flesh floated around the swirling mess of water, melting quickly as the effects of the hellfire Spell lingered. Black ... something else floated there as well, a thick liquid that seemed to move of its own volition before dissipating into dark vapor, which vanished a scant few inches above the surface.

Yeah ... trap.

A slap against the back of my neck had me reeling and I fell to my knees at the edge of the drop, looking around wildly.

From behind ... a shuffle and scrape of almost hesitant footsteps. I looked back to see horror on two legs. A young girl, perhaps ten or eleven years old in a torn white dress, skin mottled gray, mouth ugly with a dark stain that writhed around her parted lips. My stomach went icy as I realized what was staggering toward me less than twenty feet away.

Zombie!

Before I could wonder how the thing got behind me or how I missed it while meandering through the tunnels, liquid pain flushed all around my neck and I knew what the slap had been, what had hit me. Terror like I'd never felt, not even when confronting Iku-Turso, sizzled along my nerves.

Unlike the shamblers in the movies, the zombies in the really real world spit up Zombie Puke—maleficent, liquid magic that turns people into zombies in a matter of minutes. The magic can seep through skin, which takes time, or can be introduced through an orifice for speedier results.

I had just been hit with a neck-load of Zombie Puke, and I could feel it slithering around my skin, questing for an opening. Nose, ears, mouth, pores, it didn't make any difference. Once it was in, I was gone. If I couldn't remove the puke somehow, I was history. My internal organs would dissolve and my body cavity would be filled to the brim with Zombie Puke.

Perfect.

Shooting the zombie would eat what precious seconds I had left, so I hurled myself over the drop, into the pool. I hit the water in an undignified belly flop, a large chunk of ice clipping my temple, and for a brief moment I saw a universe of stars as I sank into the chilly depths. Acid pain scored my throat as the puke worked its way up and I tried to scrape it off, but it squirted through my fingers like corn syrup and my nails tore into skin made tender and raw by the terrible stuff. Somewhere along the way I lost hold of the Rail Gun, and it sank away. I tried to keep my eyes slitted, but I lost one of the nightvision contacts as well. Say goodbye to fifty grand right there. I had the almost amusing thought that BB would dock my pay.

The floor of the pool hit my butt and I thrashed and squirmed in the frigid depths. All the while my neck was on fire and I really, *really*, didn't want to be a zombie, but I mentally said goodbye to Jeanie and Canton, my lover and my friend, because I couldn't see a way out of this. It was my time to cash it in and what a way to go, to become a shambler looking to infect others. I wanted to puke myself because I knew my death wouldn't be quick or painless, quite the opposite. I'd seen a man turn into a zombie in San Francisco once and it didn't look pleasant, not at all. That was a revolting way for an Agent to go.

On my knees at the bottom of the pool—my clothes, my precious metallic hydrogen armor weighing me down—and still I wiped furiously at my skin, feeling the thick goo come away in clumps, along with some of my hair. A few seconds later it hit me: the pain in my neck and throat was gone, replaced by a brisk cold that seemed to seep deep into my flesh and nestle up close to bone. I was still me. I had no desire to puke on anyone or shamble about listlessly and quietly rot.

I was still alive.

It took a few seconds for that fact to penetrate the thick bone of my skull, and I kicked off from the bottom, going up, up and up until I breached the barrier between liquid and gas and took a breath of sweet air that tasted both burned and icy but was the best thing to pass my lips in a long, long while. My fingers fumbled at my belt for the fourth gem left of center. I was pretty sure I grasped the right one but had no time to ponder the situation as I heard a scrape, scrape, scrape from above, signaling the zombie's approach. Not bothering to aim, I flung the gem up and over the lip above and screamed, "WHALEPUDDLE!" while closing my eyes.

The gem cooked off, a napalm Spell that bathed everything in a fifteen-foot radius in ungodly heat for a few seconds, sucking in all the available oxygen. I felt the heat against my eyelids as I bumped against things better left unidentified, but I had a sneaking suspicion, thanks to the black goo I saw dissipate earlier, that they were the remains of zombies that had been lurking in the water before my Spell gems rendered them into rotting flotsam. Bits of flesh and bone and other things, even grosser. Yeech.

With a snap, the Spell ended, leaving only fading heat and stone, glowing red, above. Sighing, I paddled to the far end of the pool, away from the waterfall, absolutely certain I knew where Junior was waiting. This re-creation of the Cathedral was his way of telling me I was close and that he would be waiting nearby at a point analogous to the entrance of the original Cascade Caverns. Where this story really began. Where I helped destroy the nest of vampires belonging to his father, the master vampire.

Soon I felt stone underfoot and was able to walk to the edge where a cement path dipped into the pool. I took my time wringing out my clothes, keeping an eye out for other decaying opponents.

The Lahti was fine, but the Rail Gun was lost in the pool and I had no desire to swim among zombie pieces and parts looking for it. My antique pistol would have to do. That and the four Spell gems I had left. Seemed I'd lost a few of those as well, the belt not holding up well to the dunking. Just friggin' perfect.

And, of course, the phone Junior had provided still worked, the little LED readout showing a full charge. Not even a crack in the plastic casing. Seems God has a sense of humor and the joke was on me. The earwig and the mic were a complete loss, though, so that was some consolation.

Wet and tired, I trudged down the only other tunnel from the faux Cathedral, a wide cement ribbon that became a bridge over a chasm of waxy-looking dripstone, past several side caves I made sure were empty of life and un-life, and up to a simulated cave-in. The rubble was that in name only; all the boulders were constructed of cement and interconnected, making a solid mass I had to climb up and over, squeezing through an opening barely wide enough for my torso. The Faraday jacket ripped and platinum spilled from the inner lining. My adventure was taking a toll on my wardrobe.

Once I was past the obstruction, the cement path continued, this time with an upward slant, meandering back and forth through the cool, wet air. Once again, a copy of the Cascade Caverns. Junior, it seemed, was meticulous in his research.

Plod, plod, plod, up the winding path, sneakers *squelching* with every step. I could feel my feet become pruney as well as sore. Soon I began to limp, the cement hard on my softening calluses and a bothersome headache forming from one eye seeing just fine in the dark thanks to the remaining nightvision contact lens and the other blind as all get out. Damn Junior. Damn him and all that 'apex predator' revenge crap. He was really starting to get on my last nerve.

I rounded a hump of rock to see light ahead and above, a bare glimmer bouncing off dripping walls. Soon now. I found myself relaxing, my shoulders dropping a couple of inches. The pain in my back I didn't know I had suddenly vanished as my muscles decided to take a break. The end was near, and one way or another, this score would be settled. I found myself grinning, and it wasn't a pleasant baring of teeth. No, it was the grin of a shark, of a cat sneaking up on a bird, Heath Ledger's Joker grin as he plotted and schemed in *The Dark Knight* and it felt *good*.

Almost to the light where it bounced off the tunnel walls, and there was a spring in my step. The Lahti filled my palm—heavy, solid, and comfortable. I was ready to play the ultimate game.

Around a corner and the last cavern came into view. There he was.

Arms akimbo, a smile on his narrow face, no sunglasses and mismatched eyes shining brightly. A wooden door made of rough planks was at his back and four Coleman lanterns were placed equidistantly around the big, rough-shaped cavern I found myself in. He stood in the middle so the light would shine fully upon him.

He was the image of the ready BSI Agent: black, chitinous armor, black Faraday coat, guns holstered at the hip and an ace up his sleeve.

Said ace was Ayre Grossman. Damn. One black boot rested lightly on the Agent's neck, ready to apply crushing pressure.

The temperature of my blood dropped about ten degrees as I spied the tall Agent lying bound and gagged on the floor, blood running from nose and mouth. His face was barely recognizable through the swelling and bruising. His sad eyes implored me for forgiveness.

"How did he find you, Agent Hakala?" Junior's voice was light, as if he was talking about the weather. "And don't you dare fire that antique pistol of yours. Your friend will die before the bullet hits."

I believed him. Reluctantly, I lowered the Lahti.

"I asked you a question."

Yes he did and my mind was struggling furiously to come up with an answer. I had zero desire to tell him about the nanolocator in my butt. Fortunately, I had an angle.

Holstering the Lahti, I held up two fingers and dug into the front pocket of my jeans. I pulled forth a shiny disk the size of a half-dollar. "Radio Shack."

He was confused, which pissed him off enough to make him apply a few ounces of pressure to Ayre's neck.

"Wait, wait!" *Hurry up, Marcus!* "I'm telling the truth. This is a transmitting device you can buy at any electronics store. It emits a strong enough signal to be read a mile away and through three feet of solid rock." *You better hurry.* I didn't fail to comprehend the irony of me wishing for a master vampire to make an appearance. He'd seemed pretty confident that he could use the signal receiver, but I didn't trust that bloodsucker Marcus one inch.

"Clever," Junior grumped, easing up on Ayre's neck a bit.

"What happened to his team?" I asked. Afraid of the answer.

"They're not dead, if that's what's worrying you. Just a little … broken. They aren't near as skilled as you, or as the late Canton Alsate."

He grinned at the look on my face. "Oh, yes, I recognized Mr. Alsate. Did you really think you could fool me? The police reports say that three members of Omaha's SWAT team and Detective Nihsen were killed, with two others wounded. One in critical condition. " His smile hurt my eyes. "I must say; it did warm my heart to hear that."

Canton?

Jeanie!

"Yes, Hakala," Junior gloated. "It's down to just you and me."

What was left of my cold dead heart shattered as I stared at Junior's smug face. Even if I won this battle, Junior had won the war. My friend, my brother, was dead. *Itza-chu.*

"Okay, Junior," I drawled, hiding my fury. "Let's finish this." *Hurry up, Marcus.*

"You are quite right. Your Faraday jacket, your weapon and belt on the floor." He pointed to a spot to my right.

Jacket off, belt tossed to the side, and Lahti carefully laid on the small pile of clothes. The second the Lahti left my grasp, Junior lifted his boot from Ayre's neck and shrugged out of his own coat, revealing his full set of chest armor. It was virtually identical to what the Bureau used back in the early 2000s. My guess was that it was a Kevlar/Titanium mix; however, it seemed cruder, less polished.

"Handmade?" I asked, stalling for time.

Junior ran a hand over the rough, black material. "Yes. I wanted to see if I could do it."

"Better than I could have done." *C'mon Marcus.*

Without any effort, he dragged Ayre to the side of the cavern and I took the opportunity to examine the door on the other end. Thick planks, a steel bolt, and a simple latch. It looked like it could withstand anything short of explosives. That way lay escape, I was sure, although escape was out of the question. Only one of us would walk out of the cavern today and I had to believe it would be me.

Blur. Man shaped, the fuzzy, misty form oozed through the door and solidified into six-foot-plus of master vampire with a severe attitude problem.

Life became a flash of images, still frames as the final battle began.

Marcus lunged at Junior, fist flying faster than the eye could follow and slamming into the half-breed's kidney. There came the sound like a sledgehammer hitting a side of beef and Junior flew across the cavern to slam with bone-crushing force against the wall.

I dove for the Lahti; its comfortable heaviness filled my palm and it felt like home, like a shot of the best vodka hitting my belly and my smile showed all my teeth. I took aim.

Junior pushed off the wall, spinning, catching Marcus with a back fist strike that would've torn off a human's face. For Marcus, the blow shattered bone and scattered spiky teeth. Blood sprayed in a fine mist.

Blam! Blam! Two shots, one hitting Junior hard on the back just above his heart, but the armor absorbed the damage. The second took a goodly chunk out of his ear.

Marcus slumped to the floor, face a ruin of torn flesh and gaping holes where his teeth used to be. His eyes were half-closed and his hands twitched in pain.

Blam! A third shot, which came nowhere near the same zip code as Junior because he was jinking and juking faster than I could track. As a fourth round left the Lahti, missing him by a country mile, his booted foot came from nowhere and kicked the weapon from my hand. My flesh stung then went numb.

Junior smiled and I could see his incisors *grow*, elongate, becoming dagger-like fangs ready to pierce flesh. Fear stabbed through me.

A force like a battering ram to my midsection sent me flying and delivered a shockwave of agony that radiated from my belly to my chin. A convenient cavern wall stopped my flight, ending the worry about my abused stomach. My head bounced and I saw bright lights right before a stabbing pain exploded behind my eyeballs.

Another blow and another, my armor protecting my poor insides somewhat, but there was only so much more it could do. I puked blood, hitting Junior square in the face, but he just smiled and ran a long, pale tongue over his lips, tasting the salty fluid.

More blood sprayed as he smashed my lips and my knees gave way, all strength gone. I was done. Something was seriously broken on the inside. I hit the floor just hard enough to break my nose, adding more blood to coat my tongue.

"Too easy." That was all I heard before the lights went out.

Chapter Twenty-Eight

∼

Canton
New Player, Old Game

"I don't think we've been properly introduced," I called out, thinking furiously.

"Don't care."

She sure wasn't one for small talk. "Want to hand me a name I *can* use?"

"I have a gun to your nerdy friend's head; that's all you need to know."

Alex! Panic hit around the edges hard enough that it almost dislodged an idea that was beginning to form. I slung the Brave Bull and fumbled at the Bat Belt. "And?"

"And I will put a rather large hole in his head if you don't come in here." The mystery woman was beginning to sound cross.

There, just the Spell egg I was looking for. I pulled the strip of paper from the bottom and read the activation word, then opened the polystyrene case. A large garnet hit my palm. "How do I know you won't kill me or him if I surrender?"

"I'm not here for you. I promise you and your friends will be let go after I complete the job I've been sent to do. Last thing I need is to have the murder of Federal agents hung around my neck."

This was no spree killer. This was a professional. Do the job, limit damage and get out. "Have my people seen your face?"

The reply sure was quick. "No."

"Then let me talk to one, please. Proof of life."

A long pause, then, "It's me." Alex. Voice ragged and slurred.

"You okay? Has she hurt you?"

"Yeah, but no permanent damage." He paused for a second. "I think she's on the up and up. She subdued us rather than killing us outright."

Well that I could deal with right quick, then. "I'm coming in, don't shoot." Putting on my best face and keeping the Brave Bull slung across my back, I walked into the room at the end of the hall with hands raised toward the sky.

My tired eyes beheld an enormous media room. A flat screen that was literally wall to wall with four recliners arranged in a semi-circle in front. In each recliner lay the remaining members of my team, the fourth recliner reserved for a man so morbidly fat that I could feel my own arteries harden just looking at him. His exquisitely tailored black suit encased rolls upon rolls upon rolls of lard, which spilled over the collars of his lavender shirt and black jacket. His bald dome glistened with sweat, which ran down to soak the black cloth he was gagged with. Piggy eyes bulged from their sockets, rolling wildly.

As amazing as was the sight of a fat man overflowing a large leather recliner to the point of structural failure, I only had eyes for the lady.

Tall, slender, clad in ninja black, form-fitting linen complete with black mask that left only an amazing pair of dark blue eyes visible. Eyes that had a slight upward tilt thanks to epicanthic folds, giving her an exotic air. I would have been entranced except for the Browning Hi-Power she was pointing at Alex's head. The fat, cylindrical suppressor was planted firmly at his temple.

Alex gave me a tired grin from his reclined position. "Hi. Good to see you in one piece."

I nodded. "Me too."

"Unsling your weapon," the woman said clearly through her mask. "Carefully set it on the floor and kick it toward me."

Slowly, I unslung the auto shotgun and set it on hardwood. Let me tell you, I was mighty happy to see it scratch that expensive hardwood when I gave it the boot.

"A Brave Bull," she said, sounding impressed. "You government types have all the neat toys."

"What makes you think we're Feds?" I felt naked with no weapon in hand while she stood there embodying the grace of a crouching leopard.

Those beautiful eyes rolled. "Oh, please! You all have obviously been trained and you carry weapons that are the latest and greatest. Not to mention the funky Batman body armor. I've never met private security equipped like you."

"Now what?"

Her gaze nearly drilled a hole clean through me. "Now I finish the job I was contracted for and go on with life." She paused. "And I will leave you tied up, but alive."

I nodded. "I see. And what, if you don't mind my asking, is the job you're here to finish? Since fatty there is trussed up like the hog he is, my guess is you were paid to put a grave hurting on him, end his attempt at life, so to speak. If so, why?"

That Browning went from Alex's temple to pointing straight between my eyes in a heartbeat. She didn't bother to answer.

"Ah," I nodded. "That's it. You're the hired gunsel here to clip the two gents lounging in this pile of stone." I pointed to the fat man whose eyes, incredibly, bulged even more. "Although with him he actually counts as two men all by his lonesome. My guess fatman and his buddy screwed up something bad and have to be forcibly retired. Perhaps they were in charge of the Omaha Kiddy Operation and others feel they need to be taught a permanent lesson? Only thing is, we have the partner, so go ahead and shoot fat stuff here. We don't need him."

"Nice try. I know the other one is dead. His remote monitor signaled that his heart stopped." She considered what she said and shook her head angrily.

Oh-ho! Didn't mean to let that one slip. Heart monitors on the bigwigs. Good to know. "Well then, Ms. Assassin, I have only this to say: FLOWERQUIT."

She started. "What?"

I didn't bother to answer. Instead my feet took me at a run straight at her, my boots clomping on hardwood. As I ran, I kept my focus on the woman, but noted all the details in my peripheral vision: expensive stereo system along the far wall near the giant television, a modern-esque desk to my right under a large window covered in heavy purple drapes, and a laptop/printer setup squatting in the center in front of an impressive looking black leather office chair. Strange, the data your mind collects in high-tension situations.

Ninja chick pulled the trigger, but the Browning merely *clicked* impotently as the Spell I'd used nulled all thermal effects over 96 degrees Fahrenheit. Kal told me about a witchy woman named Solange back in 1943 who gave him the same Spell. Came in handy against the Nazis. We also ran into its twin brother while fighting the Sidhe in San Francisco, so Alex just *had* to copy it. Needless to say it took the little braniac only a very short time to figure out how it was done.

What ninja assassin lady lacked in experience in magic, she made up for in training. She managed a sidearm toss with her sidearm—I barely had time to appreciate the irony—that nearly took me in the nose, but I managed to raise an armor-clad forearm to deflect the flying pistol.

That was plenty of time for her to give fatty a good hard chop in the throat, which *crunched* his trachea quite nicely. I knew he would be dead in a matter of minutes if I didn't provide magical healing or an emergency tracheotomy. Considering that my knife skills were better for filleting rather than surgical precision, I had to get Alex free as quickly as possible.

Before that, I had to take care of Ninja Barbie here.

When I closed in, all that sleek leanness became a blur of feet and hands as she started on some serious chop-sockey. I took a ridge-hand to the cheek, but managed to plant a couple of knuckles on her left shoulder. While my cheek stung some, I gave her a palm strike between the tits that threw her straight back into the television. The high-impact plastic wasn't all *that* high impact and it cracked with sharp report.

She came back quick as a cat with a handful of stiletto that appeared as if by magic. The tip of the knife cut through the Kevlar outer layer of my armor as if it wasn't even there, only to skitter off the NewTanium underneath.

Back and back she drove me, knife hand blurring at my eyes, at my throat, and I kept backing away until I hit the far wall. It was a whole barrelful of odd for me to face a woman in a knife fight. Would rather face rabid dogs any day ... less risk.

When my back hit the wall, I knew she'd come in hard, so I prepared myself for pain. With the first soft *thonk*, her hands were everywhere, slicing armor, punching at my face, nails aiming for the eyes. A hot gash of pain; the tip of the stiletto scored my cheek as I twisted my head aside. I took the chance of grabbing her arm—that kept her knife away—but she commenced a-battering me with her free hand while simultaneously kicking at my legs with hers.

Grunting, I threw her a good five feet, but she started back at me in an instant, only to be stopped short by the sight of the Bowie in my hands.

"That's not a knife," she blurted, not even winded. "That's a damn *sword*."

I grinned. "Teach you to bring a knife to a sword fight."

And it was back on. But this time I was in the driver's seat.

The Bowie flashed, wickedly sharp, its twin edges back and front whistling through the air. An opening appeared and I took it, parting black cotton and flesh easily. I could've taken her out right then and there, but I'm an Agent, not an assassin and I wanted to question her some about who her bosses were. More blood flew from a short cut to her shoulder and she was the one to back off some, stormy eyes wary of the web of pain I created with the Bowie.

I blocked another jab with an armored forearm and lashed out again, this time cutting deep along her right arm. The stiletto clattered to the floor.

"I surrender," she said simply, raising her hands.

From behind her I heard the fat man gargle and gurgle as his life ran away from him. Not bothering to answer her, I clocked her hard across the jaw, my gloved fingers stinging with the impact. Her dark eyes rolled back into her head and she fell to the floor in a boneless heap.

Over her body to Alex, whose bonds parted to the Bowie's razor edge. I pointed to the fat man, who had turned a remarkable shade of blue. "Keep him alive."

Alex nodded and went to work while I freed the rest of the team.

"Sorry boss," said Dom when his gag was removed. "I saw her coming and still she beat me." He had a bucketful of shame and didn't know what to do with it.

"Happens," I said. "Just don't let it happen again." To Jacobs, "Strip her down to her underwear and hogtie her. If she gives you trouble, don't be gentle none. Hear?"

She heard, almost licking her chops. Dove Jacobs would make damn sure that our little ninja lady went nowhere.

Suddenly, from behind, the fat man began to breathe again, great walloping breaths that whistled strangely through his newly healed throat. The recliner creaked alarmingly. "Bag and tag him, folks," I ordered. "Alex, you're with me."

He nodded over the fat man's trussed up form. "Check, boss. This one will be okay."

I took Alex to the second floor where Patricia was still cradling Jeanie in her strong arms. The little Magician took one look at Jeanie's ashen skin and started barking orders, sounding like the world's smallest, yet toughest, DI.

"Elevate her legs. There … now hold her steady. I'm going to need complete silence, so both of you be quiet for the next minute. Got me?" The look he gave us left no room for argument.

I nodded, heart thumping up a storm in my ribcage. Jeanie was barely breathing and her skin looked waxy. The hole in my heart where Winch used to be was still raw and I didn't want Kal to feel the same ache, the same overwhelming, twisting sense of loss I dealt with every day.

Eyes closed, hands on either side of Jeanie's head, Alex concentrated, his brow furrowed. Meanwhile, Patricia held her comrade's feet in her lap while her face was pinched with worry. As for me, I had my fingers crossed. If I could've managed it, all my toes would've been crossed, too.

After a full minute, Alex sagged, face beginning to stream with sweat. "Wow," he gasped.

"What?" Fear lent my words an edge that could slice trees in half.

"What did she do, Canton?"

I pointed to the holes in the roof, floor, and outside wall. "She saved us from that. One hell of an explosion."

He nodded. "That would do it."

Now I was starting to lose my cool. "What?" I asked crossly.

Alex began to rub Jeanie's temples and her face suddenly relaxed and gained a little color. I felt a little flare of hope in my chest. "She just about used up all the magic inside of her. Almost drained her like an alkaline battery. If she would have used any more, I'd be making arrangements to move the body instead of trying to heal her. She'll be okay, by the way."

Big relief. Giant, actually. Colossal and monolithic and a few other words that meant 'damn big.' But I was a little confused, perhaps a bit slow on the uptake due to a stressful night, so I asked him to explain.

"A Magician has access to only so much magic at any given time," he explained. "And when they run low, they have to rest, to recharge, so their bodies can regain the magic used. If all the magic is drained at once, then nothing is left to keep the body going and the Magician dies. Magicians call upon dark matter and dark energy to perform magic, but it takes the body's own energy to do so." His hands continued to rub Jeanie's temples while Patricia began to work on her calves and thighs. Soon Jeanie was visibly breathing and stirring slightly.

A thought occurred to me. "So … to continue to use the battery analogy, if a person is murdered, then all that energy from their battery is discharged at once, which makes Necromancy possible?" Made sense to me, but it sure twisted my stomach up some.

Alex nodded. "Exactly. Jeanie's battery was drained almost dry. Almost. She'll be okay now. I've given her a … a … transfusion of sorts. A magic transfusion."

With a relieved sigh, I plucked my cell from my Bat Belt and dialed. "Well, that's a load off. I can't take any more stress tonight. Might have to start taking Rolaids." There came a click as a connection was made. "Hello? This is Special Agent Alsate," I said to the feds waiting patiently. "Lock this place down. We have what we need."

I hung up the phone. "Damn, but I need a vacation."

CHAPTER TWENTY-NINE

Kal

Failure Is Always an Option, Just Not a Good One

I RESTED AGAINST A SURFACE that was cold, hard, and uncomfortable. Its chill seeped deep into my flesh and made an enemy of my spine. The ache that surface caused echoed in my arms, legs, and face, which throbbed with every beat of my heart.

The darkness that cocooned me faded as my eyelids slowly rose and the sight of Junior grinning down at me did awful things to my stomach. It would serve him right if I puked on his shoes right then.

"Wakey, wakey," he crooned, mismatched eyes gleaming with delight.

"You're not a sight for sore eyes," I mumbled.

His snaky, slithery laughter hurt my ears.

Cold. Damn cold. My torso and spine, hell … my whole body ached. I couldn't glance down—my neck refused to move properly—but I knew that my shirt and armor were gone and that I was nearly naked. "If you wanted to have your way with me, all you had to do was ask."

He chuckled. "Still full of piss and vinegar, aren't you, Hakala?" That hateful face moved in close and I could smell rotting blood on his breath. I tried not to gag. There was a ripping sound, like cloth tearing in half, and a strip of duct tape was placed over my mouth.

"I'm getting sick of that mouth of yours. This ought to hold you for a while." Junior sat back on his heels and stared deep into my eyes. "I've broken both your arms and your legs and have taken your armor as my prize. Victory is mine."

"Mnph rumph," I cursed.

It only made him smile wider. "Your temporary ally, Marcus, has fled and you are all alone. I am going to let you live. For now. I want you to know that I *will* come for you one day, and I want you looking over your shoulder in fear until that day arrives. Trust me when I tell you … arrive it will."

He held my stained, metallic hydrogen vest in one large hand, splotches of my blood decorating the front. My heart leapt and I tried to work my tongue between my lips to move the tape out of the way, but Junior twigged on to what I was trying and placed his hand over my taped mouth, mashing my lips shut. His ruby ring winked at me in the warm lantern light, as if mocking my predicament. "But first, Hakala, I will destroy the Bureau. I have that power, and with this armor you so graciously provided, I am near unstoppable." He stood. "It was clever of you to recruit The Justice, but even he now knows that I cannot be beaten and has run away like the cur he is. A noble effort indeed, but now I am off. Places to go, people to kill. I will need a snack. Your colleague should do nicely."

Gaaahhh! Agony rippled across my limbs as I tried rolling over to keep Junior in sight and red spots danced in front of my vision. Through the haze of burning pain, I saw Junior heft Ayre as if he were a small sack of grain, hoist him over his shoulder, un-bolt the door and stroll way. My last sight of Ayre was his pain-ridden eyes forgiving me for my failure to save him.

Damn! I began to flop toward the door, each bump sending nails of pain through my limbs. *No! No! NO!!* The spirit was willing, but the flesh was broken. I covered ten feet in about as many minutes before I had to stop, my world now consumed by the splinters of my bones digging into tender flesh. The idea of sparing the loser had taken root in Junior's mind, a ploy I was more than grateful for. Basic psychology … if your opponent is a sadist, give him something to hurt, because the dead feel nothing. Only problem was my injuries were too extensive for me to do anything about Junior. It looked like he had won the battle.

Warm blood smell caressed my nostrils.

Through the fog of my senses, I saw a wide puddle of pinkish blood about a million miles away, where Marcus had lain. The pool was an oval, a foot long and ten inches wide. Junior had really done a number on The Justice of the vampire race. I knew Marcus would most likely give up. As acclimated to the human condition as he was, I sensed that deep down he was a creature of pragmatism and opportunity, and it would bode ill for him to tangle ass with Junior again.

So I lay there, wallowing in pain, misery, and self-loathing, arms and legs throbbing, head pounding, staring at the wooden door, an impassible barrier for a man in my condition, and I *screamed.*

Duct tape tore as my mouth opened wide, lips stinging from the pull of the adhesive. What crossed my teeth didn't sound human at all. It was primal, furious, and *insane.*

Pop.

The next scream that issued from my throat was one of agony as my right arm suddenly juddered and straightened. The shock of it drove the anger out of my mind.

What the hell? I thought as my fingers tore the remaining duct tape away.

My fingers? Yep, there they were, attached to the palm, which was connected to wrist bone, which was connected to now unbroken though still dully throbbing arm bone. I held the arm up for inspection. It looked the same, a bit sore, but still my arm. Who had healed it?

Win/Margaret's voice came to me through the mists of the past to thud against my ears as if she were right next to me. *"One thing about vampires is true … their blood does have regenerative properties."*

The thrill that went through me was electric, so intense that I didn't even question the voice from the past. Using my now somewhat healed arm, I began to pull myself across the smooth concrete toward the swiftly cooling pool of blood left behind by Marcus.

"Man, you look like hell."

Nihsen! I was so happy to hear his voice I almost wept. "Damn," I grunted, pulling myself a couple of inches closer to the precious fluid. "Not … that I'm … unhappy to … see you, Detective … but what the hell … are you doing here."

Strong hands helped me to a sitting position and the pain nearly had me swooning. "I was following that second team of Agents that arrived in town, keeping an eye on them, hoping they would lead me to you. I had them in sight, thanks to a pair of nightvision binoculars. They were in the housing development east of here acting like they were all James Bond sneaky and such when our serial killer ambushed them. Went through the whole team in less time than it took for me to understand what was going on. Then he grabbed some tall guy and headed toward this building." He looked around. "Hmph. This is weird," he said, remarking on the man-made cavern. "Anyway, I helped those who were down get all comfy and called for an ambulance. Then I heard an airplane take off. Decided to come check out what's what." The detective tossed me a crooked smile. "So this is what you do for fun, eh?"

My mind flashed back to the image of the de Havilland Beaver. Junior had made his escape. *Perfect*, I snarled silently.

Wait a minute. "Nihsen, when did the plane take off?"

"About five minutes ago."

Time. I still had time. I hoped. "Drag me to that puddle of blood over there."

"That don't look like blood." Nihsen gave me a curious look but did as I asked. When he lowered me to the floor, I intentionally fell lip-first into clotting liquid.

"Oh, man," Nihsen gagged, "that's not right."

Slurp, slurp, slurp.

Yeah, it was as disgusting as it sounds, but I forced myself to drink. Thick, metallic, it didn't taste like human blood at all. More like spicy ketchup mixed with tinfoil and bitter herbs. Nasty.

But then it happened, less than a minute later … my body began to tremble, then shake violently as spasms rocked my flesh. The splintered ends of my broken femurs *clicked* together like Legos in one moment of stupendous, piercing pain before they grew warm, the warmth lasting only a moment before it was a memory.

"Oh, that's the stuff," I breathed. Nihsen continued to make gagging noises.

I stood. Yep, legs tingled somewhat and took my weight, while a strange, electric energy swirled through my body. Oh, yeah, I felt fine … I felt more than fine. My smile nearly split my face in half.

"What's happening?" Nihsen grabbed my arm, and I smiled wider, so glad that it didn't hurt at all.

"What's happening is that now I am ready to try to take the taco." *If there was still time.*

Junior's tough plastic phone still held a charge. First ringing, then a connection. "Hey, Junior, how's hanging?" I said into the receiver.

Not sure exactly what happened next, but I think it went something like *this* ….

CHAPTER THIRTY

Maydock

Victory Dance

HE HAD DONE IT. HE had defeated Agent By-Damn Kalevi Sonofabitch Hakala! It felt so good that he was light-headed and giddy. In fact, his flesh tingled and everything seemed to possess a divine aura that was the reflection of his glory.

The de Havilland handled like a dream as he flew west, the blonde and the new snack-pack sitting in the seat behind. Her stare was vacant as her eyes tracked the ground below.

Riiiinnggg. The cell in his front pocket vibrated harshly and he swore. Somehow Hakala had managed a phone call.

"Very impressive, Kal," he said after hitting the RECEIVE button.

"Hey, Junior, how's hanging?"

Anger spiked through his forehead. Teeth gritted, he forced himself to answer amicably, "I see you managed a miracle." He cast his mind back, using his considerable ability at recall to furiously search for some clue he had missed, and with a start, figured it out. "Blood. The Justice's blood. Somehow you managed to drink his blood before it congealed. How foolish of me to have overlooked that at the time." Actually, he had been gloating quite a bit, so it was not surprising. "You are as brilliant as ever."

Hakala confirmed that fact. "That's what happens when you do your victory dance too early, big boy."

He could not contain the smugness that colored his words. "But I did win. Face it, Hakala, I am *the* apex predator on this planet. And now I am flying away, hidden from satellites and radar by the most impressive Spells ever created. You can try to use all your vaunted Bureau technology to find me, but you will fail."

"Sure. Whatever. Let me talk to Ayre."

"Ah, that's the name of my lunch? Ayre?"

"That's the name of a great Agent, Junior."

"Hmm … if you say so. I wasn't impressed."

"Let me talk to him."

He was intrigued at Hakala's insistence at speaking to his as-good-as-dead comrade. A feeling of unease rippled up his spine. "Why?"

"To … apologize for not saving him."

"That is trite."

"Nonetheless."

Interesting. Did he care for the other man? Perhaps like a pet? "Say please."

Silence.

"Say please or I will tear this creature's throat out right this instant!" he barked.

"Please." Soft, barely audible.

"Louder."

Hakala shouted, "PLEASE!"

Ah, that was much better. Smiling, he tossed the phone back over his shoulder. "Hold the phone to my lunch's ear, woman," he instructed the blonde.

The blonde fumbled for the cell from where it had fallen on the floor. Relieved to see that the connection still held, she put the cell to the Agent's ear and pulled the gag from his mouth. Drool spilled out onto his chin.

"M-master, he's unconscious," she said, cringing.

There came a harsh bark of laughter from the pilot's chair. "Then you talk to Hakala. I am sure he will find your sparkling wit most enlightening."

* * *

The laughter that followed was ugly and mean and it cut her to the bone. But she followed his directions like she always had. Like a good servant.

"H-hello?"

It was indeed the man who tried to kill the master. The kind one with the pretty eyes and the blond hair and the slightly broken smile. It was the smile she remembered most because it was nice and it promised her that no hurt would come, no matter what. It said the kind man wasn't like the master; he would never make fun of her, hurt her, feed from her, or make her suffer for some small slight. That smile said he was patient and good, and now that man was telling her things. Wonderful, unbelievable things, and she answered him monosyllabically just in case the master was listening close. She didn't want to hurt anymore and the kind man told her how she could be free.

Free!

Chapter Thirty-One

Kal
The Way Home

AYRE!

When the blonde Renfield's voice issued from the phone I nearly threw it across the cavern in frustration, but instead I raced out the thick plank door, speaking quickly lest she fly out of range, because I had an idea and I was praying there was enough of a real woman left in that docilized shell to help me out.

I found myself in a long hangar, the cavern merely a large room built specially for Junior's little tea party. Quickly I made my way across concrete until I was under a sky full of stars.

"You remember me, young lady?" I asked softly, remembering how timid she had been.

"Uh-huh."

The air was cool, but still carried enough humidity to fuzz my hair. Felt good, better than the caverns. "Do you want to be free of your master?" I crossed my fingers.

It took her a long time to answer. Almost too long. *Hurry up!* I urged. "Uh-huh," she grunted. It was a hesitant sound, full of doubt and fear and it almost brought tears to my eyes.

"I can help you be free. Seriously, it'll be easy. You'd like that, right?"

"Yeah."

Good girl. I'm so sorry. "You were so brave back in the cave where we met and I am so proud of you because I know how hard it was not to pull that trigger and shoot me. All you have to do now is to be brave for just a little while longer and then you won't have to worry about your master anymore. Easy peasy, lemon squeezy." *Please forgive me, I'm so sorry.*

"Okay."

There were metal bands around my ribs and they were squeezing my heart up through my throat. "Okay, sweetie, this is all you have to do. You listening?"

"Uh-huh."

Cool, wet air caressed my face as I walked beneath the night sky. *Please, oh please, let this work.* "Remember I told you that you could go home?" *I'm so sorry.*

"Uh-huh."

"You can go home, all you have to do is one thing. One tiny thing and everything will be good again, just like before you met your master. Would you like that?"

"Yes." Firm now.

"Are you listening carefully because I have something to tell you, something that will erase all the hurt, all the pain you've been feeling. You can now go home." *I'm so sorry.* "Are you ready?"

"Yes." No more hesitation. Her voice now had a measure of strength I'd never heard before. "Yes."

Ayre, girl, God … please forgive me. I told her the way home.

Chapter Thirty-Two

Maydock
One Last Spell

T HE BLONDE STARED WIDE-EYED AS the kind man told her what to do. It was so simple, the easiest thing in the world, actually. When he was done, she hung up.

"What did Hakala say that was so fascinating?" asked the master, his voice full of scorn. "And did you even understand it?"

The blonde knew the price of disobedience, and she knew that what the kind man told her was not really disobedience, but a choice. A small, but very important choice. "Yes. Yes I did."

The master's mismatched eyes flicked at her as his head turned. "Well?"

"Mr. Kal wanted me to tell you something important. Something he thought you should know before you got too far away. He said it was a matter of life and death."

"And what would that be, foolish woman?" The cruel, mismatched eyes were colored with genuine curiosity.

The blonde stared out the window at the ground so far below. "He wanted me to tell you this: 'I win, douchebag.'" She took a deep, cleansing breath, before saying, "RIVERPLUG."

And just like that, she was home.

Chapter Thirty-Three

Canton

Until We Meet Again

"Yeah, BB, we exfiled either Mr. G or Mr. Y," I said into the RediPad, leaning against our SUV. "Although he's big enough to be both."

The feds had occupied the mansion and were combing through it thoroughly, with the proviso that all evidence was to be vetted by my team before being logged. You never knew what was relevant.

Jeanie was back on her feet—figuratively speaking. She was actually on her butt in the backseat drinking gallons of water and resting, while Alex monitored her magic levels, clucking over her like a mother hen, which made Jacobs all jealous and stuff.

Another guard was led away in cuffs and Animal Control hauled scads of dogs away in their trucks. The majority had been killed, which was a crying shame; I hate killing dogs. The surviving guards would be processed and released. They were hired guns, no-nothing bodyguards whose worst offense was working for the wrong guys and carrying illegal weapons. As for the remaining dogs … I sure hoped they'd get good homes. Maybe I'd adopt one.

I had just finished my debrief and was looking forward to some shuteye, but I knew that moment of peace was far, far away because Kal was still out there, and even though Ayre and his team were rough and ready, Maydock was a wild card.

BB, as usual, knew what I was thinking. "Ayre has tracked Kal to the North Omaha Airport. I am sure everything is fine. Trust your comrades."

"Oh, I trust them all right, boss. I just wish Kal would've checked in today. He's been quiet as a church mouse, and that ain't like him one bit." I swiped at a buzzing insect.

BB's image on the RediPad screen gave a rare smile. A small one. "Too true."

"Any word from Ghost?"

"He is still doing what needs to be done, checking for signs of this other shadow organization. I am sure he will inform us straightaway of any relevant intel."

The buzzing insect grew louder. I realized I wasn't under attack by an invertebrate; the noise was coming from above. My eyes searched the starry sky.

There! A small black shape droned overhead making a godawful racket. My nightvision contacts were more than up to the task and I saw what was rapidly flying away. The hair on the nape of my neck stood straight up.

"Canton, what is it? What is that sound?" BB asked.

A second later Jacobs asked the same thing from inside the SUV and I sighed. "Gyrocopter."

"Do you know what's going on?" the bossman asked as the rest of the team joined me outside, staring at the dot that grew smaller and smaller. In the end, I think staring in the opposite direction saved our eyes.

"Boss, I think the feds are about to be trotting up to tell us that the ninja lady assassin has gone and staged a getaway."

Loud noises of protest. "I had her trussed up like a Christmas goose!" Jacobs exclaimed.

My eyes were still on the sky when I said, "My fault ... shouldn't have let the feds look after—"

To the west a brilliant light drowned out the stars, a horizon-blotting flare that threw our shadows crazy on the ground. Even though our backs were to the source, the reflected radiance brought tears to our eyes and I had to squint to avoid being blinded. The incandescence tossed the world into stark contrasts just before a roaring wall of sound hit, more felt than heard, bringing with it a dry, hot wind straight from hell.

It hit like a runaway freight train, sudden and unstoppable, a physical force that rocked the SUV at my back and tore away the cries of my startled teammates and feds—the piping of ants against the trumpet of an elephant.

I ducked, covering my head with my arms as the wind clutched me with insistent fingers. Briefly I wondered if this was the end of the world. Armageddon? The Rapture? Buried deep inside me was a kid who went to the Presbyterian Church every Sunday with his folks. That kid whimpered and cried and the wind and the sound raged on for several seconds before dying suddenly, the light slowly fading after.

Spinning, I looked west and saw a purple and yellow glare that faded rapidly from the night sky. Within seconds it was gone, leaving only a harsh memory and wind-scoured skin.

"What the hell was that?" screamed BB in alarm. It was the first time I'd ever heard him loose his cool, and it wasn't as neat as I thought it would be. In fact, it scared me to death.

Wait. I looked at his image … somewhat broken from interference, but still there.

"I don't—"

Before I could squeeze out a few more words, the world decided to blast me with the greatest fart ever recorded—a sharp, massive clap of noise like that of the 16-inch guns on an *Iowa*-class battleship. Instead of another rush of wind from the source of the noise, the air moved *toward* the source, a gentle pull at the back of my neck, not the fierce gush from before. Those of us still standing looked at each other in horror.

"W-what?" stammered Jacobs, spit at the corners of her mouth.

"That was the sound of air rushing back to fill a vacuum," replied Alex, taking her hand. Jeanie sat behind him in the car, rubbing her temples. "The first was an explosion."

"Nuclear?" asked Patricia, licking her lips.

I shook my head, brains somewhat a-scrambled. "No, not nuclear. The RediPad is still working. If it had been nuclear the EMP would have fried the tablet."

"Is everyone all right?" asked BB from the pad.

I nodded at his image.

"Good," he said. "Was it a thermobaric weapon?"

A fuel-air bomb would explain the size and intensity. "Not sure, boss, but I think it had something to do with Kal."

"What makes you say that?"

The whole team answered at once. "What else could it be?"

Chapter Thirty-Four

Kal

Big Bang Theory

"WHAT WAS THAT?" NIHSEN ASKED, voice colored in awe. He rubbed his eyes furiously.

"Be glad you weren't looking directly at it," I said, seeing spots. Had we been facing west, our eyes would no doubt have been dribbling down our cheeks by now.

The night was no longer cool. A violent warmth flowed across the land, the product of the explosion to the west.

"And that big boom, my dear detective, was our serial killer's airplane. I don't think we have to worry about him anymore." *I'm so sorry, Ayre.* Haltingly, I explained what had happened to the detective.

Alex used magic to create my metallic hydrogen armor, bonding a Spell Shape into the metal plates to stabilize them. My idea came when I considered the Void Spell, which effectively removes magic from a certain radius. What happens to magically stabilized metallic hydrogen when the very thing keeping it stabilized suddenly no longer works?

It goes boom.

I had placed a Void Spell gem in one of the inserts of the vest, snuggled up right next to one of the hydrogen plates … a little perfect diamond as big as my pinky nail. Small, but quality, not quantity, is paramount when it comes to magic.

The blonde had come through, repeating the activation word out loud that would set off the Void Spell. It had been a gamble … I hadn't been sure it would work, but I was sure glad it did.

Imagine all that hydrogen compressed by *millions* of pounds per square inch of pressure into metallic form. Then release those millions of pounds of pressure *all at once*. Well, the mind does some serious boggling.

It was all too easy for my imagination to fill in what must have happened: the blonde said the activation word, not knowing exactly what would happen, but overcoming years of docilization and routine. That alone was an act brave enough for any BSI Agent. The diamond released its Spell—magically creating a field devoid of magic, a paradox no Magician has been able to explain satisfactorily, not even Alex.

I imagined Junior flying the plane, hearing the word slip past the girl's lips and for a brief moment—less than a second, but lasting for a small eternity—him *knowing* that he'd been played, that he'd lost the final battle of the war. I like to think the last thing that went through his mind before a violently expanding cloud of hydrogen gas tore his body apart was my name.

The swelling cloud of hydrogen gas ripped apart the plane in less than a nanosecond and there would have been sparks, friction … just enough to set off a chain reaction similar to that produced by a nuclear device.

Four pounds of metallic hydrogen suddenly became a hydrogen bomb, resulting in an explosion so intense that a portion of the atmosphere even ignited, adding still more fuel to the fire. I reckon the heat and violence was so intense that there was nothing left of Ayre, the blond girl, or Junior except quickly cooling plasma.

Forgive me, Ayre. Forgive me, girl. I am sure, down to the deep roots of my soul, that Ayre would have done the same, would have sacrificed me and the blonde in a heartbeat had our positions been reversed. He was good Agent, a good leader, and knew when to make the really crappy calls. He would have hated it, but he would have done it. Perhaps the blonde, in that last microsecond, felt free.

I like to think she did.

As for Junior … well, rot in hell, you rat bastard.

"What do you do for an encore?" Nihsen said, staring at the fading orange tinge in the sky. "Destroy nations? Time travel?"

I shook my head. "Been there. Done that."

Chapter Thirty-Five

Kal

The Good, the Bad and the Questionable

THEY FOUND THE GYROCOPTER IN a southern suburb of Omaha, a town called La Vista, in the middle of a park. The woman Canton called the 'ninja assassin chick' has yet to be identified. Canton's team took pics of her face, of course, but she was in no database. BB would've asked Ghost to search all foreign databases, but he had sent the cybernetic spook off to address other priorities.

Ayre's team had been sent back to Warehouse. They were placed on leave until a new team leader could be chosen and were more than a little demoralized that Junior managed to toss them all around like tennis balls and make off with Ayre. It wasn't their fault ... Junior was too big a fish for any single human to handle. I think the only reason I managed to shoot him at *Foole Moon* was his arrogance.

As for his Renfields ... no one knows. There have been no suspicious deaths or incidents of sudden onset dementia. My guess is that when Junior bit the big one, his docilization Spell slowly began to unravel. Alex agreed with me.

After all the hoopla, the team stuck to me like a coat of paint, afraid that if I wasn't constantly monitored I might wander away and get lost, perhaps impale myself on a popsicle stick. Irritating and endearing in equal measure.

Alex and Jeanie had me on the couch at my hotel room at the Red Lion as soon as I finished my debrief with BB. Junior had cleared the room out of anything I'd left behind, including the Spell egg briefcase. That sucked, but what can you do?

"Just relax, Kal," Alex said softly, placing hands on my temples. "Jeanie, you don't have that much schooling in biology and anatomy, so just ride along and watch what I'm doing. If you see something anomalous, let me know."

She nodded. "Of course." Her hands rested on my stomach. It felt good enough that I wished Alex would give us a few dozen hours of privacy. Kal needed to get himself some lovin'.

Almost immediately, a soothing warmth washed over me and I began to relax, my mind hitting rewind back to the morning debrief with BB.

"What a mess," BB had said, eyes rimmed with fatigue. I almost felt sorry for him traveling to Europe to confab on the Sidhe with other Bureau-like leaders who were just as stubborn and clever as he was, only to come back to a major crap-storm.

I agreed with his assessment.

"How are you, Kal?" His shrewd eyes missed nothing, even through a RediPad.

"One tired puppy, boss. And I feel like ten miles of asshole for killing Ayre."

"This probably won't help, but you did the right thing. Ayre would have done the same, no doubt in my mind. And I firmly believe that if he hadn't been unconscious, he would have gladly killed himself if it meant destroying Maydock. All in all, it was a miracle it worked out as well as it did."

"Yeah. I know, boss. It's not Ayre I feel so bad about; he was as good as dead. Junior had him slated for his next Happy Meal." I shook my head. "No, it's the girl. I lied to her and told her it would be all right, that she would go home if she did what I asked."

"It was necessary to stop Maydock."

I felt a stab of irritation. "Don't call him that, BB. That was Two-

Hit's middle name and I don't want it sullied by using it to refer to that vamp half-breed."

My boss nodded. That was settled then.

"As for 'necessary,' " I continued, making air quotes with my fingers, "that sounds like one of those 'you can't make an omelet without breaking eggs' sort of things."

"No, Kal, not even close. That tired old chestnut is a sick rationale for committing atrocities and that is not what we do."

I raised an eyebrow. "We trample civil liberties left and right, lay on Interdictions to keep our dread secrets. Our atrocities are mostly of the legal kind." My breath rushed out in a sigh. "Except for that X-scar guy."

BB nodded slowly, his face becoming thoughtful and somewhat sad. "Yes, that is true, which is why I am logging an official reprimand in your jacket and suspending you without pay for two months upon your return to Warehouse."

Two months without pay and two months vacation. That was barely a slap on the wrist—although the black mark in my file stung. It was my first one. Oh well, those with the necessary clearance to access my file were rarer than honest politicians.

"Understood, boss." The reprimand I could handle; what was worse were the dreams to come. It would take a long time to process the guilt. *Sorry, Ayre. Sorry, blonde girl whose name I don't know.* Guilt and shame.

Damn, I needed a drink.

"That's not all," said the boss.

Oh, *there's* the other shoe dropping with a clatter. My heart flopped in my chest because I had a sneaking suspicion that—

BB finished my thought. "When you return from suspension, you will assume the position of Green Pea trainer for an as-yet-to-be-determined amount of time."

Oh, God, it was worse than I thought and the enormity of having to deal with more Green Peas clogged my throat.

However, it turned out he wasn't close to finished. "You tortured a human being, Kal," he said, face grim, voice diamond hard. Those near-colorless eyes of his bored into my baby blues and I realized with a start that BB was *pissed*. A truly angry Benjamin Bauer was something I never wanted to experience and I was ferociously happy he was on the other side of the RediPad. "You are damn lucky I don't bring you up on charges, have you prosecuted under Article 61 of your contract."

Article 61. My flesh went all goosepimply and my jaw nearly became unhinged. Article 61 was a closed-door hearing in front of the Joint Chiefs, involving some rather unpleasant, invasive truth Spells. Those affairs tended to be short, unmerciful and swift, with sentences ranging from ten years to life—out of sight and out of mind. In the last one-hundred years Article 61 had been invoked six times, the last incident having occurred in 2001. That Agent still languished in solitary confinement in ADX Florence in Colorado and is categorized by the Federal Bureau of Prisons as the most dangerous prisoner in the United States.

"I had to intervene with the president on your behalf, Kal," he continued. "You are our second most valuable asset and I will not waste such a resource on the prison system when you can be of use to the Bureau in these trying times. Luckily, he agreed with my assessment."

"Who's the first?"

"Beg pardon?"

"Who is the first," I asked slowly, still dazed by my near brush with incarceration.

"Alex."

Of course. "Is he going to be okay?" I'd read his After Action report and knew that he might be in some hot water for turning X-scar's brain into tapioca pudding, in spite of the valuable intel he had gleaned.

"I didn't have to convince the president not to press charges, although a black mark for Conduct Unbecoming has been entered into his jacket. He is not happy, but he understands. It will give him something to think about while he and Special Branch attempt to remove the crude Interdiction from Mr. G's mind." BB took a deep breath. "Regardless, you are not only on training duty, but you will also, for the foreseeable future, meet with Dr. Willows twice a week." He raised a finger as I started to protest and I closed my trap right quick. "This is nonnegotiable. And because misery loves company, Alex will also be seeing Dr. Willows twice a week."

Dr. Willows, the Bureau's head-shrinker, the resident psychologist. Looked like I'd have to spend some time on a couch trip talking about my feelings and my mother and all the really crappy things I'd done in my life.

Perfect.

"On a different note, an email was sent to your personal Bureau account. It's from ... Junior."

"Wha-a-t?" *Oh, please tell me he's dead.* "How?"

"Ghost surmises that it was a fail-safe in the event of Junior's demise. After scanning for viruses we found that it contained his journal, a personal account of his life from birth to just before his death. Best guess is that he wanted to give it to the person who beat him. Spoils of war."

I snorted. "Sounds like him."

"It sheds light on Margaret Whitcombe, her state of mind, the magic she used to create a vampire/human hybrid and vampire society. The ramifications of which will aid our efforts in hunting their nests."

Yesh. *Definitely* sounded like Junior ... screw with his kin from beyond the grave. Hybrid vengeance. "Well, at least we'll know how he planned the whole Omaha fiasco."

The boss's eyes narrowed. "Yes, no doubt it will greatly enhance your report. Which brings me to another point: why did you include the blonde girl's perspective in your brief? That sort of third-person transition is not the normal insert in your file. You were not on that plane when she uttered the activation word. You didn't have the data. Why include that bit of fancy?"

I gave that a long, hard think before saying, "There was just enough information to reconstruct that scenario." A bit of wistfulness entered my voice. "I like to think that's how it happened, though ... that she finally found a modicum of peace."

"On a different note, Kal." BB steepled his fingers, changing the subject so quickly I almost got whiplash. "We had word from the Seelie Court that the war between the Courts is keeping the Unseelie from launching any further offensives against humanity. So, for a while at least, our world will be safe from the Sidhe."

That was a load off. The Unseelie Court's plans killed millions of people and had come a gnat's whisker away from putting mankind on the endangered species list. I sat back in the couch, relief a potent narcotic flooding through my veins. "Good news is right. That means I can have my Brownie buddies back." As a member of the Faë, Brownies could be tracked by members of both Courts—that was how the Sidhe located our base of operations in San Francisco—but now that the Unseelie Court was out of the picture, the world's best drycleaners were once again available to Mama Hakala's baby boy.

The boss knew exactly what I was thinking and treated me to a patented disapproving stare. "I had an idea that might be your first reaction, juvenile as it may be, so I took the liberty of transferring them from one of our safe houses back to your room in Dorms." A long suffering sigh. It seemed that he had a flair for the dramatic. "But realize that with the first whiff of Sidhe activity, they go back into hiding ASAP."

I heroically kept the smile from my face. The boss was a big softy; he just didn't want to show it. "Sure thing, BB."

"One last item," he intoned gravely.

Uh-oh.

BB nodded at the look on my face. "Indeed. The Summit I attended not only dealt with the Sidhe issue, but also the effect of technology on our ability to hide the existence of the World Under and the various Bureaus worldwide. My counterparts in Great Britain, Europe, Scandinavia, Japan, and India and I have concluded that the World Under can no longer remain a secret, that with the advent of the Internet, the cellphone camera, and CCTV, it has grown virtually impossible to keep a jaded public blind to the Supernatural world. I made my recommendation to the president with the Joint Chief's blessing that he inform the nation of the World Under. He agreed. As of last night, I received word that the leaders of the aforementioned countries will also do so. There will be a worldwide simulcast in the next three weeks, breaking the news to the Straights."

My mouth didn't want to work and my stomach churned with fear. "What about Interdiction, boss?"

"Interdiction has worked in the past, but in the last decade we have used that Spell more than in the previous one hundred years. We have come to an information critical mass and Interdiction can no longer stop the leak. As for those who have been Interdicted, Benjamin Franklin foresaw a day where such a Spell would no longer prove useful and concocted a counter Spell. A simple phrase that will be broadcast during the simulcast. You and the other BSI employees will no longer be under Interdiction."

Visions of riots, finger-pointing, and paranoia flashed through my mind. I wasn't afraid of the rational, hard-working middle-class Joes trying to provide for their families; they tended to be sensible people who just wanted to keep their loved ones safe. No, what I worried about were the extreme paranoids, the 'love the Supernaturals' peaceniks and the bat-crap crazies. They were the ones who would put others in harm's way to advance their agendas. *Oh, Lord!* What about politicians?

The horror.

"We will have enough to worry about with the global organization of magic-using criminals uncovered," BB added. "Who knows what they will be up to?"

Through the haze of terrible possibilities that my mind kept conjuring, I said, "Don't think you'll have to worry about them too much, boss."

BB's eyes narrowed. "And you know this how, Kal?"

"Think about it, boss. The offices in Omaha were lined with *silver mesh*! That tells us that at least the higher echelons of the organization know about the Bureau and wanted to keep their magic from being detected. It also means they knew if they were discovered that all the agencies on the planet would be gunning for them, and they couldn't compete on that scale." I shook my head. "No, if I were them, I'd be turtling up, keeping my head and limbs inside a shell until we begin to relax. I'd bet my last darn nickel that most of their illegal activities around the world have abruptly stopped. Remember, they know we captured one of their capos and they can't afford to face the combined might of the world's Bureaus. They're running scared now, boss, if not dismantled permanently."

"I doubt they have closed up shop, Kal. Never underestimate the power of human greed and ambition."

And we were back to politicians again. "Okay, boss."

"We will discuss this more when you return, Kal. I need your insight on this matter. See you tonight."

I shook my head. "No can do, boss."

A refusal was the last thing he expected and he treated me to the old eyebrow trick I used on him so often. With about as much effect.

"Canton's team and I will stay here in Omaha for a while," I explained, "for the second occurrence." As I mentioned earlier, the hard and fast rule was that Supernatural intrusions into the really real world always came in twos. Besides, my suspension wouldn't take effect until I returned back to DC, so until then I was on the clock.

BB got it and nodded. He could have ordered me back and I would have obeyed, but, as a veteran Agent himself, he knew that some things had to be worked out in the field.

"Kal? Did you hear me?"

"Whumgl?" My eyes opened. Had I dozed? The world seemed a little tilty and out of focus.

"I said I have some news for you." Alex stood over me, sweaty and tired with dark circles under his eyes. Jeanie sat on the edge of the bed holding my hand.

"Good or bad?"

"Both."

Perfect. "Let me have it. You choose the news."

He nodded. "You're a Magician."

Well dip me in sh—"What?" That was it; I was going mad, ready for a room with soft, comfy walls and the only utensil available soft plastic sporks.

Jeanie drew close. "Well, love, you're not *really* a Magician."

I closed my eyes. Yep, they were coming to take me away—the nice, nice men in shiny white suits—to fit me in a coat with wraparound sleeves.

Alex's smirk was irksome. Little skink was enjoying himself immensely. *Bastard.* "What I meant to say, Kal, is that you *would* have been a Magician if your sister hadn't died."

Leena. Great, Mom and Dad could visit on weekends and I could live the rest of my life on Thorazine cocktails.

"You see, back then when you were fifteen, you most likely were coming into your powers, but hadn't popped your magical cherry yet. When your sister died and her spirit latched onto yours, she was probably attracted to the magic in your body and for fifteen years had been using *your* magic to keep you safe. Your rage, which was brought about by Leena, was most likely her using your own magic to enhance your strength and speed. She wasn't really the source of your rage. You were."

Okay, back to reality. My eyes opened. "So," I licked my lips, "you're saying I would have been a Magician if Leena hadn't been killed? Just like she would have been?"

Jeanie nodded. "Yes, love, although after all these years, your ability is a stunted, poorly formed thing, atrophied from lack of proper use." The two Magicians traded looks. "It seems that you will never really *be* a Magician."

"And that is bad news?"

Alex shook his head. "No, the bad news is that you're still ugly."

Sarky kid. I grinned. How about that? "Well, nothing has changed then. I'm still me."

Jeanie ran warm fingers across my forehead. "Kind of, love. From what Alex could tell, your magic is keeping your body healthy. In fact, almost obscenely healthy considering the damage you've accrued the last ten years. Most people would be showing signs of severe osteoarthritis, muscle fatigue, and even some respiratory distress, but you are in tip-top shape, and we believe it is due to the limited amount of magic you unconsciously use to keep yourself fit."

Stop the train, I need to get off. Magician. Me. Riiigghht. Kalevi Hakala, super agent and the dude with the mojo. It would've been laughable if Alex and Jeanie hadn't put their serious faces on and given me the squinties.

"So … what you're saying is that I am healthy as a horse because I am subconsciously using my atrophied magical ability to keep the old chassis from rusting away. Is that about it?"

They nodded. Bobblehead Magicians.

I rubbed my eyes and sighed, more than a little nonplussed.

"There's more," Jeanie said.

Perfect.

"Of course," I grumped. "Hit me."

Alex took over. "Those visions you've been having—"

"You mean memories."

"Yes, those. You had perfect recall in every detail, including smells and tactile sensations."

Uh-oh. I nodded, fearing what was going pop out of his mouth next.

"I …" he coughed, "*we* believe those memories are brought to the fore by your subconscious, given total recall by the marginal magical ability you possess."

My eyes opened wide. "I was warning myself, giving my waking mind clues by augmenting my memories and presenting them to me on a silver platter?"

"Yes."

Well … that was just damn creepy.

"One last thing."

Of course, there's always one last thing. "Shoot."

"Junior broke your arms and legs, yet you mentioned in your report your arm somehow healed itself, giving you greater mobility."

"Awww—"

"Yes," said Alex. "You know where this is going. You healed your own arm using what little magic you have, but you didn't have enough on tap to heal your other limbs."

Okay, information overload. But the sadistic little geek and my love bunny weren't done with me just yet. Alex brought out some 3x5 index cards and held them out one at a time. "Tell me what you see."

Went something like this:

"Squiggly lines. They hurt my head."

"More squiggly lines."

"An elephant eating ice cream."

"Be serious, Kal."

"Ugly squiggly lines."

"Better."

And so on and so forth until ....

A Shape opened up in front of my eyes. The ink on the index card seemed to gain depth, texture as I watched, the lines slowly lifting from paper, morphing from two-dimensional banality into a work of art given life in three dimensions. I saw everything in that shape: Picasso, Rembrandt, Degas, Dali, da Vinci and so many more. It spun before my eyes, a wonder of living magic and then it spoke to me.

Perhaps not *spoke*, per se, but it sure did communicate with me on a deep, visceral level of its purpose, its reason for being and I knew, I *knew*, that if I visualized the Shape in my mind, saw it in all its three-dimensional glory and gave it a nudge *just so*, a wondrous occurrence would be born.

"I can start a fire with this," I breathed in awe. A whole different world was in front of me, a glorious realm of magic and marvels. Then Alex had to go and put rusty nails in my Cheerios.

"It's called a Zippo Spell, Kal," he said with a small smile. "Creates a flame like that of a cigarette lighter. It's one of the weakest Spells ever invented, uses the least amount of magic ... not even a full merlin's worth. Proof that your ability is so atrophied that it's unlikely ever to grow."

And back down to reality. There went my dreams of Camelot. Jeanie placed a callused hand on my cheek and I smiled up at her. There were more marvelous things in the world than magic. "Alex, give us an hour or two, will ya?" My eyes were only for her. "Make it three."

As geeky as he was, he knew which way the wind was blowing and grinned, rising to his feet and heading toward the door. Before he touched the knob, he turned and said, "Guess I won't be making any more metallic hydrogen armor. Glad you found that flaw before anyone else could be hurt. I'm also glad you're safe." A pause. "But I wish you were easier on the equipment. I have to create *another* trench coat with deep pockets."

Couldn't help myself, had to give as good as I got. "Been thinking about that, kid," I said, briefly looking away from the woman I loved. "Why didn't you just invent a clip that can hold a bazillion bullets instead of a coat that can hold a bazillion clips? It'd save time on reloading and be more durable."

His face slowly fell. "You suck, Kal," he said before leaving.

Perfect.

"That was mean," Jeanie breathed in my ear. She gave it a lick, which did warm squishy things to my nether regions.

My arms enfolded my girlfriend. "Glad to see you are all right, hon. You could have died using up all your magic."

I could hear the smile in her voice. "Oh, we're fine, Kal."

"We?"

"Me and the baby."

Even more perfect.

Epilogue

Kal
All's Well That Ends

THE HUNTER MOVED THROUGH THE garish light of the bar, stalking his prey. He'd found the perfect one, a female with hair like spun copper and flashing green eyes that reminded him of mossy emeralds. She was tall for a human, lithe and strong and sure to be full of what he needed.

His very presence parted the crowd. A tall man with broad shoulders and a long face filled with character and confidence. There was no one like him in the bar and the human males, aggressive and drunk, sensed his power on some primal, animalistic level and stayed out of his way. The danger he posed could not have been more evident if he'd wore a sign around his neck that said 'I will freaking kill you.'

As he approached the redhead, she seemed to sense his regard. She turned her head to study him. It was evident that she approved. A small flick of the tongue over ruby lips, a slight smile and the turn of her body to display her full curves. She liked what she saw ... a lot.

The hunter stepped in close and signaled the bartender. He placed an order for them both and settled in on his game of seduction. Oh, this one was so full of life, so full of what he needed, and his need was great.

After years of observing humans, he knew the lines and how to deliver them. He knew the subtle use of body language, how the most minute gestures and facial expressions could manipulate mood and telegraph desire. He was a master of seduction and soon the woman with coppery hair signaled her willingness to depart with him.

He indicated that he was parked in the alley next to the bar and soon they were outside. Then they were sheltered in a man-made canyon, out of eyesight and earshot. Not that the hunter needed much to keep his prey quiet.

"Where's your car?" the redhead purred.

Before she could blink he was on her, hand to her throat and body pressed against the filthy brick wall of the alley. "Stay still," said the hunter in a voice like broken glass slicing flesh. "Shhh … everything will be all right."

The redhead's face relaxed into a sneer. "Yes," she said. "It will."

Pain … piercing pain like he hadn't felt in centuries took him in the side. He looked down to see the woman's hand wrapped around a dagger of blackthorn.

"What?" he gasped.

And that's when the rest of the team chimed in. Rosewood and blackthorn bullets, the only things that really gave vampires the galloping fits tore into the Supernatural's legs and sides, punching through its thousand-dollar suit and dropping it to the ground where it writhed in agony.

"Took you long enough," Pat grumped, hand bloody and blackthorn dagger dripping.

"I wanted you to get your lick in," I replied, lowering the Lahti. Beside me Canton and Dom lowered their weapons as well. From the opposite side of the alley, Jeanie and Dove Jacobs trotted up, weapons at the ready.

"No other vamps in sight, boss," said Dove. Jeanie merely smiled at the Supernatural, her eyes hard and mean.

"Good." I knelt just outside of striking range and addressed the vampire. "You know, Marcus, had you gone back to wherever you came from, I'd have been okay with that. You did, after all, try to help me kill Junior." I smiled into his boiling stare. "But you had to stick around, to be the second Supernatural occurrence and I can't have that."

Marcus hissed. One of his contacts had gone missing when he'd been shot, and his half-pink, half-brown glare was filled with hate and pain.

"Yeah, well, I could kill you myself, put another notch in my Bowie's handle, but I'm thinking back to all the women you've seduced and killed throughout the centuries. How many of them died in terror as you drank their blood? How many mothers and daughters and wives and aunts have you feasted upon and left on the cold ground to rot? Hundreds? Thousands?" My voice had become granite. "Well, big guy, I reckon it's ladies' night."

I stood. "Canton, Dom, let's grab a drink, I'm thirsty."

"As long as you're buying, white boy." My friend's grin was ear to ear.

My eyes wandered back to the broken form of Marcus, knees shot to hell, arms and guts full of rosewood and blackthorn. "Sure, why not?"

Dom's teeth shone through the blackness of his beard. "Best offer all day."

To the women I said, "Don't take too long. Only the first round is on me."

Pat and Dove gave me smiles that chilled me to the bone and I knew Marcus would not go gentle into that good night. As for my fiancée, her smile promised me more than I could have ever imagined.

Perfect.

My name is Kalevi Hakala. I am an Agent with the Bureau of Supernatural Investigation and I *hate* vampires.

* * *

Catch the further adventures of Kal Hakala in *The Spirit in St. Louis.*

B ORN IN HELSINKI, FINLAND, **MARK** **Everett Stone** arrived in the U.S. at a young age and promptly dove into the world of the fantastic. Starting at age seven with the *Iliad* and the *Odyssey*, he went on to consume every scrap of Norse Mythology he could get his grubby little paws on. At age thirteen he graduated to Tolkien and Heinlein, building up a book collection that soon rivaled the local public library's. In college Mark majored in Journalism and minored in English.

Mark has published five other books with Camel Press: *Things to Do in Denver When You're Un-Dead*, *What Happens in Vegas Dies in Vegas*, *I Left My Haunt in San Francisco*, and *Chicago, The Windigo City* (Books 1, 2, 3, and 4 of the From the Files of the BSI series) as well as *The Judas Line*, which was a finalist for the ForeWord Magazine Book of the Year Award in the Fantasy Category. Mark lives in Denver with his amazingly patient wife, Brandie, and their two sons, Aeden and Gabriel.

Next up: *The Spirit in St. Louis* and two books that continue the story that began with *The Judas Line*.

You can find Mark on the Web at markeverettstone.com.